I0674736

The Collected Supernatural and Weird Fiction of Henry James Volume 1

The Collected Supernatural and Weird Fiction of Henry James Volume 1

Including Two Novellas 'The Turn of the Screw' and 'The Lesson of the Master', Two Novelettes and Seven Short Stories of the Strange and Unusual

Henry James

LEONAUR

The Collected
Supernatural and Weird
Fiction of Henry James
Volume 1
Including Two Novellas 'The Turn of the Screw'
and 'The Lesson of the Master',
Two Novelettes and Seven Short Stories
of the Strange and Unusual
by Henry James

FIRST EDITION

Leonaur is an imprint
of Oakpast Ltd

ISBN: 978-0-85706-043-3 (hardcover)
ISBN: 978-0-85706-039-6 (softcover)

http://www.leonaur.com

Publisher's Notes

In the interests of authenticity, the spellings, grammar and place names used have been retained from the original editions.

The opinions of the authors represent a view of events in which he was a participant related from his own perspective, as such the text is relevant as an historical document.

The views expressed in this book are not necessarily those of the publisher.

Contents

The Turn of the Screw

The story had held us, round the fire, sufficiently breathless, but except the obvious remark that it was gruesome, as, on Christmas Eve in an old house, a strange tale should essentially be, I remember no comment uttered till somebody happened to say that it was the only case he had met in which such a visitation had fallen on a child. The case, I may mention, was that of an apparition in just such an old house as had gathered us for the occasion—an appearance, of a dreadful kind, to a little boy sleeping in the room with his mother and waking her up in the terror of it; waking her not to dissipate his dread and soothe him to sleep again, but to encounter also, herself, before she had succeeded in doing so, the same sight that had shaken him.

It was this observation that drew from Douglas—not immediately, but later in the evening—a reply that had the interesting consequence to which I call attention. Someone else told a story not particularly effective, which I saw he was not following. This I took for a sign that he had himself something to produce and that we should only have to wait. We waited in fact till two nights later; but that same evening, before we scattered, he brought out what was in his mind.

"I quite agree—in regard to Griffin's ghost, or whatever it was—that its appearing first to the little boy, at so tender an age, adds a particular touch. But it's not the first occurrence of its charming kind that I know to have involved a child. If the child gives the effect another turn of the screw, what do you say to TWO children—?"

"We say, of course," somebody exclaimed, "that they give two turns! Also that we want to hear about them."

I can see Douglas there before the fire, to which he had got up to present his back, looking down at his interlocutor with his hands in his pockets. "Nobody but me, till now, has ever heard. It's quite too horrible." This, naturally, was declared by several voices to give the thing the utmost price, and our friend, with quiet art, prepared his triumph by turning his eyes over the rest of us and going on: "It's beyond everything. Nothing at all that I know touches it."

"For sheer terror?" I remember asking.

He seemed to say it was not so simple as that; to be really at a loss how to qualify it. He passed his hand over his eyes, made a little wincing grimace. "For dreadful—dreadfulness!"

"Oh, how delicious!" cried one of the women.

He took no notice of her; he looked at me, but as if, instead of me, he saw what he spoke of. "For general uncanny ugliness and horror and pain."

"Well then," I said, "just sit right down and begin."

He turned round to the fire, gave a kick to a log, watched it an instant. Then as he faced us again: "I can't begin. I shall have to send to town." There was a unanimous groan at this, and much reproach; after which, in his preoccupied way, he explained. "The story's written. It's in a locked drawer—it has not been out for years. I could write to my man and enclose the key; he could send down the packet as he finds it." It was to me in particular that he appeared to propound this—appeared almost to appeal for aid not to hesitate. He had broken a thickness of ice, the formation of many a winter; had had his reasons for a long silence. The others resented postponement, but it was just his scruples that charmed me. I adjured him to write by the first post and to agree with us for an early hearing; then I asked him if the experience in question had been his own. To this his answer was prompt. "Oh, thank God, no!"

"And is the record yours? You took the thing down?"

"Nothing but the impression. I took that HERE"—he tapped

his heart. "I've never lost it."

"Then your manuscript—?"

"Is in old, faded ink, and in the most beautiful hand." He hung fire again. "A woman's. She has been dead these twenty years. She sent me the pages in question before she died." They were all listening now, and of course there was somebody to be arch, or at any rate to draw the inference. But if he put the inference by without a smile it was also without irritation.

"She was a most charming person, but she was ten years older than I. She was my sister's governess," he quietly said. "She was the most agreeable woman I've ever known in her position; she would have been worthy of any whatever. It was long ago, and this episode was long before. I was at Trinity, and I found her at home on my coming down the second summer. I was much there that year—it was a beautiful one; and we had, in her off-hours, some strolls and talks in the garden—talks in which she struck me as awfully clever and nice. Oh yes; don't grin: I liked her extremely and am glad to this day to think she liked me, too. If she hadn't she wouldn't have told me. She had never told anyone. It wasn't simply that she said so, but that I knew she hadn't. I was sure; I could see. You'll easily judge why when you hear."

"Because the thing had been such a scare?"

He continued to fix me. "You'll easily judge," he repeated: "YOU will."

I fixed him, too. "I see. She was in love."

He laughed for the first time. "You ARE acute. Yes, she was in love. That is, she had been. That came out—she couldn't tell her story without its coming out. I saw it, and she saw I saw it; but neither of us spoke of it. I remember the time and the place-the corner of the lawn, the shade of the great beeches and the long, hot summer afternoon. It wasn't a scene for a shudder; but oh—!" He quitted the fire and dropped back into his chair.

"You'll receive the packet Thursday morning?" I inquired.

"Probably not till the second post."

"Well then; after dinner—"

"You'll all meet me here?" He looked us round again. "Isn't

anybody going?" It was almost the tone of hope.

"Everybody will stay!"

"*I* will"—and "*I* will!" cried the ladies whose departure had been fixed. Mrs. Griffin, however, expressed the need for a little more light. "Who was it she was in love with?"

"The story will tell," I took upon myself to reply.

"Oh, I can't wait for the story!"

"The story WON'T tell," said Douglas; "not in any literal, vulgar way."

"More's the pity, then. That's the only way I ever understand."

"Won't YOU tell, Douglas?" somebody else inquired.

He sprang to his feet again. "Yes—tomorrow. Now I must go to bed. Goodnight." And quickly catching up a candlestick, he left us slightly bewildered. From our end of the great brown hall we heard his step on the stair; whereupon Mrs. Griffin spoke. "Well, if I don't know who she was in love with, I know who HE was."

"She was ten years older," said her husband.

"*Raison de plus*—at that age! But it's rather nice, his long reticence."

"Forty years!" Griffin put in.

"With this outbreak at last."

"The outbreak," I returned, "will make a tremendous occasion of Thursday night;" and everyone so agreed with me that, in the light of it, we lost all attention for everything else. The last story, however incomplete and like the mere opening of a serial, had been told; we handshook and "candlestuck," as somebody said, and went to bed.

I knew the next day that a letter containing the key had, by the first post, gone off to his London apartments; but in spite of—or perhaps just on account of—the eventual diffusion of this knowledge we quite let him alone till after dinner, till such an hour of the evening, in fact, as might best accord with the kind of emotion on which our hopes were fixed. Then he became as communicative as we could desire and indeed gave us his best reason for being so. We had it from him again before the fire in the hall, as we had had our mild wonders of the previous night. It appeared that the narrative he had promised to read us really required for a proper intelligence a few words of prologue.

Let me say here distinctly, to have done with it, that this narrative, from an exact transcript of my own made much later, is what I shall presently give. Poor Douglas, before his death-when it was in sight—committed to me the manuscript that reached him on the third of these days and that, on the same spot, with immense effect, he began to read to our hushed little circle on the night of the fourth. The departing ladies who had said they would stay didn't, of course, thank heaven, stay: they departed, in consequence of arrangements made, in a rage of curiosity, as they professed, produced by the touches with which he had already worked us up. But that only made his little final auditory more compact and select, kept it, round the hearth, subject to a common thrill.

The first of these touches conveyed that the written statement took up the tale at a point after it had, in a manner, begun. The fact to be in possession of was therefore that his old friend, the youngest of several daughters of a poor country parson, had, at the age of twenty, on taking service for the first time in the schoolroom, come up to London, in trepidation, to answer in person an advertisement that had already placed her in brief correspondence with the advertiser. This person proved, on her presenting herself, for judgment, at a house in Harley Street, that impressed her as vast and imposing—this prospective patron proved a gentleman, a bachelor in the prime of life, such a figure as had never risen, save in a dream or an old novel, before a fluttered, anxious girl out of a Hampshire vicarage.

One could easily fix his type; it never, happily, dies out. He was handsome and bold and pleasant, offhand and gay and kind. He struck her, inevitably, as gallant and splendid, but what took her most of all and gave her the courage she afterward showed was that he put the whole thing to her as a kind of favour, an obligation he should gratefully incur. She conceived him as rich, but as fearfully extravagant—saw him all in a glow of high fashion, of good looks, of expensive habits, of charming ways with women. He had for his own town residence a big house filled with the spoils of travel and the trophies of the chase; but it was to his country home, an old family place in Essex, that he wished her immediately to proceed.

He had been left, by the death of their parents in India, guardian to a small nephew and a small niece, children of a younger, a military brother, whom he had lost two years before. These children were, by the strangest of chances for a man in his position—a lone man without the right sort of experience or a grain of patience—very heavily on his hands. It had all been a great worry and, on his own part doubtless, a series of blunders, but he immensely pitied the poor chicks and had done all he could; had in particular sent them down to his other house, the proper place for them being of course the country, and kept them there, from the first, with the best people he could find to look after them, parting even with his own servants to wait on them and going down himself, whenever he might, to see how they were doing.

The awkward thing was that they had practically no other relations and that his own affairs took up all his time. He had put them in possession of Bly, which was healthy and secure, and had placed at the head of their little establishment—but below stairs only—an excellent woman, Mrs. Grose, whom he was sure his visitor would like and who had formerly been maid to his mother. She was now housekeeper and was also acting for the time as superintendent to the little girl, of whom, without children of her own, she was, by good luck, extremely fond. There were plenty of people to help, but of course the young lady who should go down as governess would be in supreme authority. She would also have, in holidays, to look after the small boy, who had been for a term at school—young as he was to be sent, but what else could be done?—and who, as the holidays were about to begin, would be back from one day to the other.

There had been for the two children at first a young lady

whom they had had the misfortune to lose. She had done for them quite beautifully—she was a most respectable person—till her death, the great awkwardness of which had, precisely, left no alternative but the school for little Miles. Mrs. Grose, since then, in the way of manners and things, had done as she could for Flora; and there were, further, a cook, a housemaid, a dairy-woman, an old pony, an old groom, and an old gardener, all like-wise thoroughly respectable.

So far had Douglas presented his picture when someone put a question. "And what did the former governess die of?—of so much respectability?"

Our friend's answer was prompt. "That will come out. I don't anticipate."

"Excuse me—I thought that was just what you ARE doing."

"In her successor's place," I suggested, "I should have wished to learn if the office brought with it—"

"Necessary danger to life?" Douglas completed my thought. "She did wish to learn, and she did learn. You shall hear tomorrow what she learned. Meanwhile, of course, the prospect struck her as slightly grim. She was young, untried, nervous: it was a vision of serious duties and little company, of really great loneliness. She hesitated—took a couple of days to consult and consider. But the salary offered much exceeded her modest measure, and on a second interview she faced the music, she engaged." And Douglas, with this, made a pause that, for the benefit of the company, moved me to throw in—

"The moral of which was of course the seduction exercised by the splendid young man. She succumbed to it."

He got up and, as he had done the night before, went to the fire, gave a stir to a log with his foot, then stood a moment with his back to us. "She saw him only twice."

"Yes, but that's just the beauty of her passion."

A little to my surprise, on this, Douglas turned round to me. "It WAS the beauty of it. There were others," he went on, "who hadn't succumbed. He told her frankly all his difficulty-that for several applicants the conditions had been prohibitive. They were, somehow, simply afraid. It sounded dull—it sounded strange; and all the more so because of his main condition."

"Which was—?"

"That she should never trouble him—but never, never: neither appeal nor complain nor write about anything; only meet all questions herself, receive all moneys from his solicitor, take the whole thing over and let him alone. She promised to do this, and she mentioned to me that when, for a moment, disburdened, delighted, he held her hand, thanking her for the sacrifice, she already felt rewarded."

"But was that all her reward?" one of the ladies asked.

"She never saw him again."

"Oh!" said the lady; which, as our friend immediately left us again, was the only other word of importance contributed to the subject till, the next night, by the corner of the hearth, in the best chair, he opened the faded red cover of a thin old-fashioned gilt-edged album. The whole thing took indeed more nights than one, but on the first occasion the same lady put another question. "What is your title?"

"I haven't one."

"Oh, *I* have!" I said. But Douglas, without heeding me, had begun to read with a fine clearness that was like a rendering to the ear of the beauty of his author's hand.

1

I remember the whole beginning as a succession of flights and drops, a little seesaw of the right throbs and the wrong. After rising, in town, to meet his appeal, I had at all events a couple of very bad days—found myself doubtful again, felt indeed sure I had made a mistake. In this state of mind I spent the long hours of bumping, swinging coach that carried me to the stopping place at which I was to be met by a vehicle from the house. This convenience, I was told, had been ordered, and I found, toward the close of the June afternoon, a commodious fly in waiting for me. Driving at that hour, on a lovely day, through a country to which the summer sweetness seemed to offer me a friendly welcome, my fortitude mounted afresh and, as we turned into the avenue, encountered a reprieve that was probably but a proof of the point to which it had sunk.

I suppose I had expected, or had dreaded, something so melancholy that what greeted me was a good surprise. I remember as a most pleasant impression the broad, clear front, its open windows and fresh curtains and the pair of maids looking out; I remember the lawn and the bright flowers and the crunch of my wheels on the gravel and the clustered treetops over which the rooks circled and cawed in the golden sky. The scene had a greatness that made it a different affair from my own scant home, and there immediately appeared at the door, with a little girl in her hand, a civil person who dropped me as decent a curtsy as if I had been the mistress or a distinguished visitor. I had received in Harley Street a narrower notion of the place, and that, as I recalled it, made me think the proprietor still more of a gentleman, suggested that what I was to enjoy might be something beyond his promise.

I had no drop again till the next day, for I was carried triumphantly through the following hours by my introduction to the younger of my pupils. The little girl who accompanied Mrs. Grose appeared to me on the spot a creature so charming as to make it a great fortune to have to do with her. She was the most beautiful child I had ever seen, and I afterward wondered that my employer had not told me more of her. I slept little that night—I was too much excited; and this astonished me, too, I recollect, remained with me, adding to my sense of the liberality with which I was treated.

The large, impressive room, one of the best in the house, the great state bed, as I almost felt it, the full, figured draperies, the long glasses in which, for the first time, I could see myself from head to foot, all struck me—like the extraordinary charm of my small charge—as so many things thrown in. It was thrown in as well, from the first moment, that I should get on with Mrs. Grose in a relation over which, on my way, in the coach, I fear I had rather brooded.

The only thing indeed that in this early outlook might have made me shrink again was the clear circumstance of her being so glad to see me. I perceived within half an hour that she was so glad—stout, simple, plain, clean, wholesome woman—as to be positively on her guard against showing it too much. I wondered even then a little why she should wish not to show it, and that, with reflection, with suspicion, might of course have made me uneasy.

But it was a comfort that there could be no uneasiness in a connection with anything so beatific as the radiant image of my little girl, the vision of whose angelic beauty had probably more than anything else to do with the restlessness that, before morning, made me several times rise and wander about my room to take in the whole picture and prospect; to watch, from my open window, the faint summer dawn, to look at such portions of the rest of the house as I could catch, and to listen, while, in the fading dusk, the first birds began to twitter, for the possible recurrence of a sound or two, less natural and not without, but within, that I had fancied I heard.

There had been a moment when I believed I recognized, faint and far, the cry of a child; there had been another when I found myself just consciously starting as at the passage, before my door, of a light footstep. But these fancies were not marked enough not to be thrown off, and it is only in the light, or the gloom, I should rather say, of other and subsequent matters that they now come back to me. To watch, teach, "form" little Flora would too evidently be the making of a happy and useful life. It had been agreed between us downstairs that after this first occasion I should have her as a matter of course at night, her small white bed being already arranged, to that end, in my room.

What I had undertaken was the whole care of her, and she had remained, just this last time, with Mrs. Grose only as an effect of our consideration for my inevitable strangeness and her natural timidity. In spite of this timidity—which the child herself, in the oddest way in the world, had been perfectly frank and brave about, allowing it, without a sign of uncomfortable consciousness, with the deep, sweet serenity indeed of one of Raphael's holy infants, to be discussed, to be imputed to her, and to determine us—I feel quite sure she would presently like me. It was part of what I already liked Mrs. Grose herself for, the pleasure I could see her feel in my admiration and wonder as I sat at supper with four tall candles and with my pupil, in a high chair and a bib, brightly facing me, between them, over bread and milk. There were naturally things that in Flora's presence could pass between us only as prodigious and gratified looks, obscure and roundabout allusions.

"And the little boy—does he look like her? Is he too so very remarkable?"

One wouldn't flatter a child. "Oh, miss, MOST remarkable. If you think well of this one!"—and she stood there with a plate in her hand, beaming at our companion, who looked from one of us to the other with placid heavenly eyes that contained nothing to check us.

"Yes; if I do—?"

"You WILL be carried away by the little gentleman!"

"Well, that, I think, is what I came for—to be carried away. I'm afraid, however," I remember feeling the impulse to add, "I'm rather easily carried away. I was carried away in London!"

I can still see Mrs. Grose's broad face as she took this in. "In Harley Street?"

"In Harley Street."

"Well, miss, you're not the first—and you won't be the last."

"Oh, I've no pretension," I could laugh, "to being the only one. My other pupil, at any rate, as I understand, comes back tomorrow?"

"Not tomorrow—Friday, miss. He arrives, as you did, by the coach, under care of the guard, and is to be met by the same carriage."

I forthwith expressed that the proper as well as the pleasant and friendly thing would be therefore that on the arrival of the public conveyance I should be in waiting for him with his little sister; an idea in which Mrs. Grose concurred so heartily that I somehow took her manner as a kind of comforting pledge-never falsified, thank heaven!—that we should on every question be quite at one. Oh, she was glad I was there!

What I felt the next day was, I suppose, nothing that could be fairly called a reaction from the cheer of my arrival; it was probably at the most only a slight oppression produced by a fuller measure of the scale, as I walked round them, gazed up at them, took them in, of my new circumstances. They had, as it were, an extent and mass for which I had not been prepared and in the presence of which I found myself, freshly, a little scared as well as a little proud. Lessons, in this agitation, certainly suffered some delay; I reflected that my first duty was, by the gentlest arts I could contrive, to win the child into the sense of knowing me.

I spent the day with her out-of-doors; I arranged with her, to her great satisfaction, that it should be she, she only, who might show me the place. She showed it step by step and room by room and secret by secret, with droll, delightful, childish talk about it and with the result, in half an hour, of our becoming immense friends. Young as she was, I was struck, throughout our little tour, with her confidence and courage with the way, in empty chambers and dull corridors, on crooked staircases that made me pause and even on the summit of an old machicolated square tower that made me dizzy, her morning music, her disposition to tell me so many more things than she asked, rang out and led me on.

I have not seen Bly since the day I left it, and I daresay that to my older and more informed eyes it would now appear sufficiently contracted. But as my little conductress, with her hair of gold and her frock of blue, danced before me round corners and pattered down passages, I had the view of a castle of romance inhabited by a rosy sprite, such a place as would somehow, for diversion of the young idea, take all colour out of storybooks and fairytales. Wasn't it just a storybook over which I had fallen adoze and adream? No; it was a big, ugly, antique, but convenient house, embodying a few features of a building still older, half-replaced and half-utilized, in which I had the fancy of our being almost as lost as a handful of passengers in a great drifting ship. Well, I was, strangely, at the helm!

2

This came home to me when, two days later, I drove over with Flora to meet, as Mrs. Grose said, the little gentleman; and all the more for an incident that, presenting itself the second evening, had deeply disconcerted me. The first day had been, on the whole, as I have expressed, reassuring; but I was to see it wind up in keen apprehension. The postbag, that evening—it came late—contained a letter for me, which, however, in the hand of my employer, I found to be composed but of a few words enclosing another, addressed to himself, with a seal still unbroken. "This, I recognize, is from the headmaster, and the headmaster's an awful bore. Read him, please; deal with him; but mind you don't report. Not a word. I'm off!"

I broke the seal with a great effort—so great a one that I was a long time coming to it; took the unopened missive at last up to my room and only attacked it just before going to bed. I had better have let it wait till morning, for it gave me a second sleepless night. With no counsel to take, the next day, I was full of distress; and it finally got so the better of me that I determined to open myself at least to Mrs. Grose.

"What does it mean? The child's dismissed his school."

She gave me a look that I remarked at the moment; then, visibly, with a quick blankness, seemed to try to take it back. "But aren't they all—?"

"Sent home—yes. But only for the holidays. Miles may never go back at all."

Consciously, under my attention, she reddened. "They won't take him?"

"They absolutely decline."

At this she raised her eyes, which she had turned from me; I saw them fill with good tears. "What has he done?"

I hesitated; then I judged best simply to hand her my letter-which, however, had the effect of making her, without taking it, simply put her hands behind her. She shook her head sadly. "Such things are not for me, miss."

My counsellor couldn't read! I winced at my mistake, which I attenuated as I could, and opened my letter again to repeat it to her; then, faltering in the act and folding it up once more, I put it back in my pocket. "Is he really BAD?"

The tears were still in her eyes. "Do the gentlemen say so?"

"They go into no particulars. They simply express their regret that it should be impossible to keep him. That can have only one meaning." Mrs. Grose listened with dumb emotion; she forbore to ask me what this meaning might be; so that, presently, to put the thing with some coherence and with the mere aid of her presence to my own mind, I went on: "That he's an injury to the others."

At this, with one of the quick turns of simple folk, she suddenly flamed up. "Master Miles! HIM an injury?"

There was such a flood of good faith in it that, though I had not yet seen the child, my very fears made me jump to the absurdity of the idea. I found myself, to meet my friend the better, offering it, on the spot, sarcastically. "To his poor little innocent mates!"

"It's too dreadful," cried Mrs. Grose, "to say such cruel things! Why, he's scarce ten years old."

"Yes, yes; it would be incredible."

She was evidently grateful for such a profession. "See him, miss, first. THEN believe it!" I felt forthwith a new impatience to see him; it was the beginning of a curiosity that, for all the next hours, was to deepen almost to pain. Mrs. Grose was aware, I could judge, of what she had produced in me, and she followed it up with assurance. "You might as well believe it of the little lady. Bless her," she added the next moment—"LOOK at her!"

I turned and saw that Flora, whom, ten minutes before, I had established in the schoolroom with a sheet of white paper, a pencil, and a copy of nice "round o's," now presented herself to view at the open door. She expressed in her little way an extraordinary detachment from disagreeable duties, looking to me, however, with a great childish light that seemed to offer it as a mere result of the affection she had conceived for my person, which had rendered necessary that she should follow me. I needed nothing more than this to feel the full force of Mrs. Grose's comparison, and, catching my pupil in my arms, covered her with kisses in which there was a sob of atonement.

Nonetheless, the rest of the day I watched for further occasion to approach my colleague, especially as, toward evening, I began to fancy she rather sought to avoid me. I overtook her, I remember, on the staircase; we went down together, and at the bottom I detained her, holding her there with a hand on her arm. "I take what you said to me at noon as a declaration that YOU'VE never known him to be bad."

She threw back her head; she had clearly, by this time, and very honestly, adopted an attitude. "Oh, never known him—I don't pretend THAT!"

I was upset again. "Then you HAVE known him—?"

"Yes indeed, miss, thank God!"

On reflection I accepted this. "You mean that a boy who never is—?"

"Is no boy for ME!"

I held her tighter. "You like them with the spirit to be naughty?" Then, keeping pace with her answer, "So do I!" I eagerly brought out. "But not to the degree to contaminate—"

"To contaminate?"—my big word left her at a loss. I explained it. "To corrupt."

She stared, taking my meaning in; but it produced in her an odd laugh. "Are you afraid he'll corrupt YOU?" She put the question with such a fine bold humour that, with a laugh, a little silly doubtless, to match her own, I gave way for the time to the apprehension of ridicule.

But the next day, as the hour for my drive approached, I cropped up in another place. "What was the lady who was here before?"

"The last governess? She was also young and pretty—almost

as young and almost as pretty, miss, even as you."

"Ah, then, I hope her youth and her beauty helped her!" I recollect throwing off. "He seems to like us young and pretty!"

"Oh, he DID," Mrs. Grose assented: "it was the way he liked everyone!" She had no sooner spoken indeed than she caught herself up. "I mean that's HIS way—the master's."

I was struck. "But of whom did you speak first?"

She looked blank, but she coloured. "Why, of HIM."

"Of the master?"

"Of who else?"

There was so obviously no one else that the next moment I had lost my impression of her having accidentally said more than she meant; and I merely asked what I wanted to know. "Did SHE see anything in the boy—?"

"That wasn't right? She never told me."

I had a scruple, but I overcame it. "Was she careful—particular?"

Mrs. Grose appeared to try to be conscientious. "About some things—yes."

"But not about all?"

Again she considered. "Well, miss—she's gone. I won't tell tales."

"I quite understand your feeling," I hastened to reply; but I thought it, after an instant, not opposed to this concession to pursue: "Did she die here?"

"No—she went off."

I don't know what there was in this brevity of Mrs. Grose's that struck me as ambiguous. "Went off to die?" Mrs. Grose looked straight out of the window, but I felt that, hypothetically, I had a right to know what young persons engaged for Bly were expected to do. "She was taken ill, you mean, and went home?"

"She was not taken ill, so far as appeared, in this house. She left it, at the end of the year, to go home, as she said, for a short holiday, to which the time she had put in had certainly given her a right. We had then a young woman—a nursemaid who had stayed on and who was a good girl and clever; and SHE took the children altogether for the interval. But our young lady never came back, and at the very moment I was expecting her I heard from the master that she was dead."

I turned this over. "But of what?"

"He never told me! But please, miss," said Mrs. Grose, "I must get to my work."

3

Her thus turning her back on me was fortunately not, for my just preoccupations, a snub that could check the growth of our mutual esteem. We met, after I had brought home little Miles, more intimately than ever on the ground of my stupefaction, my general emotion: so monstrous was I then ready to pronounce it that such a child as had now been revealed to me should be under an interdict. I was a little late on the scene, and I felt, as he stood wistfully looking out for me before the door of the inn at which the coach had put him down, that I had seen him, on the instant, without and within, in the great glow of freshness, the same positive fragrance of purity, in which I had, from the first moment, seen his little sister.

He was incredibly beautiful, and Mrs. Grose had put her finger on it: everything but a sort of passion of tenderness for him was swept away by his presence. What I then and there took him to my heart for was something divine that I have never found to the same degree in any child—his indescribable little air of knowing nothing in the world but love. It would have been impossible to carry a bad name with a greater sweetness of innocence, and by the time I had got back to Bly with him I remained merely bewildered—so far, that is, as I was not outraged—by the sense of the horrible letter locked up in my room, in a drawer. As soon as I could compass a private word with Mrs. Grose I declared to her that it was grotesque.

She promptly understood me. "You mean the cruel charge—?"

"It doesn't live an instant. My dear woman, LOOK at him!"

She smiled at my pretention to have discovered his charm. "I assure you, miss, I do nothing else! What will you say, then?" she immediately added.

"In answer to the letter?" I had made up my mind. "Nothing."

"And to his uncle?"

I was incisive. "Nothing."

"And to the boy himself?"

I was wonderful. "Nothing."

She gave with her apron a great wipe to her mouth. "Then I'll stand by you. We'll see it out."

"We'll see it out!" I ardently echoed, giving her my hand to make it a vow.

She held me there a moment, then whisked up her apron again with her detached hand. "Would you mind, miss, if I used the freedom—"

"To kiss me? No!" I took the good creature in my arms and, after we had embraced like sisters, felt still more fortified and indignant.

This, at all events, was for the time: a time so full that, as I recall the way it went, it reminds me of all the art I now need to make it a little distinct. What I look back at with amazement is the situation I accepted. I had undertaken, with my companion, to see it out, and I was under a charm, apparently, that could smooth away the extent and the far and difficult connections of such an effort. I was lifted aloft on a great wave of infatuation and pity. I found it simple, in my ignorance, my confusion, and perhaps my conceit, to assume that I could deal with a boy whose education for the world was all on the point of beginning.

I am unable even to remember at this day what proposal I framed for the end of his holidays and the resumption of his studies. Lessons with me, indeed, that charming summer, we all had a theory that he was to have; but I now feel that, for weeks, the lessons must have been rather my own. I learned something—at first, certainly—that had not been one of the teachings of my small, smothered life; learned to be amused, and even amusing, and not to think for the morrow. It was the first time, in a manner, that I had known space and air and freedom, all the music of summer and all the mystery of nature. And then there was consideration—and consideration was sweet.

Oh, it was a trap—not designed, but deep—to my imagination, to my delicacy, perhaps to my vanity; to whatever, in me, was most excitable. The best way to picture it all is to say that I was off my guard. They gave me so little trouble—they were of a gentleness so extraordinary. I used to speculate—but even this with a dim disconnectedness—as to how the rough future (for all futures are rough!) would handle them and might bruise them. They had the bloom of health and happiness; and yet, as if I had been in charge of a pair of little grandees, of princes of the blood, for whom everything, to be right, would have to be enclosed and protected, the only form that, in my fancy, the afteryears could take for them was that of a romantic, a really royal extension of the garden and the park. It may be, of course, above all, that what suddenly broke into this gives the previous time a charm of stillness—that hush in which something gathers or crouches. The change was actually like the spring of a beast.

In the first weeks the days were long; they often, at their finest, gave me what I used to call my own hour, the hour when, for my pupils, teatime and bedtime having come and gone, I had, before my final retirement, a small interval alone. Much as I liked my companions, this hour was the thing in the day I liked most; and I liked it best of all when, as the light faded—or rather, I should say, the day lingered and the last calls of the last birds sounded, in a flushed sky, from the old trees—I could take a turn into the grounds and enjoy, almost with a sense of property that amused and flattered me, the beauty and dignity of the place.

It was a pleasure at these moments to feel myself tranquil and justified; doubtless, perhaps, also to reflect that by my discretion, my quiet good sense and general high propriety, I was giving pleasure—if he ever thought of it!—to the person to whose pressure I had responded. What I was doing was what he had earnestly hoped and directly asked of me, and that I COULD, after all, do it proved even a greater joy than I had expected. I daresay I fancied myself, in short, a remarkable young woman and took comfort in the faith that this would more publicly appear. Well, I needed to be remarkable to offer a front to the remarkable things that presently gave their first sign.

It was plump, one afternoon, in the middle of my very hour: the children were tucked away, and I had come out for my stroll. One of the thoughts that, as I don't in the least shrink now from noting, used to be with me in these wanderings was that it would be as charming as a charming story suddenly to meet someone. Someone would appear there at the turn of a path and would stand before me and smile and approve. I didn't ask more than that—I only asked that he should KNOW; and the only way to be sure he knew would be to see it, and the kind light of it, in his handsome face.

That was exactly present to me—by which I mean the face was—when, on the first of these occasions, at the end of a long June day, I stopped short on emerging from one of the plantations and coming into view of the house. What arrested me on the spot—and with a shock much greater than any vision had allowed for—was the sense that my imagination had, in a flash, turned real. He did stand there!—but high up, beyond the lawn and at the very top of the tower to which, on that first morning, little Flora had conducted me. This tower was one of a pair—square, incongruous, crenelated structures—that were distinguished, for some reason, though I could see little difference, as the new and the old.

They flanked opposite ends of the house and were probably architectural absurdities, redeemed in a measure indeed by not being wholly disengaged nor of a height too pretentious, dating, in their gingerbread antiquity, from a romantic revival that was already a respectable past. I admired them, had fancies about them, for we could all profit in a degree, especially when they loomed through the dusk, by the grandeur of their actual battlements; yet it was not at such an elevation that the figure I had so often invoked seemed most in place.

It produced in me, this figure, in the clear twilight, I remember, two distinct gasps of emotion, which were, sharply, the shock of my first and that of my second surprise. My second was a violent perception of the mistake of my first: the man who met my eyes was not the person I had precipitately supposed. There came to me thus a bewilderment of vision of which, after these years, there is no living view that I can hope to give. An unknown man in a lonely place is a permitted object of fear to a young woman privately bred; and the figure that faced me was—a few more seconds assured me—as little anyone else I knew as it was the image that had been in my mind. I had not seen it in Harley Street—I had not seen it anywhere.

The place, moreover, in the strangest way in the world, had, on the instant, and by the very fact of its appearance, become a solitude. To me at least, making my statement here with a deliberation with which I have never made it, the whole feeling of the moment returns. It was as if, while I took in—what I did take in—all the rest of the scene had been stricken with death. I can hear again, as I write, the intense hush in which the sounds of evening dropped. The rooks stopped cawing in the golden sky, and the friendly hour lost, for the minute, all its voice. But there was no other change in nature, unless indeed it were a change that I saw with a stranger sharpness.

The gold was still in the sky, the clearness in the air, and the man who looked at me over the battlements was as definite as a picture in a frame. That's how I thought, with extraordinary quickness, of each person that he might have been and that he was not. We were confronted across our distance quite long enough for me to ask myself with intensity who then he was and to feel, as an effect of my inability to say, a wonder that in a few instants more became intense.

The great question, or one of these, is, afterward, I know, with regard to certain matters, the question of how long they have lasted. Well, this matter of mine, think what you will of it, lasted while I caught at a dozen possibilities, none of which made a difference for the better, that I could see, in there having been in the house—and for how long, above all?—a person of whom I was in ignorance. It lasted while I just bridled a little with the sense that my office demanded that there should be no such ignorance and no such person. It lasted while this visitant, at all events—and there was a touch of the strange freedom, as I remember, in the sign of familiarity of his wearing no hat—seemed to fix me, from his position, with just the question, just the scrutiny through the fading light, that his own presence provoked.

We were too far apart to call to each other, but there was a moment at which, at shorter range, some challenge between us, breaking the hush, would have been the right result of our straight mutual stare. He was in one of the angles, the one away from the house, very erect, as it struck me, and with both hands on the ledge. So I saw him as I see the letters I form on this page; then, exactly, after a minute, as if to add to the spectacle, he slowly changed his place—passed, looking at me hard all the while, to the opposite corner of the platform. Yes, I had the sharpest sense that during this transit he never took his eyes from me, and I can see at this moment the way his hand, as he went, passed from one of the crenelations to the next. He stopped at the other corner, but less long, and even as he turned away still markedly fixed me. He turned away; that was all I knew.

4

It was not that I didn't wait, on this occasion, for more, for I was rooted as deeply as I was shaken. Was there a "secret" at Bly—a mystery of Udolpho or an insane, an unmentionable relative kept in unsuspected confinement? I can't say how long I turned it over, or how long, in a confusion of curiosity and dread, I remained where I had had my collision; I only recall that when I re-entered the house darkness had quite closed in. Agitation, in the interval, certainly had held me and driven me, for I must, in circling about the place, have walked three miles; but I was to be, later on, so much more overwhelmed that this mere dawn of alarm was a comparatively human chill.

The most singular part of it, in fact—singular as the rest had been—was the part I became, in the hall, aware of in meeting Mrs. Grose. This picture comes back to me in the general train—the impression, as I received it on my return, of the wide white panelled space, bright in the lamplight and with its portraits and red carpet, and of the good surprised look of my friend, which immediately told me she had missed me. It came to me straightway, under her contact, that, with plain heartiness, mere relieved anxiety at my appearance, she knew nothing whatever that could bear upon the incident I had there ready for her. I had not suspected in advance that her comfortable face would pull me up, and I somehow measured the importance of what I had seen by my thus finding myself hesitate to mention it.

Scarce anything in the whole history seems to me so odd as this fact that my real beginning of fear was one, as I may say, with the instinct of sparing my companion. On the spot, accordingly, in the pleasant hall and with her eyes on me, I, for a reason that I couldn't then have phrased, achieved an inward resolution-offered a vague pretext for my lateness and, with the plea of the beauty of the night and of the heavy dew and wet feet, went as soon as possible to my room.

Here it was another affair; here, for many days after, it was a queer affair enough. There were hours, from day to day—or at least there were moments, snatched even from clear duties-when I had to shut myself up to think. It was not so much yet that I was more nervous than I could bear to be as that I was remarkably afraid of becoming so; for the truth I had now to turn over was, simply and clearly, the truth that I could arrive at no account whatever of the visitor with whom I had been so inexplicably and yet, as it seemed to me, so intimately concerned. It took little time to see that I could sound without forms of inquiry and without exciting remark any domestic complications.

The shock I had suffered must have sharpened all my senses; I felt sure, at the end of three days and as the result of mere closer attention, that I had not been practiced upon by the servants nor made the object of any "game." Of whatever it was that I knew, nothing was known around me. There was but one sane inference: someone had taken a liberty rather gross. That was what, repeatedly, I dipped into my room and locked the door to say to myself. We had been, collectively, subject to an intrusion; some unscrupulous traveller, curious in old houses, had made his way in unobserved, enjoyed the prospect from the best point of view, and then stolen out as he came. If he had given me such a bold hard stare, that was but a part of his indiscretion. The good thing, after all, was that we should surely see no more of him.

This was not so good a thing, I admit, as not to leave me to judge that what, essentially, made nothing else much signify was simply my charming work. My charming work was just my life with Miles and Flora, and through nothing could I so like it as through feeling that I could throw myself into it in trouble. The attraction of my small charges was a constant joy, leading me to wonder afresh at the vanity of my original fears, the distaste I had begun by entertaining for the probable gray prose of my office.

There was to be no gray prose, it appeared, and no long grind; so how could work not be charming that presented itself as daily beauty? It was all the romance of the nursery and the poetry of the schoolroom. I don't mean by this, of course, that we studied only fiction and verse; I mean I can express no otherwise the sort of interest my companions inspired. How can I describe that except by saying that instead of growing used to them—and it's a marvel for a governess: I call the sisterhood to witness!—I made constant fresh discoveries. There was one direction, assuredly, in which these discoveries stopped: deep obscurity continued to cover the region of the boy's conduct at school. It had been promptly given me, I have noted, to face that mystery without a pang.

Perhaps even it would be nearer the truth to say that—without a word—he himself had cleared it up. He had made the whole charge absurd. My conclusion bloomed there with the real rose flush of his innocence: he was only too fine and fair for the little horrid, unclean school world, and he had paid a price for it. I reflected acutely that the sense of such differences, such superiorities of quality, always, on the part of the majority—which could include even stupid, sordid headmasters—turn infallibly to the vindictive.

Both the children had a gentleness (it was their only fault, and it never made Miles a muff) that kept them—how shall I express it?—almost impersonal and certainly quite unpunishable. They were like the cherubs of the anecdote, who had—morally, at any rate—nothing to whack! I remember feeling with Miles in especial as if he had had, as it were, no history. We expect of a small child a scant one, but there was in this beautiful little boy something extraordinarily sensitive, yet extraordinarily happy, that, more than in any creature of his age I have seen, struck me as beginning anew each day. He had never for a second suffered. I took this as a direct disproof of his having really been chastised. If he had been wicked he would have "caught" it, and I should have caught it by the rebound—I should have found the trace.

I found nothing at all, and he was therefore an angel. He never spoke of his school, never mentioned a comrade or a master; and I, for my part, was quite too much disgusted to allude to them. Of course I was under the spell, and the wonderful part is that, even at the time, I perfectly knew I was. But I gave myself up to it; it was an antidote to any pain, and I had more pains than one. I was in receipt in these days of disturbing letters from home, where things were not going well. But with my children, what things in the world mattered? That was the question I used to put to my scrappy retirements. I was dazzled by their loveliness.

There was a Sunday—to get on—when it rained with such force and for so many hours that there could be no procession to church; in consequence of which, as the day declined, I had arranged with Mrs. Grose that, should the evening show improvement, we would attend together the late service. The rain happily stopped, and I prepared for our walk, which, through the park and by the good road to the village, would be a matter of twenty minutes. Coming downstairs to meet my colleague in the hall, I remembered a pair of gloves that had required three stitches and that had received them—with a publicity perhaps not edifying—while I sat with the children at their tea, served on Sundays, by exception, in that cold, clean temple of mahogany and brass, the "grown-up" dining room.

The gloves had been dropped there, and I turned in to recover them. The day was gray enough, but the afternoon light still lingered, and it enabled me, on crossing the threshold, not only to recognize, on a chair near the wide window, then closed, the articles I wanted, but to become aware of a person on the other side of the window and looking straight in. One step into the room had sufficed; my vision was instantaneous; it was all there. The person looking straight in was the person who had already appeared to me. He appeared thus again with I won't say greater distinctness, for that was impossible, but with a nearness that represented a forward stride in our intercourse and made me, as I met him, catch my breath and turn cold.

He was the same—he was the same, and seen, this time, as he had been seen before, from the waist up, the window, though the dining room was on the ground floor, not going down to the terrace on which he stood. His face was close to the glass, yet the effect of this better view was, strangely, only to show me how intense the former had been. He remained but a few seconds-long enough to convince me he also saw and recognized; but it was as if I had been looking at him for years and had known him always.

Something, however, happened this time that had not happened before; his stare into my face, through the glass and across the room, was as deep and hard as then, but it quitted me for a moment during which I could still watch it, see it fix successively several other things. On the spot there came to me the added shock of a certitude that it was not for me he had come there. He had come for someone else. The flash of this knowledge—for it was knowledge in the midst of dread—produced in me the most extraordinary effect, started as I stood there, a sudden vibration of duty and courage. I say courage because I was beyond all doubt already far gone. I bounded straight out of the door again, reached that of the house, got, in an instant, upon the drive, and, passing along the terrace as fast as I could rush, turned a corner and came full in sight. But it was in sight of nothing now—my visitor had vanished. I stopped, I almost dropped, with the real relief of this; but I took in the whole scene—I gave him time to reappear. I call it time, but how long was it? I can't speak to the purpose today of the duration of these things.

That kind of measure must have left me: they couldn't have lasted as they actually appeared to me to last. The terrace and the whole place, the lawn and the garden beyond it, all I could see of the park, were empty with a great emptiness. There were shrubberies and big trees, but I remember the clear assurance I felt that none of them concealed him. He was there or was not there: not there if I didn't see him. I got hold of this; then, instinctively, instead of returning as I had come, went to the window. It was confusedly present to me that I ought to place myself where he had stood. I did so; I applied my face to the pane and looked, as he had looked, into the room.

As if, at this moment, to show me exactly what his range had been, Mrs. Grose, as I had done for himself just before, came in from the hall. With this I had the full image of a repetition of what had already occurred. She saw me as I had seen my own visitant; she pulled up short as I had done; I gave her something of the shock that I had received. She turned white, and this made me ask myself if I had blanched as much. She stared, in short, and retreated on just MY lines, and I knew she had then passed out and come round to me and that I should presently meet her. I remained where I was, and while I waited I thought of more things than one. But there's only one I take space to mention. I wondered why SHE should be scared.

5

Oh, she let me know as soon as, round the corner of the house, she loomed again into view. "What in the name of goodness is the matter—?" She was now flushed and out of breath.

I said nothing till she came quite near. "With me?" I must have made a wonderful face. "Do I show it?"

"You're as white as a sheet. You look awful."

I considered; I could meet on this, without scruple, any innocence. My need to respect the bloom of Mrs. Grose's had dropped, without a rustle, from my shoulders, and if I wavered for the instant it was not with what I kept back. I put out my hand to her and she took it; I held her hard a little, liking to feel her close to me. There was a kind of support in the shy heave of her surprise. "You came for me for church, of course, but I can't go."

"Has anything happened?"

"Yes. You must know now. Did I look very queer?"

"Through this window? Dreadful!"

"Well," I said, "I've been frightened." Mrs. Grose's eyes expressed plainly that SHE had no wish to be, yet also that she knew too well her place not to be ready to share with me any marked inconvenience. Oh, it was quite settled that she MUST share! "Just what you saw from the dining room a minute ago was the effect of that. What *I* saw—just before—was much worse."

Her hand tightened. "What was it?"

"An extraordinary man. Looking in."

"What extraordinary man?"

"I haven't the least idea."

Mrs. Grose gazed round us in vain. "Then where is he gone?"

"I know still less."

"Have you seen him before?"

"Yes—once. On the old tower."

She could only look at me harder. "Do you mean he's a stranger?"

"Oh, very much!"

"Yet you didn't tell me?"

"No—for reasons. But now that you've guessed—"

Mrs. Grose's round eyes encountered this charge. "Ah, I haven't guessed!" she said very simply. "How can I if YOU don't imagine?"

"I don't in the very least."

"You've seen him nowhere but on the tower?"

"And on this spot just now."

Mrs. Grose looked round again. "What was he doing on the tower?"

"Only standing there and looking down at me."

She thought a minute. "Was he a gentleman?"

I found I had no need to think. "No." She gazed in deeper wonder. "No."

"Then nobody about the place? Nobody from the village?"

"Nobody—nobody. I didn't tell you, but I made sure."

She breathed a vague relief: this was, oddly, so much to the good. It only went indeed a little way. "But if he isn't a gentleman—"

"What IS he? He's a horror."

"A horror?"

"He's—God help me if I know WHAT he is!"

Mrs. Grose looked round once more; she fixed her eyes on the duskier distance, then, pulling herself together, turned to me with abrupt inconsequence. "It's time we should be at church."

"Oh, I'm not fit for church!"

"Won't it do you good?"

"It won't do THEM—! I nodded at the house.

"The children?"

"I can't leave them now."

"You're afraid—?"

I spoke boldly. "I'm afraid of HIM."

Mrs. Grose's large face showed me, at this, for the first time, the faraway faint glimmer of a consciousness more acute: I somehow made out in it the delayed dawn of an idea I myself had not given her and that was as yet quite obscure to me. It comes back to me that I thought instantly of this as something I could get from her; and I felt it to be connected with the desire she presently showed to know more. "When was it—on the tower?"

"About the middle of the month. At this same hour."

"Almost at dark," said Mrs. Grose.

"Oh, no, not nearly. I saw him as I see you."

"Then how did he get in?"

"And how did he get out?" I laughed. "I had no opportunity to ask him! This evening, you see," I pursued, "he has not been able to get in."

"He only peeps?"

"I hope it will be confined to that!" She had now let go my hand; she turned away a little. I waited an instant; then I brought out: "Go to church. Goodbye. I must watch."

Slowly she faced me again. "Do you fear for them?"

We met in another long look. "Don't YOU?" Instead of answering she came nearer to the window and, for a minute, applied her face to the glass. "You see how he could see," I meanwhile went on.

She didn't move. "How long was he here?"

"Till I came out. I came to meet him."

Mrs. Grose at last turned round, and there was still more in her face. "*I* couldn't have come out."

"Neither could I!" I laughed again. "But I did come. I have my duty."

"So have I mine," she replied; after which she added: "What is he like?"

"I've been dying to tell you. But he's like nobody."

"Nobody?" she echoed.

"He has no hat." Then seeing in her face that she already, in this, with a deeper dismay, found a touch of picture, I quickly added stroke to stroke. "He has red hair, very red, close-curling, and a pale face, long in shape, with straight, good features and little, rather queer whiskers that are as red as his hair. His eyebrows are, somehow, darker; they look particularly arched and as if they might move a good deal. His eyes are sharp, strange-awfully; but I only know clearly that they're rather small and very fixed. His mouth's wide, and his lips are thin, and except for his little whiskers he's quite clean-shaven. He gives me a sort of sense of looking like an actor."

"An actor!" It was impossible to resemble one less, at least, than Mrs. Grose at that moment.

"I've never seen one, but so I suppose them. He's tall, active, erect," I continued, "but never—no, never!—a gentleman."

My companion's face had blanched as I went on; her round eyes started and her mild mouth gaped. "A gentleman?" she gasped, confounded, stupefied: "a gentleman HE?"

"You know him then?"

She visibly tried to hold herself. "But he IS handsome?"

I saw the way to help her. "Remarkably!"

"And dressed—?"

"In somebody's clothes." "They're smart, but they're not his own."

She broke into a breathless affirmative groan: "They're the master's!"

I caught it up. "You DO know him?"

She faltered but a second. "Quint!" she cried.

"Quint?"

"Peter Quint—his own man, his valet, when he was here!"

"When the master was?"

Gaping still, but meeting me, she pieced it all together. "He never wore his hat, but he did wear—well, there were waistcoats missed. They were both here—last year. Then the master went, and Quint was alone."

I followed, but halting a little. "Alone?"

"Alone with US." Then, as from a deeper depth, "In charge," she added.

"And what became of him?"

She hung fire so long that I was still more mystified. "He went, too," she brought out at last.

"Went where?"

Her expression, at this, became extraordinary. "God knows where! He died."

"Died?" I almost shrieked.

She seemed fairly to square herself, plant herself more firmly to utter the wonder of it. "Yes. Mr. Quint is dead."

6

It took of course more than that particular passage to place us together in presence of what we had now to live with as we could—my dreadful liability to impressions of the order so vividly exemplified, and my companion's knowledge, henceforth—a knowledge half consternation and half compassion-of that liability. There had been, this evening, after the revelation left me, for an hour, so prostrate—there had been, for either of us, no attendance on any service but a little service of tears and vows, of prayers and promises, a climax to the series of mutual challenges and pledges that had straightway ensued on our retreating together to the schoolroom and shutting ourselves up there to have everything out.

The result of our having everything out was simply to reduce our situation to the last rigor of its elements. She herself had seen nothing, not the shadow of a shadow, and nobody in the house but the governess was in the governess's plight; yet she accepted without directly impugning my sanity the truth as I gave it to her, and ended by showing me, on this ground, an awe-stricken tenderness, an expression of the sense of my more than questionable privilege, of which the very breath has remained with me as that of the sweetest of human charities.

What was settled between us, accordingly, that night, was that we thought we might bear things together; and I was not even sure that, in spite of her exemption, it was she who had the best of the burden. I knew at this hour, I think, as well as I knew later, what I was capable of meeting to shelter my pupils; but it took me some time to be wholly sure of what my honest ally was prepared for to keep terms with so compromising a contract. I was queer company enough—quite as queer as the company I received; but as I trace over what we went through I see how much common ground we must have found in the one idea that, by good fortune, COULD steady us.

It was the idea, the second movement, that led me straight out, as I may say, of the inner chamber of my dread. I could take the air in the court, at least, and there Mrs. Grose could join me. Perfectly can I recall now the particular way strength came to me before we separated for the night. We had gone over and over every feature of what I had seen.

"He was looking for someone else, you say—someone who was not you?"

"He was looking for little Miles." A portentous clearness now possessed me. "THAT'S whom he was looking for."

"But how do you know?"

"I know, I know, I know!" My exaltation grew. "And YOU know, my dear!"

She didn't deny this, but I required, I felt, not even so much telling as that. She resumed in a moment, at any rate: "What if HE should see him?"

"Little Miles? That's what he wants!"

She looked immensely scared again. "The child?"

"Heaven forbid! The man. He wants to appear to THEM." That he might was an awful conception, and yet, somehow, I could keep it at bay; which, moreover, as we lingered there, was what I succeeded in practically proving. I had an absolute certainty that I should see again what I had already seen, but something within me said that by offering myself bravely as the sole subject of such experience, by accepting, by inviting, by surmounting it all, I should serve as an expiatory victim and guard the tranquility of my companions. The children, in especial, I should thus fence about and absolutely save. I recall one of the last things I said that night to Mrs. Grose.

"It does strike me that my pupils have never mentioned—"

She looked at me hard as I musingly pulled up. "His having been here and the time they were with him?"

"The time they were with him, and his name, his presence, his history, in any way."

"Oh, the little lady doesn't remember. She never heard or knew."

"The circumstances of his death?" I thought with some intensity. "Perhaps not. But Miles would remember—Miles would know."

"Ah, don't try him!" broke from Mrs. Grose.

I returned her the look she had given me. "Don't be afraid." I continued to think. "It IS rather odd."

"That he has never spoken of him?"

"Never by the least allusion. And you tell me they were 'great friends'?"

"Oh, it wasn't HIM!" Mrs. Grose with emphasis declared. "It was Quint's own fancy. To play with him, I mean—to spoil him." She paused a moment; then she added: "Quint was much too free."

This gave me, straight from my vision of his face—SUCH a face!—a sudden sickness of disgust. "Too free with MY boy?"

"Too free with everyone!"

I forbore, for the moment, to analyze this description further than by the reflection that a part of it applied to several of the members of the household, of the half-dozen maids and men who were still of our small colony. But there was everything, for our apprehension, in the lucky fact that no discomfortable legend, no perturbation of scullions, had ever, within anyone's memory attached to the kind old place. It had neither bad name nor ill fame, and Mrs. Grose, most apparently, only desired to cling to me and to quake in silence. I even put her, the very last thing of all, to the test. It was when, at midnight, she had her hand on the schoolroom door to take leave. "I have it from you then—for it's of great importance—that he was definitely and admittedly bad?"

"Oh, not admittedly. *I* knew it—but the master didn't."

"And you never told him?"

"Well, he didn't like tale-bearing—he hated complaints. He was terribly short with anything of that kind, and if people were all right to HIM—"

"He wouldn't be bothered with more?" This squared well enough with my impressions of him: he was not a trouble-loving gentleman, nor so very particular perhaps about some of the company HE kept. All the same, I pressed my interlocutress. "I promise you I would have told!"

She felt my discrimination. "I daresay I was wrong. But, really, I was afraid."

"Afraid of what?"

"Of things that man could do. Quint was so clever—he was so deep."

I took this in still more than, probably, I showed. "You weren't afraid of anything else? Not of his effect—?"

"His effect?" she repeated with a face of anguish and waiting while I faltered.

"On innocent little precious lives. They were in your charge."

"No, they were not in mine!" she roundly and distressfully returned. "The master believed in him and placed him here because he was supposed not to be well and the country air so good for him. So he had everything to say. Yes"—she let me have it—"even about THEM."

"Them—that creature?" I had to smother a kind of howl. "And you could bear it!"

"No. I couldn't—and I can't now!" And the poor woman burst into tears.

A rigid control, from the next day, was, as I have said, to follow them; yet how often and how passionately, for a week, we came back together to the subject! Much as we had discussed it that Sunday night, I was, in the immediate later hours in especial—for it may be imagined whether I slept—still haunted with the shadow of something she had not told me. I myself had kept back nothing, but there was a word Mrs. Grose had kept back. I was sure, moreover, by morning, that this was not from a failure of frankness, but because on every side there were fears.

It seems to me indeed, in retrospect, that by the time the morrow's sun was high I had restlessly read into the fact before us almost all the meaning they were to receive from subsequent and more cruel occurrences. What they gave me above all was just the sinister figure of the living man—the dead one would keep awhile!—and of the months he had continuously passed at Bly, which, added up, made a formidable stretch. The limit of this evil time had arrived only when, on the dawn of a winter's morning, Peter Quint was found, by a laborer going to early work, stone dead on the road from the village: a catastrophe explained—superficially at least—by a visible wound to his head; such a wound as might have been produced—and as, on the final evidence, HAD been—by a fatal slip, in the dark and after leaving the public house, on the steepish icy slope, a wrong path altogether, at the bottom of which he lay.

The icy slope, the turn mistaken at night and in liquor, accounted for much—practically, in the end and after the inquest and boundless chatter, for everything; but there had been matters in his life—strange passages and perils, secret disorders, vices more than suspected—that would have accounted for a good deal more.

I scarce know how to put my story into words that shall be a credible picture of my state of mind; but I was in these days literally able to find a joy in the extraordinary flight of heroism the occasion demanded of me. I now saw that I had been asked for a service admirable and difficult; and there would be a greatness in letting it be seen—oh, in the right quarter!—that I could succeed where many another girl might have failed. It was an immense help to me—I confess I rather applaud myself as I look back!—that I saw my service so strongly and so simply. I was there to protect and defend the little creatures in the world the most bereaved and the most lovable, the appeal of whose helplessness had suddenly become only too explicit, a deep, constant ache of one's own committed heart.

We were cut off, really, together; we were united in our danger. They had nothing but me, and I—well, I had THEM. It was in short a magnificent chance. This chance presented itself to me in an image richly material. I was a screen—I was to stand before them. The more I saw, the less they would. I began to watch them in a stifled suspense, a disguised excitement that might well, had it continued too long, have turned to something like madness. What saved me, as I now see, was that it turned to something else altogether. It didn't last as suspense—it was superseded by horrible proofs. Proofs, I say, yes—from the moment I really took hold.

This moment dated from an afternoon hour that I happened to spend in the grounds with the younger of my pupils alone. We had left Miles indoors, on the red cushion of a deep window seat; he had wished to finish a book, and I had been glad to encourage a purpose so laudable in a young man whose only defect was an occasional excess of the restless. His sister, on the contrary, had been alert to come out, and I strolled with her half an hour, seeking the shade, for the sun was still high and the day exceptionally warm. I was aware afresh, with her, as we went, of how, like her brother, she contrived—it was the charming thing in both children—to let me alone without appearing to drop me and to accompany me without appearing to surround.

They were never importunate and yet never listless. My attention to them all really went to seeing them amuse themselves immensely without me: this was a spectacle they seemed actively to prepare and that engaged me as an active admirer. I walked in a world of their invention—they had no occasion whatever to draw upon mine; so that my time was taken only with being, for them, some remarkable person or thing that the game of the moment required and that was merely, thanks to my superior, my exalted stamp, a happy and highly distinguished sinecure. I forget what I was on the present occasion; I only remember that I was something very important and very quiet and that Flora was playing very hard. We were on the edge of the lake, and, as we had lately begun geography, the lake was the Sea of Azof.

Suddenly, in these circumstances, I became aware that, on the other side of the Sea of Azof, we had an interested spectator. The way this knowledge gathered in me was the strangest thing in the world—the strangest, that is, except the very much stranger in which it quickly merged itself. I had sat down with a piece of work—for I was something or other that could sit—on the old stone bench which overlooked the pond; and in this position I began to take in with certitude, and yet without direct vision, the presence, at a distance, of a third person. The old trees, the thick shrubbery, made a great and pleasant shade, but it was all suffused with the brightness of the hot, still hour.

There was no ambiguity in anything; none whatever, at least, in the conviction I from one moment to another found myself forming as to what I should see straight before me and across the lake as a consequence of raising my eyes. They were attached at this juncture to the stitching in which I was engaged, and I can feel once more the spasm of my effort not to move them till I should so have steadied myself as to be able to make up my mind what to do.

There was an alien object in view—a figure whose right of presence I instantly, passionately questioned. I recollect counting over perfectly the possibilities, reminding myself that nothing was more natural, for instance, then the appearance of one of the men about the place, or even of a messenger, a postman, or a tradesman's boy, from the village. That reminder had as little effect on my practical certitude as I was conscious—still even without looking—of its having upon the character and attitude of our visitor. Nothing was more natural than that these things should be the other things that they absolutely were not.

Of the positive identity of the apparition I would assure myself as soon as the small clock of my courage should have ticked out the right second; meanwhile, with an effort that was already sharp enough, I transferred my eyes straight to little Flora, who, at the moment, was about ten yards away. My heart had stood still for an instant with the wonder and terror of the question whether she too would see; and I held my breath while I waited for what a cry from her, what some sudden innocent sign either of interest or of alarm, would tell me. I waited, but nothing came; then, in the first place—and there is something more dire in this, I feel, than in anything I have to relate—I was determined by a sense that, within a minute, all sounds from her had previously dropped; and, in the second, by the circumstance that, also within the minute, she had, in her play, turned her back to the water.

This was her attitude when I at last looked at her—looked with the confirmed conviction that we were still, together, under direct personal notice. She had picked up a small flat piece of wood, which happened to have in it a little hole that had evidently suggested to her the idea of sticking in another fragment that might figure as a mast and make the thing a boat. This second morsel, as I watched her, she was very markedly and intently attempting to tighten in its place. My apprehension of what she was doing sustained me so that after some seconds I felt I was ready for more. Then I again shifted my eyes—I faced what I had to face.

7

I got hold of Mrs. Grose as soon after this as I could; and I can give no intelligible account of how I fought out the interval. Yet I still hear myself cry as I fairly threw myself into her arms: "They KNOW—it's too monstrous: they know, they know!"

"And what on earth—?" I felt her incredulity as she held me.

"Why, all that WE know—and heaven knows what else besides!" Then, as she released me, I made it out to her, made it out perhaps only now with full coherency even to myself. "Two hours ago, in the garden"—I could scarce articulate—"Flora SAW!"

Mrs. Grose took it as she might have taken a blow in the stomach. "She has told you?" she panted.

"Not a word—that's the horror. She kept it to herself! The child of eight, THAT child!" Unutterable still, for me, was the stupefaction of it.

Mrs. Grose, of course, could only gape the wider. "Then how do you know?"

"I was there—I saw with my eyes: saw that she was perfectly aware."

"Do you mean aware of HIM?"

"No—of HER." I was conscious as I spoke that I looked prodigious things, for I got the slow reflection of them in my companion's face. "Another person—this time; but a figure of quite as unmistakable horror and evil: a woman in black, pale and dreadful—with such an air also, and such a face!—on the other side of the lake. I was there with the child—quiet for the hour; and in the midst of it she came."

"Came how—from where?"

"From where they come from! She just appeared and stood there—but not so near."

"And without coming nearer?"

"Oh, for the effect and the feeling, she might have been as close as you!"

My friend, with an odd impulse, fell back a step. "Was she someone you've never seen?"

"Yes. But someone the child has. Someone YOU have." Then, to show how I had thought it all out: "My predecessor—the one who died."

"Miss Jessel?"

"Miss Jessel. You don't believe me?" I pressed.

She turned right and left in her distress. "How can you be sure?"

This drew from me, in the state of my nerves, a flash of impatience. "Then ask Flora—SHE'S sure!" But I had no sooner spoken than I caught myself up. "No, for God's sake, DON'T! She'll say she isn't—she'll lie!"

Mrs. Grose was not too bewildered instinctively to protest. "Ah, how CAN you?"

"Because I'm clear. Flora doesn't want me to know."

"It's only then to spare you."

"No, no—there are depths, depths! The more I go over it, the more I see in it, and the more I see in it, the more I fear. I don't know what I DON'T see—what I DON'T fear!"

Mrs. Grose tried to keep up with me. "You mean you're afraid of seeing her again?"

"Oh, no; that's nothing—now!" Then I explained. "It's of

NOT seeing her."

But my companion only looked wan. "I don't understand you."

"Why, it's that the child may keep it up—and that the child assuredly WILL—without my knowing it."

At the image of this possibility Mrs. Grose for a moment collapsed, yet presently to pull herself together again, as if from the positive force of the sense of what, should we yield an inch, there would really be to give way to. "Dear, dear—we must keep our heads! And after all, if she doesn't mind it—!" She even tried a grim joke. "Perhaps she likes it!"

"Likes SUCH things—a scrap of an infant!"

"Isn't it just a proof of her blessed innocence?" my friend bravely inquired.

She brought me, for the instant, almost round. "Oh, we must clutch at THAT—we must cling to it! If it isn't a proof of what you say, it's a proof of—God knows what! For the woman's a horror of horrors."

Mrs. Grose, at this, fixed her eyes a minute on the ground; then at last raising them, "Tell me how you know," she said.

"Then you admit it's what she was?" I cried.

"Tell me how you know," my friend simply repeated.

"Know? By seeing her! By the way she looked."

"At you, do you mean—so wickedly?"

"Dear me, no—I could have borne that. She gave me never a glance. She only fixed the child."

Mrs. Grose tried to see it. "Fixed her?"

"Ah, with such awful eyes!"

She stared at mine as if they might really have resembled them. "Do you mean of dislike?"

"God help us, no. Of something much worse."

"Worse than dislike?—this left her indeed at a loss.

"With a determination—indescribable. With a kind of fury of intention."

I made her turn pale. "Intention?"

"To get hold of her." Mrs. Grose—her eyes just lingering on

mine—gave a shudder and walked to the window; and while she stood there looking out I completed my statement. "THAT'S what Flora knows."

After a little she turned round. "The person was in black, you say?"

"In mourning—rather poor, almost shabby. But—yes—with extraordinary beauty." I now recognized to what I had at last, stroke by stroke, brought the victim of my confidence, for she quite visibly weighed this. "Oh, handsome—very, very," I insisted; "wonderfully handsome. But infamous."

She slowly came back to me. "Miss Jessel—WAS infamous." She once more took my hand in both her own, holding it as tight as if to fortify me against the increase of alarm I might draw from this disclosure. "They were both infamous," she finally said.

So, for a little, we faced it once more together; and I found absolutely a degree of help in seeing it now so straight. "I appreciate," I said, "the great decency of your not having hitherto spoken; but the time has certainly come to give me the whole thing." She appeared to assent to this, but still only in silence; seeing which I went on: "I must have it now. Of what did she die? Come, there was something between them."

"There was everything."

"In spite of the difference—?"

"Oh, of their rank, their condition"—she brought it woefully out. "SHE was a lady."

I turned it over; I again saw. "Yes—she was a lady."

"And he so dreadfully below," said Mrs. Grose.

I felt that I doubtless needn't press too hard, in such company, on the place of a servant in the scale; but there was nothing to prevent an acceptance of my companion's own measure of my predecessor's abasement. There was a way to deal with that, and I dealt; the more readily for my full vision—on the evidence—of our employer's late clever, good-looking "own" man; impudent, assured, spoiled, depraved. "The fellow was a hound."

Mrs. Grose considered as if it were perhaps a little a case for a sense of shades. "I've never seen one like him. He did what he wished."

"With HER?"

"With them all."

It was as if now in my friend's own eyes Miss Jessel had again appeared. I seemed at any rate, for an instant, to see their evocation of her as distinctly as I had seen her by the pond; and I brought out with decision: "It must have been also what SHE wished!"

Mrs. Grose's face signified that it had been indeed, but she said at the same time: "Poor woman—she paid for it!"

"Then you do know what she died of?" I asked.

"No—I know nothing. I wanted not to know; I was glad enough I didn't; and I thanked heaven she was well out of this!"

"Yet you had, then, your idea—"

"Of her real reason for leaving? Oh, yes—as to that. She couldn't have stayed. Fancy it here—for a governess! And afterward I imagined—and I still imagine. And what I imagine is dreadful."

"Not so dreadful as what *I* do," I replied; on which I must have shown her—as I was indeed but too conscious—a front of miserable defeat. It brought out again all her compassion for me, and at the renewed touch of her kindness my power to resist broke down. I burst, as I had, the other time, made her burst, into tears; she took me to her motherly breast, and my lamentation overflowed. "I don't do it!" I sobbed in despair; "I don't save or shield them! It's far worse than I dreamed—they're lost!"

8

What I had said to Mrs. Grose was true enough: there were in the matter I had put before her depths and possibilities that I lacked resolution to sound; so that when we met once more in the wonder of it we were of a common mind about the duty of resistance to extravagant fancies. We were to keep our heads if we should keep nothing else—difficult indeed as that might be in the face of what, in our prodigious experience, was least to be questioned. Late that night, while the house slept, we had another talk in my room, when she went all the way with me as to its being beyond doubt that I had seen exactly what I had seen.

To hold her perfectly in the pinch of that, I found I had only to ask her how, if I had "made it up," I came to be able to give, of each of the persons appearing to me, a picture disclosing, to the last detail, their special marks—a portrait on the exhibition of which she had instantly recognized and named them. She wished of course—small blame to her!—to sink the whole subject; and I was quick to assure her that my own interest in it had now violently taken the form of a search for the way to escape from it. I encountered her on the ground of a probability that with recurrence—for recurrence we took for granted—I should get used to my danger, distinctly professing that my personal exposure had suddenly become the least of my discomforts. It was my new suspicion that was intolerable; and yet even to this complication the later hours of the day had brought a little ease.

On leaving her, after my first outbreak, I had of course returned to my pupils, associating the right remedy for my dismay with that sense of their charm which I had already found to be a thing I could positively cultivate and which had never failed me yet. I had simply, in other words, plunged afresh into Flora's special society and there become aware—it was almost a luxury!-that she could put her little conscious hand straight upon the spot that ached. She had looked at me in sweet speculation and then had accused me to my face of having "cried." I had supposed I had brushed away the ugly signs: but I could literally-for the time, at all events—rejoice, under this fathomless charity, that they had not entirely disappeared.

To gaze into the depths of blue of the child's eyes and pronounce their loveliness a trick of premature cunning was to be guilty of a cynicism in preference to which I naturally preferred to abjure my judgment and, so far as might be, my agitation. I couldn't abjure for merely wanting to, but I could repeat to Mrs. Grose—as I did there, over and over, in the small hours—that with their voices in the air, their pressure on one's heart, and their fragrant faces against one's cheek, everything fell to the ground but their incapacity and their beauty. It was a pity that, somehow, to settle this once for all, I had equally to re-enumerate the signs of subtlety that, in the afternoon, by the lake had made a miracle of my show of self-possession.

It was a pity to be obliged to reinvestigate the certitude of the moment itself and repeat how it had come to me as a revelation that the inconceivable communion I then surprised was a matter, for either party, of habit. It was a pity that I should have had to quaver out again the reasons for my not having, in my delusion, so much as questioned that the little girl saw our visitant even as I actually saw Mrs. Grose herself, and that she wanted, by just so much as she did thus see, to make me suppose she didn't, and at the same time, without showing anything, arrive at a guess as to whether I myself did! It was a pity that I needed once more to describe the portentous little activity by which she sought to divert my attention—the perceptible increase of movement, the greater intensity of play, the singing, the gabbling of nonsense, and the invitation to romp.

Yet if I had not indulged, to prove there was nothing in it, in this review, I should have missed the two or three dim elements of comfort that still remained to me. I should not for instance have been able to asseverate to my friend that I was certain-which was so much to the good—that *I* at least had not betrayed myself. I should not have been prompted, by stress of need, by desperation of mind—I scarce know what to call it—to invoke such further aid to intelligence as might spring from pushing my colleague fairly to the wall.

She had told me, bit by bit, under pressure, a great deal; but a small shifty spot on the wrong side of it all still sometimes brushed my brow like the wing of a bat; and I remember how on this occasion—for the sleeping house and the concentration alike of our danger and our watch seemed to help—I felt the importance of giving the last jerk to the curtain. "I don't believe anything so horrible," I recollect saying; "no, let us put it definitely, my dear, that I don't. But if I did, you know, there's a thing I should require now, just without sparing you the least bit more—oh, not a scrap, come!—to get out of you. What was it you had in mind when, in our distress, before Miles came back, over the letter from his school, you said, under my insistence, that you didn't pretend for him that he had not literally EVER been 'bad'? He has NOT literally 'ever,' in these weeks that I myself have lived with him and so closely watched him; he has been an imperturbable little prodigy of delightful, lovable goodness. Therefore you might perfectly have made the claim for him if you had not, as it happened, seen an exception to take. What was your exception, and to what passage in your personal observation of him did you refer?"

It was a dreadfully austere inquiry, but levity was not our note, and, at any rate, before the gray dawn admonished us to separate I had got my answer. What my friend had had in mind proved to be immensely to the purpose. It was neither more nor less than the circumstance that for a period of several months Quint and the boy had been perpetually together. It was in fact the very appropriate truth that she had ventured to criticize the propriety, to hint at the incongruity, of so close an alliance, and even to go so far on the subject as a frank overture to Miss Jessel. Miss Jessel had, with a most strange manner, requested her to mind her business, and the good woman had, on this, directly approached little Miles. What she had said to him, since I pressed, was that SHE liked to see young gentlemen not forget their station.

I pressed again, of course, at this. "You reminded him that Quint was only a base menial?"

"As you might say! And it was his answer, for one thing, that was bad."

"And for another thing?" I waited. "He repeated your words to Quint?"

"No, not that. It's just what he WOULDN'T!" she could still impress upon me. "I was sure, at any rate," she added, "that he didn't. But he denied certain occasions."

"What occasions?"

"When they had been about together quite as if Quint were his tutor—and a very grand one—and Miss Jessel only for the little lady. When he had gone off with the fellow, I mean, and spent hours with him."

"He then prevaricated about it—he said he hadn't?" Her assent was clear enough to cause me to add in a moment: "I see. He lied."

"Oh!" Mrs. Grose mumbled. This was a suggestion that it didn't matter; which indeed she backed up by a further remark. "You see, after all, Miss Jessel didn't mind. She didn't forbid him."

I considered. "Did he put that to you as a justification?"

At this she dropped again. "No, he never spoke of it."

"Never mentioned her in connection with Quint?"

She saw, visibly flushing, where I was coming out. "Well, he didn't show anything. He denied," she repeated; "he denied."

Lord, how I pressed her now! "So that you could see he knew what was between the two wretches?"

"I don't know—I don't know!" the poor woman groaned.

"You do know, you dear thing," I replied; "only you haven't my dreadful boldness of mind, and you keep back, out of timidity and modesty and delicacy, even the impression that, in the past, when you had, without my aid, to flounder about in silence, most of all made you miserable. But I shall get it out of you yet! There was something in the boy that suggested to you," I continued, "that he covered and concealed their relation."

"Oh, he couldn't prevent—"

"Your learning the truth? I daresay! But, heavens," I fell, with vehemence, athinking, "what it shows that they must, to that extent, have succeeded in making of him!"

"Ah, nothing that's not nice NOW!" Mrs. Grose lugubriously pleaded.

"I don't wonder you looked queer," I persisted, "when I mentioned to you the letter from his school!"

"I doubt if I looked as queer as you!" she retorted with

homely force. "And if he was so bad then as that comes to, how is he such an angel now?"

"Yes, indeed—and if he was a fiend at school! How, how, how? Well," I said in my torment, "you must put it to me again, but I shall not be able to tell you for some days. Only, put it to me again!" I cried in a way that made my friend stare. "There are directions in which I must not for the present let myself go." Meanwhile I returned to her first example—the one to which she had just previously referred—of the boy's happy capacity for an occasional slip. "If Quint—on your remonstrance at the time you speak of—was a base menial, one of the things Miles said to you, I find myself guessing, was that you were another." Again her admission was so adequate that I continued: "And you forgave him that?"

"Wouldn't YOU?"

"Oh, yes!" And we exchanged there, in the stillness, a sound of the oddest amusement. Then I went on: "At all events, while he was with the man—"

"Miss Flora was with the woman. It suited them all!"

It suited me, too, I felt, only too well; by which I mean that it suited exactly the particularly deadly view I was in the very act of forbidding myself to entertain. But I so far succeeded in checking the expression of this view that I will throw, just here, no further light on it than may be offered by the mention of my final observation to Mrs. Grose. "His having lied and been impudent are, I confess, less engaging specimens than I had hoped to have from you of the outbreak in him of the little natural man. Still," I mused, "They must do, for they make me feel more than ever that I must watch."

It made me blush, the next minute, to see in my friend's face how much more unreservedly she had forgiven him than her anecdote struck me as presenting to my own tenderness an occasion for doing. This came out when, at the schoolroom door, she quitted me. "Surely you don't accuse HIM—"

"Of carrying on an intercourse that he conceals from me? Ah, remember that, until further evidence, I now accuse nobody." Then, before shutting her out to go, by another passage, to her own place, "I must just wait," I wound up.

9

I waited and waited, and the days, as they elapsed, took something from my consternation. A very few of them, in fact, passing, in constant sight of my pupils, without a fresh incident, sufficed to give to grievous fancies and even to odious memories a kind of brush of the sponge. I have spoken of the surrender to their extraordinary childish grace as a thing I could actively cultivate, and it may be imagined if I neglected now to address myself to this source for whatever it would yield. Stranger than I can express, certainly, was the effort to struggle against my new lights; it would doubtless have been, however, a greater tension still had it not been so frequently successful.

I used to wonder how my little charges could help guessing that I thought strange things about them; and the circumstances that these things only made them more interesting was not by itself a direct aid to keeping them in the dark. I trembled lest they should see that they WERE so immensely more interesting. Putting things at the worst, at all events, as in meditation I so often did, any clouding of their innocence could only be—blameless and foredoomed as they were—a reason the more for taking risks. There were moments when, by an irresistible impulse, I found myself catching them up and pressing them to my heart.

As soon as I had done so I used to say to myself: "What will they think of that? Doesn't it betray too much?" It would have been easy to get into a sad, wild tangle about how much I might betray; but the real account, I feel, of the hours of peace that I could still enjoy was that the immediate charm of my companions was a beguilement still effective even under the shadow of the possibility that it was studied. For if it occurred to me that I might occasionally excite suspicion by the little outbreaks of my sharper passion for them, so too I remember wondering if I mightn't see a queerness in the traceable increase of their own demonstrations.

They were at this period extravagantly and preternaturally fond of me; which, after all, I could reflect, was no more than a graceful response in children perpetually bowed over and hugged. The homage of which they were so lavish succeeded, in truth, for my nerves, quite as well as if I never appeared to myself, as I may say, literally to catch them at a purpose in it. They had never, I think, wanted to do so many things for their poor protectress; I mean—though they got their lessons better and better, which was naturally what would please her most-in the way of diverting, entertaining, surprising her; reading her passages, telling her stories, acting her charades, pouncing out at her, in disguises, as animals and historical characters, and above all astonishing her by the "pieces" they had secretly got by heart and could interminably recite. I should never get to the bottom—were I to let myself go even now—of the prodigious private commentary, all under still more private correction, with which, in these days, I overscored their full hours.

They had shown me from the first a facility for everything, a general faculty which, taking a fresh start, achieved remarkable flights. They got their little tasks as if they loved them, and indulged, from the mere exuberance of the gift, in the most unimposed little miracles of memory. They not only popped out at me as tigers and as Romans, but as Shakespeareans, astronomers, and navigators. This was so singularly the case that it had presumably much to do with the fact as to which, at the present day, I am at a loss for a different explanation: I allude to my unnatural composure on the subject of another school for Miles.

What I remember is that I was content not, for the time, to open the question, and that contentment must have sprung from the sense of his perpetually striking show of cleverness. He was too clever for a bad governess, for a parson's daughter, to spoil; and the strangest if not the brightest thread in the pensive embroidery I just spoke of was the impression I might have got, if I had dared to work it out, that he was under some influence operating in his small intellectual life as a tremendous incitement.

If it was easy to reflect, however, that such a boy could postpone school, it was at least as marked that for such a boy to have been "kicked out" by a schoolmaster was a mystification without end. Let me add that in their company now—and I was careful almost never to be out of it—I could follow no scent very far. We lived in a cloud of music and love and success and private theatricals. The musical sense in each of the children was of the quickest, but the elder in especial had a marvellous knack of catching and repeating. The schoolroom piano broke into all gruesome fancies; and when that failed there were confabulations in corners, with a sequel of one of them going out in the highest spirits in order to "come in" as something new. I had had brothers myself, and it was no revelation to me that little girls could be slavish idolaters of little boys.

What surpassed everything was that there was a little boy in the world who could have for the inferior age, sex, and intelligence so fine a consideration. They were extraordinarily at one, and to say that they never either quarrelled or complained is to make the note of praise coarse for their quality of sweetness. Sometimes, indeed, when I dropped into coarseness, I perhaps came across traces of little understandings between them by which one of them should keep me occupied while the other slipped away. There is a naive side, I suppose, in all diplomacy; but if my pupils practiced upon me, it was surely with the minimum of grossness. It was all in the other quarter that, after a lull, the grossness broke out.

I find that I really hang back; but I must take my plunge. In going on with the record of what was hideous at Bly, I not only challenge the most liberal faith—for which I little care; but—and this is another matter—I renew what I myself suffered, I again push my way through it to the end. There came suddenly an hour after which, as I look back, the affair seems to me to have been all pure suffering; but I have at least reached the heart of it, and the straightest road out is doubtless to advance.

One evening—with nothing to lead up or to prepare it—I felt the cold touch of the impression that had breathed on me the night of my arrival and which, much lighter then, as I have mentioned, I should probably have made little of in memory had my subsequent sojourn been less agitated. I had not gone to bed; I sat reading by a couple of candles. There was a roomful of old books at Bly—last-century fiction, some of it, which, to the extent of a distinctly deprecated renown, but never to so much as that of a stray specimen, had reached the sequestered home and appealed to the unavowed curiosity of my youth.

I remember that the book I had in my hand was Fielding's *Amelia*; also that I was wholly awake. I recall further both a general conviction that it was horribly late and a particular objection to looking at my watch. I figure, finally, that the white curtain draping, in the fashion of those days, the head of Flora's little bed, shrouded, as I had assured myself long before, the perfection of childish rest. I recollect in short that, though I was deeply interested in my author, I found myself, at the turn of a page and with his spell all scattered, looking straight up from him and hard at the door of my room.

There was a moment during which I listened, reminded of the faint sense I had had, the first night, of there being something undefinably astir in the house, and noted the soft breath of the open casement just move the half-drawn blind. Then, with all the marks of a deliberation that must have seemed magnificent had there been anyone to admire it, I laid down my book, rose to my feet, and, taking a candle, went straight out of the room and, from the passage, on which my light made little impression, noiselessly closed and locked the door.

I can say now neither what determined nor what guided me, but I went straight along the lobby, holding my candle high, till I came within sight of the tall window that presided over the great turn of the staircase. At this point I precipitately found myself aware of three things. They were practically simultaneous, yet they had flashes of succession. My candle, under a bold flourish, went out, and I perceived, by the uncovered window, that the yielding dusk of earliest morning rendered it unnecessary. Without it, the next instant, I saw that there was someone on the stair. I speak of sequences, but I required no lapse of seconds to stiffen myself for a third encounter with Quint.

The apparition had reached the landing halfway up and was therefore on the spot nearest the window, where at sight of me, it stopped short and fixed me exactly as it had fixed me from the tower and from the garden. He knew me as well as I knew him; and so, in the cold, faint twilight, with a glimmer in the high glass and another on the polish of the oak stair below, we faced each other in our common intensity. He was absolutely, on this occasion, a living, detestable, dangerous presence. But that was not the wonder of wonders; I reserve this distinction for quite another circumstance: the circumstance that dread had unmistakably quitted me and that there was nothing in me there that didn't meet and measure him.

I had plenty of anguish after that extraordinary moment, but I had, thank God, no terror. And he knew I had not—I found myself at the end of an instant magnificently aware of this. I felt, in a fierce rigor of confidence, that if I stood my ground a minute I should cease—for the time, at least—to have him to reckon with; and during the minute, accordingly, the thing was as human and hideous as a real interview: hideous just because it WAS human, as human as to have met alone, in the small hours, in a sleeping house, some enemy, some adventurer, some criminal. It was the dead silence of our long gaze at such close quarters that gave the whole horror, huge as it was, its only note of the unnatural.

If I had met a murderer in such a place and at such an hour, we still at least would have spoken. Something would have passed, in life, between us; if nothing had passed, one of us would have moved. The moment was so prolonged that it would have taken but little more to make me doubt if even *I* were in life. I can't express what followed it save by saying that the silence itself—which was indeed in a manner an attestation of my strength—became the element into which I saw the figure disappear; in which I definitely saw it turn as I might have seen the low wretch to which it had once belonged turn on receipt of an order, and pass, with my eyes on the villainous back that no hunch could have more disfigured, straight down the staircase and into the darkness in which the next bend was lost.

10

I remained awhile at the top of the stair, but with the effect presently of understanding that when my visitor had gone, he had gone: then I returned to my room. The foremost thing I saw there by the light of the candle I had left burning was that Flora's little bed was empty; and on this I caught my breath with all the terror that, five minutes before, I had been able to resist. I dashed at the place in which I had left her lying and over which (for the small silk counterpane and the sheets were disarranged) the white curtains had been deceivingly pulled forward; then my step, to my unutterable relief, produced an answering sound: I perceived an agitation of the window blind, and the child, ducking down, emerged rosily from the other side of it.

She stood there in so much of her candour and so little of her nightgown, with her pink bare feet and the golden glow of her curls. She looked intensely grave, and I had never had such a sense of losing an advantage acquired (the thrill of which had just been so prodigious) as on my consciousness that she addressed me with a reproach. "You naughty: where HAVE you been?"—instead of challenging her own irregularity I found myself arraigned and explaining. She herself explained, for that matter, with the loveliest, eagerest simplicity. She had known suddenly, as she lay there, that I was out of the room, and had jumped up to see what had become of me.

I had dropped, with the joy of her reappearance, back into my chair—feeling then, and then only, a little faint; and she had pattered straight over to me, thrown herself upon my knee, given herself to be held with the flame of the candle full in the wonderful little face that was still flushed with sleep. I remember closing my eyes an instant, yieldingly, consciously, as before the excess of something beautiful that shone out of the blue of her own. "You were looking for me out of the window?" I said.

"You thought I might be walking in the grounds?"

"Well, you know, I thought someone was"—she never blanched as she smiled out that at me.

Oh, how I looked at her now! "And did you see anyone?"

"Ah, NO!" she returned, almost with the full privilege of childish inconsequence, resentfully, though with a long sweetness in her little drawl of the negative.

At that moment, in the state of my nerves, I absolutely believed she lied; and if I once more closed my eyes it was before the dazzle of the three or four possible ways in which I might take this up. One of these, for a moment, tempted me with such singular intensity that, to withstand it, I must have gripped my little girl with a spasm that, wonderfully, she submitted to without a cry or a sign of fright. Why not break out at her on the spot and have it all over?—give it to her straight in her lovely little lighted face? "You see, you see, you KNOW that you do and that you already quite suspect I believe it; therefore, why not frankly confess it to me, so that we may at least live with it together and learn perhaps, in the strangeness of our fate, where we are and what it means?"

This solicitation dropped, alas, as it came: if I could immediately have succumbed to it I might have spared myself—well, you'll see what. Instead of succumbing I sprang again to my feet, looked at her bed, and took a helpless middle way. "Why did you pull the curtain over the place to make me think you were still there?"

Flora luminously considered; after which, with her little divine smile: "Because I don't like to frighten you!"

"But if I had, by your idea, gone out—?"

She absolutely declined to be puzzled; she turned her eyes to the flame of the candle as if the question were as irrelevant, or at any rate as impersonal, as Mrs. Marcet or nine-times-nine. "Oh, but you know," she quite adequately answered, "that you might come back, you dear, and that you HAVE!" And after a little, when she had got into bed, I had, for a long time, by almost sitting on her to hold her hand, to prove that I recognized the pertinence of my return.

You may imagine the general complexion, from that moment, of my nights. I repeatedly sat up till I didn't know when; I selected moments when my roommate unmistakably slept, and, stealing out, took noiseless turns in the passage and even pushed as far as to where I had last met Quint. But I never met him there again; and I may as well say at once that I on no other occasion saw him in the house. I just missed, on the staircase, on the other hand, a different adventure. Looking down it from the top I once recognized the presence of a woman seated on one of the lower steps with her back presented to me, her body half-bowed and her head, in an attitude of woe, in her hands. I had been there but an instant, however, when she vanished without looking round at me.

I knew, nonetheless, exactly what dreadful face she had to show; and I wondered whether, if instead of being above I had been below, I should have had, for going up, the same nerve I had lately shown Quint. Well, there continued to be plenty of chance for nerve. On the eleventh night after my latest encounter with that gentleman—they were all numbered now—I had an alarm that perilously skirted it and that indeed, from the particular quality of its unexpectedness, proved quite my sharpest shock. It was precisely the first night during this series that, weary with watching, I had felt that I might again without laxity lay myself down at my old hour. I slept immediately and, as I afterward knew, till about one o'clock; but when I woke it was to sit straight up, as completely roused as if a hand had shook me. I had left a light burning, but it was now out, and I felt an instant certainty that Flora had extinguished it. This brought me to my feet and straight, in the darkness, to her bed, which I found she had left. A glance at the window enlightened me further, and the striking of a match completed the picture.

The child had again got up—this time blowing out the taper, and had again, for some purpose of observation or response, squeezed in behind the blind and was peering out into the night. That she now saw—as she had not, I had satisfied myself, the previous time—was proved to me by the fact that she was disturbed neither by my reillumination nor by the haste I made to get into slippers and into a wrap. Hidden, protected, absorbed, she evidently rested on the sill—the casement opened forward—and gave herself up. There was a great still moon to help her, and this fact had counted in my quick decision. She was face to face with the apparition we had met at the lake, and could now communicate with it as she had not then been able to do.

What I, on my side, had to care for was, without disturbing her, to reach, from the corridor, some other window in the same quarter. I got to the door without her hearing me; I got out of it, closed it, and listened, from the other side, for some sound from her. While I stood in the passage I had my eyes on her brother's door, which was but ten steps off and which, indescribably, produced in me a renewal of the strange impulse that I lately spoke of as my temptation. What if I should go straight in and march to HIS window?—what if, by risking to his boyish bewilderment a revelation of my motive, I should throw across the rest of the mystery the long halter of my boldness?

This thought held me sufficiently to make me cross to his threshold and pause again. I preternaturally listened; I figured to myself what might portentously be; I wondered if his bed were also empty and he too were secretly at watch. It was a deep, soundless minute, at the end of which my impulse failed. He was quiet; he might be innocent; the risk was hideous; I turned away. There was a figure in the grounds—a figure prowling for a sight, the visitor with whom Flora was engaged; but it was not the visitor most concerned with my boy. I hesitated afresh, but on other grounds and only for a few seconds; then I had made my choice.

There were empty rooms at Bly, and it was only a question of choosing the right one. The right one suddenly presented itself to me as the lower one—though high above the gardens—in the solid corner of the house that I have spoken of as the old tower. This was a large, square chamber, arranged with some state as a bedroom, the extravagant size of which made it so inconvenient that it had not for years, though kept by Mrs. Grose in exemplary order, been occupied. I had often admired it and I knew my way about in it; I had only, after just faltering at the first chill gloom of its disuse, to pass across it and unbolt as quietly as I could one of the shutters.

Achieving this transit, I uncovered the glass without a sound and, applying my face to the pane, was able, the darkness without being much less than within, to see that I commanded the right direction. Then I saw something more. The moon made the night extraordinarily penetrable and showed me on the lawn a person, diminished by distance, who stood there motionless and as if fascinated, looking up to where I had appeared—looking, that is, not so much straight at me as at something that was apparently above me. There was clearly another person above me—there was a person on the tower; but the presence on the lawn was not in the least what I had conceived and had confidently hurried to meet. The presence on the lawn—I felt sick as I made it out—was poor little Miles himself.

11

It was not till late next day that I spoke to Mrs. Grose; the rigor with which I kept my pupils in sight making it often difficult to meet her privately, and the more as we each felt the importance of not provoking—on the part of the servants quite as much as on that of the children—any suspicion of a secret flurry or that of a discussion of mysteries. I drew a great security in this particular from her mere smooth aspect. There was nothing in her fresh face to pass on to others my horrible confidences. She believed me, I was sure, absolutely: if she hadn't I don't know what would have become of me, for I couldn't have borne the business alone. But she was a magnificent monument to the blessing of a want of imagination, and if she could see in our little charges nothing but their beauty and amiability, their happiness and cleverness, she had no direct communication with the sources of my trouble.

If they had been at all visibly blighted or battered, she would doubtless have grown, on tracing it back, haggard enough to match them; as matters stood, however, I could feel her, when she surveyed them, with her large white arms folded and the habit of serenity in all her look, thank the Lord's mercy that if they were ruined the pieces would still serve. Flights of fancy gave place, in her mind, to a steady fireside glow, and I had already begun to perceive how, with the development of the conviction that—as time went on without a public accident-our young things could, after all, look out for themselves, she addressed her greatest solicitude to the sad case presented by their instructress. That, for myself, was a sound simplification: I could engage that, to the world, my face should tell no tales, but it would have been, in the conditions, an immense added strain to find myself anxious about hers.

At the hour I now speak of she had joined me, under pressure, on the terrace, where, with the lapse of the season, the afternoon sun was now agreeable; and we sat there together while, before us, at a distance, but within call if we wished, the children strolled to and fro in one of their most manageable moods. They moved slowly, in unison, below us, over the lawn, the boy, as they went, reading aloud from a storybook and passing his arm round his sister to keep her quite in touch. Mrs. Grose watched them with positive placidity; then I caught the suppressed intellectual creak with which she conscientiously turned to take from me a view of the back of the tapestry.

I had made her a receptacle of lurid things, but there was an odd recognition of my superiority—my accomplishments and my function—in her patience under my pain. She offered her mind to my disclosures as, had I wished to mix a witch's broth and proposed it with assurance, she would have held out a large clean saucepan. This had become thoroughly her attitude by the time that, in my recital of the events of the night, I reached the point of what Miles had said to me when, after seeing him, at such a monstrous hour, almost on the very spot where he happened now to be, I had gone down to bring him in; choosing then, at the window, with a concentrated need of not alarming the house, rather that method than a signal more resonant.

I had left her meanwhile in little doubt of my small hope of representing with success even to her actual sympathy my sense of the real splendour of the little inspiration with which, after I had got him into the house, the boy met my final articulate challenge. As soon as I appeared in the moonlight on the terrace, he had come to me as straight as possible; on which I had taken his hand without a word and led him, through the dark spaces, up the staircase where Quint had so hungrily hovered for him, along the lobby where I had listened and trembled, and so to his forsaken room.

Not a sound, on the way, had passed between us, and I had wondered—oh, HOW I had wondered!—if he were groping about in his little mind for something plausible and not too grotesque. It would tax his invention, certainly, and I felt, this time, over his real embarrassment, a curious thrill of triumph. It was a sharp trap for the inscrutable! He couldn't play any longer at innocence; so how the deuce would he get out of it? There beat in me indeed, with the passionate throb of this question an equal dumb appeal as to how the deuce *I* should. I was confronted at last, as never yet, with all the risk attached even now to sounding my own horrid note.

I remember in fact that as we pushed into his little chamber, where the bed had not been slept in at all and the window, uncovered to the moonlight, made the place so clear that there was no need of striking a match—I remember how I suddenly dropped, sank upon the edge of the bed from the force of the idea that he must know how he really, as they say, "had" me. He could do what he liked, with all his cleverness to help him, so long as I should continue to defer to the old tradition of the criminality of those caretakers of the young who minister to superstitions and fears. He "had" me indeed, and in a cleft stick; for who would ever absolve me, who would consent that I should go unhung, if, by the faintest tremor of an overture, I were the first to introduce into our perfect intercourse an element so dire?

No, no: it was useless to attempt to convey to Mrs. Grose, just as it is scarcely less so to attempt to suggest here, how, in our short, stiff brush in the dark, he fairly shook me with admiration. I was of course thoroughly kind and merciful; never, never yet had I placed on his little shoulders hands of such tenderness as those with which, while I rested against the bed, I held him there well under fire. I had no alternative but, in form at least, to put it to him.

"You must tell me now—and all the truth. What did you go out for? What were you doing there?"

I can still see his wonderful smile, the whites of his beautiful eyes, and the uncovering of his little teeth shine to me in the dusk. "If I tell you why, will you understand?" My heart, at this, leaped into my mouth. WOULD he tell me why? I found no sound on my lips to press it, and I was aware of replying only with a vague, repeated, grimacing nod. He was gentleness itself, and while I wagged my head at him he stood there more than ever a little fairy prince. It was his brightness indeed that gave me a respite. Would it be so great if he were really going to tell me? "Well," he said at last, "just exactly in order that you should do this."

"Do what?"

"Think me—for a change—BAD!" I shall never forget the sweetness and gaiety with which he brought out the word, nor how, on top of it, he bent forward and kissed me. It was practically the end of everything. I met his kiss and I had to make, while I folded him for a minute in my arms, the most stupendous effort not to cry. He had given exactly the account of himself that permitted least of my going behind it, and it was only with the effect of confirming my acceptance of it that, as I presently glanced about the room, I could say—

"Then you didn't undress at all?"

He fairly glittered in the gloom. "Not at all. I sat up and read."

"And when did you go down?"

"At midnight. When I'm bad I AM bad!"

"I see, I see—it's charming. But how could you be sure I would know it?"

"Oh, I arranged that with Flora." His answers rang out with a readiness! "She was to get up and look out."

"Which is what she did do." It was I who fell into the trap!

"So she disturbed you, and, to see what she was looking at, you also looked—you saw."

"While you," I concurred, "caught your death in the night air!"

He literally bloomed so from this exploit that he could afford radiantly to assent. "How otherwise should I have been bad enough?" he asked. Then, after another embrace, the incident and our interview closed on my recognition of all the reserves of goodness that, for his joke, he had been able to draw upon.

12

The particular impression I had received proved in the morning light, I repeat, not quite successfully presentable to Mrs. Grose, though I reinforced it with the mention of still another remark that he had made before we separated. "It all lies in half a dozen words," I said to her, "words that really settle the matter. 'Think, you know, what I MIGHT do!' He threw that off to show me how good he is. He knows down to the ground what he 'might' do. That's what he gave them a taste of at school."

"Lord, you do change!" cried my friend.

"I don't change—I simply make it out. The four, depend upon it, perpetually meet. If on either of these last nights you had been with either child, you would clearly have understood. The more I've watched and waited the more I've felt that if there were nothing else to make it sure it would be made so by the systematic silence of each. NEVER, by a slip of the tongue, have they so much as alluded to either of their old friends, any more than Miles has alluded to his expulsion.

"Oh, yes, we may sit here and look at them, and they may show off to us there to their fill; but even while they pretend to be lost in their fairytale they're steeped in their vision of the dead restored. He's not reading to her," I declared; "they're talking of THEM—they're talking horrors! I go on, I know, as if I were crazy; and it's a wonder I'm not. What I've seen would have made YOU so; but it has only made me more lucid, made me get hold of still other things."

My lucidity must have seemed awful, but the charming creatures who were victims of it, passing and repassing in their interlocked sweetness, gave my colleague something to hold on by; and I felt how tight she held as, without stirring in the breath of my passion, she covered them still with her eyes. "Of what other things have you got hold?"

"Why, of the very things that have delighted, fascinated, and yet, at bottom, as I now so strangely see, mystified and troubled me. Their more than earthly beauty, their absolutely unnatural goodness. It's a game," I went on; "it's a policy and a fraud!"

"On the part of little darlings—?"

"As yet mere lovely babies? Yes, mad as that seems!" The very act of bringing it out really helped me to trace it—follow it all up and piece it all together. "They haven't been good—they've only been absent. It has been easy to live with them, because they're simply leading a life of their own. They're not mine-they're not ours. They're his and they're hers!"

"Quint's and that woman's?"

"Quint's and that woman's. They want to get to them."

Oh, how, at this, poor Mrs. Grose appeared to study them! "But for what?"

"For the love of all the evil that, in those dreadful days, the pair put into them. And to ply them with that evil still, to keep up the work of demons, is what brings the others back."

"Laws!" said my friend under her breath. The exclamation was homely, but it revealed a real acceptance of my further proof of what, in the bad time—for there had been a worse even than this!—must have occurred. There could have been no such justification for me as the plain assent of her experience to whatever depth of depravity I found credible in our brace of scoundrels. It was in obvious submission of memory that she brought out after a moment: "They WERE rascals! But what can they now do?" she pursued.

"Do?" I echoed so loud that Miles and Flora, as they passed at their distance, paused an instant in their walk and looked at us. "Don't they do enough?" I demanded in a lower tone, while the children, having smiled and nodded and kissed hands to us, resumed their exhibition. We were held by it a minute; then I answered: "They can destroy them!" At this my companion did turn, but the inquiry she launched was a silent one, the effect of which was to make me more explicit. "They don't know, as yet, quite how—but they're trying hard. They're seen only across, as it were, and beyond—in strange places and on high places, the top of towers, the roof of houses, the outside of windows, the further edge of pools; but there's a deep design, on either side, to shorten the distance and overcome the obstacle; and the success of the tempters is only a question of time. They've only to keep to their suggestions of danger."

"For the children to come?"

"And perish in the attempt!" Mrs. Grose slowly got up, and I scrupulously added: "Unless, of course, we can prevent!"

Standing there before me while I kept my seat, she visibly turned things over. "Their uncle must do the preventing. He must take them away."

"And who's to make him?"

She had been scanning the distance, but she now dropped on me a foolish face. "You, miss."

"By writing to him that his house is poisoned and his little nephew and niece mad?"

"But if they ARE, miss?"

"And if I am myself, you mean? That's charming news to be sent him by a governess whose prime undertaking was to give him no worry."

Mrs. Grose considered, following the children again. "Yes, he do hate worry. That was the great reason—"

"Why those fiends took him in so long? No doubt, though his indifference must have been awful. As I'm not a fiend, at any rate, I shouldn't take him in."

My companion, after an instant and for all answer, sat down again and grasped my arm. "Make him at any rate come to you."

I stared. "To ME?" I had a sudden fear of what she might do. "'Him'?"

"He ought to BE here—he ought to help."

I quickly rose, and I think I must have shown her a queerer face than ever yet. "You see me asking him for a visit?" No, with her eyes on my face she evidently couldn't. Instead of it even—as a woman reads another—she could see what I myself saw: his derision, his amusement, his contempt for the breakdown of my resignation at being left alone and for the fine machinery I had set in motion to attract his attention to my slighted charms. She didn't know—no one knew—how proud I had been to serve him and to stick to our terms; yet she nonetheless took the measure, I think, of the warning I now gave her. "If you should so lose your head as to appeal to him for me—"

She was really frightened. "Yes, miss?"

"I would leave, on the spot, both him and you."

13

It was all very well to join them, but speaking to them proved quite as much as ever an effort beyond my strength—offered, in close quarters, difficulties as insurmountable as before. This situation continued a month, and with new aggravations and particular notes, the note above all, sharper and sharper, of the small ironic consciousness on the part of my pupils. It was not, I am as sure today as I was sure then, my mere infernal imagination: it was absolutely traceable that they were aware of my predicament and that this strange relation made, in a manner, for a long time, the air in which we moved.

I don't mean that they had their tongues in their cheeks or did anything vulgar, for that was not one of their dangers: I do mean, on the other hand, that the element of the unnamed and untouched became, between us, greater than any other, and that so much avoidance could not have been so successfully effected without a great deal of tacit arrangement. It was as if, at moments, we were perpetually coming into sight of subjects before which we must stop short, turning suddenly out of alleys that we perceived to be blind, closing with a little bang that made us look at each other—for, like all bangs, it was something louder than we had intended—the doors we had indiscreetly opened.

All roads lead to Rome, and there were times when it might have struck us that almost every branch of study or subject of conversation skirted forbidden ground. Forbidden ground was the question of the return of the dead in general and of whatever, in especial, might survive, in memory, of the friends little children had lost. There were days when I could have sworn that one of them had, with a small invisible nudge, said to the other: "She thinks she'll do it this time—but she WON'T!"

To "do it" would have been to indulge for instance—and for once in a way—in some direct reference to the lady who had prepared them for my discipline. They had a delightful endless appetite for passages in my own history, to which I had again and again treated them; they were in possession of everything that had ever happened to me, had had, with every circumstance the story of my smallest adventures and of those of my brothers and sisters and of the cat and the dog at home, as well as many particulars of the eccentric nature of my father, of the furniture and arrangement of our house, and of the conversation of the old women of our village.

There were things enough, taking one with another, to chatter about, if one went very fast and knew by instinct when to go round. They pulled with an art of their own the strings of my invention and my memory; and nothing else perhaps, when I thought of such occasions afterward, gave me so the suspicion of being watched from under cover. It was in any case over MY life, MY past, and MY friends alone that we could take anything like our ease—a state of affairs that led them sometimes without the least pertinence to break out into sociable reminders. I was invited—with no visible connection—to repeat afresh Goody Gosling's celebrated *mot* or to confirm the details already supplied as to the cleverness of the vicarage pony.

It was partly at such junctures as these and partly at quite different ones that, with the turn my matters had now taken, my predicament, as I have called it, grew most sensible. The fact that the days passed for me without another encounter ought, it would have appeared, to have done something toward soothing my nerves. Since the light brush, that second night on the upper landing, of the presence of a woman at the foot of the stair, I had seen nothing, whether in or out of the house, that one had better not have seen. There was many a corner round which I expected to come upon Quint, and many a situation that, in a merely sinister way, would have favoured the appearance of Miss Jessel. The summer had turned, the summer had gone; the autumn had dropped upon Bly and had blown out half our lights.

The place, with its gray sky and withered garlands, its bared spaces and scattered dead leaves, was like a theatre after the performance—all strewn with crumpled playbills. There were exactly states of the air, conditions of sound and of stillness, unspeakable impressions of the KIND of ministering moment, that brought back to me, long enough to catch it, the feeling of the medium in which, that June evening out of doors, I had had my first sight of Quint, and in which, too, at those other instants, I had, after seeing him through the window, looked for him in vain in the circle of shrubbery.

I recognized the signs, the portents—I recognized the moment, the spot. But they remained unaccompanied and empty, and I continued unmolested; if unmolested one could call a young woman whose sensibility had, in the most extraordinary fashion, not declined but deepened. I had said in my talk with Mrs. Grose on that horrid scene of Flora's by the lake—and had perplexed her by so saying—that it would from that moment distress me much more to lose my power than to keep it. I had then expressed what was vividly in my mind: the truth that, whether the children really saw or not—since, that is, it was not yet definitely proved—I greatly preferred, as a safeguard, the fullness of my own exposure.

I was ready to know the very worst that was to be known. What I had then had an ugly glimpse of was that my eyes might be sealed just while theirs were most opened. Well, my eyes WERE sealed, it appeared, at present—a consummation for which it seemed blasphemous not to thank God. There was, alas, a difficulty about that: I would have thanked him with all my soul had I not had in a proportionate measure this conviction of the secret of my pupils.

How can I retrace today the strange steps of my obsession? There were times of our being together when I would have been ready to swear that, literally, in my presence, but with my direct sense of it closed, they had visitors who were known and were welcome. Then it was that, had I not been deterred by the very chance that such an injury might prove greater than the injury to be averted, my exultation would have broken out. "They're here, they're here, you little wretches," I would have cried, "and you can't deny it now!" The little wretches denied it with all the added volume of their sociability and their tenderness, in just the crystal depths of which—like the flash of a fish in a stream—the mockery of their advantage peeped up.

The shock, in truth, had sunk into me still deeper than I knew on the night when, looking out to see either Quint or Miss Jessel under the stars, I had beheld the boy over whose rest I watched and who had immediately brought in with him-had straightway, there, turned it on me—the lovely upward look with which, from the battlements above me, the hideous apparition of Quint had played. If it was a question of a scare, my discovery on this occasion had scared me more than any other, and it was in the condition of nerves produced by it that I made my actual inductions.

They harassed me so that sometimes, at odd moments, I shut myself up audibly to rehearse—it was at once a fantastic relief and a renewed despair—the manner in which I might come to the point. I approached it from one side and the other while, in my room, I flung myself about, but I always broke down in the monstrous utterance of names. As they died away on my lips, I said to myself that I should indeed help them to represent something infamous, if, by pronouncing them, I should violate as rare a little case of instinctive delicacy as any schoolroom, probably, had ever known.

When I said to myself: "THEY have the manners to be silent, and you, trusted as you are, the baseness to speak!" I felt myself crimson and I covered my face with my hands. After these secret scenes I chattered more than ever, going on volubly enough till one of our prodigious, palpable hushes occurred—I can call them nothing else—the strange, dizzy lift or swim (I try for terms!) into a stillness, a pause of all life, that had nothing to do with the more or less noise that at the moment we might be engaged in making and that I could hear through any deepened exhilaration or quickened recitation or louder strum of the piano. Then it was that the others, the outsiders, were there. Though they were not angels, they "passed," as the French say, causing me, while they stayed, to tremble with the fear of their addressing to their younger victims some yet more infernal message or more vivid image than they had thought good enough for myself.

What it was most impossible to get rid of was the cruel idea that, whatever I had seen, Miles and Flora saw MORE—things terrible and unguessable and that sprang from dreadful passages of intercourse in the past. Such things naturally left on the surface, for the time, a chill which we vociferously denied that we felt; and we had, all three, with repetition, got into such splendid training that we went, each time, almost automatically, to mark the close of the incident, through the very same movements. It was striking of the children, at all events, to kiss me inveterately with a kind of wild irrelevance and never to fail—one or the other—of the precious question that had helped us through many a peril. "When do you think he WILL come? Don't you think we OUGHT to write?"—there was nothing like that inquiry, we found by experience, for carrying off an awkwardness.

"He" of course was their uncle in Harley Street; and we lived in much profusion of theory that he might at any moment arrive to mingle in our circle. It was impossible to have given less encouragement than he had done to such a doctrine, but if we had not had the doctrine to fall back upon we should have deprived each other of some of our finest exhibitions. He never wrote to them—that may have been selfish, but it was a part of the flattery of his trust of me; for the way in which a man pays his highest tribute to a woman is apt to be but by the more festal celebration of one of the sacred laws of his comfort; and I held that I carried out the spirit of the pledge given not to appeal to him when I let my charges understand that their own letters were but charming literary exercises.

They were too beautiful to be posted; I kept them myself; I have them all to this hour. This was a rule indeed which only added to the satiric effect of my being plied with the supposition that he might at any moment be among us. It was exactly as if my charges knew how almost more awkward than anything else that might be for me. There appears to me, moreover, as I look back, no note in all this more extraordinary than the mere fact that, in spite of my tension and of their triumph, I never lost patience with them. Adorable they must in truth have been, I now reflect, that I didn't in these days hate them! Would exasperation, however, if relief had longer been postponed, finally have betrayed me? It little matters, for relief arrived. I call it relief, though it was only the relief that a snap brings to a strain or the burst of a thunderstorm to a day of suffocation. It was at least change, and it came with a rush.

14

Walking to church a certain Sunday morning, I had little Miles at my side and his sister, in advance of us and at Mrs. Grose's, well in sight. It was a crisp, clear day, the first of its order for some time; the night had brought a touch of frost, and the autumn air, bright and sharp, made the church bells almost gay. It was an odd accident of thought that I should have happened at such a moment to be particularly and very gratefully struck with the obedience of my little charges. Why did they never resent my inexorable, my perpetual society? Something or other had brought nearer home to me that I had all but pinned the boy to my shawl and that, in the way our companions were marshalled before me, I might have appeared to provide against some danger of rebellion.

I was like a gaoler with an eye to possible surprises and escapes. But all this belonged—I mean their magnificent little surrender—just to the special array of the facts that were most abysmal. Turned out for Sunday by his uncle's tailor, who had had a free hand and a notion of pretty waistcoats and of his grand little air, Miles's whole title to independence, the rights of his sex and situation, were so stamped upon him that if he had suddenly struck for freedom I should have had nothing to say. I was by the strangest of chances wondering how I should meet him when the revolution unmistakably occurred. I call it a revolution because I now see how, with the word he spoke, the curtain rose on the last act of my dreadful drama, and the catastrophe was precipitated. "Look here, my dear, you know," he charmingly said, "when in the world, please, am I going back to school?"

Transcribed here the speech sounds harmless enough, particularly as uttered in the sweet, high, casual pipe with which, at all interlocutors, but above all at his eternal governess, he threw off intonations as if he were tossing roses. There was something in them that always made one "catch," and I caught, at any rate, now so effectually that I stopped as short as if one of the trees of the park had fallen across the road. There was something new, on the spot, between us, and he was perfectly aware that I recognized it, though, to enable me to do so, he had no need to look a whit less candid and charming than usual. I could feel in him how he already, from my at first finding nothing to reply, perceived the advantage he had gained.

I was so slow to find anything that he had plenty of time, after a minute, to continue with his suggestive but inconclusive smile: "You know, my dear, that for a fellow to be with a lady

ALWAYS—!" His "my dear" was constantly on his lips for me, and nothing could have expressed more the exact shade of the sentiment with which I desired to inspire my pupils than its fond familiarity. It was so respectfully easy.

But, oh, how I felt that at present I must pick my own phrases! I remember that, to gain time, I tried to laugh, and I seemed to see in the beautiful face with which he watched me how ugly and queer I looked. "And always with the same lady?" I returned.

He neither blanched nor winked. The whole thing was virtually out between us. "Ah, of course, she's a jolly, 'perfect' lady; but, after all, I'm a fellow, don't you see? that's—well, getting on."

I lingered there with him an instant ever so kindly. "Yes, you're getting on." Oh, but I felt helpless!

I have kept to this day the heartbreaking little idea of how he seemed to know that and to play with it. "And you can't say I've not been awfully good, can you?"

I laid my hand on his shoulder, for, though I felt how much better it would have been to walk on, I was not yet quite able. "No, I can't say that, Miles."

"Except just that one night, you know—!"

"That one night?" I couldn't look as straight as he.

"Why, when I went down—went out of the house."

"Oh, yes. But I forget what you did it for."

"You forget?"—he spoke with the sweet extravagance of childish reproach. "Why, it was to show you I could!"

"Oh, yes, you could."

"And I can again."

I felt that I might, perhaps, after all, succeed in keeping my wits about me. "Certainly. But you won't."

"No, not THAT again. It was nothing."

"It was nothing," I said. "But we must go on."

He resumed our walk with me, passing his hand into my arm. "Then when AM I going back?"

I wore, in turning it over, my most responsible air. "Were you very happy at school?"

He just considered. "Oh, I'm happy enough anywhere!"

"Well, then," I quavered, "if you're just as happy here—!"

"Ah, but that isn't everything! Of course YOU know a lot—"

"But you hint that you know almost as much?" I risked as he paused.

"Not half I want to!" Miles honestly professed. "But it isn't so much that."

"What is it, then?"

"Well—I want to see more life."

"I see; I see." We had arrived within sight of the church and of various persons, including several of the household of Bly, on their way to it and clustered about the door to see us go in. I quickened our step; I wanted to get there before the question between us opened up much further; I reflected hungrily that, for more than an hour, he would have to be silent; and I thought with envy of the comparative dusk of the pew and of the almost spiritual help of the hassock on which I might bend my knees. I seemed literally to be running a race with some confusion to which he was about to reduce me, but I felt that he had got in first when, before we had even entered the churchyard, he threw out—

"I want my own sort!"

It literally made me bound forward. "There are not many of your own sort, Miles!" I laughed. "Unless perhaps dear little Flora!"

"You really compare me to a baby girl?"

This found me singularly weak. "Don't you, then, LOVE our sweet Flora?"

"If I didn't—and you, too; if I didn't—!" he repeated as if retreating for a jump, yet leaving his thought so unfinished that, after we had come into the gate, another stop, which he imposed on me by the pressure of his arm, had become inevitable. Mrs. Grose and Flora had passed into the church, the other worshippers had followed, and we were, for the minute, alone among the old, thick graves. We had paused, on the path from the gate, by a low, oblong, tablelike tomb.

"Yes, if you didn't—?"

He looked, while I waited, at the graves. "Well, you know what!" But he didn't move, and he presently produced something that made me drop straight down on the stone slab, as if suddenly to rest. "Does my uncle think what YOU think?"

I markedly rested. "How do you know what I think?"

"Ah, well, of course I don't; for it strikes me you never tell me. But I mean does HE know?"

"Know what, Miles?"

"Why, the way I'm going on."

I perceived quickly enough that I could make, to this inquiry, no answer that would not involve something of a sacrifice of my employer. Yet it appeared to me that we were all, at Bly, sufficiently sacrificed to make that venial. "I don't think your uncle much cares."

Miles, on this, stood looking at me. "Then don't you think he can be made to?"

"In what way?"

"Why, by his coming down."

"But who'll get him to come down?"

"*I* will!" the boy said with extraordinary brightness and emphasis. He gave me another look charged with that expression and then marched off alone into church.

15

The business was practically settled from the moment I never followed him. It was a pitiful surrender to agitation, but my being aware of this had somehow no power to restore me. I only sat there on my tomb and read into what my little friend had said to me the fullness of its meaning; by the time I had grasped the whole of which I had also embraced, for absence, the pretext that I was ashamed to offer my pupils and the rest of the congregation such an example of delay. What I said to myself above all was that Miles had got something out of me and that the proof of it, for him, would be just this awkward collapse. He had got out of me that there was something I was much afraid of and that he should probably be able to make use of my fear to gain, for his own purpose, more freedom.

My fear was of having to deal with the intolerable question of the grounds of his dismissal from school, for that was really but the question of the horrors gathered behind. That his uncle should arrive to treat with me of these things was a solution that, strictly speaking, I ought now to have desired to bring on; but I could so little face the ugliness and the pain of it that I simply procrastinated and lived from hand to mouth.

The boy, to my deep discomposure, was immensely in the right, was in a position to say to me: "Either you clear up with my guardian the mystery of this interruption of my studies, or you cease to expect me to lead with you a life that's so unnatural for a boy." What was so unnatural for the particular boy I was concerned with was this sudden revelation of a consciousness and a plan.

That was what really overcame me, what prevented my going in. I walked round the church, hesitating, hovering; I reflected that I had already, with him, hurt myself beyond repair. Therefore I could patch up nothing, and it was too extreme an effort to squeeze beside him into the pew: he would be so much more sure than ever to pass his arm into mine and make me sit there for an hour in close, silent contact with his commentary on our talk. For the first minute since his arrival I wanted to get away from him. As I paused beneath the high east window and listened to the sounds of worship, I was taken with an impulse that might master me, I felt, completely should I give it the least encouragement.

I might easily put an end to my predicament by getting away altogether. Here was my chance; there was no one to stop me; I could give the whole thing up—turn my back and retreat. It was only a question of hurrying again, for a few preparations, to the house which the attendance at church of so many of the servants would practically have left unoccupied. No one, in short, could blame me if I should just drive desperately off. What was it to get away if I got away only till dinner? That would be in a couple of hours, at the end of which—I had the acute prevision—my little pupils would play at innocent wonder about my nonappearance in their train.

"What DID you do, you naughty, bad thing? Why in the world, to worry us so—and take our thoughts off, too, don't you know?—did you desert us at the very door?" I couldn't meet such questions nor, as they asked them, their false little lovely eyes; yet it was all so exactly what I should have to meet that, as the prospect grew sharp to me, I at last let myself go.

I got, so far as the immediate moment was concerned, away; I came straight out of the churchyard and, thinking hard, retraced my steps through the park. It seemed to me that by the time I reached the house I had made up my mind I would fly. The Sunday stillness both of the approaches and of the interior, in which I met no one, fairly excited me with a sense of opportunity. Were I to get off quickly, this way, I should get off without a scene, without a word. My quickness would have to be remarkable, however, and the question of a conveyance was the great one to settle.

Tormented, in the hall, with difficulties and obstacles, I remember sinking down at the foot of the staircase—suddenly collapsing there on the lowest step and then, with a revulsion, recalling that it was exactly where more than a month before, in the darkness of night and just so bowed with evil things, I had seen the specter of the most horrible of women. At this I was able to straighten myself; I went the rest of the way up; I made, in my bewilderment, for the schoolroom, where there were objects belonging to me that I should have to take. But I opened the door to find again, in a flash, my eyes unsealed. In the presence of what I saw I reeled straight back upon my resistance.

Seated at my own table in clear noonday light I saw a person whom, without my previous experience, I should have taken at the first blush for some housemaid who might have stayed at home to look after the place and who, availing herself of rare relief from observation and of the schoolroom table and my pens, ink, and paper, had applied herself to the considerable effort of a letter to her sweetheart. There was an effort in the way that, while her arms rested on the table, her hands with evident weariness supported her head; but at the moment I took this in I had already become aware that, in spite of my entrance, her attitude strangely persisted.

Then it was—with the very act of its announcing itself—that her identity flared up in a change of posture. She rose, not as if she had heard me, but with an indescribable grand melancholy of indifference and detachment, and, within a dozen feet of me, stood there as my vile predecessor. Dishonoured and tragic, she was all before me; but even as I fixed and, for memory, secured it, the awful image passed away. Dark as midnight in her black dress, her haggard beauty and her unutterable woe, she had looked at me long enough to appear to say that her right to sit at my table was as good as mine to sit at hers.

While these instants lasted, indeed, I had the extraordinary chill of feeling that it was I who was the intruder. It was as a wild protest against it that, actually addressing her—"You terrible, miserable woman!"—I heard myself break into a sound that, by the open door, rang through the long passage and the empty house. She looked at me as if she heard me, but I had recovered myself and cleared the air. There was nothing in the room the next minute but the sunshine and a sense that I must stay.

16

I had so perfectly expected that the return of my pupils would be marked by a demonstration that I was freshly upset at having to take into account that they were dumb about my absence. Instead of gaily denouncing and caressing me, they made no allusion to my having failed them, and I was left, for the time, on perceiving that she too said nothing, to study Mrs. Grose's odd face. I did this to such purpose that I made sure they had in some way bribed her to silence; a silence that, however, I would engage to break down on the first private opportunity.

This opportunity came before tea: I secured five minutes with her in the housekeeper's room, where, in the twilight, amid a smell of lately baked bread, but with the place all swept and garnished, I found her sitting in pained placidity before the fire. So I see her still, so I see her best: facing the flame from her straight chair in the dusky, shining room, a large clean image of the "put away"—of drawers closed and locked and rest without a remedy.

"Oh, yes, they asked me to say nothing; and to please them-so long as they were there—of course I promised. But what had happened to you?"

"I only went with you for the walk," I said. "I had then to come back to meet a friend."

She showed her surprise. "A friend—YOU?"

"Oh, yes, I have a couple!" I laughed. "But did the children give you a reason?"

"For not alluding to your leaving us? Yes; they said you would like it better. Do you like it better?"

My face had made her rueful. "No, I like it worse!" But after an instant I added: "Did they say why I should like it better?"

"No; Master Miles only said, 'We must do nothing but what she likes!'"

"I wish indeed he would. And what did Flora say?"

"Miss Flora was too sweet. She said, 'Oh, of course, of course!'—and I said the same."

I thought a moment. "You were too sweet, too—I can hear you all. But nonetheless, between Miles and me, it's now all out."

"All out?" My companion stared. "But what, miss?"

"Everything. It doesn't matter. I've made up my mind. I came home, my dear," I went on, "for a talk with Miss Jessel."

I had by this time formed the habit of having Mrs. Grose literally well in hand in advance of my sounding that note; so that even now, as she bravely blinked under the signal of my word, I could keep her comparatively firm. "A talk! Do you mean she spoke?"

"It came to that. I found her, on my return, in the schoolroom."

"And what did she say?" I can hear the good woman still, and the candour of her stupefaction.

"That she suffers the torments—!"

It was this, of a truth, that made her, as she filled out my picture, gape. "Do you mean," she faltered, "—of the lost?"

"Of the lost. Of the damned. And that's why, to share them-" I faltered myself with the horror of it.

But my companion, with less imagination, kept me up. "To share them—?"

"She wants Flora." Mrs. Grose might, as I gave it to her, fairly have fallen away from me had I not been prepared. I still held her there, to show I was. "As I've told you, however, it doesn't matter."

"Because you've made up your mind? But to what?"

"To everything."

"And what do you call 'everything'?"

"Why, sending for their uncle."

"Oh, miss, in pity do," my friend broke out. "ah, but I will, I WILL! I see it's the only way. What's 'out,' as I told you, with Miles is that if he thinks I'm afraid to—and has ideas of what he gains by that—he shall see he's mistaken. Yes, yes; his uncle shall have it here from me on the spot (and before the boy himself, if necessary) that if I'm to be reproached with having done nothing again about more school—"

"Yes, miss—" my companion pressed me.

"Well, there's that awful reason."

There were now clearly so many of these for my poor colleague that she was excusable for being vague. "But—a—which?"

"Why, the letter from his old place."

"You'll show it to the master?"

"I ought to have done so on the instant."

"Oh, no!" said Mrs. Grose with decision.

"I'll put it before him," I went on inexorably, "that I can't undertake to work the question on behalf of a child who has been expelled—"

"For we've never in the least known what!" Mrs. Grose declared.

"For wickedness. For what else—when he's so clever and beautiful and perfect? Is he stupid? Is he untidy? Is he infirm? Is he ill-natured? He's exquisite—so it can be only THAT; and that would open up the whole thing. After all," I said, "it's their uncle's fault. If he left here such people—!"

"He didn't really in the least know them. The fault's mine." She had turned quite pale.

"Well, you shan't suffer," I answered.

"The children shan't!" she emphatically returned.

I was silent awhile; we looked at each other. "Then what am I to tell him?"

"You needn't tell him anything. *I'll* tell him."

I measured this. "Do you mean you'll write—?" Remembering she couldn't, I caught myself up. "How do you communicate?"

"I tell the bailiff. HE writes."

"And should you like him to write our story?"

My question had a sarcastic force that I had not fully intended, and it made her, after a moment, inconsequently break down. The tears were again in her eyes. "Ah, miss, YOU write!"

"Well—tonight," I at last answered; and on this we separated.

17

I went so far, in the evening, as to make a beginning. The weather had changed back, a great wind was abroad, and beneath the lamp, in my room, with Flora at peace beside me, I sat for a long time before a blank sheet of paper and listened to the lash of the rain and the batter of the gusts. Finally I went out, taking a candle; I crossed the passage and listened a minute at Miles's door. What, under my endless obsession, I had been impelled to listen for was some betrayal of his not being at rest, and I presently caught one, but not in the form I had expected. His voice tinkled out. "I say, you there—come in." It was a gaiety in the gloom!

I went in with my light and found him, in bed, very wide awake, but very much at his ease. "Well, what are YOU up to?" he asked with a grace of sociability in which it occurred to me that Mrs. Grose, had she been present, might have looked in vain for proof that anything was "out."

I stood over him with my candle. "How did you know I was there?"

"Why, of course I heard you. Did you fancy you made no noise? You're like a troop of cavalry!" he beautifully laughed.

"Then you weren't asleep?"

"Not much! I lie awake and think."

I had put my candle, designedly, a short way off, and then, as he held out his friendly old hand to me, had sat down on the edge of his bed. "What is it," I asked, "that you think of?"

"What in the world, my dear, but YOU?"

"Ah, the pride I take in your appreciation doesn't insist on that! I had so far rather you slept."

"Well, I think also, you know, of this queer business of ours."

I marked the coolness of his firm little hand. "Of what queer business, Miles?"

"Why, the way you bring me up. And all the rest!"

I fairly held my breath a minute, and even from my glimmering taper there was light enough to show how he smiled up at me from his pillow. "What do you mean by all the rest?"

"Oh, you know, you know!"

I could say nothing for a minute, though I felt, as I held his hand and our eyes continued to meet, that my silence had all the air of admitting his charge and that nothing in the whole world of reality was perhaps at that moment so fabulous as our actual relation. "Certainly you shall go back to school," I said, "if it be that that troubles you. But not to the old place—we must find another, a better. How could I know it did trouble you, this question, when you never told me so, never spoke of it at all?" His clear, listening face, framed in its smooth whiteness, made him for the minute as appealing as some wistful patient in a children's hospital; and I would have given, as the resemblance came to me, all I possessed on earth really to be the nurse or the sister of charity who might have helped to cure him. Well, even as it was, I perhaps might help! "Do you know you've never said a word to me about your school—I mean the old one; never mentioned it in any way?"

He seemed to wonder; he smiled with the same loveliness. But he clearly gained time; he waited, he called for guidance. "Haven't I?" It wasn't for ME to help him—it was for the thing I had met!

Something in his tone and the expression of his face, as I got this from him, set my heart aching with such a pang as it had never yet known; so unutterably touching was it to see his little brain puzzled and his little resources taxed to play, under the spell laid on him, a part of innocence and consistency. "No, never—from the hour you came back. You've never mentioned to me one of your masters, one of your comrades, nor the least little thing that ever happened to you at school. Never, little Miles—no, never—have you given me an inkling of anything that MAY have happened there.

"Therefore you can fancy how much I'm in the dark. Until you came out, that way, this morning, you had, since the first hour I saw you, scarce even made a reference to anything in your previous life. You seemed so perfectly to accept the present." It was extraordinary how my absolute conviction of his secret precocity (or whatever I might call the poison of an influence that I dared but half to phrase) made him, in spite of the faint breath of his inward trouble, appear as accessible as an older person—imposed him almost as an intellectual equal. "I thought you wanted to go on as you are."

It struck me that at this he just faintly coloured. He gave, at any rate, like a convalescent slightly fatigued, a languid shake of his head. "I don't—I don't. I want to get away."

"You're tired of Bly?"

"Oh, no, I like Bly."

"Well, then—?"

"Oh, YOU know what a boy wants!"

I felt that I didn't know so well as Miles, and I took temporary refuge. "You want to go to your uncle?"

Again, at this, with his sweet ironic face, he made a movement on the pillow. "Ah, you can't get off with that!"

I was silent a little, and it was I, now, I think, who changed colour. "My dear, I don't want to get off!"

"You can't, even if you do. You can't, you can't!"—he lay beautifully staring. "My uncle must come down, and you must completely settle things."

"If we do," I returned with some spirit, "you may be sure it will be to take you quite away."

"Well, don't you understand that that's exactly what I'm working for? You'll have to tell him—about the way you've let it all drop: you'll have to tell him a tremendous lot!"

The exultation with which he uttered this helped me somehow, for the instant, to meet him rather more. "And how much will YOU, Miles, have to tell him? There are things he'll ask you!"

He turned it over. "Very likely. But what things?"

"The things you've never told me. To make up his mind what to do with you. He can't send you back—"

"Oh, I don't want to go back!" he broke in. "I want a new field."

He said it with admirable serenity, with positive unimpeachable gaiety; and doubtless it was that very note that most evoked for me the poignancy, the unnatural childish tragedy, of his probable reappearance at the end of three months with all this bravado and still more dishonour. It overwhelmed me now that I should never be able to bear that, and it made me let myself go. I threw myself upon him and in the tenderness of my pity I embraced him. "Dear little Miles, dear little Miles—!"

My face was close to his, and he let me kiss him, simply taking it with indulgent good humour. "Well, old lady?"

"Is there nothing—nothing at all that you want to tell me?"

He turned off a little, facing round toward the wall and holding up his hand to look at as one had seen sick children look. "I've told you—I told you this morning."

Oh, I was sorry for him! "That you just want me not to worry you?"

He looked round at me now, as if in recognition of my understanding him; then ever so gently, "To let me alone," he replied.

There was even a singular little dignity in it, something that made me release him, yet, when I had slowly risen, linger beside him. God knows I never wished to harass him, but I felt that merely, at this, to turn my back on him was to abandon or, to put it more truly, to lose him. "I've just begun a letter to your uncle," I said.

"Well, then, finish it!"

I waited a minute. "What happened before?"

He gazed up at me again. "Before what?"

"Before you came back. And before you went away."

For some time he was silent, but he continued to meet my eyes. "What happened?"

It made me, the sound of the words, in which it seemed to me that I caught for the very first time a small faint quaver of consenting consciousness—it made me drop on my knees beside the bed and seize once more the chance of possessing him. "Dear little Miles, dear little Miles, if you KNEW how I want to help you! It's only that, it's nothing but that, and I'd rather die than give you a pain or do you a wrong—I'd rather die than hurt a hair of you. Dear little Miles"—oh, I brought it out now even if I SHOULD go too far—"I just want you to help me to save you!"

But I knew in a moment after this that I had gone too far. The answer to my appeal was instantaneous, but it came in the form of an extraordinary blast and chill, a gust of frozen air, and a shake of the room as great as if, in the wild wind, the casement had crashed in. The boy gave a loud, high shriek, which, lost in the rest of the shock of sound, might have seemed, indistinctly, though I was so close to him, a note either of jubilation or of terror. I jumped to my feet again and was conscious of darkness. So for a moment we remained, while I stared about me and saw that the drawn curtains were unstirred and the window tight. "Why, the candle's out!" I then cried.

"It was I who blew it, dear!" said Miles.

18

The next day, after lessons, Mrs. Grose found a moment to say to me quietly: "Have you written, miss?"

"Yes—I've written." But I didn't add—for the hour—that my letter, sealed and directed, was still in my pocket. There would be time enough to send it before the messenger should go to the village. Meanwhile there had been, on the part of my pupils, no more brilliant, more exemplary morning. It was exactly as if they had both had at heart to gloss over any recent little friction. They performed the dizziest feats of arithmetic, soaring quite out of MY feeble range, and perpetrated, in higher spirits than ever, geographical and historical jokes. It was conspicuous of course in Miles in particular that he appeared to wish to show how easily he could let me down.

This child, to my memory, really lives in a setting of beauty and misery that no words can translate; there was a distinction all his own in every impulse he revealed; never was a small natural creature, to the uninitiated eye all frankness and freedom, a more ingenious, a more extraordinary little gentleman. I had perpetually to guard against the wonder of contemplation into which my initiated view betrayed me; to check the irrelevant gaze and discouraged sigh in which I constantly both attacked and renounced the enigma of what such a little gentleman could have done that deserved a penalty. Say that, by the dark prodigy I knew, the imagination of all evil HAD been opened up to him: all the justice within me ached for the proof that it could ever have flowered into an act.

He had never, at any rate, been such a little gentleman as

when, after our early dinner on this dreadful day, he came round to me and asked if I shouldn't like him, for half an hour, to play to me. David playing to Saul could never have shown a finer sense of the occasion. It was literally a charming exhibition of tact, of magnanimity, and quite tantamount to his saying outright: "The true knights we love to read about never push an advantage too far. I know what you mean now: you mean that—to be let alone yourself and not followed up—you'll cease to worry and spy upon me, won't keep me so close to you, will let me go and come. Well, I 'come,' you see—but I don't go! There'll be plenty of time for that. I do really delight in your society, and I only want to show you that I contended for a principle."

It may be imagined whether I resisted this appeal or failed to accompany him again, hand in hand, to the schoolroom. He sat down at the old piano and played as he had never played; and if there are those who think he had better have been kicking a football I can only say that I wholly agree with them. For at the end of a time that under his influence I had quite ceased to measure, I started up with a strange sense of having literally slept at my post. It was after luncheon, and by the schoolroom fire, and yet I hadn't really, in the least, slept: I had only done something much worse—I had forgotten. Where, all this time, was Flora? When I put the question to Miles, he played on a minute before answering and then could only say: "Why, my dear, how do *I* know?"—breaking moreover into a happy laugh which, immediately after, as if it were a vocal accompaniment, he prolonged into incoherent, extravagant song.

I went straight to my room, but his sister was not there; then, before going downstairs, I looked into several others. As she was nowhere about she would surely be with Mrs. Grose, whom, in the comfort of that theory, I accordingly proceeded in quest of. I found her where I had found her the evening before, but she met my quick challenge with blank, scared ignorance. She had only supposed that, after the repast, I had carried off both the children; as to which she was quite in her right, for it was the very first time I had allowed the little girl out of my sight without some special provision.

Of course now indeed she might be with the maids, so that the immediate thing was to look for her without an air of alarm. This we promptly arranged between us; but when, ten minutes later and in pursuance of our arrangement, we met in the hall, it was only to report on either side that after guarded inquiries we had altogether failed to trace her. For a minute there, apart from observation, we exchanged mute alarms, and I could feel with what high interest my friend returned me all those I had from the first given her.

"She'll be above," she presently said—"in one of the rooms you haven't searched."

"No; she's at a distance." I had made up my mind. "She has gone out."

Mrs. Grose stared. "Without a hat?"

I naturally also looked volumes. "Isn't that woman always without one?"

"She's with HER?"

"She's with HER!" I declared. "We must find them."

My hand was on my friend's arm, but she failed for the moment, confronted with such an account of the matter, to respond to my pressure. She communed, on the contrary, on the spot, with her uneasiness. "And where's Master Miles?"

"Oh, HE'S with Quint. They're in the schoolroom."

"Lord, miss!" My view, I was myself aware—and therefore I suppose my tone—had never yet reached so calm an assurance.

"The trick's played," I went on; "they've successfully worked their plan. He found the most divine little way to keep me quiet while she went off."

"'Divine'?" Mrs. Grose bewilderedly echoed.

"Infernal, then!" I almost cheerfully rejoined. "He has provided for himself as well. But come!"

She had helplessly gloomed at the upper regions. "You leave him—?"

"So long with Quint? Yes—I don't mind that now."

She always ended, at these moments, by getting possession of my hand, and in this manner she could at present still stay me. But after gasping an instant at my sudden resignation, "Because of your letter?" she eagerly brought out.

I quickly, by way of answer, felt for my letter, drew it forth, held it up, and then, freeing myself, went and laid it on the great hall table. "Luke will take it," I said as I came back. I reached the house door and opened it; I was already on the steps.

My companion still demurred: the storm of the night and the early morning had dropped, but the afternoon was damp and gray. I came down to the drive while she stood in the doorway. "You go with nothing on?"

"What do I care when the child has nothing? I can't wait to dress," I cried, "and if you must do so, I leave you. Try meanwhile, yourself, upstairs."

"With THEM?" Oh, on this, the poor woman promptly joined me!

19

We went straight to the lake, as it was called at Bly, and I daresay rightly called, though I reflect that it may in fact have been a sheet of water less remarkable than it appeared to my untraveled eyes. My acquaintance with sheets of water was small, and the pool of Bly, at all events on the few occasions of my consenting, under the protection of my pupils, to affront its surface in the old flat-bottomed boat moored there for our use, had impressed me both with its extent and its agitation.

The usual place of embarkation was half a mile from the house, but I had an intimate conviction that, wherever Flora might be, she was not near home. She had not given me the slip for any small adventure, and, since the day of the very great one that I had shared with her by the pond, I had been aware, in our walks, of the quarter to which she most inclined. This was why I had now given to Mrs. Grose's steps so marked a direction—a direction that made her, when she perceived it, oppose a resistance that showed me she was freshly mystified. "You're going to the water, Miss?—you think she's IN—?"

"She may be, though the depth is, I believe, nowhere very great. But what I judge most likely is that she's on the spot from which, the other day, we saw together what I told you."

"When she pretended not to see—?"

"With that astounding self-possession? I've always been sure she wanted to go back alone. And now her brother has managed it for her."

Mrs. Grose still stood where she had stopped. "You suppose they really TALK of them?"

"I could meet this with a confidence! They say things that, if we heard them, would simply appal us."

"And if she IS there—"

"Yes?"

"Then Miss Jessel is?"

"Beyond a doubt. You shall see."

"Oh, thank you!" my friend cried, planted so firm that, taking it in, I went straight on without her. By the time I reached the pool, however, she was close behind me, and I knew that, whatever, to her apprehension, might befall me, the exposure of my society struck her as her least danger. She exhaled a moan of relief as we at last came in sight of the greater part of the water without a sight of the child. There was no trace of Flora on that nearer side of the bank where my observation of her had been most startling, and none on the opposite edge, where, save for a margin of some twenty yards, a thick copse came down to the water.

The pond, oblong in shape, had a width so scant compared to its length that, with its ends out of view, it might have been taken for a scant river. We looked at the empty expanse, and then I felt the suggestion of my friend's eyes. I knew what she meant and I replied with a negative headshake.

"No, no; wait! She has taken the boat."

My companion stared at the vacant mooring place and then again across the lake. "Then where is it?"

"Our not seeing it is the strongest of proofs. She has used it to go over, and then has managed to hide it."

"All alone—that child?"

"She's not alone, and at such times she's not a child: she's an old, old woman." I scanned all the visible shore while Mrs. Grose took again, into the queer element I offered her, one of her plunges of submission; then I pointed out that the boat might perfectly be in a small refuge formed by one of the recesses of the pool, an indentation masked, for the hither side, by a projection of the bank and by a clump of trees growing close to the water.

"But if the boat's there, where on earth's SHE?" my colleague anxiously asked.

"That's exactly what we must learn." And I started to walk further.

"By going all the way round?"

"Certainly, far as it is. It will take us but ten minutes, but it's far enough to have made the child prefer not to walk. She went straight over."

"Laws!" cried my friend again; the chain of my logic was ever too much for her. It dragged her at my heels even now, and when we had got halfway round—a devious, tiresome process, on ground much broken and by a path choked with overgrowth—I paused to give her breath. I sustained her with a grateful arm, assuring her that she might hugely help me; and this started us afresh, so that in the course of but few minutes more we reached a point from which we found the boat to be where I had supposed it.

It had been intentionally left as much as possible out of sight and was tied to one of the stakes of a fence that came, just there, down to the brink and that had been an assistance to disembarking. I recognized, as I looked at the pair of short, thick oars, quite safely drawn up, the prodigious character of the feat for a little girl; but I had lived, by this time, too long among wonders and had panted to too many livelier measures. There was a gate in the fence, through which we passed, and that brought us, after a trifling interval, more into the open. Then, "There she is!" we both exclaimed at once.

Flora, a short way off, stood before us on the grass and smiled as if her performance was now complete. The next thing she did, however, was to stoop straight down and pluck—quite as if it were all she was there for—a big, ugly spray of withered fern. I instantly became sure she had just come out of the copse. She waited for us, not herself taking a step, and I was conscious of the rare solemnity with which we presently approached her. She smiled and smiled, and we met; but it was all done in a silence by this time flagrantly ominous. Mrs. Grose was the first to break the spell: she threw herself on her knees and, drawing the child to her breast, clasped in a long embrace the little tender, yielding body.

While this dumb convulsion lasted I could only watch it—which I did the more intently when I saw Flora's face peep at me over our companion's shoulder. It was serious now—the flicker had left it; but it strengthened the pang with which I at that moment envied Mrs. Grose the simplicity of HER relation. Still, all this while, nothing more passed between us save that Flora had let her foolish fern again drop to the ground. What she and I had virtually said to each other was that pretexts were useless now. When Mrs. Grose finally got up she kept the child's hand, so that the two were still before me; and the singular reticence of our communion was even more marked in the frank look she launched me. "I'll be hanged," it said, "if *I'll* speak!"

It was Flora who, gazing all over me in candid wonder, was the first. She was struck with our bareheaded aspect. "Why, where are your things?"

"Where yours are, my dear!" I promptly returned.

She had already got back her gaiety, and appeared to take this as an answer quite sufficient. "And where's Miles?" she went on.

There was something in the small valour of it that quite finished me: these three words from her were, in a flash like the glitter of a drawn blade, the jostle of the cup that my hand, for weeks and weeks, had held high and full to the brim that now, even before speaking, I felt overflow in a deluge. "I'll tell you if you'll tell ME—" I heard myself say, then heard the tremor in which it broke.

"Well, what?"

Mrs. Grose's suspense blazed at me, but it was too late now, and I brought the thing out handsomely. "Where, my pet, is Miss Jessel?"

20

Just as in the churchyard with Miles, the whole thing was upon us. Much as I had made of the fact that this name had never once, between us, been sounded, the quick, smitten glare with which the child's face now received it fairly likened my breach of the silence to the smash of a pane of glass. It added to the interposing cry, as if to stay the blow, that Mrs. Grose, at the same instant, uttered over my violence—the shriek of a creature scared, or rather wounded, which, in turn, within a few seconds, was completed by a gasp of my own. I seized my colleague's arm. "She's there, she's there!"

Miss Jessel stood before us on the opposite bank exactly as she had stood the other time, and I remember, strangely, as the first feeling now produced in me, my thrill of joy at having brought on a proof. She was there, and I was justified; she was there, and I was neither cruel nor mad. She was there for poor scared Mrs. Grose, but she was there most for Flora; and no moment of my monstrous time was perhaps so extraordinary as that in which I consciously threw out to her—with the sense that, pale and ravenous demon as she was, she would catch and understand it—an inarticulate message of gratitude. She rose erect on the spot my friend and I had lately quitted, and there was not, in all the long reach of her desire, an inch of her evil that fell short.

This first vividness of vision and emotion were things of a few seconds, during which Mrs. Grose's dazed blink across to where I pointed struck me as a sovereign sign that she too at last saw, just as it carried my own eyes precipitately to the child. The revelation then of the manner in which Flora was affected startled me, in truth, far more than it would have done to find her also merely agitated, for direct dismay was of course not what I had expected. Prepared and on her guard as our pursuit had actually made her, she would repress every betrayal; and I was therefore shaken, on the spot, by my first glimpse of the particular one for which I had not allowed.

To see her, without a convulsion of her small pink face, not even feign to glance in the direction of the prodigy I announced, but only, instead of that, turn at ME an expression of hard, still gravity, an expression absolutely new and unprecedented and that appeared to read and accuse and judge me—this was a stroke that somehow converted the little girl herself into the very presence that could make me quail. I quailed even though my certitude that she thoroughly saw was never greater than at that instant, and in the immediate need to defend myself I called it passionately to witness.

"She's there, you little unhappy thing—there, there, THERE, and you see her as well as you see me!" I had said shortly before to Mrs. Grose that she was not at these times a child, but an old, old woman, and that description of her could not have been more strikingly confirmed than in the way in which, for all answer to this, she simply showed me, without a concession, an admission, of her eyes, a countenance of deeper and deeper, of indeed suddenly quite fixed, reprobation. I was by this time—if I can put the whole thing at all together—more appalled at what I may properly call her manner than at anything else, though it was simultaneously with this that I became aware of having Mrs. Grose also, and very formidably, to reckon with. My elder companion, the next moment, at any rate, blotted out everything but her own flushed face and her loud, shocked protest, a burst of high disapproval. "What a dreadful turn, to be sure, miss! Where on earth do you see anything?"

I could only grasp her more quickly yet, for even while she spoke the hideous plain presence stood undimmed and undaunted. It had already lasted a minute, and it lasted while I continued, seizing my colleague, quite thrusting her at it and presenting her to it, to insist with my pointing hand. "You don't see her exactly as WE see?—you mean to say you don't now—NOW? She's as big as a blazing fire! Only look, dearest woman, LOOK—!" She looked, even as I did, and gave me, with her deep groan of negation, repulsion, compassion—the mixture with her pity of her relief at her exemption—a sense, touching to me even then, that she would have backed me up if she could.

I might well have needed that, for with this hard blow of the proof that her eyes were hopelessly sealed I felt my own situation horribly crumble, I felt—I saw—my livid predecessor press, from her position, on my defeat, and I was conscious, more than all, of what I should have from this instant to deal with in the astounding little attitude of Flora. Into this attitude Mrs. Grose immediately and violently entered, breaking, even while there pierced through my sense of ruin a prodigious private triumph, into breathless reassurance.

"She isn't there, little lady, and nobody's there—and you never see nothing, my sweet! How can poor Miss Jessel—when poor Miss Jessel's dead and buried? WE know, don't we, love?"—and she appealed, blundering in, to the child. "It's all a mere mistake and a worry and a joke—and we'll go home as fast as we can!"

Our companion, on this, had responded with a strange, quick primness of propriety, and they were again, with Mrs. Grose on her feet, united, as it were, in pained opposition to me. Flora continued to fix me with her small mask of reprobation, and even at that minute I prayed God to forgive me for seeming to see that, as she stood there holding tight to our friend's dress, her incomparable childish beauty had suddenly failed, had quite vanished.

I've said it already—she was literally, she was hideously, hard; she had turned common and almost ugly. "I don't know what you mean. I see nobody. I see nothing. I never HAVE. I think you're cruel. I don't like you!" Then, after this deliverance, which might have been that of a vulgarly pert little girl in the street, she hugged Mrs. Grose more closely and buried in her skirts the dreadful little face.

In this position she produced an almost furious wail. "Take

me away, take me away—oh, take me away from HER!"

"From ME?" I panted.

"From you—from you!" she cried.

Even Mrs. Grose looked across at me dismayed, while I had nothing to do but communicate again with the figure that, on the opposite bank, without a movement, as rigidly still as if catching, beyond the interval, our voices, was as vividly there for my disaster as it was not there for my service. The wretched child had spoken exactly as if she had got from some outside source each of her stabbing little words, and I could therefore, in the full despair of all I had to accept, but sadly shake my head at her.

"If I had ever doubted, all my doubt would at present have gone. I've been living with the miserable truth, and now it has only too much closed round me. Of course I've lost you: I've interfered, and you've seen—under HER dictation"—with which I faced, over the pool again, our infernal witness—"the easy and perfect way to meet it. I've done my best, but I've lost you. Goodbye." For Mrs. Grose I had an imperative, an almost frantic "Go, go!" before which, in infinite distress, but mutely possessed of the little girl and clearly convinced, in spite of her blindness, that something awful had occurred and some collapse engulfed us, she retreated, by the way we had come, as fast as she could move.

Of what first happened when I was left alone I had no subsequent memory. I only knew that at the end of, I suppose, a quarter of an hour, an odorous dampness and roughness, chilling and piercing my trouble, had made me understand that I must have thrown myself, on my face, on the ground and given way to a wildness of grief. I must have lain there long and cried and sobbed, for when I raised my head the day was almost done. I got up and looked a moment, through the twilight, at the gray pool and its blank, haunted edge, and then I took, back to the house, my dreary and difficult course.

When I reached the gate in the fence the boat, to my surprise, was gone, so that I had a fresh reflection to make on Flora's extraordinary command of the situation. She passed that night, by the most tacit, and I should add, were not the word so grotesque a false note, the happiest of arrangements, with Mrs. Grose. I saw neither of them on my return, but, on the other hand, as by an ambiguous compensation, I saw a great deal of Miles. I saw—I can use no other phrase—so much of him that it was as if it were more than it had ever been.

No evening I had passed at Bly had the portentous quality of this one; in spite of which—and in spite also of the deeper depths of consternation that had opened beneath my feet—there was literally, in the ebbing actual, an extraordinarily sweet sadness. On reaching the house I had never so much as looked for the boy; I had simply gone straight to my room to change what I was wearing and to take in, at a glance, much material testimony to Flora's rupture. Her little belongings had all been removed.

When later, by the schoolroom fire, I was served with tea by the usual maid, I indulged, on the article of my other pupil, in no inquiry whatever. He had his freedom now—he might have it to the end! Well, he did have it; and it consisted—in part at least—of his coming in at about eight o'clock and sitting down with me in silence. On the removal of the tea things I had blown out the candles and drawn my chair closer: I was conscious of a mortal coldness and felt as if I should never again be warm. So, when he appeared, I was sitting in the glow with my thoughts. He paused a moment by the door as if to look at me; then—as if to share them—came to the other side of the hearth and sank into a chair. We sat there in absolute stillness; yet he wanted, I felt, to be with me.

21

Before a new day, in my room, had fully broken, my eyes opened to Mrs. Grose, who had come to my bedside with worse news. Flora was so markedly feverish that an illness was perhaps at hand; she had passed a night of extreme unrest, a night agitated above all by fears that had for their subject not in the least her former, but wholly her present, governess. It was not against the possible re-entrance of Miss Jessel on the scene that she protested—it was conspicuously and passionately against mine. I was promptly on my feet of course, and with an immense deal to ask; the more that my friend had discernibly now girded her loins to meet me once more. This I felt as soon as I had put to her the question of her sense of the child's sincerity as against my own. "She persists in denying to you that she saw, or has ever seen, anything?"

My visitor's trouble, truly, was great. "Ah, miss, it isn't a matter on which I can push her! Yet it isn't either, I must say, as if I much needed to. It has made her, every inch of her, quite old."

"Oh, I see her perfectly from here. She resents, for all the world like some high little personage, the imputation on her truthfulness and, as it were, her respectability. 'Miss Jessel indeed—SHE!' Ah, she's 'respectable,' the chit! The impression she gave me there yesterday was, I assure you, the very strangest of all; it was quite beyond any of the others. I DID put my foot in it! She'll never speak to me again."

Hideous and obscure as it all was, it held Mrs. Grose briefly silent; then she granted my point with a frankness which, I made sure, had more behind it. "I think indeed, miss, she never will. She do have a grand manner about it!"

"And that manner"—I summed it up—"is practically what's the matter with her now!"

Oh, that manner, I could see in my visitor's face, and not a little else besides! "She asks me every three minutes if I think you're coming in."

"I see—I see." I, too, on my side, had so much more than worked it out. "Has she said to you since yesterday—except to repudiate her familiarity with anything so dreadful—a single other word about Miss Jessel?"

"Not one, miss. And of course you know," my friend added, "I took it from her, by the lake, that, just then and there at least, there WAS nobody."

"Rather! and, naturally, you take it from her still."

"I don't contradict her. What else can I do?"

"Nothing in the world! You've the cleverest little person to deal with. They've made them—their two friends, I mean—still cleverer even than nature did; for it was wondrous material to play on! Flora has now her grievance, and she'll work it to the end."

"Yes, miss; but to WHAT end?"

"Why, that of dealing with me to her uncle. She'll make me out to him the lowest creature—!"

I winced at the fair show of the scene in Mrs. Grose's face; she looked for a minute as if she sharply saw them together. "And him who thinks so well of you!"

"He has an odd way—it comes over me now," I laughed,"—of proving it! But that doesn't matter. What Flora wants, of course, is to get rid of me."

My companion bravely concurred. "Never again to so much as look at you."

"So that what you've come to me now for," I asked, "is to speed me on my way?" Before she had time to reply, however, I had her in check. "I've a better idea—the result of my reflections. My going WOULD seem the right thing, and on Sunday I was terribly near it. Yet that won't do. It's YOU who must go. You must take Flora."

My visitor, at this, did speculate. "But where in the world—?"

"Away from here. Away from THEM. Away, even most of all, now, from me. Straight to her uncle."

"Only to tell on you—?"

"No, not 'only'! To leave me, in addition, with my remedy."

She was still vague. "And what IS your remedy?"

"Your loyalty, to begin with. And then Miles's."

She looked at me hard. "Do you think he—?"

"Won't, if he has the chance, turn on me? Yes, I venture still to think it. At all events, I want to try. Get off with his sister as soon as possible and leave me with him alone." I was amazed, myself, at the spirit I had still in reserve, and therefore perhaps a trifle the more disconcerted at the way in which, in spite of this fine example of it, she hesitated. "There's one thing, of course," I went on: "they mustn't, before she goes, see each other for three seconds." Then it came over me that, in spite of Flora's presumable sequestration from the instant of her return from the pool, it might already be too late. "Do you mean," I anxiously asked, "that they HAVE met?"

At this she quite flushed. "Ah, miss, I'm not such a fool as that! If I've been obliged to leave her three or four times, it has been each time with one of the maids, and at present, though she's alone, she's locked in safe. And yet—and yet!" There were too many things.

"And yet what?"

"Well, are you so sure of the little gentleman?"

"I'm not sure of anything but YOU. But I have, since last evening, a new hope. I think he wants to give me an opening. I do believe that—poor little exquisite wretch!—he wants to speak. Last evening, in the firelight and the silence, he sat with me for two hours as if it were just coming."

Mrs. Grose looked hard, through the window, at the gray, gathering day. "And did it come?"

"No, though I waited and waited, I confess it didn't, and it was without a breach of the silence or so much as a faint allusion to his sister's condition and absence that we at last kissed for good night. All the same," I continued, "I can't, if her uncle sees her, consent to his seeing her brother without my having given the boy—and most of all because things have got so bad—a little more time."

My friend appeared on this ground more reluctant than I could quite understand. "What do you mean by more time?"

"Well, a day or two—really to bring it out. He'll then be on MY side—of which you see the importance. If nothing comes, I shall only fail, and you will, at the worst, have helped me by doing, on your arrival in town, whatever you may have found possible." So I put it before her, but she continued for a little so inscrutably embarrassed that I came again to her aid. "Unless, indeed," I wound up, "you really want NOT to go."

I could see it, in her face, at last clear itself; she put out her hand to me as a pledge. "I'll go—I'll go. I'll go this morning."

I wanted to be very just. "If you SHOULD wish still to wait, I would engage she shouldn't see me."

"No, no: it's the place itself. She must leave it." She held me a moment with heavy eyes, then brought out the rest. "Your idea's the right one. I myself, miss—"

"Well?"

"I can't stay."

The look she gave me with it made me jump at possibilities. "You mean that, since yesterday, you HAVE seen—?"

She shook her head with dignity. "I've HEARD—!"

"Heard?"

"From that child—horrors! There!" she sighed with tragic relief. "On my honour, miss, she says things—!" But at this evocation she broke down; she dropped, with a sudden sob, upon my sofa and, as I had seen her do before, gave way to all the grief of it.

It was quite in another manner that I, for my part, let myself go. "Oh, thank God!"

She sprang up again at this, drying her eyes with a groan. "'Thank God'?"

"It so justifies me!"

"It does that, miss!"

I couldn't have desired more emphasis, but I just hesitated. "She's so horrible?"

I saw my colleague scarce knew how to put it. "Really shocking."

"And about me?"

"About you, miss—since you must have it. It's beyond everything, for a young lady; and I can't think wherever she must have picked up—"

"The appalling language she applied to me? I can, then!" I broke in with a laugh that was doubtless significant enough.

It only, in truth, left my friend still more grave. "Well, perhaps

I ought to also—since I've heard some of it before! Yet I can't bear it," the poor woman went on while, with the same movement, she glanced, on my dressing table, at the face of my watch. "But I must go back."

I kept her, however. "Ah, if you can't bear it—!"

"How can I stop with her, you mean? Why, just FOR that: to get her away. Far from this," she pursued, "far from THEM-"

"She may be different? She may be free?" I seized her almost with joy. "Then, in spite of yesterday, you BELIEVE—"

"In such doings?" Her simple description of them required, in the light of her expression, to be carried no further, and she gave me the whole thing as she had never done. "I believe."

Yes, it was a joy, and we were still shoulder to shoulder: if I might continue sure of that I should care but little what else happened. My support in the presence of disaster would be the same as it had been in my early need of confidence, and if my friend would answer for my honesty, I would answer for all the rest. On the point of taking leave of her, nonetheless, I was to some extent embarrassed. "There's one thing, of course—it occurs to me—to remember. My letter, giving the alarm, will have reached town before you."

I now perceived still more how she had been beating about the bush and how weary at last it had made her. "Your letter won't have got there. Your letter never went."

"What then became of it?"

"Goodness knows! Master Miles—"

"Do you mean HE took it?" I gasped.

She hung fire, but she overcame her reluctance. "I mean that I saw yesterday, when I came back with Miss Flora, that it wasn't where you had put it. Later in the evening I had the chance to question Luke, and he declared that he had neither noticed nor touched it." We could only exchange, on this, one of our deeper mutual soundings, and it was Mrs. Grose who first brought up the plumb with an almost elated "You see!"

"Yes, I see that if Miles took it instead he probably will have read it and destroyed it."

"And don't you see anything else?"

I faced her a moment with a sad smile. "It strikes me that by this time your eyes are open even wider than mine."

They proved to be so indeed, but she could still blush, almost, to show it. "I make out now what he must have done at school." And she gave, in her simple sharpness, an almost droll disillusioned nod. "He stole!"

I turned it over—I tried to be more judicial. "Well—perhaps."

She looked as if she found me unexpectedly calm. "He stole LETTERS!"

She couldn't know my reasons for a calmness after all pretty shallow; so I showed them off as I might. "I hope then it was to more purpose than in this case! The note, at any rate, that I put on the table yesterday," I pursued, "will have given him so scant an advantage—for it contained only the bare demand for an interview—that he is already much ashamed of having gone so far for so little, and that what he had on his mind last evening was precisely the need of confession." I seemed to myself, for the instant, to have mastered it, to see it all. "Leave us, leave us"—I was already, at the door, hurrying her off. "I'll get it out of him. He'll meet me—he'll confess. If he confesses, he's saved. And if he's saved—"

"Then YOU are?" The dear woman kissed me on this, and I took her farewell. "I'll save you without him!" she cried as she went.

22

Yet it was when she had got off—and I missed her on the spot—that the great pinch really came. If I had counted on what it would give me to find myself alone with Miles, I speedily perceived, at least, that it would give me a measure. No hour of my stay in fact was so assailed with apprehensions as that of my coming down to learn that the carriage containing Mrs. Grose and my younger pupil had already rolled out of the gates. Now I WAS, I said to myself, face to face with the elements, and for much of the rest of the day, while I fought my weakness, I could consider that I had been supremely rash. It was a tighter place still than I had yet turned round in; all the more that, for the first time, I could see in the aspect of others a confused reflection of the crisis. What had happened naturally caused them all to stare; there was too little of the explained, throw out whatever we might, in the suddenness of my colleague's act.

The maids and the men looked blank; the effect of which on my nerves was an aggravation until I saw the necessity of making it a positive aid. It was precisely, in short, by just clutching the helm that I avoided total wreck; and I dare say that, to bear up at all, I became, that morning, very grand and very dry. I welcomed the consciousness that I was charged with much to do, and I caused it to be known as well that, left thus to myself, I was quite remarkably firm. I wandered with that manner, for the next hour or two, all over the place and looked, I have no doubt, as if I were ready for any onset. So, for the benefit of whom it might concern, I paraded with a sick heart.

The person it appeared least to concern proved to be, till dinner, little Miles himself. My perambulations had given me, meanwhile, no glimpse of him, but they had tended to make more public the change taking place in our relation as a consequence of his having at the piano, the day before, kept me, in Flora's interest, so beguiled and befooled. The stamp of publicity had of course been fully given by her confinement and departure, and the change itself was now ushered in by our non-observance of the regular custom of the schoolroom.

He had already disappeared when, on my way down, I pushed open his door, and I learned below that he had breakfasted—in the presence of a couple of the maids—with Mrs. Grose and his sister. He had then gone out, as he said, for a stroll; than which nothing, I reflected, could better have expressed his frank view of the abrupt transformation of my office. What he would not permit this office to consist of was yet to be settled: there was a queer relief, at all events—I mean for myself in especial—in the renouncement of one pretension.

If so much had sprung to the surface, I scarce put it too strongly in saying that what had perhaps sprung highest was the absurdity of our prolonging the fiction that I had anything more to teach him. It sufficiently stuck out that, by tacit little tricks in which even more than myself he carried out the care for my dignity, I had had to appeal to him to let me off straining to meet him on the ground of his true capacity.

He had at any rate his freedom now; I was never to touch it again; as I had amply shown, moreover, when, on his joining me in the schoolroom the previous night, I had uttered, on the subject of the interval just concluded, neither challenge nor hint. I had too much, from this moment, my other ideas. Yet when he at last arrived, the difficulty of applying them, the accumulations of my problem, were brought straight home to me by the beautiful little presence on which what had occurred had as yet, for the eye, dropped neither stain nor shadow.

To mark, for the house, the high state I cultivated I decreed that my meals with the boy should be served, as we called it, downstairs; so that I had been awaiting him in the ponderous pomp of the room outside of the window of which I had had from Mrs. Grose, that first scared Sunday, my flash of something it would scarce have done to call light. Here at present I felt afresh—for I had felt it again and again—how my equilibrium depended on the success of my rigid will, the will to shut my eyes as tight as possible to the truth that what I had to deal with was, revoltingly, against nature.

I could only get on at all by taking "nature" into my confidence and my account, by treating my monstrous ordeal as a push in a direction unusual, of course, and unpleasant, but demanding, after all, for a fair front, only another turn of the screw of ordinary human virtue. No attempt, nonetheless, could well require more tact than just this attempt to supply, one's self, ALL the nature. How could I put even a little of that article into a suppression of reference to what had occurred? How, on the other hand, could I make reference without a new plunge into the hideous obscure?

Well, a sort of answer, after a time, had come to me, and it was so far confirmed as that I was met, incontestably, by the quickened vision of what was rare in my little companion. It was indeed as if he had found even now—as he had so often found at lessons—still some other delicate way to ease me off. Wasn't there light in the fact which, as we shared our solitude, broke out with a specious glitter it had never yet quite worn?—the fact that (opportunity aiding, precious opportunity which had now come) it would be preposterous, with a child so endowed, to forego the help one might wrest from absolute intelligence?

What had his intelligence been given him for but to save him? Mightn't one, to reach his mind, risk the stretch of an angular arm over his character? It was as if, when we were face to face in the dining room, he had literally shown me the way. The roast mutton was on the table, and I had dispensed with attendance. Miles, before he sat down, stood a moment with his hands in his pockets and looked at the joint, on which he seemed on the point of passing some humorous judgment. But what he presently produced was: "I say, my dear, is she really very awfully ill?"

"Little Flora? Not so bad but that she'll presently be better. London will set her up. Bly had ceased to agree with her. Come here and take your mutton."

He alertly obeyed me, carried the plate carefully to his seat, and, when he was established, went on. "Did Bly disagree with her so terribly suddenly?"

"Not so suddenly as you might think. One had seen it coming on."

"Then why didn't you get her off before?"

"Before what?"

"Before she became too ill to travel."

I found myself prompt. "She's NOT too ill to travel: she only might have become so if she had stayed. This was just the moment to seize. The journey will dissipate the influence"—oh, I was grand!—"and carry it off."

"I see, I see"—Miles, for that matter, was grand, too. He settled to his repast with the charming little "table manner" that, from the day of his arrival, had relieved me of all grossness of admonition. Whatever he had been driven from school for, it was not for ugly feeding. He was irreproachable, as always, today; but he was unmistakably more conscious. He was discernibly trying to take for granted more things than he found, without assistance, quite easy; and he dropped into peaceful silence while he felt his situation.

Our meal was of the briefest—mine a vain pretence, and I had the things immediately removed. While this was done Miles stood again with his hands in his little pockets and his back to me—stood and looked out of the wide window through which, that other day, I had seen what pulled me up. We continued silent while the maid was with us—as silent, it whimsically occurred to me, as some young couple who, on their wedding journey, at the inn, feel shy in the presence of the waiter. He turned round only when the waiter had left us. "Well—so we're alone!"

23

"Oh, more or less." I fancy my smile was pale. "Not absolutely. We shouldn't like that!" I went on.

"No—I suppose we shouldn't. Of course we have the others."

"We have the others—we have indeed the others," I concurred.

"Yet even though we have them," he returned, still with his hands in his pockets and planted there in front of me, "they don't much count, do they?"

I made the best of it, but I felt wan. "It depends on what you call 'much'!"

"Yes"—with all accommodation—"everything depends!" On this, however, he faced to the window again and presently reached it with his vague, restless, cogitating step. He remained there awhile, with his forehead against the glass, in contemplation of the stupid shrubs I knew and the dull things of November. I had always my hypocrisy of "work," behind which, now, I gained the sofa. Steadying myself with it there as I had repeatedly done at those moments of torment that I have described as the moments of my knowing the children to be given to something from which I was barred, I sufficiently obeyed my habit of being prepared for the worst.

But an extraordinary impression dropped on me as I extracted a meaning from the boy's embarrassed back—none other than the impression that I was not barred now. This inference grew in a few minutes to sharp intensity and seemed bound up with the direct perception that it was positively HE who was. The frames and squares of the great window were a kind of image, for him, of a kind of failure. I felt that I saw him, at any rate, shut in or shut out. He was admirable, but not comfortable: I took it in with a throb of hope. Wasn't he looking, through the haunted pane, for something he couldn't see?—and wasn't it the first time in the whole business that he had known such a lapse?

The first, the very first: I found it a splendid portent. It made him anxious, though he watched himself; he had been anxious all day and, even while in his usual sweet little manner he sat at table, had needed all his small strange genius to give it a gloss. When he at last turned round to meet me, it was almost as if this genius had succumbed. "Well, I think I'm glad Bly agrees with ME!"

"You would certainly seem to have seen, these twenty-four hours, a good deal more of it than for some time before. I hope," I went on bravely, "that you've been enjoying yourself."

"Oh, yes, I've been ever so far; all round about—miles and miles away. I've never been so free."

He had really a manner of his own, and I could only try to keep up with him. "Well, do you like it?"

He stood there smiling; then at last he put into two words- "Do YOU?"—more discrimination than I had ever heard two words contain. Before I had time to deal with that, however, he continued as if with the sense that this was an impertinence to be softened. "Nothing could be more charming than the way you take it, for of course if we're alone together now it's you that are alone most. But I hope," he threw in, "you don't particularly mind!"

"Having to do with you?" I asked. "My dear child, how can I help minding? Though I've renounced all claim to your company—you're so beyond me—I at least greatly enjoy it. What else should I stay on for?"

He looked at me more directly, and the expression of his face, graver now, struck me as the most beautiful I had ever found in it. "You stay on just for THAT?"

"Certainly. I stay on as your friend and from the tremendous interest I take in you till something can be done for you that may be more worth your while. That needn't surprise you." My voice trembled so that I felt it impossible to suppress the shake. "Don't you remember how I told you, when I came and sat on your bed the night of the storm, that there was nothing in the world I wouldn't do for you?"

"Yes, yes!" He, on his side, more and more visibly nervous, had a tone to master; but he was so much more successful than I that, laughing out through his gravity, he could pretend we were pleasantly jesting. "Only that, I think, was to get me to do something for YOU!"

"It was partly to get you to do something," I conceded. "But, you know, you didn't do it."

"Oh, yes," he said with the brightest superficial eagerness, "you wanted me to tell you something."

"That's it. Out, straight out. What you have on your mind, you know."

"Ah, then, is THAT what you've stayed over for?"

He spoke with a gaiety through which I could still catch the finest little quiver of resentful passion; but I can't begin to express the effect upon me of an implication of surrender even so faint. It was as if what I had yearned for had come at last only to astonish me. "Well, yes—I may as well make a clean breast of it, it was precisely for that."

He waited so long that I supposed it for the purpose of repudiating the assumption on which my action had been founded;

but what he finally said was: "Do you mean now—here?"

"There couldn't be a better place or time." He looked round him uneasily, and I had the rare—oh, the queer!—impression of the very first symptom I had seen in him of the approach of immediate fear. It was as if he were suddenly afraid of me—which struck me indeed as perhaps the best thing to make him. Yet in the very pang of the effort I felt it vain to try sternness, and I heard myself the next instant so gentle as to be almost grotesque. "You want so to go out again?"

"Awfully!" He smiled at me heroically, and the touching little bravery of it was enhanced by his actually flushing with pain. He had picked up his hat, which he had brought in, and stood twirling it in a way that gave me, even as I was just nearly reaching port, a perverse horror of what I was doing. To do it in ANY way was an act of violence, for what did it consist of but the obtrusion of the idea of grossness and guilt on a small helpless creature who had been for me a revelation of the possibilities of beautiful intercourse?

Wasn't it base to create for a being so exquisite a mere alien awkwardness? I suppose I now read into our situation a clearness it couldn't have had at the time, for I seem to see our poor eyes already lighted with some spark of a prevision of the anguish that was to come. So we circled about, with terrors and scruples, like fighters not daring to close. But it was for each other we feared! That kept us a little longer suspended and unbruised. "I'll tell you everything," Miles said—"I mean I'll tell you anything you like. You'll stay on with me, and we shall both be all right, and I WILL tell you—I WILL. But not now."

"Why not now?"

My insistence turned him from me and kept him once more at his window in a silence during which, between us, you might have heard a pin drop. Then he was before me again with the air of a person for whom, outside, someone who had frankly to be reckoned with was waiting. "I have to see Luke."

I had not yet reduced him to quite so vulgar a lie, and I felt proportionately ashamed. But, horrible as it was, his lies made up my truth. I achieved thoughtfully a few loops of my knitting. "Well, then, go to Luke, and I'll wait for what you promise. Only, in return for that, satisfy, before you leave me, one very much smaller request."

He looked as if he felt he had succeeded enough to be able still a little to bargain. "Very much smaller—?"

"Yes, a mere fraction of the whole. Tell me"—oh, my work preoccupied me, and I was offhand!—"if, yesterday afternoon, from the table in the hall, you took, you know, my letter."

24

My sense of how he received this suffered for a minute from something that I can describe only as a fierce split of my attention—a stroke that at first, as I sprang straight up, reduced me to the mere blind movement of getting hold of him, drawing him close, and, while I just fell for support against the nearest piece of furniture, instinctively keeping him with his back to the window. The appearance was full upon us that I had already had to deal with here: Peter Quint had come into view like a sentinel before a prison. The next thing I saw was that, from outside, he had reached the window, and then I knew that, close to the glass and glaring in through it, he offered once more to the room his white face of damnation.

It represents but grossly what took place within me at the sight to say that on the second my decision was made; yet I believe that no woman so overwhelmed ever in so short a time recovered her grasp of the ACT. It came to me in the very horror of the immediate presence that the act would be, seeing and facing what I saw and faced, to keep the boy himself unaware. The inspiration—I can call it by no other name—was that I felt how voluntarily, how transcendently, I MIGHT. It was like fighting with a demon for a human soul, and when I had fairly so appraised it I saw how the human soul—held out, in the tremor of my hands, at arm's length—had a perfect dew of sweat on a lovely childish forehead. The face that was close to mine was as white as the face against the glass, and out of it presently came a sound, not low nor weak, but as if from much further away, that I drank like a waft of fragrance.

"Yes—I took it."

At this, with a moan of joy, I enfolded, I drew him close; and while I held him to my breast, where I could feel in the sudden fever of his little body the tremendous pulse of his little heart, I kept my eyes on the thing at the window and saw it move and shift its posture. I have likened it to a sentinel, but its slow wheel, for a moment, was rather the prowl of a baffled beast. My present quickened courage, however, was such that, not too much to let it through, I had to shade, as it were, my flame. Meanwhile the glare of the face was again at the window, the scoundrel fixed as if to watch and wait. It was the very confidence that I might now defy him, as well as the positive certitude, by this time, of the child's unconsciousness, that made me go on. "What did you take it for?"

"To see what you said about me."

"You opened the letter?"

"I opened it."

My eyes were now, as I held him off a little again, on Miles's own face, in which the collapse of mockery showed me how complete was the ravage of uneasiness. What was prodigious was that at last, by my success, his sense was sealed and his communication stopped: he knew that he was in presence, but knew not of what, and knew still less that I also was and that I did know. And what did this strain of trouble matter when my eyes went back to the window only to see that the air was clear again and—by my personal triumph—the influence quenched? There was nothing there. I felt that the cause was mine and that I should surely get ALL. "And you found nothing!"—I let my elation out.

He gave the most mournful, thoughtful little headshake. "Nothing."

"Nothing, nothing!" I almost shouted in my joy.

"Nothing, nothing," he sadly repeated.

I kissed his forehead; it was drenched. "So what have you

done with it?"

"I've burned it."

"Burned it?" It was now or never. "Is that what you did at school?"

Oh, what this brought up! "At school?"

"Did you take letters?—or other things?"

"Other things?" He appeared now to be thinking of something far off and that reached him only through the pressure of his anxiety. Yet it did reach him. "Did I STEAL?"

I felt myself redden to the roots of my hair as well as wonder if it were more strange to put to a gentleman such a question or to see him take it with allowances that gave the very distance of his fall in the world. "Was it for that you mightn't go back?"

The only thing he felt was rather a dreary little surprise. "Did you know I mightn't go back?"

"I know everything."

He gave me at this the longest and strangest look. "Everything?"

"Everything. Therefore DID you—?" But I couldn't say it again.

Miles could, very simply. "No. I didn't steal."

My face must have shown him I believed him utterly; yet my hands—but it was for pure tenderness—shook him as if to ask him why, if it was all for nothing, he had condemned me to months of torment. "What then did you do?"

He looked in vague pain all round the top of the room and drew his breath, two or three times over, as if with difficulty. He might have been standing at the bottom of the sea and raising his eyes to some faint green twilight. "Well—I said things."

"Only that?"

"They thought it was enough!"

"To turn you out for?"

Never, truly, had a person "turned out" shown so little to explain it as this little person! He appeared to weigh my question, but in a manner quite detached and almost helpless. "Well, I suppose I oughtn't."

"But to whom did you say them?"

He evidently tried to remember, but it dropped—he had lost it. "I don't know!"

He almost smiled at me in the desolation of his surrender, which was indeed practically, by this time, so complete that I ought to have left it there. But I was infatuated—I was blind with victory, though even then the very effect that was to have brought him so much nearer was already that of added separation. "Was it to everyone?" I asked.

"No; it was only to—" But he gave a sick little headshake. "I don't remember their names."

"Were they then so many?"

"No—only a few. Those I liked."

Those he liked? I seemed to float not into clearness, but into a darker obscure, and within a minute there had come to me out of my very pity the appalling alarm of his being perhaps innocent. It was for the instant confounding and bottomless, for if he WERE innocent, what then on earth was *I*? Paralyzed, while it lasted, by the mere brush of the question, I let him go a little, so that, with a deep-drawn sigh, he turned away from me again; which, as he faced toward the clear window, I suffered, feeling that I had nothing now there to keep him from. "And did they repeat what you said?" I went on after a moment.

He was soon at some distance from me, still breathing hard and again with the air, though now without anger for it, of being confined against his will. Once more, as he had done before, he looked up at the dim day as if, of what had hitherto sustained him, nothing was left but an unspeakable anxiety. "Oh, yes," he nevertheless replied—"they must have repeated them. To those THEY liked," he added.

There was, somehow, less of it than I had expected; but I turned it over. "And these things came round—?"

"To the masters? Oh, yes!" he answered very simply. "But I didn't know they'd tell."

"The masters? They didn't—they've never told. That's why I ask you."

He turned to me again his little beautiful fevered face. "Yes, it was too bad."

"Too bad?"

"What I suppose I sometimes said. To write home."

I can't name the exquisite pathos of the contradiction given to such a speech by such a speaker; I only know that the next instant I heard myself throw off with homely force: "Stuff and nonsense!" But the next after that I must have sounded stern enough. "What WERE these things?"

My sternness was all for his judge, his executioner; yet it made him avert himself again, and that movement made ME, with a single bound and an irrepressible cry, spring straight upon him. For there again, against the glass, as if to blight his confession and stay his answer, was the hideous author of our woe—the white face of damnation. I felt a sick swim at the drop of my victory and all the return of my battle, so that the wildness of my veritable leap only served as a great betrayal. I saw him, from the midst of my act, meet it with a divination, and on the perception that even now he only guessed, and that the window was still to his own eyes free, I let the impulse flame up to convert the climax of his dismay into the very proof of his liberation. "No more, no more, no more!" I shrieked, as I tried to press him against me, to my visitant.

"Is she HERE?" Miles panted as he caught with his sealed eyes the direction of my words. Then as his strange "she" staggered me and, with a gasp, I echoed it, "Miss Jessel, Miss Jessel!" he with a sudden fury gave me back.

I seized, stupefied, his supposition—some sequel to what we had done to Flora, but this made me only want to show him that it was better still than that. "It's not Miss Jessel! But it's at the window—straight before us. It's THERE—the coward horror, there for the last time!"

At this, after a second in which his head made the movement of a baffled dog's on a scent and then gave a frantic little shake for air and light, he was at me in a white rage, bewildered, glaring vainly over the place and missing wholly, though it now, to my sense, filled the room like the taste of poison, the wide, overwhelming presence. "It's HE?"

I was so determined to have all my proof that I flashed into ice to challenge him. "Whom do you mean by 'he'?"

"Peter Quint—you devil!" His face gave again, round the room, its convulsed supplication. "WHERE?"

They are in my ears still, his supreme surrender of the name and his tribute to my devotion. "What does he matter now, my own?—what will he EVER matter? *I* have you," I launched at the beast, "but he has lost you forever!" Then, for the demonstration of my work, "There, THERE!" I said to Miles.

But he had already jerked straight round, stared, glared again, and seen but the quiet day. With the stroke of the loss I was so proud of he uttered the cry of a creature hurled over an abyss, and the grasp with which I recovered him might have been that of catching him in his fall. I caught him, yes, I held him—it may be imagined with what a passion; but at the end of a minute I began to feel what it truly was that I held. We were alone with the quiet day, and his little heart, dispossessed, had stopped.

The Lesson of the Master

Chapter 1

He had been told the ladies were at church, but this was corrected by what he saw from the top of the steps—they descended from a great height in two arms, with a circular sweep of the most charming effect—at the threshold of the door which, from the long bright gallery, overlooked the immense lawn. Three gentlemen, on the grass, at a distance, sat under the great trees, while the fourth figure showed a crimson dress that told as a "bit of colour" amid the fresh rich green. The servant had so far accompanied Paul Overt as to introduce him to this view, after asking him if he wished first to go to his room. The young man declined that privilege, conscious of no disrepair from so short and easy a journey and always liking to take at once a general perceptive possession of a new scene. He stood there a little with his eyes on the group and on the admirable picture, the wide grounds of an old country-house near London—that only made it better—on a splendid Sunday in June. "But that lady, who's *she*?" he said to the servant before the man left him.

"I think she's Mrs. St. George, sir."

"Mrs. St. George, the wife of the distinguished—"Then Paul Overt checked himself, doubting if a footman would know.

"Yes, sir—probably, sir," said his guide, who appeared to wish to intimate that a person staying at Summersoft would naturally be, if only by alliance, distinguished. His tone, however, made poor Overt himself feel for the moment scantly so.

"And the gentlemen?" Overt went on.

"Well, sir, one of them's General Fancourt."

"Ah yes, I know; thank you." General Fancourt was distinguished, there was no doubt of that, for something he had done, or perhaps even hadn't done—the young man couldn't remember which—some years before in India. The servant went away, leaving the glass doors open into the gallery, and Paul Overt remained at the head of the wide double staircase, saying to himself that the place was sweet and promised a pleasant visit, while he leaned on the balustrade of fine old ironwork which, like all the other details, was of the same period as the house. It all went together and spoke in one voice—a rich English voice of the early part of the eighteenth century.

It might have been church-time on a summer's day in the reign of Queen Anne; the stillness was too perfect to be modern, the nearness counted so as distance, and there was something so fresh and sound in the originality of the large smooth house, the expanse of beautiful brickwork that showed for pink rather than red and that had been kept clear of messy creepers by the law under which a woman with a rare complexion disdains a veil. When Paul Overt became aware that the people under the trees had noticed him he turned back through the open doors into the great gallery which was the pride of the place.

It marched across from end to end and seemed—with its bright colours, its high panelled windows, its faded flowered chintzes, its quickly-recognised portraits and pictures, the blue-and-white china of its cabinets and the attenuated festoons and rosettes of its ceiling—a cheerful upholstered avenue into the other century.

Our friend was slightly nervous; that went with his character as a student of fine prose, went with the artist's general disposition to vibrate; and there was a particular thrill in the idea that Henry St. George might be a member of the party. For the young aspirant he had remained a high literary figure, in spite of the lower range of production to which he had fallen after his first three great successes, the comparative absence of quality in his later work. There had been moments when Paul Overt almost shed tears for this; but now that he was near him—he had never met him—he was conscious only of the fine original source and of his own immense debt. After he had taken a turn or two up and down the gallery he came out again and descended the steps. He was but slenderly supplied with a certain social boldness—it was really a weakness in him—so that, conscious of a want of acquaintance with the four persons in the distance, he gave way to motions recommended by their not committing him to a positive approach.

There was a fine English awkwardness in this—he felt that too as he sauntered vaguely and obliquely across the lawn, taking an independent line. Fortunately there was an equally fine English directness in the way one of the gentlemen presently rose and made as if to "stalk" him, though with an air of conciliation and reassurance. To this demonstration Paul Overt instantly responded, even if the gentleman were not his host. He was tall, straight and elderly and had, like the great house itself, a pink smiling face, and into the bargain a white moustache.

Our young man met him halfway while he laughed and said: "Er—Lady Watermouth told us you were coming; she asked me just to look after you." Paul Overt thanked him, liking him on the spot, and turned round with him to walk toward the others. "They've all gone to church—all except us," the stranger continued as they went; "we're just sitting here—it's so jolly." Overt pronounced it jolly indeed: it was such a lovely place. He mentioned that he was having the charming impression for the first time.

"Ah you've not been here before?" said his companion. "It's a nice little place—not much to *do*, you know". Overt wondered what he wanted to "do"—he felt that he himself was doing so much. By the time they came to where the others sat he had recognised his initiator for a military man and—such was the turn of Overt's imagination—had found him thus still more sympathetic. He would naturally have a need for action, for deeds at variance with the pacific pastoral scene. He was evidently so good-natured, however, that he accepted the inglorious hour for what it was worth. Paul Overt shared it with him and with his companions for the next twenty minutes; the latter looked at him and he looked at them without knowing much who they were, while the talk went on without much telling him even what it meant.

It seemed indeed to mean nothing in particular; it wandered, with casual pointless pauses and short terrestrial flights, amid names of persons and places—names which, for our friend, had no great power of evocation. It was all sociable and slow, as was right and natural of a warm Sunday morning.

His first attention was given to the question, privately considered, of whether one of the two younger men would be Henry St. George. He knew many of his distinguished contemporaries by their photographs, but had never, as happened, seen a portrait of the great misguided novelist. One of the gentlemen was unimaginable—he was too young; and the other scarcely looked clever enough, with such mild undiscriminating eyes. If those eyes were St. George's the problem, presented by the ill-matched parts of his genius would be still more difficult of solution.

Besides, the deportment of their proprietor was not, as regards the lady in the red dress, such as could be natural, toward the wife of his bosom, even to a writer accused by several critics of sacrificing too much to manner. Lastly Paul Overt had a vague sense that if the gentleman with the expressionless eyes bore the name that had set his heart beating faster (he also had contradictory conventional whiskers—the young admirer of the celebrity had never in a mental vision seen *his* face in so vulgar a frame) he would have given him a sign of recognition or of friendliness, would have heard of him a little, would know something about "Ginistrella," would have an impression of how that fresh fiction had caught the eye of real criticism.

Paul Overt had a dread of being grossly proud, but even morbid modesty might view the authorship of *Ginistrella* as constituting a degree of identity. His soldierly friend became clear enough: he was "Fancourt," but was also "the General"; and he mentioned to the new visitor in the course of a few moments that he had but lately returned from twenty years service abroad.

"And now you remain in England?" the young man asked.

"Oh yes; I've bought a small house in London."

"And I hope you like it," said Overt, looking at Mrs. St. George.

"Well, a little house in Manchester Square—there's a limit to the enthusiasm *that* inspires."

"Oh I meant being at home again—being back in Piccadilly."

"My daughter likes Piccadilly—that's the main thing. She's very fond of art and music and literature and all that kind of thing. She missed it in India and she finds it in London, or she hopes she'll find it. Mr. St. George has promised to help her-he has been awfully kind to her. She has gone to church—she's fond of that too—but they'll all be back in a quarter of an hour. You must let me introduce you to her—she'll be so glad to know you. I dare say she has read every blest word you've written."

"I shall be delighted—I haven't written so very many," Overt pleaded, feeling, and without resentment, that the General at least was vagueness itself about that. But he wondered a little why, expressing this friendly disposition, it didn't occur to the doubtless eminent soldier to pronounce the word that would put him in relation with Mrs. St. George. If it was a question of introductions Miss Fancourt—apparently as yet unmarried-was far away, while the wife of his illustrious confrere was almost between them. This lady struck Paul Overt as altogether pretty, with a surprising juvenility and a high smartness of aspect, something that—he could scarcely have said why—served for mystification.

St. George certainly had every right to a charming wife, but he himself would never have imagined the important little woman in the aggressively Parisian dress the partner for life, the alter ego, of a man of letters. That partner in general, he knew, that second self, was far from presenting herself in a single type: observation had taught him that she was not inveterately, not necessarily plain. But he had never before seen her look so much as if her prosperity had deeper foundations than an ink-spotted study-table littered with proof-sheets. Mrs. St. George might have been the wife of a gentleman who "kept" books rather than wrote them, who carried on great affairs in the City and made better bargains than those that poets mostly make with publishers.

With this she hinted at a success more personal—a success peculiarly stamping the age in which society, the world of conversation, is a great drawing-room with the City for its ante-chamber. Overt numbered her years at first as some thirty, and then ended by believing that she might approach her fiftieth. But she somehow in this case juggled away the excess and the difference—you only saw them in a rare glimpse, like the rabbit in the conjurer's sleeve. She was extraordinarily white, and her every element and item was pretty; her eyes, her ears, her hair, her voice, her hands, her feet—to which her relaxed attitude in her wicker chair gave a great publicity—and the numerous ribbons and trinkets with which she was bedecked.

She looked as if she had put on her best clothes to go to church and then had decided they were too good for that and had stayed at home. She told a story of some length about the shabby way Lady Jane had treated the Duchess, as well as an anecdote in relation to a purchase she had made in Paris—on her way back from Cannes; made for Lady Egbert, who had never refunded the money. Paul Overt suspected her of a tendency to figure great people as larger than life, until he noticed the manner in which she handled Lady Egbert, which was so sharply mutinous that it reassured him. He felt he should have understood her better if he might have met her eye; but she scarcely so much as glanced at him.

"Ah here they come—all the good ones!" she said at last; and Paul Overt admired at his distance the return of the church-goers—several persons, in couples and threes, advancing in a flicker of sun and shade at the end of a large green vista formed by the level grass and the overarching boughs.

"If you mean to imply that *we're* bad, I protest," said one of the gentlemen—"after making one's self agreeable all the morning!"

"Ah if they've found you agreeable—!" Mrs. St. George gaily cried. "But if we're good the others are better."

"They must be angels then," said the amused General.

"Your husband was an angel, the way he went off at your bidding," the gentleman who had first spoken declared to Mrs. St. George.

"At my bidding?"

"Didn't you make him go to church?"

"I never made him do anything in my life but once—when I made him burn up a bad book. That's all!" At her "That's all!" our young friend broke into an irrepressible laugh; it lasted only a second, but it drew her eyes to him. His own met them, though not long enough to help him to understand her; unless it were a step towards this that he saw on the instant how the burnt book—the way she alluded to it!—would have been one of her husband's finest things.

"A bad book?" her interlocutor repeated.

"I didn't like it. He went to church because your daughter went," she continued to General Fancourt. "I think it my duty to call your attention to his extraordinary demonstrations to your daughter."

"Well, if you don't mind them I don't," the General laughed.

"*Il s'attache e ses pas*. But I don't wonder—she's so charming."

"I hope she won't make him burn any books!" Paul Overt ventured to exclaim.

"If she'd make him write a few it would be more to the purpose," said Mrs. St. George. "He has been of a laziness of late—!"

Our young man stared—he was so struck with the lady's phraseology. Her "Write a few" seemed to him almost as good as her "That's all." Didn't she, as the wife of a rare artist, know what it was to produce one perfect work of art? How in the world did she think they were turned on? His private conviction was that, admirably as Henry St. George wrote, he had written for the last ten years, and especially for the last five, only too much, and there was an instant during which he felt inwardly solicited to make this public.

But before he had spoken a diversion was effected by the return of the absentees. They strolled up dispersedly—there were eight or ten of them—and the circle under the trees rearranged itself as they took their place in it. They made it much larger, so that Paul Overt could feel—he was always feeling that sort of thing, as he said to himself—that if the company had already been interesting to watch the interest would now become intense. He shook hands with his hostess, who welcomed him without many words, in the manner of a woman able to trust him to understand and conscious that so pleasant an occasion would in every way speak for itself. She offered him no particular facility for sitting by her, and when they had all subsided again he found himself still next General Fancourt, with an unknown lady on his other flank.

"That's my daughter—that one opposite," the General said to him without lose of time. Overt saw a tall girl, with magnificent red hair, in a dress of a pretty grey-green tint and of a limp silken texture, a garment that clearly shirked every modern effect. It had therefore somehow the stamp of the latest thing, so that our beholder quickly took her for nothing if not contemporaneous.

"She's very handsome—very handsome," he repeated while he considered her. There was something noble in her head, and she appeared fresh and strong.

Her good father surveyed her with complacency, remarking soon: "She looks too hot—that's her walk. But she'll be all right presently. Then I'll make her come over and speak to you."

"I should be sorry to give you that trouble. If you were to take me over *there*—!" the young man murmured.

"My dear sir, do you suppose I put myself out that way? I

don't mean for you, but for Marian," the General added.

"I would put myself out for her soon enough," Overt replied; after which he went on: "Will you be so good as to tell me which of those gentlemen is Henry St. George?"

"The fellow talking to my girl. By Jove, he *is* making up to her—they're going off for another walk."

"Ah is that he—really?" Our friend felt a certain surprise, for the personage before him seemed to trouble a vision which had been vague only while not confronted with the reality. As soon as the reality dawned the mental image, retiring with a sigh, became substantial enough to suffer a slight wrong. Overt, who had spent a considerable part of his short life in foreign lands, made now, but not for the first time, the reflexion that whereas in those countries he had almost always recognised the artist and the man of letters by his personal "type," the mould of his face, the character of his head, the expression of his figure and even the indications of his dress, so in England this identification was as little as possible a matter of course, thanks to the greater conformity, the habit of sinking the profession instead of advertising it, the general diffusion of the air of the gentleman—the gentleman committed to no particular set of ideas.

More than once, on returning to his own country, he had said to himself about people met in society: "One sees them in this place and that, and one even talks with them; but to find out what they *do* one would really have to be a detective." In respect to several individuals whose work he was the opposite of "drawn to"—perhaps he was wrong—he found himself adding "No wonder they conceal it—when it's so bad!" He noted that oftener than in France and in Germany his artist looked like a gentleman—that is like an English one—while, certainly outside a few exceptions, his gentlemen didn't look like an artist.

St. George was not one of the exceptions; that circumstance he definitely apprehended before the great man had turned his back to walk off with Miss Fancourt. He certainly looked better behind than any foreign man of letters—showed for beautifully correct in his tall black hat and his superior frock coat. Somehow, all the same, these very garments—he wouldn't have minded them so much on a weekday—were disconcerting to Paul Overt, who forgot for the moment that the head of the profession was not a bit better dressed than himself. He had caught a glimpse of a regular face, a fresh colour, a brown moustache and a pair of eyes surely never visited by a fine frenzy, and he promised himself to study these denotements on the first occasion.

His superficial sense was that their owner might have passed for a lucky stockbroker—a gentleman driving eastward every morning from a sanitary suburb in a smart dog-cart. That carried out the impression already derived from his wife. Paul's glance, after a moment, travelled back to this lady, and he saw how her own had followed her husband as he moved off with Miss Fancourt. Overt permitted himself to wonder a little if she were jealous when another woman took him away. Then he made out that Mrs. St. George wasn't glaring at the indifferent maiden. Her eyes rested but on her husband, and with unmistakeable serenity. That was the way she wanted him to be—she liked his conventional uniform. Overt longed to hear more about the book she had induced him to destroy.

Chapter 2

As they all came out from luncheon General Fancourt took hold of him with an "I say, I want you to know my girl!" as if the idea had just occurred to him and he hadn't spoken of it before. With the other hand he possessed himself all paternally of the young lady. "You know all about him. I've seen you with his books. She reads everything—everything!" he went on to Paul. The girl smiled at him and then laughed at her father. The General turned away and his daughter spoke—"Isn't papa delightful?"

"He is indeed, Miss Fancourt."

"As if I read you because I read 'everything'!"

"Oh I don't mean for saying that," said Paul Overt. "I liked him from the moment he began to be kind to me. Then he promised me this privilege."

"It isn't for you he means it—it's for me. If you flatter yourself that he thinks of anything in life but me you'll find you're mistaken. He introduces every one. He thinks me insatiable."

"You speak just like him," laughed our youth.

"Ah but sometimes I want to"—and the girl coloured. "I don't read everything—I read very little. But I *have* read you."

"Suppose we go into the gallery," said Paul Overt. She pleased him greatly, not so much because of this last remark—though that of course was not too disconcerting—as because, seated opposite to him at luncheon, she had given him for half an hour the impression of her beautiful face. Something else had come with it—a sense of generosity, of an enthusiasm which, unlike many enthusiasms, was not all manner. That was not spoiled for him by his seeing that the repast had placed her again in familiar contact with Henry St. George. Sitting next her this celebrity was also opposite our young man, who had been able to note that he multiplied the attentions lately brought by his wife to the General's notice.

Paul Overt had gathered as well that this lady was not in the least discomposed by these fond excesses and that she gave every sign of an unclouded spirit. She had Lord Masham on one side of her and on the other the accomplished Mr. Mulliner, editor of the new high-class lively evening paper which was expected to meet a want felt in circles increasingly conscious that Conservatism must be made amusing, and unconvinced when assured by those of another political colour that it was already amusing enough. At the end of an hour spent in her company Paul Overt thought her still prettier than at the first radiation, and if her profane allusions to her husband's work had not still rung in his ears he should have liked her—so far as it could be a question of that in connexion with a woman to whom he had not yet spoken and to whom probably he should never speak if it were left to her.

Pretty women were a clear need to this genius, and for the hour it was Miss Fancourt who supplied the want. If Overt had promised himself a closer view the occasion was now of the best, and it brought consequences felt by the young man as important. He saw more in St. George's face, which he liked the better for its not having told its whole story in the first three minutes. That story came out as one read, in short instalments—it was excusable that one's analogies should be somewhat professional—and the text was a style considerably involved, a language not easy to translate at sight.

There were shades of meaning in it and a vague perspective of history which receded as you advanced. Two facts Paul had particularly heeded. The first of these was that he liked the measured mask much better at inscrutable rest than in social agitation; its almost convulsive smile above all displeased him (as much as any impression from that source could), whereas the quiet face had a charm that grew in proportion as stillness settled again. The change to the expression of gaiety excited, he made out, very much the private protest of a person sitting gratefully in the twilight when the lamp is brought in too soon.

His second reflexion was that, though generally averse to the flagrant use of ingratiating arts by a man of age "making up" to a pretty girl, he was not in this case too painfully affected: which seemed to prove either that St. George had a light hand or the air of being younger than he was, or else that Miss Fancourt's own manner somehow made everything right.

Overt walked with her into the gallery, and they strolled to the end of it, looking at the pictures, the cabinets, the charming vista, which harmonised with the prospect of the summer afternoon, resembling it by a long brightness, with great divans and old chairs that figured hours of rest. Such a place as that had the added merit of giving those who came into it plenty to talk about. Miss Fancourt sat down with her new acquaintance on a flowered sofa, the cushions of which, very numerous, were tight ancient cubes of many sizes, and presently said: "I'm so glad to have a chance to thank you."

"To thank me—?" He had to wonder.

"I liked your book so much. I think it splendid."

She sat there smiling at him, and he never asked himself

which book she meant; for after all he had written three or four. That seemed a vulgar detail, and he wasn't even gratified by the idea of the pleasure she told him—her handsome bright face told him—he had given her. The feeling she appealed to, or at any rate the feeling she excited, was something larger, something that had little to do with any quickened pulsation of his own vanity. It was responsive admiration of the life she embodied, the young purity and richness of which appeared to imply that real success was to resemble *that*, to live, to bloom, to present the perfection of a fine type, not to have hammered out headachy fancies with a bent back at an ink-stained table.

While her grey eyes rested on him—there was a wideish space between these, and the division of her rich-coloured hair, so thick that it ventured to be smooth, made a free arch above them—he was almost ashamed of that exercise of the pen which it was her present inclination to commend. He was conscious he should have liked better to please her in some other way. The lines of her face were those of a woman grown, but the child lingered on in her complexion and in the sweetness of her mouth.

Above all she was natural—that was indubitable now; more natural than he had supposed at first, perhaps on account of her aesthetic toggery, which was conventionally unconventional, suggesting what he might have called a tortuous spontaneity. He had feared that sort of thing in other cases, and his fears had been justified; for, though he was an artist to the essence, the modern reactionary nymph, with the brambles of the woodland caught in her folds and a look as if the satyrs had toyed with her hair, made him shrink not as a man of starch and patent leather, but as a man potentially himself a poet or even a faun.

The girl was really more candid than her costume, and the best proof of it was her supposing her liberal character suited by any uniform. This was a fallacy, since if she was draped as a pessimist he was sure she liked the taste of life. He thanked her for her appreciation—aware at the same time that he didn't appear to thank her enough and that she might think him ungracious.

He was afraid she would ask him to explain something he had written, and he always winced at that—perhaps too timidly-for to his own ear the explanation of a work of art sounded fatuous.

But he liked her so much as to feel a confidence that in the long run he should be able to show her he wasn't rudely evasive. Moreover she surely wasn't quick to take offence, wasn't irritable; she could be trusted to wait. So when he said to her, "Ah don't talk of anything I've done, don't talk of it *here*; there's another man in the house who's the actuality!"—when he uttered this short sincere protest it was with the sense that she would see in the words neither mock humility nor the impatience of a successful man bored with praise.

"You mean Mr. St. George—isn't he delightful?"

Paul Overt met her eyes, which had a cool morning-light that would have half-broken his heart if he hadn't been so young. "Alas I don't know him. I only admire him at a distance."

"Oh you must know him—he wants so to talk to you," returned Miss Fancourt, who evidently had the habit of saying the things that, by her quick calculation, would give people pleasure. Paul saw how she would always calculate on everything's being simple between others.

"I shouldn't have supposed he knew anything about me," he professed.

"He does then—everything. And if he didn't I should be able to tell him."

"To tell him everything?" our friend smiled.

"You talk just like the people in your book!" she answered.

"Then they must all talk alike."

She thought a moment, not a bit disconcerted. "Well, it must be so difficult. Mr. St. George tells me it *is*—terribly. I've tried too—and I find it so. I've tried to write a novel."

"Mr. St. George oughtn't to discourage you," Paul went so far as to say.

"You do much more—when you wear that expression."

"Well, after all, why try to be an artist?" the young man pursued. "It's so poor—so poor!"

"I don't know what you mean," said Miss Fancourt, who looked grave.

"I mean as compared with being a person of action—as living your works."

"But what's art but an intense life—if it be real?" she asked. "I think it's the only one—everything else is so clumsy!" Her companion laughed, and she brought out with her charming serenity what next struck her. "It's so interesting to meet so many celebrated people."

"So I should think—but surely it isn't new to you."

"Why I've never seen anyone—anyone: living always in Asia."

The way she talked of Asia somehow enchanted him. "But doesn't that continent swarm with great figures? Haven't you administered provinces in India and had captive *rajahs* and tributary princes chained to your car?"

It was as if she didn't care even *should* he amuse himself at her cost. "I was with my father, after I left school to go out there. It was delightful being with him—we're alone together in the world, he and I—but there was none of the society I like best. One never heard of a picture—never of a book, except bad ones."

"Never of a picture? Why, wasn't all life a picture?"

She looked over the delightful place where they sat. "Nothing to compare to this. I adore England!" she cried.

It fairly stirred in him the sacred chord. "Ah of course I don't deny that we must do something with her, poor old dear, yet."

"She hasn't been touched, really," said the girl.

"Did Mr. St. George say that?"

There was a small and, as he felt, harmless spark of irony in his question; which, however, she answered very simply, not noticing the insinuation. "Yes, he says England hasn't been touched-not considering all there is," she went on eagerly. "He's so interesting about our country. To listen to him makes one want so to do something."

"It would make *me* want to," said Paul Overt, feeling strongly, on the instant, the suggestion of what she said and that of the emotion with which she said it, and well aware of what an incentive, on St. George's lips, such a speech might be.

"Oh you—as if you hadn't! I should like so to hear you talk together," she added ardently.

"That's very genial of you; but he'd have it all his own way. I'm prostrate before him."

She had an air of earnestness. "Do you think then he's so perfect?"

"Far from it. Some of his later books seem to me of a queerness—!"

"Yes, yes—he knows that."

Paul Overt stared. "That they seem to me of a queerness—!"

"Well yes, or at any rate that they're not what they should be. He told me he didn't esteem them. He has told me such wonderful things—he's so interesting."

There was a certain shock for Paul Overt in the knowledge that the fine genius they were talking of had been reduced to so explicit a confession and had made it, in his misery, to the first comer; for though Miss Fancourt was charming what was she after all but an immature girl encountered at a country-house? Yet precisely this was part of the sentiment he himself had just expressed: he would make way completely for the poor peccable great man not because he didn't read him clear, but altogether because he did.

His consideration was half composed of tenderness for superficialities which he was sure their perpetrator judged privately, judged more ferociously than any one, and which represented some tragic intellectual secret. He would have his reasons for his psychology *e fleur de peau*, and these reasons could only be cruel ones, such as would make him dearer to those who already were fond of him. "You excite my envy. I have my reserves, I discriminate—but I love him," Paul said in a moment. "And seeing him for the first time this way is a great event for me."

"How momentous—how magnificent!" cried the girl. "How delicious to bring you together!"

"Your doing it—that makes it perfect," our friend returned.

"He's as eager as you," she went on. "But it's so odd you shouldn't have met."

"It's not really so odd as it strikes you. I've been out of England so much—made repeated absences all these last years."

She took this in with interest. "And yet you write of it as well as if you were always here."

"It's just the being away perhaps. At any rate the best bits, I suspect, are those that were done in dreary places abroad."

"And why were they dreary?"

"Because they were health-resorts—where my poor mother was dying."

"Your poor mother?"—she was all sweet wonder.

"We went from place to place to help her to get better. But she never did. To the deadly Riviera (I hate it!) to the high Alps, to Algiers, and far away—a hideous journey—to Colorado."

"And she isn't better?" Miss Fancourt went on.

"She died a year ago."

"Really?—like mine! Only that's years since. Some day you must tell me about your mother," she added.

He could at first, on this, only gaze at her. "What right things you say! If you say them to St. George I don't wonder he's in bondage."

It pulled her up for a moment. "I don't know what you mean. He doesn't make speeches and professions at all—he isn't ridiculous."

"I'm afraid you consider then that I am."

"No, I don't"—she spoke it rather shortly. And then she added: "He understands—understands everything."

The young man was on the point of saying jocosely: "And I don't—is that it?" But these words, in time, changed themselves to others slightly less trivial: "Do you suppose he understands his wife?"

Miss Fancourt made no direct answer, but after a moment's

hesitation put it: "Isn't she charming?"

"Not in the least!"

"Here he comes. Now you must know him," she went on. A small group of visitors had gathered at the other end of the gallery and had been there overtaken by Henry St. George, who strolled in from a neighbouring room. He stood near them a moment, not falling into the talk but taking up an old miniature from a table and vaguely regarding it. At the end of a minute he became aware of Miss Fancourt and her companion in the distance; whereupon, laying down his miniature, he approached them with the same procrastinating air, his hands in his pockets and his eyes turned, right and left, to the pictures. The gallery was so long that this transit took some little time, especially as there was a moment when he stopped to admire the fine Gainsborough. "He says Mrs. St. George has been the making of him," the girl continued in a voice slightly lowered.

"Ah he's often obscure!" Paul laughed.

"Obscure?" she repeated as if she heard it for the first time. Her eyes rested on her other friend, and it wasn't lost upon Paul that they appeared to send out great shafts of softness. "He's going to speak to us!" she fondly breathed. There was a sort of rapture in her voice, and our friend was startled. "Bless my soul, does she care for him like *that*?—is she in love with him?" he mentally enquired. "Didn't I tell you he was eager?" she had meanwhile asked of him.

"It's eagerness dissimulated," the young man returned as the subject of their observation lingered before his Gainsborough. "He edges toward us shyly. Does he mean that she saved him by burning that book?"

"That book? what book did she burn?" The girl quickly turned her face to him.

"Hasn't he told you then?"

"Not a word."

"Then he doesn't tell you everything!" Paul had guessed that she pretty much supposed he did. The great man had now resumed his course and come nearer; in spite of which his more qualified admirer risked a profane observation: "St. George and the Dragon is what the anecdote suggests!"

His companion, however, didn't hear it; she smiled at the dragon's adversary. "He *is* eager—he is!" she insisted.

"Eager for you—yes."

But meanwhile she had called out: "I'm sure you want to know Mr. Overt. You'll be great friends, and it will always be delightful to me to remember I was here when you first met and that I had something to do with it."

There was a freshness of intention in the words that carried them off; nevertheless our young man was sorry for Henry St. George, as he was sorry at any time for any person publicly invited to be responsive and delightful. He would have been so touched to believe that a man he deeply admired should care a straw for him that he wouldn't play with such a presumption if it were possibly vain. In a single glance of the eye of the pardonable Master he read—having the sort of divination that belonged to his talent—that this personage had ever a store of friendly patience, which was part of his rich outfit, but was versed in no printed page of a rising scribbler.

There was even a relief, a simplification, in that: liking him so much already for what he had done, how could one have liked him any more for a perception which must at the best have been vague? Paul Overt got up, trying to show his compassion, but at the same instant he found himself encompassed by St. George's happy personal art—a manner of which it was the essence to conjure away false positions. It all took place in a moment. Paul was conscious that he knew him now, conscious of his handshake and of the very quality of his hand; of his face, seen nearer and consequently seen better, of a general fraternising assurance, and in particular of the circumstance that St. George didn't dislike him (as yet at least) for being imposed by a charming but too gushing girl, attractive enough without such danglers.

No irritation at any rate was reflected in the voice with which he questioned Miss Fancourt as to some project of a walk—a general walk of the company round the park. He had soon said something to Paul about a talk—"We must have a tremendous lot of talk; there are so many things, aren't there?"—but our friend could see this idea wouldn't in the present case take very immediate effect. All the same he was extremely happy, even after the matter of the walk had been settled—the three presently passed back to the other part of the gallery, where it was discussed with several members of the party; even when, after they had all gone out together, he found himself for half an hour conjoined with Mrs. St. George.

Her husband had taken the advance with Miss Fancourt, and this pair were quite out of sight. It was the prettiest of rambles for a summer afternoon—a grassy circuit, of immense extent, skirting the limit of the park within. The park was completely surrounded by its old mottled but perfect red wall, which, all the way on their left, constituted in itself an object of interest. Mrs. St. George mentioned to him the surprising number of acres thus enclosed, together with numerous other facts relating to the property and the family, and the family's other properties: she couldn't too strongly urge on him the importance of seeing their other houses.

She ran over the names of these and rang the changes on them with the facility of practice, making them appear an almost endless list. She had received Paul Overt very amiably on his breaking ground with her by the mention of his joy in having just made her husband's acquaintance, and struck him as so alert and so accommodating a little woman that he was rather ashamed of his *mot* about her to Miss Fancourt; though he reflected that a hundred other people, on a hundred occasions, would have been sure to make it. He got on with Mrs. St. George, in short, better than he expected; but this didn't prevent her suddenly becoming aware that she was faint with fatigue and must take her way back to the house by the shortest cut. She professed that she hadn't the strength of a kitten and was a miserable wreck; a character he had been too preoccupied to discern in her while he wondered in what sense she could be held to have been the making of her husband.

He had arrived at a glimmering of the answer when she announced that she must leave him, though this perception was of course provisional. While he was in the very act of placing himself at her disposal for the return the situation underwent a change; Lord Masham had suddenly turned up, coming back to them, overtaking them, emerging from the shrubbery—Overt could scarcely have said how he appeared—and Mrs. St. George had protested that she wanted to be left alone and not to break up the party. A moment later she was walking off with Lord Masham. Our friend fell back and joined Lady Watermouth, to whom he presently mentioned that Mrs. St. George had been obliged to renounce the attempt to go further.

"She oughtn't to have come out at all," her ladyship rather grumpily remarked.

"Is she so very much of an invalid?"

"Very bad indeed." And his hostess added with still greater austerity: "She oughtn't really to come to one!" He wondered what was implied by this, and presently gathered that it was not a reflexion on the lady's conduct or her moral nature: it only represented that her strength was not equal to her aspirations.

Chapter 3

The smoking-room at Summersoft was on the scale of the rest of the place; high light commodious and decorated with such refined old carvings and mouldings that it seemed rather a bower for ladies who should sit at work at fading crewels than a parliament of gentlemen smoking strong cigars. The gentlemen mustered there in considerable force on the Sunday evening, collecting mainly at one end, in front of one of the cool fair fireplaces of white marble, the entablature of which was adorned with a delicate little Italian "subject." There was another in the wall that faced it, and, thanks to the mild summer night, a fire in neither; but a nucleus for aggregation was furnished on one side by a table in the chimney-corner laden with bottles, decanters and tall tumblers.

Paul Overt was a faithless smoker; he would puff a cigarette for reasons with which tobacco had nothing to do. This was particularly the case on the occasion of which I speak; his motive was the vision of a little direct talk with Henry St. George. The "tremendous" communion of which the great man had held out hopes to him earlier in the day had not yet come off, and this saddened him considerably, for the party was to go its several ways immediately after breakfast on the morrow.

He had, however, the disappointment of finding that apparently the author of *Shadowmere* was not disposed to prolong his vigil. He wasn't among the gentlemen assembled when Paul entered, nor was he one of those who turned up, in bright habiliments, during the next ten minutes. The young man waited a little, wondering if he had only gone to put on something extraordinary; this would account for his delay as well as contribute further to Overt's impression of his tendency to do the approved superficial thing. But he didn't arrive—he must have been putting on something more extraordinary than was probable.

Our hero gave him up, feeling a little injured, a little wounded, at this loss of twenty coveted words. He wasn't angry, but he puffed his cigarette sighingly, with the sense of something rare possibly missed. He wandered away with his regret and moved slowly round the room, looking at the old prints on the walls. In this attitude he presently felt a hand on his shoulder and a friendly voice in his ear "This is good. I hoped I should find you. I came down on purpose." St. George was there without a change of dress and with a fine face—his graver one—to which our young man all in a flutter responded. He explained that it was only for the Master—the idea of a little talk—that he had sat up, and that, not finding him, he had been on the point of going to bed.

"Well, you know, I don't smoke—my wife doesn't let me," said St. George, looking for a place to sit down. "It's very good for me—very good for me. Let us take that sofa."

"Do you mean smoking's good for you?"

"No no—her not letting me. It's a great thing to have a wife who's so sure of all the things one can do without. One might never find them out one's self. She doesn't allow me to touch a cigarette." They took possession of a sofa at a distance from the group of smokers, and St. George went on: "Have you got one yourself?"

"Do you mean a cigarette?"

"Dear no—a wife."

"No; and yet I'd give up my cigarette for one."

"You'd give up a good deal more than that," St. George returned. "However, you'd get a great deal in return. There's a something to be said for wives," he added, folding his arms and crossing his outstretched legs. He declined tobacco altogether and sat there without returning fire. His companion stopped smoking, touched by his courtesy; and after all they were out of the fumes, their sofa was in a far-away corner. It would have been a mistake, St. George went on, a great mistake for them to have separated without a little chat; "for I know all about you," he said, "I know you're very remarkable. You've written a very distinguished book."

"And how do you know it?" Paul asked.

"Why, my dear fellow, it's in the air, it's in the papers, it's everywhere." St. George spoke with the immediate familiarity of a confrere—a tone that seemed to his neighbour the very rustle of the laurel. "You're on all men's lips and, what's better, on all women's. And I've just been reading your book."

"Just? You hadn't read it this afternoon," said Overt.

"How do you know that?"

"I think you should know how I know it," the young man laughed.

"I suppose Miss Fancourt told you."

"No indeed—she led me rather to suppose you had."

"Yes—that's much more what she'd do. Doesn't she shed a rosy glow over life? But you didn't believe her?" asked St. George.

"No, not when you came to us there."

"Did I pretend? did I pretend badly?" But without waiting

for an answer to this St. George went on: "You ought always to believe such a girl as that—always, always. Some women are meant to be taken with allowances and reserves; but you must take *her* just as she is."

"I like her very much," said Paul Overt.

Something in his tone appeared to excite on his companion's part a momentary sense of the absurd; perhaps it was the air of deliberation attending this judgement. St. George broke into a laugh to reply. "It's the best thing you can do with her. She's a rare young lady! In point of fact, however, I confess I hadn't read you this afternoon."

"Then you see how right I was in this particular case not to believe Miss Fancourt."

"How right? how can I agree to that when I lost credit by it?"

"Do you wish to pass exactly for what she represents you? Certainly you needn't be afraid," Paul said.

"Ah, my dear young man, don't talk about passing—for the likes of me! I'm passing away—nothing else than that. She has a better use for her young imagination (isn't it fine?) than in 'representing' in any way such a weary wasted used-up animal!" The Master spoke with a sudden sadness that produced a protest on Paul's part; but before the protest could be uttered he went on, reverting to the latter's striking novel: "I had no idea you were so good—one hears of so many things. But you're surprisingly good."

"I'm going to be surprisingly better," Overt made bold to reply.

"I see that, and it's what fetches me. I don't see so much else—as one looks about—that's going to be surprisingly better. They're going to be consistently worse—most of the things. It's so much easier to be worse—heaven knows I've found it so. I'm not in a great glow, you know, about what's breaking out all over the place. But you *must* be better—you really must keep it up. I haven't of course. It's very difficult—that's the devil of the whole thing, keeping it up. But I see you'll be able to. It will be a great disgrace if you don't."

"It's very interesting to hear you speak of yourself; but I don't know what you mean by your allusions to your having fallen off," Paul Overt observed with pardonable hypocrisy. He liked his companion so much now that the fact of any decline of talent or of care had ceased for the moment to be vivid to him.

"Don't say that—don't say that," St. George returned gravely, his head resting on the top of the sofa-back and his eyes on the ceiling. "You know perfectly what I mean. I haven't read twenty pages of your book without seeing that you can't help it."

"You make me very miserable," Paul ecstatically breathed.

"I'm glad of that, for it may serve as a kind of warning. Shocking enough it must be, especially to a young fresh mind, full of faith—the spectacle of a man meant for better things sunk at my age in such dishonour." St. George, in the same contemplative attitude, spoke softly but deliberately, and without perceptible emotion. His tone indeed suggested an impersonal lucidity that was practically cruel—cruel to himself—and made his young friend lay an argumentative hand on his arm.

"But he went on while his eyes seemed to follow the graces of the eighteenth-century ceiling: "Look at me well, take my lesson to heart—for it *is* a lesson. Let that good come of it at least that you shudder with your pitiful impression, and that this may help to keep you straight in the future. Don't become in your old age what I have in mine—the depressing, the deplorable illustration of the worship of false gods!"

"What do you mean by your old age?" the young man asked.

"It has made me old. But I like your youth."

Paul answered nothing—they sat for a minute in silence. They heard the others going on about the governmental majority. Then "What do you mean by false gods?" he enquired.

His companion had no difficulty whatever in saying, "The idols of the market; money and luxury and 'the world;' placing one's children and dressing one's wife; everything that drives one to the short and easy way. Ah the vile things they make one do!"

"But surely one's right to want to place one's children."

"One has no business to have any children," St. George placidly declared. "I mean of course if one wants to do anything good."

"But aren't they an inspiration—an incentive?"

"An incentive to damnation, artistically speaking."

"You touch on very deep things—things I should like to discuss with you," Paul said. "I should like you to tell me volumes about yourself. This is a great feast for *me*!"

"Of course it is, cruel youth. But to show you I'm still not incapable, degraded as I am, of an act of faith, I'll tie my vanity to the stake for you and burn it to ashes. You must come and see me—you must come and see us," the Master quickly substituted. "Mrs. St. George is charming; I don't know whether you've had any opportunity to talk with her. She'll be delighted to see you; she likes great celebrities, whether incipient or predominant. You must come and dine—my wife will write to you. Where are you to be found?"

"This is my little address"—and Overt drew out his pocket-book and extracted a visiting-card. On second thoughts, however, he kept it back, remarking that he wouldn't trouble his friend to take charge of it but would come and see him straightway in London and leave it at his door if he should fail to obtain entrance.

"Ah you'll probably fail; my wife's always out—or when she isn't out is knocked up from having been out. You must come and dine—though that won't do much good either, for my wife insists on big dinners." St. George turned it over further, but then went on: "You must come down and see us in the country, that's the best way; we've plenty of room, and it isn't bad."

"You've a house in the country?" Paul asked enviously.

"Ah not like this! But we have a sort of place we go to—an hour from Euston. That's one of the reasons."

"One of the reasons?"

"Why my books are so bad."

"You must tell me all the others!" Paul longingly laughed.

His friend made no direct rejoinder to this, but spoke again abruptly. "Why have I never seen you before?"

The tone of the question was singularly flattering to our hero, who felt it to imply the great man's now perceiving he had for years missed something. "Partly, I suppose, because there has been no particular reason why you should see me. I haven't lived in the world—in your world. I've spent many years out of England, in different places abroad."

"Well, please don't do it anymore. You must do England-there's such a lot of it."

"Do you mean I must write about it?" and Paul struck the note of the listening candour of a child.

"Of course you must. And tremendously well, do you mind? That takes off a little of my esteem for this thing of yours—that it goes on abroad. Hang 'abroad!' Stay at home and do things here—do subjects we can measure."

"I'll do whatever you tell me," Overt said, deeply attentive. "But pardon me if I say I don't understand how you've been reading my book," he added. "I've had you before me all the afternoon, first in that long walk, then at tea on the lawn, till we went to dress for dinner, and all the evening at dinner and in this place."

St. George turned his face about with a smile. "I gave it but a quarter of an hour."

"A quarter of an hour's immense, but I don't understand where you put it in. In the drawing-room after dinner you weren't reading—you were talking to Miss Fancourt."

"It comes to the same thing, because we talked about *Ginistrella*. She described it to me—she lent me her copy."

"Lent it to you?"

"She travels with it."

"It's incredible," Paul blushed.

"It's glorious for you, but it also turned out very well for me. When the ladies went off to bed she kindly offered to send the book down to me. Her maid brought it to me in the hall and I went to my room with it. I hadn't thought of coming here, I do that so little. But I don't sleep early, I always have to read an hour or two. I sat down to your novel on the spot, without undressing, without taking off anything but my coat. I think that's a sign my curiosity had been strongly roused about it. I read a quarter of an hour, as I tell you, and even in a quarter of an hour I was greatly struck."

"Ah the beginning isn't very good—it's the whole thing!" said Overt, who had listened to this recital with extreme interest. "And you laid down the book and came after me?" he asked.

"That's the way it moved me. I said to myself 'I see it's off his own bat, and he's there, by the way, and the day's over and I haven't said twenty words to him.' It occurred to me that you'd probably be in the smoking-room and that it wouldn't be too late to repair my omission. I wanted to do something civil to you, so I put on my coat and came down. I shall read your book again when I go up."

Our friend faced round in his place—he was touched as he had scarce ever been by the picture of such a demonstration in his favour. "You're really the kindest of men. *Cela s'est passe comme ca*?—and I've been sitting here with you all this time and never apprehended it and never thanked you!"

"Thank Miss Fancourt—it was she who wound me up. She has made me feel as if I had read your novel."

"She's an angel from heaven!" Paul declared.

"She is indeed. I've never seen any one like her. Her interest in literature's touching—something quite peculiar to herself; she takes it all so seriously. She feels the arts and she wants to feel them more. To those who practise them it's almost humiliating—her curiosity, her sympathy, her good faith. How can anything be as fine as she supposes it?"

"She's a rare organisation," the younger man sighed.

"The richest I've ever seen—an artistic intelligence really of the first order. And lodged in such a form!" St. George exclaimed.

"One would like to represent such a girl as that," Paul continued.

"Ah there it is—there's nothing like life!" said his companion. "When you're finished, squeezed dry and used up and you think the sack's empty, you're still appealed to, you still get touches and thrills, the idea springs up—out of the lap of the actual—and shows you there's always something to be done. But I shan't do it—she's not for me!"

"How do you mean, not for you?"

"Oh it's all over—she's for you, if you like."

"Ah much less!" said Paul. "She's not for a dingy little man of letters; she's for the world, the bright rich world of bribes and rewards. And the world will take hold of her—it will carry her away."

"It will try—but it's just a case in which there may be a fight. It would be worth fighting, for a man who had it in him, with youth and talent on his side."

These words rang not a little in Paul Overt's consciousness-they held him briefly silent. "It's a wonder she has remained as she is; giving herself away so—with so much to give away."

"Remaining, you mean, so ingenuous—so natural? Oh she doesn't care a straw—she gives away because she overflows. She has her own feelings, her own standards; she doesn't keep remembering that she must be proud. And then she hasn't been here long enough to be spoiled; she has picked up a fashion or two, but only the amusing ones. She's a provincial—a provincial of genius," St. George went on; "her very blunders are charming, her mistakes are interesting. She has come back from Asia with all sorts of excited curiosities and unappeased *appetities*. She's first-rate herself and she expends herself on the second-rate. She's life herself and she takes a rare interest in imitations. She mixes all things up, but there are none in regard to which she hasn't perceptions. She sees things in a perspective—as if from the top of the Himalayas—and she enlarges everything she touches. Above all she exaggerates—to herself, I mean. She exaggerates you and me!"

There was nothing in that description to allay the agitation caused in our younger friend by such a sketch of a fine subject. It seemed to him to show the art of St. George's admired hand, and he lost himself in gazing at the vision—this hovered there before him—of a woman's figure which should be part of the glory of a novel. But at the end of a moment the thing had turned into smoke, and out of the smoke—the last puff of a big cigar—proceeded the voice of General Fancourt, who had left the others and come and planted himself before the gentlemen on the sofa. "I suppose that when you fellows get talking you sit up half the night."

"Half the night?—*jamais de la vie*! I follow a hygiene"—and St. George rose to his feet.

"I see—you're hothouse plants," laughed the General. "That's the way you produce your flowers."

"I produce mine between ten and one every morning—I bloom with a regularity!" St. George went on.

"And with a splendour!" added the polite General, while Paul noted how little the author of *Shadowmere* minded, as he phrased it to himself, when addressed as a celebrated story-teller. The young man had an idea *he* should never get used to that; it would always make him uncomfortable—from the suspicion that people would think they had to—and he would want to prevent it. Evidently his great colleague had toughened and hardened—had made himself a surface. The group of men had finished their cigars and taken up their bedroom candlesticks; but before they all passed out Lord Watermouth invited the pair of guests who had been so absorbed together to "have" something. It happened that they both declined; upon which General Fancourt said: "Is that the hygiene? You don't water the flowers?"

"Oh I should drown them!" St. George replied; but, leaving the room still at his young friend's side, he added whimsically, for the latter's benefit, in a lower tone: "My wife doesn't let me."

"Well I'm glad I'm not one of you fellows!" the General richly concluded.

The nearness of Summersoft to London had this consequence, chilling to a person who had had a vision of sociability in a railway-carriage, that most of the company, after breakfast, drove back to town, entering their own vehicles, which had come out to fetch them, while their servants returned by train with their luggage.

Three or four young men, among whom was Paul Overt, also availed themselves of the common convenience; but they stood in the portico of the house and saw the others roll away. Miss Fancourt got into a victoria with her father after she had shaken hands with our hero and said, smiling in the frankest way in the world, "I *must* see you more. Mrs. St. George is so nice: she has promised to ask us both to dinner together." This lady and her husband took their places in a perfectly-appointed brougham-she required a closed carriage—and as our young man waved his hat to them in response to their nods and flourishes he reflected that, taken together, they were an honourable image of success, of the material rewards and the social credit of literature. Such things were not the full measure, but he nevertheless felt a little proud for literature.

CHAPTER 4

Before a week had elapsed he met Miss Fancourt in Bond Street, at a private view of the works of a young artist in "black-and-white" who had been so good as to invite him to the stuffy scene. The drawings were admirable, but the crowd in the one little room was so dense that he felt himself up to his neck in a sack of wool. A fringe of people at the outer edge endeavoured by curving forward their backs and presenting, below them, a still more convex surface of resistance to the pressure of the mass, to preserve an interval between their noses and the glazed mounts of the pictures; while the central body, in the comparative gloom projected by a wide horizontal screen hung under the skylight and allowing only a margin for the day, remained upright dense and vague, lost in the contemplation of its own ingredients.

This contemplation sat especially in the sad eyes of certain female heads, surmounted with hats of strange convolution and plumage, which rose on long necks above the others. One of the heads Paul perceived, was much the so most beautiful of the collection, and his next discovery was that it belonged to Miss Fancourt. Its beauty was enhanced by the glad smile she sent him across surrounding obstructions, a smile that drew him to her as fast as he could make his way. He had seen for himself at Summersoft that the last thing her nature contained was an affectation of indifference; yet even with this circumspection he took a fresh satisfaction in her not having pretended to await his arrival with composure. She smiled as radiantly as if she wished to make him hurry, and as soon as he came within earshot she broke out in her voice of joy: "He's here—he's here—he's coming back in a moment!"

"Ah your father?" Paul returned as she offered him her hand.

"Oh dear no, this isn't in my poor father's line. I mean Mr. St. George. He has just left me to speak to some one—he's coming back. It's he who brought me—wasn't it charming?"

"Ah that gives him a pull over me—I couldn't have 'brought' you, could I?"

"If you had been so kind as to propose it—why not you as well as he?" the girl returned with a face that, expressing no cheap *coquetry*, simply affirmed a happy fact.

"Why he's a *pere de famille.* They've privileges," Paul explained. And then quickly: "Will you go to see places with *me*?" he asked.

"Anything you like!" she smiled. "I know what you mean, that girls have to have a lot of people—" Then she broke off: "I don't know; I'm free. I've always been like that—I can go about with anyone. I'm so glad to meet you," she added with a sweet distinctness that made those near her turn round.

"Let me at least repay that speech by taking you out of this squash," her friend said. "Surely people aren't happy here!"

"No, they're awfully *mornes*, aren't they? But I'm very happy indeed and I promised Mr. St. George to remain in this spot till he comes back. He's going to take me away. They send him invitations for things of this sort—more than he wants. It was so kind of him to think of me."

"They also send me invitations of this kind—more than I want. And if thinking of *you* will do it—!" Paul went on.

"Oh I delight in them—everything that's life—everything that's London!"

"They don't have private views in Asia, I suppose," he laughed. "But what a pity that for this year, even in this gorged city, they're pretty well over."

"Well, next year will do, for I hope you believe we're going to be friends always. Here he comes!" Miss Fancourt continued before Paul had time to respond.

He made out St. George in the gaps of the crowd, and this perhaps led to his hurrying a little to say: "I hope that doesn't mean I'm to wait till next year to see you."

"No, no—aren't we to meet at dinner on the twenty-fifth?" she panted with an eagerness as happy as his own.

"That's almost next year. Is there no means of seeing you before?"

She stared with all her brightness. "Do you mean you'd *come*?"

"Like a shot, if you'll be so good as to ask me!"

"On Sunday then—this next Sunday?"

"What have I done that you should doubt it?" the young man asked with delight.

Miss Fancourt turned instantly to St. George, who had now joined them, and announced triumphantly: "He's coming on Sunday—this next Sunday!"

"Ah my day—my day too!" said the famous novelist, laughing, to their companion.

"Yes, but not yours only. You shall meet in Manchester Square; you shall talk—you shall be wonderful!"

"We don't meet often enough," St. George allowed, shaking hands with his disciple. "Too many things—ah too many things! But we must make it up in the country in September. You won't forget you've promised me that?"

"Why he's coming on the twenty-fifth—you'll see him then," said the girl.

"On the twenty-fifth?" St. George asked vaguely.

"We dine with you; I hope you haven't forgotten. He's dining out that day," she added gaily to Paul.

"Oh bless me, yes—that's charming! And you're coming? My wife didn't tell me," St. George said to him. "Too many things-too many things!" he repeated.

"Too many people—too many people!" Paul exclaimed, giving ground before the penetration of an elbow.

"You oughtn't to say that. They all read you."

"Me? I should like to see them! Only two or three at most," the young man returned.

"Did you ever hear anything like that? He knows, haughtily, how good he is!" St. George declared, laughing to Miss Fancourt. "They read *me*, but that doesn't make me like them any better. Come away from them, come away!" And he led the way out of the exhibition.

"He's going to take me to the Park," Miss Fancourt observed to Overt with elation as they passed along the corridor that led to the street.

"Ah does he go there?" Paul asked, taking the fact for a somewhat unexpected illustration of St. George's *moeurs*.

"It's a beautiful day—there'll be a great crowd. We're going to look at the people, to look at types," the girl went on. "We shall sit under the trees; we shall walk by the Row."

"I go once a year—on business," said St. George, who had overheard Paul's question.

"Or with a country cousin, didn't you tell me? I'm the country cousin!" she continued over her shoulder to Paul as their friend drew her toward a hansom to which he had signalled. The young man watched them get in; he returned, as he stood there, the friendly wave of the hand with which, ensconced in the vehicle beside her, St. George took leave of him. He even lingered to see the vehicle start away and lose itself in the confusion of Bond Street. He followed it with his eyes; it put to him embarrassing things. "She's not for *me*!" the great novelist had said emphatically at Summersoft; but his manner of conducting himself toward her appeared not quite in harmony with such a conviction.

How could he have behaved differently if she *had* been for him? An indefinite envy rose in Paul Overt's heart as he took his way on foot alone; a feeling addressed alike strangely enough, to each of the occupants of the hansom. How much he should like to rattle about London with such a girl! How much he should like to go and look at "types" with St. George!

The next Sunday at four o'clock he called in Manchester Square, where his secret wish was gratified by his finding Miss Fancourt alone. She was in a large bright friendly occupied room, which was painted red all over, draped with the quaint cheap florid stuffs that are represented as coming from southern and eastern countries, where they are fabled to serve as the counterpanes of the peasantry, and bedecked with pottery of vivid hues, ranged on casual shelves, and with many water-colour drawings from the hand (as the visitor learned) of the young lady herself, commemorating with a brave breadth the sunsets, the mountains, the temples and palaces of India.

He sat an hour—more than an hour, two hours—and all the while no one came in. His hostess was so good as to remark, with her liberal humanity, that it was delightful they weren't interrupted; it was so rare in London, especially at that season, that people got a good talk. But luckily now, of a fine Sunday, half the world went out of town, and that made it better for those who didn't go, when these others were in sympathy. It was the defect of London—one of two or three, the very short list of those she recognised in the teeming world-city she adored—that there were too few good chances for talk; you never had time to carry anything far.

"Too many things—too many things!" Paul said, quoting St. George's exclamation of a few days before.

"Ah yes, for him there are too many—his life's too complicated."

"Have you seen it *near*? That's what I should like to do; it might explain some mysteries," her visitor went on. She asked him what mysteries he meant, and he said: "Oh peculiarities of his work, inequalities, superficialities. For one who looks at it from the artistic point of view it contains a bottomless ambiguity."

She became at this, on the spot, all intensity. "Ah do describe that more—it's so interesting. There are no such suggestive questions. I'm so fond of them. He thinks he's a failure—fancy!" she beautifully wailed.

"That depends on what his ideal may have been. With his gifts it ought to have been high. But till one knows what he really proposed to himself—? Do *you* know by chance?" the young man broke off.

"Oh he doesn't talk to me about himself. I can't make him. It's too provoking."

Paul was on the point of asking what then he did talk about, but discretion checked it and he said instead: "Do you think he's unhappy at home?"

She seemed to wonder. "At home?"

"I mean in his relations with his wife. He has a mystifying little way of alluding to her."

"Not to me," said Marian Fancourt with her clear eyes. "That wouldn't be right, would it?" she asked gravely.

"Not particularly; so I'm glad he doesn't mention her to you. To praise her might bore you, and he has no business to do anything else. Yet he knows you better than me."

"Ah but he respects *you*!" the girl cried as with envy.

Her visitor stared a moment, then broke into a laugh. "Doesn't he respect you?"

"Of course, but not in the same way. He respects what you've done—he told me so, the other day."

Paul drank it in, but retained his faculties. "When you went to look at types?"

"Yes—we found so many: he has such an observation of them! He talked a great deal about your book. He says it's really important."

"Important! Ah the grand creature!"—and the author of the work in question groaned for joy.

"He was wonderfully amusing, he was inexpressibly droll, while we walked about. He sees everything; he has so many comparisons and images, and they're always exactly right. *C'est d'un trouve*, as they say."

"Yes, with his gifts, such things as he ought to have done!" Paul sighed.

"And don't you think he *has* done them?"

Ah it was just the point. "A part of them, and of course even that part's immense. But he might have been one of the greatest. However, let us not make this an hour of qualifications. Even as they stand," our friend earnestly concluded, "his writings are a mine of gold."

To this proposition she ardently responded, and for half an hour the pair talked over the Master's principal productions. She knew them well—she knew them even better than her visitor, who was struck with her critical intelligence and with something large and bold in the movement in her mind. She said things that startled him and that evidently had come to her directly; they weren't picked-up phrases—she placed them too well. St. George had been right about her being first-rate, about her not being afraid to gush, not remembering that she must be proud. Suddenly something came back to her, and she said: "I recollect that he did speak of Mrs. St. George to me once. He said, *apropos* of something or other, that she didn't care for perfection."

"That's a great crime in an artist's wife," Paul returned.

"Yes, poor thing!" and the girl sighed with a suggestion of many reflexions, some of them mitigating. But she presently added: "Ah perfection, perfection—how one ought to go in for it! I wish I could."

"Everyone can in his way," her companion opined.

"In *his* way, yes—but not in hers. Women are so hampered-so condemned! Yet it's a kind of dishonour if you don't, when you want to *do* something, isn't it?" Miss Fancourt pursued, dropping one train in her quickness to take up another, an accident that was common with her. So these two young persons sat discussing high themes in their eclectic drawing-room, in their London "season"—discussing, with extreme seriousness, the high theme of perfection. It must be said in extenuation of this eccentricity that they were interested in the business. Their tone had truth and their emotion beauty; they weren't posturing for each other or for someone else.

The subject was so wide that they found themselves reducing it; the perfection to which for the moment they agreed to confine their speculations was that of the valid, the exemplary work of art. Our young woman's imagination, it appeared, had wandered far in that direction, and her guest had the rare delight of feeling in their conversation a full interchange. This episode will have lived for years in his memory and even in his wonder; it had the quality that fortune distils in a single drop at a time—the quality that lubricates many ensuing frictions.

He still, whenever he likes, has a vision of the room, the bright red sociable talkative room with the curtains that, by a stroke of successful audacity, had the note of vivid blue. He remembers where certain things stood, the particular book open on the table and the almost intense odour of the flowers placed, at the left, somewhere behind him. These facts were the fringe, as it were, of a fine special agitation which had its birth in those two hours and of which perhaps the main sign was in its leading him inwardly and repeatedly to breathe "I had no idea there was any one like this—I had no idea there was any one like this!" Her freedom amazed him and charmed him—it seemed so to simplify the practical question.

She was on the footing of an independent personage—a motherless girl who had passed out of her teens and had a position and responsibilities, who wasn't held down to the limitations of a little miss. She came and went with no dragged *duenna*, she received people alone, and, though she was totally without hardness, the question of protection or patronage had no relevancy in regard to her. She gave such an impression of the clear and the noble combined with the easy and the natural that in spite of her eminent modern situation she suggested no sort of sister-hood with the "fast" girl. Modern she was indeed, and made Paul Overt, who loved old colour, the golden glaze of time, think with some alarm of the muddled palette of the future. He couldn't get used to her interest in the arts he cared for; it seemed too good to be real—it was so unlikely an adventure to tumble into such a well of sympathy.

One might stray into the desert easily—that was on the cards and that was the law of life; but it was too rare an accident to stumble on a crystal well. Yet if her aspirations seemed at one moment too extravagant to be real they struck him at the next as too intelligent to be false. They were both high and lame, and, whims for whims, he preferred them to any he had met in a like relation. It was probable enough she would leave them behind—exchange them for politics or "smartness" or mere prolific maternity, as was the custom of scribbling daubing educated flattered girls in an age of luxury and a society of leisure.

He noted that the water-colours on the walls of the room she sat in had mainly the quality of being naives, and reflected that *naivete* in art is like a zero in a number: its importance depends on the figure it is united with. Meanwhile, however, he had fallen in love with her. Before he went away, at any rate, he said to her: "I thought St. George was coming to see you today, but he doesn't turn up."

For a moment he supposed she was going to cry "*Comment donc*? Did you come here only to meet him?" But the next he became aware of how little such a speech would have fallen in with any note of flirtation he had as yet perceived in her. She only replied: "Ah yes, but I don't think he'll come. He recommended me not to expect him." Then she gaily but all gently added: "He said it wasn't fair to you. But I think I could manage two."

"So could I," Paul Overt returned, stretching the point a little to meet her. In reality his appreciation of the occasion was so completely an appreciation of the woman before him that another figure in the scene, even so esteemed a one as St. George, might for the hour have appealed to him vainly. He left the house wondering what the great man had meant by its not being fair to him; and, still more than that, whether he had actually stayed away from the force of that idea.

As he took his course through the Sunday solitude of Manchester Square, swinging his stick and with a good deal of emotion fermenting in his soul, it appeared to him he was living in a world strangely magnanimous. Miss Fancourt had told him it was possible she should be away, and that her father should be, on the following Sunday, but that she had the hope of a visit from him in the other event. She promised to let him know should their absence fail, and then he might act accordingly.

After he had passed into one of the streets that open from the Square he stopped, without definite intentions, looking sceptically for a cab. In a moment he saw a hansom roll through the place from the other side and come a part of the way toward him. He was on the point of hailing the driver when he noticed a "fare" within; then he waited, seeing the man prepare to deposit his passenger by pulling up at one of the houses. The house was apparently the one he himself had just quitted; at least he drew that inference as he recognised Henry St. George in the person who stepped out of the hansom. Paul turned off as quickly as if he had been caught in the act of spying.

He gave up his cab—he preferred to walk; he would go nowhere else. He was glad St. George hadn't renounced his visit altogether—that would have been too absurd. Yes, the world was magnanimous, and even he himself felt so as, on looking at his watch, he noted but six o'clock, so that he could mentally congratulate his successor on having an hour still to sit in Miss Fancourt's drawing-room. He himself might use that hour for another visit, but by the time he reached the Marble Arch the idea of such a course had become incongruous to him.

He passed beneath that architectural effort and walked into the Park till he got upon the spreading grass. Here he continued to walk; he took his way across the elastic turf and came out by the Serpentine. He watched with a friendly eye the diversions of the London people, he bent a glance almost encouraging on the young ladies paddling their sweethearts about the lake and the guardsmen tickling tenderly with their bearskins the artificial flowers in the Sunday hats of their partners. He prolonged his meditative walk; he went into Kensington Gardens, he sat upon the penny chairs, he looked at the little sail-boats launched upon the round pond and was glad he had no engagement to dine.

He repaired for this purpose, very late, to his club, where he found himself unable to order a repast and told the waiter to bring whatever there was. He didn't even observe what he was served with, and he spent the evening in the library of the establishment, pretending to read an article in an American magazine. He failed to discover what it was about; it appeared in a dim way to be about Marian Fancourt.

Quite late in the week she wrote to him that she was not to go into the country—it had only just been settled. Her father, she added, would never settle anything, but put it all on her. She felt her responsibility—she had to—and since she was forced this was the way she had decided. She mentioned no reasons, which gave our friend all the clearer field for bold conjecture about them. In Manchester Square on this second Sunday he esteemed his fortune less good, for she had three or four other visitors.

But there were three or four compensations; perhaps the greatest of which was that, learning how her father had after all, at the last hour, gone out of town alone, the bold conjecture I just now spoke of found itself becoming a shade more bold. And then her presence was her presence, and the personal red room was there and was full of it, whatever phantoms passed and vanished, emitting incomprehensible sounds. Lastly, he had the resource of staying till everyone had come and gone and of believing this grateful to her, though she gave no particular sign. When they were alone together he came to his point. "But St. George did come—last Sunday. I saw him as I looked back."

"Yes; but it was the last time."

"The last time?"

"He said he would never come again."

Paul Overt stared. "Does he mean he wishes to cease to see you?"

"I don't know what he means," the girl bravely smiled. "He won't at any rate see me here."

"And pray why not?"

"I haven't the least idea," said Marian Fancourt, whose visitor found her more perversely sublime than ever yet as she professed this clear helplessness.

Chapter 5

"Oh I say, I want you to stop a little," Henry St. George said to him at eleven o'clock the night he dined with the head of the profession. The company—none of it indeed *of* the profession-had been numerous and was taking its leave; our young man, after bidding goodnight to his hostess, had put out his hand in farewell to the master of the house. Besides drawing from the latter the protest I have cited this movement provoked a further priceless word about their chance now to have a talk, their going into his room, his having still everything to say. Paul Overt was all delight at this kindness; nevertheless he mentioned in weak jocose qualification the bare fact that he had promised to go to another place which was at a considerable distance.

"Well then you'll break your promise, that's all. You quite awful humbug!" St. George added in a tone that confirmed our young man's ease.

"Certainly I'll break it—but it was a real promise."

"Do you mean to Miss Fancourt? You're following her?" his friend asked.

He answered by a question. "Oh is *she* going?"

"Base impostor!" his ironic host went on. "I've treated you handsomely on the article of that young lady: I won't make another concession. Wait three minutes—I'll be with you." He gave himself to his departing guests, accompanied the long-trained ladies to the door. It was a hot night, the windows were open, the sound of the quick carriages and of the linkmen's call came into the house. The affair had rather glittered; a sense of festal things was in the heavy air: not only the influence of that particular entertainment, but the suggestion of the wide hurry of pleasure which in London on summer nights fills so many of the happier quarters of the complicated town.

Gradually Mrs. St. George's drawing-room emptied itself; Paul was left alone with his hostess, to whom he explained the motive of his waiting. "Ah yes, some intellectual, some *professional*, talk," she leered; "at this season doesn't one miss it? Poor dear Henry, I'm so glad!" The young man looked out of the window a moment, at the called hansoms that lurched up, at the smooth broughams that rolled away.

When he turned round Mrs. St. George had disappeared; her husband's voice rose to him from below—he was laughing and talking, in the portico, with some lady who awaited her carriage. Paul had solitary possession, for some minutes, of the warm deserted rooms where the covered tinted lamplight was soft, the seats had been pushed about and the odour of flowers lingered. They were large, they were pretty, they contained objects of value; everything in the picture told of a "good house." At the end of five minutes a servant came in with a request from the Master that he would join him downstairs; upon which, descending, he followed his conductor through a long passage to an apartment thrown out, in the rear of the habitation, for the special requirements, as he guessed, of a busy man of letters.

St. George was in his shirt-sleeves in the middle of a large high room—a room without windows, but with a wide skylight at the top, that of a place of exhibition. It was furnished as a library, and the serried bookshelves rose to the ceiling, a surface of incomparable tone produced by dimly-gilt "backs" interrupted here and there by the suspension of old prints and drawings.

At the end furthest from the door of admission was a tall desk, of great extent, at which the person using it could write only in the erect posture of a clerk in a counting-house; and stretched from the entrance to this structure was a wide plain band of crimson cloth, as straight as a garden-path and almost as long, where, in his mind's eye, Paul at once beheld the Master pace to and fro during vexed hours—hours, that is, of admirable composition. The servant gave him a coat, an old jacket with a hang of experience, from a cupboard in the wall, retiring afterwards with the garment he had taken off.

Paul Overt welcomed the coat; it was a coat for talk, it promised confidences—having visibly received so many—and had tragic literary elbows. "Ah we're practical—we're practical!" St. George said as he saw his visitor look the place over. "Isn't it a good big cage for going round and round? My wife invented it and she locks me up here every morning."

Our young man breathed—by way of tribute—with a certain oppression. "You don't miss a window—a place to look out?"

"I did at first awfully; but her calculation was just. It saves time, it has saved me many months in these ten years. Here I stand, under the eye of day—in London of course, very often, it's rather a bleared old eye—walled in to my trade. I can't get away—so the room's a fine lesson in concentration. I've learnt the lesson, I think; look at that big bundle of proof and acknowledge it." He pointed to a fat roll of papers, on one of the tables, which had not been undone.

"Are you bringing out another—?" Paul asked in a tone the fond deficiencies of which he didn't recognise till his companion burst out laughing, and indeed scarce even then.

"You humbug, you humbug!"—St. George appeared to enjoy caressing him, as it were, with that opprobrium. "Don't I know what you think of them?" he asked, standing there with his hands in his pockets and with a new kind of smile. It was as if he were going to let his young votary see him all now.

"Upon my word in that case you know more than I do!" the latter ventured to respond, revealing a part of the torment of being able neither clearly to esteem nor distinctly to renounce him.

"My dear fellow," said the more and more interesting Master, "don't imagine I talk about my books specifically; they're not a decent subject—*il ne manquerait plus que ca*! I'm not so bad as you may apprehend! About myself, yes, a little, if you like; though it wasn't for that I brought you down here. I want to ask you something—very much indeed; I value this chance. Therefore sit down. We're practical, but there *is* a sofa, you see—for she does humour my poor bones so far. Like all really great administrators and disciplinarians she knows when wisely to relax."

Paul sank into the corner of a deep leathern couch, but his friend remained standing and explanatory. "If you don't mind, in this room, this is my habit. From the door to the desk and from the desk to the door. That shakes up my imagination gently; and don't you see what a good thing it is that there's no window for her to fly out of? The eternal standing as I write (I stop at that bureau and put it down, when anything comes, and so we go on) was rather wearisome at first, but we adopted it with an eye to the long run; you're in better order—if your legs don't break down!—and you can keep it up for more years. Oh we're practical—we're practical!" St. George repeated, going to the table and taking up all mechanically the bundle of proofs. But, pulling off the wrapper, he had a change of attention that appealed afresh to our hero. He lost himself a moment, examining the sheets of his new book, while the younger man's eyes wandered over the room again.

"Lord, what good things I should do if I had such a charming place as this to do them in!" Paul reflected. The outer world, the world of accident and ugliness, was so successfully excluded, and within the rich protecting square, beneath the patronising sky, the dream- figures, the summoned company, could hold their particular revel. It was a fond prevision of Overt's rather than an observation on actual data, for which occasions had been too few, that the Master thus more closely viewed would have the quality, the charming gift, of flashing out, all surprisingly, in personal intercourse and at moments of suspended or perhaps even of diminished expectation. A happy relation with him would be a thing proceeding by jumps, not by traceable stages.

"Do you read them—really?" he asked, laying down the proofs on Paul's enquiring of him how soon the work would be published. And when the young man answered "Oh yes, always," he was moved to mirth again by something he caught in his manner of saying that. "You go to see your grandmother on her birthday—and very proper it is, especially as she won't last forever. She has lost every faculty and every sense; she neither sees, nor hears, nor speaks; but all customary pieties and kindly habits are respectable. Only you're strong if you *do* read 'em! I couldn't, my dear fellow. You are strong, I know; and that's just a part of what I wanted to say to you. You're very strong indeed. I've been going into your other things—they've interested me immensely. Someone ought to have told me about them before—someone I could believe. But whom can one believe? You're wonderfully on the right road—it's awfully decent work. Now do you mean to keep it up?—that's what I want to ask you."

"Do I mean to do others?" Paul asked, looking up from his sofa at his erect inquisitor and feeling partly like a happy little boy when the school-master is gay, and partly like some pilgrim of old who might have consulted a world-famous oracle. St. George's own performance had been infirm, but as an adviser he would be infallible.

"Others—others? Ah the number won't matter; one other would do, if it were really a further step—a throb of the same effort. What I mean is have you it in your heart to go in for some sort of decent perfection?"

"Ah decency, ah perfection—!" the young man sincerely sighed. "I talked of them the other Sunday with Miss Fancourt."

It produced on the Master's part a laugh of odd acrimony. "Yes, they'll 'talk' of them as much as you like! But they'll do little to help one to them. There's no obligation of course; only you strike me as capable," he went on. "You must have thought it all over. I can't believe you're without a plan. That's the sensation you give me, and it's so rare that it really stirs one up—it makes you remarkable. If you haven't a plan, if you *don't* mean to keep it up, surely you're within your rights; it's nobody's business, no one can force you, and not more than two or three people will notice you don't go straight. The others—*all* the rest, every blest soul in England, will think you do—will think you are keeping it up: upon my honour they will! I shall be one of the two or three who know better. Now the question is whether you can do it for two or three. Is that the stuff you're made of?"

It locked his guest a minute as in closed throbbing arms. "I could do it for one, if you were the one."

"Don't say that; I don't deserve it; it scorches me," he protested with eyes suddenly grave and glowing. "The 'one' is of course one's self, one's conscience, one's idea, the singleness of one's aim. I think of that pure spirit as a man thinks of a woman he has in some detested hour of his youth loved and forsaken. She haunts him with reproachful eyes, she lives forever before him. As an artist, you know, I've married for money."

Paul stared and even blushed a little, confounded by this avowal; whereupon his host, observing the expression of his face, dropped a quick laugh and pursued: "You don't follow my figure. I'm not speaking of my dear wife, who had a small fortune—which, however, was not my bribe. I fell in love with her, as many other people have done. I refer to the mercenary muse whom I led to the altar of literature. Don't, my boy, put your nose into *that* yoke. The awful jade will lead you a life!"

Our hero watched him, wondering and deeply touched. "Haven't you been happy!"

"Happy? It's a kind of hell."

"There are things I should like to ask you," Paul said after a pause.

"Ask me anything in all the world. I'd turn myself inside out to save you."

"To 'save' me?" he quavered.

"To make you stick to it—to make you see it through. As I said to you the other night at Summersoft, let my example be vivid to you."

"Why your books are not so bad as that," said Paul, fairly

laughing and feeling that if ever a fellow had breathed the air of art—!

"So bad as what?"

"Your talent's so great that it's in everything you do, in what's less good as well as in what's best. You've some forty volumes to show for it—forty volumes of wonderful life, of rare observation, of magnificent ability."

"I'm very clever, of course I know that"—but it was a thing, in fine, this author made nothing of. "Lord, what rot they'd all be if I hadn't been I'm a successful charlatan," he went on—"I've been able to pass off my system. But do you know what it is? It's *carton-pierre*."

"*Carton-pierre*?" Paul was struck, and gaped.

"Lincrusta-Walton!"

"Ah don't say such things—you make me bleed!" the younger man protested. "I see you in a beautiful fortunate home, living in comfort and honour."

"Do you call it honour?"—his host took him up with an intonation that often comes back to him. "That's what I want *you* to go in for. I mean the real thing. This is *brummagem*."

"*Brummagem*?" Paul ejaculated while his eyes wandered, by a movement natural at the moment, over the luxurious room.

"Ah they make it so well today—it's wonderfully deceptive!"

Our friend thrilled with the interest and perhaps even more with the pity of it. Yet he wasn't afraid to seem to patronise when he could still so far envy. "Is it deceptive that I find you living with every appearance of domestic felicity—blest with a devoted, accomplished wife, with children whose acquaintance I haven't yet had the pleasure of making, but who *must* be delightful young people, from what I know of their parents?"

St. George smiled as for the candour of his question. "It's all excellent, my dear fellow—heaven forbid I should deny it. I've made a great deal of money; my wife has known how to take care of it, to use it without wasting it, to put a good bit of it by, to make it fructify. I've got a loaf on the shelf; I've got everything in fact but the great thing."

"The great thing?" Paul kept echoing.

"The sense of having done the best—the sense which is the real life of the artist and the absence of which is his death, of having drawn from his intellectual instrument the finest music that nature had hidden in it, of having played it as it should be played. He either does that or he doesn't—and if he doesn't he isn't worth speaking of. Therefore, precisely, those who really know *don't* speak of him. He may still hear a great chatter, but what he hears most is the incorruptible silence of Fame. I've squared her, you may say, for my little hour—but what's my little hour? Don't imagine for a moment," the Master pursued, "that I'm such a cad as to have brought you down here to abuse or to complain of my wife to you. She's a woman of distinguished qualities, to whom my obligations are immense; so that, if you please, we'll say nothing about her.

"My boys—my children are all boys—are straight and strong, thank God, and have no poverty of growth about them, no penury of needs. I receive periodically the most satisfactory attestation from Harrow, from Oxford, from Sandhurst—oh we've done the best for them!—of their eminence as living thriving consuming organisms."

"It must be delightful to feel that the son of one's loins is at Sandhurst," Paul remarked enthusiastically.

"It is—it's charming. Oh I'm a patriot!"

The young man then could but have the greater tribute of questions to pay. "Then what did you mean—the other night at Summersoft—by saying that children are a curse?"

"My dear youth, on what basis are we talking?" and St. George dropped upon the sofa at a short distance from him. Sitting a little sideways he leaned back against the opposite arm with his hands raised and interlocked behind his head. "On the supposition that a certain perfection's possible and even desirable—isn't it so? Well, all I say is that one's children interfere with perfection. One's wife interferes. Marriage interferes."

"You think then the artist shouldn't marry?"

"He does so at his peril—he does so at his cost."

"Not even when his wife's in sympathy with his work?"

"She never is—she can't be! Women haven't a conception of such things."

"Surely they on occasion work themselves," Paul objected.

"Yes, very badly indeed. Oh of course, often, they think they understand, they think they sympathise. Then it is they're most dangerous. Their idea is that you shall do a great lot and get a great lot of money. Their great nobleness and virtue, their exemplary conscientiousness as British females, is in keeping you up to that. My wife makes all my bargains with my publishers for me, and has done so for twenty years. She does it consummately well—that's why I'm really pretty well off. Aren't you the father of their innocent babes, and will you withhold from them their natural sustenance? You asked me the other night if they're not an immense incentive. Of course they are—there's no doubt of that!"

Paul turned it over: it took, from eyes he had never felt open so wide, so much looking at. "For myself I've an idea I need incentives."

"Ah well then, *n'en parlons plus*!" his companion handsomely smiled.

"*You* are an incentive, I maintain," the young man went on. "You don't affect me in the way you'd apparently like to. Your great success is what I see—the pomp of Ennismore Gardens!"

"Success?"—St. George's eyes had a cold fine light. "Do you call it success to be spoken of as you'd speak of me if you were sitting here with another artist—a young man intelligent and sincere like yourself? Do you call it success to make you blush—as you would blush!—if some foreign critic (some fellow, of course I mean, who should know what he was talking about and should have shown you he did, as foreign critics like to show it) were to say to you: 'He's the one, in this country, whom they consider the most perfect, isn't he?' Is it success to be the occasion of a young Englishman's having to stammer as you would have to stammer at such a moment for old England? No, no;

success is to have made people wriggle to another tune. Do try it!"

Paul continued all gravely to glow. "Try what?"

"Try to do some really good work."

"Oh I want to, heaven knows!"

"Well, you can't do it without sacrifices—don't believe that for a moment," the Master said. "I've made none. I've had everything. In other words I've missed everything."

"You've had the full rich masculine human general life, with all the responsibilities and duties and burdens and sorrows and joys—all the domestic and social initiations and complications. They must be immensely suggestive, immensely amusing," Paul anxiously submitted.

"Amusing?"

"For a strong man—yes."

"They've given me subjects without number, if that's what you mean; but they've taken away at the same time the power to use them. I've touched a thousand things, but which one of them have I turned into gold? The artist has to do only with that—he knows nothing of any baser metal. I've led the life of the world, with my wife and my progeny; the clumsy conventional expensive materialised vulgarised brutalised life of London. We've got everything handsome, even a carriage—we're perfect Philistines and prosperous hospitable eminent people. But, my dear fellow, don't try to stultify yourself and pretend you don't know what we *haven't* got. It's bigger than all the rest. Between artists—come!" the Master wound up. "You know as well as you sit there that you'd put a pistol-ball into your brain if you had written my books!"

It struck his listener that the tremendous talk promised by him at Summersoft had indeed come off, and with a promptitude, a fullness, with which the latter's young imagination had scarcely reckoned. His impression fairly shook him and he throbbed with the excitement of such deep soundings and such strange confidences. He throbbed indeed with the conflict of his feelings—bewilderment and recognition and alarm, enjoyment and protest and assent, all commingled with tenderness (and a kind of shame in the participation) for the sores and bruises exhibited by so fine a creature, and with a sense of the tragic secret nursed under his trappings. The idea of *his*, Paul Overt's, becoming the occasion of such an act of humility made him flush and pant, at the same time that his consciousness was in certain directions too much alive not to swallow—and not intensely to taste—every offered spoonful of the revelation.

It had been his odd fortune to blow upon the deep waters, to make them surge and break in waves of strange eloquence. But how couldn't he give out a passionate contradiction of his host's last extravagance, how couldn't he enumerate to him the parts of his work he loved, the splendid things he had found in it, beyond the compass of any other writer of the day? St. George listened a while, courteously; then he said, laying his hand on his visitor's: "That's all very well; and if your idea's to do nothing better there's no reason you shouldn't have as many good things as I—as many human and material appendages, as many sons or daughters, a wife with as many gowns, a house with as many servants, a stable with as many horses, a heart with as many aches." The Master got up when he had spoken thus—he stood a moment—near the sofa looking down on his agitated pupil. "Are you possessed of any property?" it occurred to him to ask.

"None to speak of."

"Oh well then there's no reason why you shouldn't make a goodish income—if you set about it the right way. Study *me* for that—study me well. You may really have horses."

Paul sat there some minutes without speaking. He looked straight before him—he turned over many things. His friend had wandered away, taking up a parcel of letters from the table where the roll of proofs had lain. "What was the book Mrs. St. George made you burn—the one she didn't like?" our young man brought out.

"The book she made me burn—how did you know that?" The Master looked up from his letters quite without the facial convulsion the pupil had feared.

"I heard her speak of it at Summersoft."

"Ah yes—she's proud of it. I don't know—it was rather good."

"What was it about?"

"Let me see." And he seemed to make an effort to remember. "Oh yes—it was about myself." Paul gave an irrepressible groan for the disappearance of such a production, and the elder man went on: "Oh but *you* should write it—*you* should do me." And he pulled up—from the restless motion that had come upon him; his fine smile a generous glare. "There's a subject, my boy: no end of stuff in it!"

Again Paul was silent, but it was all tormenting. "Are there no women who really understand—who can take part in a sacrifice?"

"How can they take part? They themselves are the sacrifice. They're the idol and the altar and the flame."

"Isn't there even *one* who sees further?" Paul continued.

For a moment St. George made no answer; after which, having torn up his letters, he came back to the point all ironic. "Of course I know the one you mean. But not even Miss Fancourt."

"I thought you admired her so much."

"It's impossible to admire her more. Are you in love with her?" St. George asked.

"Yes," Paul Overt presently said.

"Well then give it up."

Paul stared. "Give up my 'love'?"

"Bless me, no. Your idea." And then as our hero but still gazed: "The one you talked with her about. The idea of a decent perfection."

"She'd help it—she'd help it!" the young man cried.

"For about a year—the first year, yes. After that she'd be as a millstone round its neck."

Paul frankly wondered. "Why she has a passion for the real thing, for good work—for everything you and I care for most."

"'You and I' is charming, my dear fellow!" his friend laughed.

"She has it indeed, but she'd have a still greater passion for her children—and very proper too. She'd insist on everything's being made comfortable, advantageous, propitious for them. That isn't the artist's business."

"The artist—the artist! Isn't he a man all the same?"

St. George had a grand grimace. "I mostly think not. You know as well as I what he has to do: the concentration, the finish, the independence he must strive for from the moment he begins to wish his work really decent. Ah my young friend, his relation to women, and especially to the one he's most intimately concerned with, is at the mercy of the damning fact that whereas he can in the nature of things have but one standard, they have about fifty. That's what makes them so superior," St. George amusingly added. "Fancy an artist with a change of standards as you'd have a change of shirts or of dinner-plates. To *do* it—to do it and make it divine—is the only thing he has to think about. 'Is it done or not?' is his only question. Not 'Is it done as well as a proper solicitude for my dear little family will allow?' He has nothing to do with the relative—he has only to do with the absolute; and a dear little family may represent a dozen relatives."

"Then you don't allow him the common passions and affections of men?" Paul asked.

"Hasn't he a passion, an affection, which includes all the rest? Besides, let him have all the passions he likes—if he only keeps his independence. He must be able to be poor."

Paul slowly got up. "Why then did you advise me to make up to her?"

St. George laid his hand on his shoulder. "Because she'd make a splendid wife! And I hadn't read you then."

The young man had a strained smile. "I wish you had left me alone!"

"I didn't know that that wasn't good enough for you," his host returned.

"What a false position, what a condemnation of the artist, that he's a mere disfranchised monk and can produce his effect only by giving up personal happiness. What an arraignment of art!" Paul went on with a trembling voice.

"Ah you don't imagine by chance that I'm defending art? 'Arraignment'—I should think so! Happy the societies in which it hasn't made its appearance, for from the moment it comes they have a consuming ache, they have an incurable corruption, in their breast. Most assuredly is the artist in a false position! But I thought we were taking him for granted. Pardon me," St. George continued: "*Ginistrella*' made me!"

Paul stood looking at the floor—one o'clock struck, in the stillness, from a neighbouring church-tower. "Do you think she'd ever look at me?" he put to his friend at last.

"Miss Fancourt—as a suitor? Why shouldn't I think it? That's why I've tried to favour you—I've had a little chance or two of bettering your opportunity."

"Forgive my asking you, but do you mean by keeping away yourself?" Paul said with a blush.

"I'm an old idiot—my place isn't there," St. George stated gravely.

"I'm nothing yet, I've no fortune; and there must be so many others," his companion pursued.

The Master took this considerably in, but made little of it. "You're a gentleman and a man of genius. I think you might do something."

"But if I must give that up—the genius?"

"Lots of people, you know, think I've kept mine," St. George wonderfully grinned.

"You've a genius for mystification!" Paul declared; but grasping his hand gratefully in attenuation of this judgement.

"Poor dear boy, I do worry you! But try, try, all the same. I think your chances are good and you'll win a great prize."

Paul held fast the other's hand a minute; he looked into the strange deep face. "No, I *am* an artist—I can't help it!"

"Ah show it then!" St. George pleadingly broke out. "Let me see before I die the thing I most want, the thing I yearn for: a life in which the passion—ours—is really intense. If you can be rare don't fail of it! Think what it is—how it counts—how it lives!"

They had moved to the door and he had closed both his hands over his companion's. Here they paused again and our hero breathed deep. "I want to live!"

"In what sense?"

"In the greatest."

"Well then stick to it—see it through."

"With your sympathy—your help?"

"Count on that—you'll be a great figure to me. Count on my highest appreciation, my devotion. You'll give me satisfaction-if that has any weight with you." After which, as Paul appeared still to waver, his host added: "Do you remember what you said to me at Summersoft?"

"Something infatuated, no doubt!"

"'I'll do anything in the world you tell me.' You said that."

"And you hold me to it?"

"Ah what am I?" the Master expressively sighed.

"Lord, what things I shall have to do!" Paul almost moaned as be departed.

Chapter 6

"It goes on too much abroad—hang abroad!" These or something like them had been the Master's remarkable words in relation to the action of *Ginistrella*; and yet, though they had made a sharp impression on the author of that work, like almost all spoken words from the same source, he a week after the conversation I have noted left England for a long absence and full of brave intentions. It is not a perversion of the truth to pronounce that encounter the direct cause of his departure. If the oral utterance of the eminent writer had the privilege of moving him deeply it was especially on his turning it over at leisure, hours and days later, that it appeared to yield him its full meaning and exhibit its extreme importance.

He spent the summer in Switzerland and, having in September begun a new task, determined not to cross the Alps till he should have made a good start. To this end he returned to a quiet corner he knew well, on the edge of the Lake of Geneva and within sight of the towers of Chillon: a region and a view for which he had an affection that sprang from old associations and was capable of mysterious revivals and refreshments. Here he lingered late, till the snow was on the nearer hills, almost down to the limit to which he could climb when his stint, on the shortening afternoons, was performed.

The autumn was fine, the lake was blue and his book took form and direction. These felicities, for the time, embroidered his life, which he suffered to cover him with its mantle. At the end of six weeks he felt he had learnt St. George's lesson by heart, had tested and proved its doctrine. Nevertheless he did a very inconsistent thing: before crossing the Alps he wrote to Marian Fancourt. He was aware of the perversity of this act, and it was only as a luxury, an amusement, the reward of a strenuous autumn, that he justified it. She had asked of him no such favour when, shortly before he left London, three days after their dinner in Ennismore Gardens, he went to take leave of her.

It was true she had had no ground—he hadn't named his intention of absence. He had kept his counsel for want of due assurance: it was that particular visit that was, the next thing, to settle the matter. He had paid the visit to see how much he really cared for her, and quick departure, without so much as an explicit farewell, was the sequel to this enquiry, the answer to which had created within him a deep yearning. When he wrote her from Clarens he noted that he owed her an explanation (more than three months after!) for not having told her what he was doing.

She replied now briefly but promptly, and gave him a striking piece of news: that of the death, a week before, of Mrs. St. George. This exemplary woman had succumbed, in the country, to a violent attack of inflammation of the lungs—he would remember that for a long time she had been delicate. Miss Fancourt added that she believed her husband overwhelmed by the blow; he would miss her too terribly—she had been everything in life to him.

Paul Overt, on this, immediately wrote to St. George. He would from the day of their parting have been glad to remain in communication with him, but had hitherto lacked the right excuse for troubling so busy a man. Their long nocturnal talk came back to him in every detail, but this was no bar to an expression of proper sympathy with the head of the profession, for hadn't that very talk made it clear that the late accomplished lady was the influence that ruled his life? What catastrophe could be more cruel than the extinction of such an influence?

This was to be exactly the tone taken by St. George in answering his young friend upwards of a month later. He made no allusion of course to their important discussion. He spoke of his wife as frankly and generously as if he had quite forgotten that occasion, and the feeling of deep bereavement was visible in his words. "She took everything off my hands—off my mind. She carried on our life with the greatest art, the rarest devotion, and I was free, as few men can have been, to drive my pen, to shut myself up with my trade. This was a rare service—the highest she could have rendered me. Would I could have acknowledged it more fitly!"

A certain bewilderment, for our hero, disengaged itself from these remarks: they struck him as a contradiction, a retractation, strange on the part of a man who hadn't the excuse of witlessness. He had certainly not expected his correspondent to rejoice in the death of his wife, and it was perfectly in order that the rupture of a tie of more than twenty years should have left him sore. But if she had been so clear a blessing what in the name of consistency had the dear man meant by turning him upside down that night—by dosing him to that degree, at the most sensitive hour of his life, with the doctrine of renunciation? If Mrs. St. George was an irreparable loss, then her husband's inspired advice had been a bad joke and renunciation was a mistake.

Overt was on the point of rushing back to London to show that, for his part, he was perfectly willing to consider it so, and he went so far as to take the manuscript of the first chapters of his new book out of his table-drawer, to insert it into a pocket of his portmanteau. This led to his catching a glimpse of certain pages he hadn't looked at for months, and that accident, in turn, to his being struck with the high promise they revealed—a rare result of such retrospections, which it was his habit to avoid as much as possible: they usually brought home to him that the glow of composition might be a purely subjective and misleading emotion.

On this occasion a certain belief in himself disengaged itself whimsically from the serried erasures of his first draft, making him think it best after all to pursue his present trial to the end. If he could write as well under the rigour of privation it might be a mistake to change the conditions before that spell had spent itself. He would go back to London of course, but he would go back only when he should have finished his book. This was the vow he privately made, restoring his manuscript to the table-drawer.

It may be added that it took him a long time to finish his book, for the subject was as difficult as it was fine, and he was literally embarrassed by the fullness of his notes. Something within him warned him that he must make it supremely good—otherwise he should lack, as regards his private behaviour, a handsome excuse. He had a horror of this deficiency and found himself as firm as need be on the question of the lamp and the file. He crossed the Alps at last and spent the winter, the spring, the ensuing summer, in Italy, where still, at the end of a twelvemonth, his task was unachieved. "Stick to it—see it through": this general injunction of St. George's was good also for the particular case. He applied it to the utmost, with the result that when in its slow order the summer had come round again he felt he had given all that was in him. This time he put his papers into his portmanteau, with the address of his publisher attached, and took his way northward.

He had been absent from London for two years—two years which, seeming to count as more, had made such a difference in his own life—through the production of a novel far stronger, he believed, than *Ginistrella*—that he turned out into Piccadilly, the morning after his arrival, with a vague expectation of changes, of finding great things had happened. But there were few transformations in Piccadilly—only three or four big red houses where there had been low black ones—and the brightness of the end of June peeped through the rusty railings of the Green Park and glittered in the varnish of the rolling carriages as he had seen it in other, more cursory Junes.

It was a greeting he appreciated; it seemed friendly and pointed, added to the exhilaration of his finished book, of his having his own country and the huge oppressive amusing city that suggested everything, that contained everything, under his hand again. "Stay at home and do things here—do subjects we can measure," St. George had said; and now it struck him he should ask nothing better than to stay at home for ever.

Late in the afternoon he took his way to Manchester Square, looking out for a number he hadn't forgotten. Miss Fancourt, however, was not at home, so that he turned rather dejectedly from the door. His movement brought him face to face with a gentleman just approaching it and recognised on another glance as Miss Fancourt's father. Paul saluted this personage, and the General returned the greeting with his customary good manner—a manner so good, however, that you could never tell whether it meant he placed you.

The disappointed caller felt the impulse to address him; then, hesitating, became both aware of having no particular remark to make, and convinced that though the old soldier remembered him he remembered him wrong. He therefore went his way without computing the irresistible effect his own evident recognition would have on the General, who never neglected a chance to gossip. Our young man's face was expressive, and observation seldom let it pass. He hadn't taken ten steps before he heard himself called after with a friendly semi-articulate "Er—I beg your pardon!"

He turned round and the General, smiling at him from the porch, said: "Won't you come in? I won't leave you the advantage of me!" Paul declined to come in, and then felt regret, for

Miss Fancourt, so late in the afternoon, might return at any moment. But her father gave him no second chance; he appeared mainly to wish not to have struck him as ungracious.

A further look at the visitor had recalled something, enough at least to enable him to say: "You've come back, you've come back?" Paul was on the point of replying that he had come back the night before, but he suppressed, the next instant, this strong light on the immediacy of his visit and, giving merely a general assent, alluded to the young lady he deplored not having found. He had come late in the hope she would be in. "I'll tell her—I'll tell her," said the old man; and then he added quickly, gallantly: "You'll be giving us something new? It's a long time, isn't it?" Now he remembered him right.

"Rather long. I'm very slow." Paul explained. "I met you at Summersoft a long time ago."

"Oh yes—with Henry St. George. I remember very well. Before his poor wife—" General Fancourt paused a moment, smiling a little less. "I dare say you know."

"About Mrs. St. George's death? Certainly—I heard at the time."

"Oh no, I mean—I mean he's to be married."

"Ah I've not heard that!" But just as Paul was about to add "To whom?" the General crossed his intention.

"When did you come back? I know you've been away—by my daughter. She was very sorry. You ought to give her something new."

"I came back last night," said our young man, to whom something had occurred which made his speech for the moment a little thick.

"Ah most kind of you to come so soon. Couldn't you turn up at dinner?"

"At dinner?" Paul just mechanically repeated, not liking to ask whom St. George was going to marry, but thinking only of that.

"There are several people, I believe. Certainly St. George. Or afterwards if you like better. I believe my daughter expects—"

He appeared to notice something in the visitor's raised face (on his steps he stood higher) which led him to interrupt himself, and the interruption gave him a momentary sense of awkwardness, from which he sought a quick issue. "Perhaps then you haven't heard she's to be married."

Paul gaped again. "To be married?"

"To Mr. St. George—it has just been settled. Odd marriage, isn't it?" Our listener uttered no opinion on this point: he only continued to stare. "But I dare say it will do—she's so awfully literary!" said the General.

Paul had turned very red. "Oh it's a surprise—very interesting, very charming! I'm afraid I can't dine—so many thanks!"

"Well, you must come to the wedding!" cried the General. "Oh I remember that day at Summersoft. He's a great man, you know."

"Charming—charming!" Paul stammered for retreat. He shook hands with the General and got off. His face was red and he had the sense of its growing more and more crimson. All the evening at home—he went straight to his rooms and remained there dinnerless—his cheek burned at intervals as if it had been smitten. He didn't understand what had happened to him, what trick had been played him, what treachery practised. "None, none," he said to himself. "I've nothing to do with it. I'm out of it—it s none of my business." But that bewildered murmur was followed again and again by the incongruous ejaculation: "Was it a plan—was it a plan?" Sometimes he cried to himself, breathless, "Have I been duped, sold, swindled?" If at all, he was an absurd, an abject victim.

It was as if he hadn't lost her till now. He had renounced her, yes; but that was another affair—that was a closed but not a locked door. Now he seemed to see the door quite slammed in his face. Did he expect her to wait—was she to give him his time like that: two years at a stretch? He didn't know what he had expected—he only knew what he hadn't. It wasn't this—it wasn't this. Mystification bitterness and wrath rose and boiled in him when he thought of the deference, the devotion, the credulity with which he had listened to St. George.

The evening wore on and the light was long; but even when it had darkened he remained without a lamp. He had flung himself on the sofa, where he lay through the hours with his eyes either closed or gazing at the gloom, in the attitude of a man teaching himself to bear something, to bear having been made a fool of. He had made it too easy—that idea passed over him like a hot wave.

Suddenly, as he heard eleven o'clock strike, he jumped up, remembering what General Fancourt had said about his coming after dinner. He'd go—he'd see her at least; perhaps he should see what it meant. He felt as if some of the elements of a hard sum had been given him and the others were wanting: he couldn't do his sum till he had got all his figures.

He dressed and drove quickly, so that by half-past eleven he was at Manchester Square. There were a good many carriages at the door—a party was going on; a circumstance which at the last gave him a slight relief, for now he would rather see her in a crowd. People passed him on the staircase; they were going away, going "on" with the hunted herdlike movement of London society at night. But sundry groups remained in the drawing-room, and it was some minutes, as she didn't hear him announced, before he discovered and spoke to her.

In this short interval he had seen St. George talking to a lady before the fireplace; but he at once looked away, feeling unready for an encounter, and therefore couldn't be sure the author of *Shadowmere* noticed him. At all events he didn't come over though Miss Fancourt did as soon as she saw him—she almost rushed at him, smiling rustling radiant beautiful. He had forgotten what her head, what her face offered to the sight; she was in white, there were gold figures on her dress and her hair was a *casque* of gold. He saw in a single moment that she was happy, happy with an aggressive splendour. But she wouldn't speak to him of that, she would speak only of himself.

"I'm so delighted; my father told me. How kind of you to come!" She struck him as so fresh and brave, while his eyes moved over her, that he said to himself irresistibly: "Why to him, why not to youth, to strength, to ambition, to a future? Why, in her rich young force, to failure, to abdication to superannuation?" In his thought at that sharp moment he blasphemed even against all that had been left of his faith in the peccable Master. "I'm so sorry I missed you," she went on. "My father told me. How charming of you to have come so soon!"

"Does that surprise you?" Paul Overt asked.

"The first day? No, from you—nothing that's nice." She was interrupted by a lady who bade her goodnight, and he seemed to read that it cost her nothing to speak to him in that tone; it was her old liberal lavish way, with a certain added amplitude that time had brought; and if this manner began to operate on the spot, at such a juncture in her history, perhaps in the other days too it had meant just as little or as much—a mere mechanical charity, with the difference now that she was satisfied, ready to give but in want of nothing. Oh she was satisfied—and why shouldn't she be? Why shouldn't she have been surprised at his coming the first day—for all the good she had ever got from him?

As the lady continued to hold her attention Paul turned from her with a strange irritation in his complicated artistic soul and a sort of disinterested disappointment. She was so happy that it was almost stupid—a disproof of the extraordinary intelligence he had formerly found in her. Didn't she know how bad St. George could be, hadn't she recognised the awful thinness—? If she didn't she was nothing, and if she did why such an insolence of serenity? This question expired as our young man's eyes settled at last on the genius who had advised him in a great crisis. St. George was still before the chimney-piece, but now he was alone—fixed, waiting, as if he meant to stop after every one—and he met the clouded gaze of the young friend so troubled as to the degree of his right (the right his resentment would have enjoyed) to regard himself as a victim.

Somehow the ravage of the question was checked by the Master's radiance. It was as fine in its way as Marian Fancourt's, it denoted the happy human being; but also it represented to Paul Overt that the author of *Shadowmere* had now definitely ceased to count—ceased to count as a writer. As he smiled a welcome across the place he was almost banal, was almost smug. Paul fancied that for a moment he hesitated to make a movement, as if for all the world he *had* his bad conscience; then they had already met in the middle of the room and had shaken hands—expressively, cordially on St. George's part. With which they had passed back together to where the elder man had been standing, while St. George said: "I hope you're never going away again. I've been dining here; the General told me."

He was handsome, he was young, he looked as if he had still a great fund of life. He bent the friendliest, most unconfessing eyes on his disciple of a couple of years before; asked him about everything, his health, his plans, his late occupations, the new book. "When will it be out—soon, soon, I hope? Splendid, eh? That's right; you're a comfort, you're a luxury! I've read you all over again these last six months." Paul waited to see if he would tell him what the General had told him in the afternoon and what Miss Fancourt, verbally at least, of course hadn't. But as it didn't come out he at last put the question.

"Is it true, the great news I hear—that you're to be married?"

"Ah you have heard it then?"

"Didn't the General tell you?" Paul asked.

The Master's face was wonderful. "Tell me what?"

"That he mentioned it to me this afternoon?"

"My dear fellow, I don't remember. We've been in the midst of people. I'm sorry, in that case, that I lose the pleasure, myself, of announcing to you a fact that touches me so nearly. It *is* a fact, strange as it may appear. It has only just become one. Isn't it ridiculous?" St. George made this speech without confusion, but on the other hand, so far as our friend could judge, without latent impudence. It struck his interlocutor that, to talk so comfortably and coolly, he must simply have forgotten what had passed between them. His next words, however, showed he hadn't, and they produced, as an appeal to Paul's own memory, an effect which would have been ludicrous if it hadn't been cruel. "Do you recall the talk we had at my house that night, into which Miss Fancourt's name entered? I've often thought of it since."

"Yes; no wonder you said what you did"—Paul was careful to meet his eyes.

"In the light of the present occasion? Ah but there was no light then. How could I have foreseen this hour?"

"Didn't you think it probable?"

"Upon my honour, no," said Henry St. George. "Certainly I owe you that assurance. Think how my situation has changed."

"I see—I see," our young man murmured.

His companion went on as if, now that the subject had been broached, he was, as a person of imagination and tact, quite ready to give every satisfaction—being both by his genius and his method so able to enter into everything another might feel. "But it's not only that; for honestly, at my age, I never dreamed—a widower with big boys and with so little else! It has turned out differently from anything one could have dreamed, and I'm fortunate beyond all measure. She has been so free, and yet she consents. Better than anyone else perhaps—for I remember how you liked her before you went away, and how she liked you-you can intelligently congratulate me."

"She has been so free!" Those words made a great impression on Paul Overt, and he almost writhed under that irony in them as to which it so little mattered whether it was designed or casual. Of course she had been free, and appreciably perhaps by his own act; for wasn't the Master's allusion to her having liked him a part of the irony too? "I thought that by your theory you disapproved of a writer's marrying."

"Surely—surely. But you don't call me a writer?"

"You ought to be ashamed," said Paul.

"Ashamed of marrying again?"

"I won't say that—but ashamed of your reasons."

The elder man beautifully smiled. "You must let me judge of

them, my good friend."

"Yes; why not? For you judged wonderfully of mine."

The tone of these words appeared suddenly, for St. George, to suggest the unsuspected. He stared as if divining a bitterness. "Don't you think I've been straight?"

"You might have told me at the time perhaps."

"My dear fellow, when I say I couldn't pierce futurity—!"

"I mean afterwards."

The Master wondered. "After my wife's death?"

"When this idea came to you."

"Ah never, never! I wanted to save you, rare and precious as you are."

Poor Overt looked hard at him. "Are you marrying Miss Fancourt to save me?"

"Not absolutely, but it adds to the pleasure. I shall be the making of you," St. George smiled. "I was greatly struck, after our talk, with the brave devoted way you quitted the country, and still more perhaps with your force of character in remaining abroad. You're very strong—you're wonderfully strong."

Paul tried to sound his shining eyes; the strange thing was that he seemed sincere—not a mocking fiend. He turned away, and as he did so heard the Master say something about his giving them all the proof, being the joy of his old age. He faced him again, taking another look. "Do you mean to say you've stopped writing?"

"My dear fellow, of course I have. It's too late. Didn't I tell you?"

"I can't believe it!"

"Of course you can't—with your own talent! No, no; for the rest of my life I shall only read *you*."

"Does she know that—Miss Fancourt?"

"She will—she will." Did he mean this, our young man wondered, as a covert intimation that the assistance he should derive from that young lady's fortune, moderate as it was, would make the difference of putting it in his power to cease to work ungratefully an exhausted vein? Somehow, standing there in the ripeness of his successful manhood, he didn't suggest that any of his veins were exhausted. "Don't you remember the moral I offered myself to you that night as pointing?" St. George continued. "Consider at any rate the warning I am at present."

This was too much—he *was* the mocking fiend. Paul turned from him with a mere nod for goodnight and the sense in a sore heart that he might come back to him and his easy grace, his fine way of arranging things, sometime in the far future, but couldn't fraternise with him now. It was necessary to his soreness to believe for the hour in the intensity of his grievance—all the more cruel for its not being a legal one. It was doubtless in the attitude of hugging this wrong that he descended the stairs without taking leave of Miss Fancourt, who hadn't been in view at the moment he quitted the room.

He was glad to get out into the honest dusky unsophisticating night, to move fast, to take his way home on foot. He walked a long time, going astray, paying no attention. He was thinking of too many other things. His steps recovered their direction, however, and at the end of an hour he found himself before his door in the small inexpensive empty street. He lingered, questioning himself still before going in, with nothing around and above him but moonless blackness, a bad lamp or two and a few far-away dim stars.

To these last faint features he raised his eyes; he had been saying to himself that he should have been "sold" indeed, diabolically sold, if now, on his new foundation, at the end of a year, St. George were to put forth something of his prime quality—something of the type of *Shadowmere* and finer than his finest. Greatly as he admired his talent Paul literally hoped such an incident wouldn't occur; it seemed to him just then that he shouldn't be able to bear it. His late adviser's words were still in his ears—"You're very strong, wonderfully strong."

Was he really? Certainly he would have to be, and it might a little serve for revenge. *Is* he? the reader may ask in turn, if his interest has followed the perplexed young man so far. The best answer to that perhaps is that he's doing his best, but that it's too soon to say. When the new book came out in the autumn Mr. and Mrs. St. George found it really magnificent. The former still has published nothing but Paul doesn't even yet feel safe. I may say for him, however, that if this event were to occur he would really be the very first to appreciate it: which is perhaps a proof that the Master was essentially right and that Nature had dedicated him to intellectual, not to personal passion.

The Marriages

Chapter 1

"Won't you stay a little longer?" the hostess asked while she held the girl's hand and smiled. "It's too early for everyone to go—it's too absurd." Mrs. Churchley inclined her head to one side and looked gracious; she flourished about her face, in a vaguely protecting sheltering way, an enormous fan of red feathers. Everything in her composition, for Adela Chart, was enormous. She had big eyes, big teeth, big shoulders, big hands, big rings and bracelets, big jewels of every sort and many of them. The train of her crimson dress was longer than any other; her house was huge; her drawing-room, especially now that the company had left it, looked vast, and it offered to the girl's eyes a collection of the largest sofas and chairs, pictures, mirrors, clocks, that she had ever beheld.

Was Mrs. Churchley's fortune also large, to account for so many immensities? Of this Adela could know nothing, but it struck her, while she smiled sweetly back at their entertainer, that she had better try to find out. Mrs. Churchley had at least a high-hung carriage drawn by the tallest horses, and in the Row she was to be seen perched on a mighty hunter. She was high and extensive herself, though not exactly fat; her bones were big, her limbs were long, and her loud hurrying voice resembled the bell of a steamboat. While she spoke to his daughter she had the air of hiding from Colonel Chart, a little shyly, behind the wide ostrich fan. But Colonel Chart was not a man to be either ignored or eluded.

"Of course every one's going on to something else," he said. "I believe there are a lot of things to-night."

"And where are YOU going?" Mrs. Churchley asked, dropping her fan and turning her bright hard eyes on the Colonel.

"Oh I don't do that sort of thing!"—he used a tone of familiar resentment that fell with a certain effect on his daughter's ear. She saw in it that he thought Mrs. Churchley might have done him a little more justice. But what made the honest soul suppose her a person to look to for a perception of fine shades? Indeed the shade was one it might have been a little difficult to seize—the difference between "going on" and coming to a dinner of twenty people. The pair were in mourning; the second year had maintained it for Adela, but the Colonel hadn't objected to dining with Mrs. Churchley, any more than he had objected at Easter to going down to the Millwards', where he had met her and where the girl had her reasons for believing him to have known he should meet her. Adela wasn't clear about the occasion of their original meeting, to which a certain mystery attached.

In Mrs. Churchley's exclamation now there was the fullest concurrence in Colonel Chart's idea; she didn't say "Ah yes, dear friend, I understand!" but this was the note of sympathy she plainly wished to sound. It immediately made Adela say to her "Surely you must be going on somewhere yourself."

"Yes, you must have a lot of places," the Colonel concurred, while his view of her shining raiment had an invidious directness. Adela could read the tacit implication: "You're not in sorrow, in desolation."

Mrs. Churchley turned away from her at this and just waited before answering. The red fan was up again, and this time it sheltered her from Adela. "I'll give everything up—for YOU," were the words that issued from behind it. "DO stay a little. I always think this is such a nice hour. One can really talk," Mrs. Churchley went on. The Colonel laughed; he said it wasn't fair. But their hostess pressed his daughter. "Do sit down; it's the only time to have any talk." The girl saw her father sit down, but she wandered away, turning her back and pretending to look at a picture. She was so far from agreeing with Mrs. Churchley that it was an hour she particularly disliked. She was conscious of the queerness, the shyness, in London, of the gregarious flight of guests after a dinner, the general *sauve qui peut* and panic fear of being left with the host and hostess. But personally she always felt the contagion, always conformed to the rush. Besides, she knew herself turn red now, flushed with a conviction that had come over her and that she wished not to show.

Her father sat down on one of the big sofas with Mrs. Churchley; fortunately he was also a person with a presence that could hold its own. Adela didn't care to sit and watch them while they made love, as she crudely imaged it, and she cared still less to join in their strange commerce. She wandered further away, went into another of the bright "handsome," rather nude rooms—they were like women dressed for a ball—where the displaced chairs, at awkward angles to each other, seemed to retain the attitudes of bored talkers. Her heart beat as she had seldom known it, but she continued to make a pretence of looking at the pictures on the walls and the ornaments on the tables, while she hoped that, as she preferred it, it would be also the course her father would like best.

She hoped "awfully," as she would have said, that he wouldn't think her rude. She was a person of courage, and he was a kind, an intensely good-natured man; nevertheless she went in some fear of him. At home it had always been a religion with them to be nice to the people he liked. How, in the old days, her mother, her incomparable mother, so clever, so unerring, so perfect, how in the precious days her mother had practised that art! Oh her mother, her irrecoverable mother! One of the pictures she was looking at swam before her eyes. Mrs. Churchley, in the natural course, would have begun immediately to climb staircases.

Adela could see the high bony shoulders and the long crimson tail and the universal coruscating nod wriggle their horribly practical way through the rest of the night. Therefore she MUST have had her reasons for detaining them. There were mothers who thought everyone wanted to marry their eldest son, and the girl sought to be clear as to whether she herself belonged to the class of daughters who thought everyone wanted to marry their father. Her companions left her alone; and though she didn't want to be near them it angered her that Mrs. Churchley didn't call her. That proved she was conscious of the situation. She would have called her, only Colonel Chart had perhaps dreadfully murmured "Don't, love, don't."

This proved he also was conscious. The time was really not long—ten minutes at the most elapsed—when he cried out gaily, pleasantly, as if with a small jocular reproach, "I say, Adela, we must release this dear lady!" He spoke of course as if it had been Adela's fault that they lingered. When they took leave she gave Mrs. Churchley, without intention and without defiance, but from the simple sincerity of her pain, a longer look into the eyes than she had ever given her before. Mrs. Churchley's onyx pupils reflected the question as distant dark windows reflect the sunset; they seemed to say: "Yes, I AM, if that's what you want to know!"

What made the case worse, what made the girl more sure, was the silence preserved by her companion in the brougham on their way home. They rolled along in the June darkness from Prince's Gate to Seymour Street, each looking out of a window in conscious prudence; watching but not seeing the hurry of the London night, the flash of lamps, the quick roll on the wood of hansoms and other broughams. Adela had expected her father would say something about Mrs. Churchley; but when he said nothing it affected her, very oddly, still more as if he had spoken. In Seymour Street he asked the footman if Mr. Godfrey had come in, to which the servant replied that he had come in early and gone straight to his room.

Adela had gathered as much, without saying so, from a lighted window on the second floor; but she contributed no remark to the question. At the foot of the stairs her father halted as if he had something on his mind; but what it amounted to seemed only the dry "Goodnight" with which he presently ascended. It was the first time since her mother's death that he had bidden her goodnight without kissing her. They were a kissing family, and after that dire event the habit had taken a fresh spring. She had left behind her such a general passion of regret that in kissing each other they felt themselves a little to be kissing her. Now, as, standing in the hall, with the stiff watching footman-she could have said to him angrily "Go away!"—planted near her, she looked with unspeakable pain at her father's back while he mounted, the effect was of his having withheld from another and a still more slighted cheek the touch of his lips.

He was going to his room, and after a moment she heard his door close. Then she said to the servant "Shut up the house"-she tried to do everything her mother had done, to be a little of what she had been, conscious only of falling woefully short-and took her own way upstairs.

After she had reached her room she waited, listening, shaken by the apprehension that she should hear her father come out again and go up to Godfrey. He would go up to tell him, to have it over without delay, precisely because it would be so difficult. She asked herself indeed why he should tell Godfrey when he hadn't taken the occasion—their drive home being an occasion—to tell herself. However, she wanted no announcing, no telling; there was such a horrible clearness in her mind that what she now waited for was only to be sure her father wouldn't proceed as she had imagined.

At the end of the minutes she saw this particular danger was over, upon which she came out and made her own way to her brother. Exactly what she wanted to say to him first, if their parent counted on the boy's greater indulgence, and before he could say anything, was: "Don't forgive him; don't, don't!"

He was to go up for an examination, poor lad, and during these weeks his lamp burned till the small hours. It was for the Foreign Office, and there was to be some frightful number of competitors; but Adela had great hopes of him—she believed so in his talents and saw with pity how hard he worked. This would have made her spare him, not trouble his night, his scanty rest, if anything less dreadful had been at stake. It was a blessing however that one could count on his coolness, young as he was—his bright good-looking discretion, the thing that already made him half a man of the world.

Moreover he was the one who would care most. If Basil was the eldest son—he had as a matter of course gone into the army and was in India, on the staff, by good luck, of a governor-general—it was exactly this that would make him comparatively indifferent. His life was elsewhere, and his father and he had been in a measure military comrades, so that he would be deterred by a certain delicacy from protesting; he wouldn't have liked any such protest in an affair of HIS. Beatrice and Muriel would care, but they were too young to speak, and this was just why her own responsibility was so great.

Godfrey was in working-gear—shirt and trousers and slippers and a beautiful silk jacket. His room felt hot, though a window was open to the summer night; the lamp on the table shed its studious light over a formidable heap of text-books and papers, the bed moreover showing how he had flung himself down to think out a problem. As soon as she got in she began. "Father's going to marry Mrs. Churchley, you know."

She saw his poor pink face turn pale. "How do you know?"

"I've seen with my eyes. We've been dining there—we've just come home. He's in love with her. She's in love with HIM. They'll arrange it."

"Oh I say!" Godfrey exclaimed, incredulous.

"He will, he will, he will!" cried the girl; and with it she burst into tears.

Godfrey, who had a cigarette in his hand, lighted it at one of the candles on the mantelpiece as if he were embarrassed. As Adela, who had dropped into his armchair, continued to sob, he said after a moment: "He oughtn't to—he oughtn't to."

"Oh think of mamma—think of mamma!" she wailed almost louder than was safe.

"Yes, he ought to think of mamma." With which Godfrey looked at the tip of his cigarette.

"To such a woman as that—after HER!"

"Dear old mamma!" said Godfrey while he smoked.

Adela rose again, drying her eyes. "It's like an insult to her; it's as if he denied her." Now that she spoke of it she felt herself rise to a height. "He rubs out at a stroke all the years of their happiness."

"They were awfully happy," Godfrey agreed.

"Think what she was—think how no one else will ever again be like her!" the girl went on.

"I suppose he's not very happy now," her brother vaguely contributed.

"Of course he isn't, any more than you and I are; and it's dreadful of him to want to be."

"Well, don't make yourself miserable till you're sure," the young man said.

But Adela showed him confidently that she WAS sure, from the way the pair had behaved together and from her father's attitude on the drive home. If Godfrey had been there he would have seen everything; it couldn't be explained, but he would have felt. When he asked at what moment the girl had first had her suspicion she replied that it had all come at once, that evening; or that at least she had had no conscious fear till then. There had been signs for two or three weeks, but she hadn't understood them—ever since the day Mrs. Churchley had dined in Seymour Street. Adela had on that occasion thought it odd her father should have wished to invite her, given the quiet way they were living; she was a person they knew so little.

He had said something about her having been very civil to him, and that evening, already, she had guessed that he must have frequented their portentous guest herself more than there had been signs of. To-night it had come to her clearly that he would have called on her every day since the time of her dining with them; every afternoon about the hour he was ostensibly at his club. Mrs. Churchley WAS his club—she was for all the world just like one. At this Godfrey laughed; he wanted to know what his sister knew about clubs. She was slightly disappointed in his laugh, even wounded by it, but she knew perfectly what she meant: she meant that Mrs. Churchley was public and florid, promiscuous and mannish.

"Oh I daresay she's all right," he said as if he wanted to get on with his work. He looked at the clock on the mantel-shelf; he would have to put in another hour.

"All right to come and take darling mamma's place—to sit where SHE used to sit, to lay her horrible hands on HER things?" Adela was appalled—all the more that she hadn't expected it-at her brother's apparent acceptance of such a prospect.

He coloured; there was something in her passionate piety that scorched him. She glared at him with tragic eyes—he might have profaned an altar. "Oh I mean that nothing will come of it."

"Not if we do our duty," said Adela. And then as he looked as if he hadn't an idea of what that could be: "You must speak to him—tell him how we feel; that we shall never forgive him, that we can't endure it."

"He'll think I'm cheeky," her brother returned, looking down at his papers with his back to her and his hands in his pockets.

"Cheeky to plead for HER memory?"

"He'll say it's none of my business."

"Then you believe he'll do it?" cried the girl.

"Not a bit. Go to bed!"

"I'LL speak to him"—she had turned as pale as a young priestess.

"Don't cry out till you're hurt; wait till he speaks to YOU."

"He won't, he won't!" she declared. "He'll do it without telling us."

Her brother had faced round to her again; he started a little at this, and again, at one of the candles, lighted his cigarette, which had gone out. She looked at him a moment; then he said something that surprised her. "Is Mrs. Churchley very rich?"

"I haven't the least idea. What on earth has that to do with it?"

Godfrey puffed his cigarette. "Does she live as if she were?"

"She has a lot of hideous showy things."

"Well, we must keep our eyes open," he concluded. "And now you must let me get on." He kissed his visitor as if to make up for dismissing her, or for his failure to take fire; and she held him a moment, burying her head on his shoulder.

A wave of emotion surged through her, and again she quavered out: "Ah why did she leave us? Why did she leave us?"

"Yes, why indeed?" the young man sighed, disengaging himself with a movement of oppression.

Chapter 2

Adela was so far right as that by the end of the week, though she remained certain, her father had still not made the announcement she dreaded. What convinced her was the sense of her changed relations with him—of there being between them something unexpressed, something she was aware of as she would have been of an open wound. When she spoke of this to Godfrey he said the change was of her own making—also that she was cruelly unjust to the governor. She suffered even more from her brother's unexpected perversity; she had had so different a theory about him that her disappointment was almost an humiliation and she needed all her fortitude to pitch her faith lower. She wondered what had happened to him and why he so failed her. She would have trusted him to feel right about anything, above all about such a question.

Their worship of their mother's memory, their recognition of her sacred place in their past, her exquisite influence in their father's life, his fortune, his career, in the whole history of the family and welfare of the house—accomplished clever gentle good beautiful and capable as she had been, a woman whose quiet distinction was universally admired, so that on her death one of the Princesses, the most august of her friends, had written Adela such a note about her as princesses were understood very seldom to write: their hushed tenderness over all this was like a religion, and was also an attributive honour, to fall away from which was a form of treachery.

This wasn't the way people usually felt in London, she knew; but strenuous ardent observant girl as she was, with secrecies of sentiment and dim originalities of attitude, she had already made up her mind that London was no treasure-house of delicacies. Remembrance there was hammered thin—to be faithful was to make society gape. The patient dead were sacrificed; they had no shrines, for people were literally ashamed of mourning. When they had hustled all sensibility out of their lives they invented the fiction that they felt too much to utter.

Adela said nothing to her sisters; this reticence was part of the virtue it was her idea to practise for them. SHE was to be their mother, a direct deputy and representative. Before the vision of that other woman parading in such a character she felt capable of ingenuities, of deep diplomacies. The essence of these indeed was just tremulously to watch her father. Five days after they had dined together at Mrs. Churchley's he asked her if she had been to see that lady.

"No indeed, why should I?" Adela knew that he knew she hadn't been, since Mrs. Churchley would have told him.

"Don't you call on people after you dine with them?" said Colonel Chart.

"Yes, in the course of time. I don't rush off within the week."

Her father looked at her, and his eyes were colder than she had ever seen them, which was probably, she reflected, just the way hers appeared to himself. "Then you'll please rush off to-morrow. She's to dine with us on the 12th, and I shall expect your sisters to come down."

Adela stared. "To a dinner-party?"

"It's not to be a dinner-party. I want them to know Mrs. Churchley."

"Is there to be nobody else?"

"Godfrey of course. A family party," he said with an assurance before which she turned cold.

The girl asked her brother that evening if THAT wasn't tantamount to an announcement. He looked at her queerly and then said: "I'VE been to see her."

"What on earth did you do that for?"

"Father told me he wished it."

"Then he HAS told you?"

"Told me what?" Godfrey asked while her heart sank with the sense of his making difficulties for her.

"That they're engaged, of course. What else can all this mean?"

"He didn't tell me that, but I like her."

"LIKE her!" the girl shrieked.

"She's very kind, very good."

"To thrust herself upon us when we hate her? Is that what you call kind? Is that what you call decent?"

"Oh *I* don't hate her"—and he turned away as if she bored him.

She called the next day on Mrs. Churchley, designing to break out somehow, to plead, to appeal—"Oh spare us! have mercy on us! let him alone! go away!" But that wasn't easy when they were face to face. Mrs. Churchley had every intention of getting, as she would have said—she was perpetually using the expression—into touch; but her good intentions were as depressing as a tailor's misfits. She could never understand that they had no place for her vulgar charity, that their life was filled with a fragrance of perfection for which she had no sense fine enough. She was as undomestic as a shop-front and as out of tune as a parrot. She would either make them live in the streets or bring the streets into their life—it was the same thing. She had evidently never read a book, and she used intonations that Adela had never heard, as if she had been an Australian or an American.

She understood everything in a vulgar sense; speaking of Godfrey's visit to her and praising him according to her idea, saying horrid things about him—that he was awfully good-looking, a perfect gentleman, the kind she liked. How could her father, who was after all in everything else such a dear, listen to a woman, or endure her, who thought she pleased him when she called the son of his dead wife a perfect gentleman? What would he have been, pray? Much she knew about what any of them were! When she told Adela she wanted her to like her the girl thought for an instant her opportunity had come—the chance to plead with her and beg her off. But she presented such an impenetrable surface that it would have been like giving a message to a varnished door. She wasn't a woman, said Adela; she was an address.

When she dined in Seymour Street the "children," as the girl called the others, including Godfrey, liked her. Beatrice and Muriel stared shyly and silently at the wonders of her apparel (she was brutally over-dressed) without of course guessing the danger that tainted the air. They supposed her in their innocence to be amusing, and they didn't know, any more than she did herself, how she patronised them. When she was upstairs with them after dinner Adela could see her look round the room at the things she meant to alter—their mother's things, not a bit like her own and not good enough for her.

After a quarter of an hour of this our young lady felt sure she was deciding that Seymour Street wouldn't do at all, the dear old home that had done for their mother those twenty years. Was she plotting to transport them all to her horrible Prince's Gate? Of one thing at any rate Adela was certain: her father, at that moment alone in the dining-room with Godfrey, pretending to drink another glass of wine to make time, was coming to the point, was telling the news. When they reappeared they both, to her eyes, looked unnatural: the news had been told.

She had it from Godfrey before Mrs. Churchley left the house, when, after a brief interval, he followed her out of the drawing-room on her taking her sisters to bed. She was waiting for him at the door of her room. Her father was then alone with his fiancee—the word was grotesque to Adela; it was already as if the place were her home.

"What did you say to him?" our young woman asked when her brother had told her.

"I said nothing." Then he added, colouring—the expression

of her face was such—"There was nothing to say."

"Is that how it strikes you?"—and she stared at the lamp.

"He asked me to speak to her," Godfrey went on.

"In what hideous sense?"

"To tell her I was glad."

"And did you?" Adela panted.

"I don't know. I said something. She kissed me."

"Oh how COULD you?" shuddered the girl, who covered her face with her hands.

"He says she's very rich," her brother returned.

"Is that why you kissed her?"

"I didn't kiss her. Goodnight." And the young man, turning his back, went out.

When he had gone Adela locked herself in as with the fear she should be overtaken or invaded, and during a sleepless feverish memorable night she took counsel of her uncompromising spirit. She saw things as they were, in all the indignity of life. The levity, the mockery, the infidelity, the ugliness, lay as plain as a map before her; it was a world of gross practical jokes, a world pour rire; but she cried about it all the same. The morning dawned early, or rather it seemed to her there had been no night, nothing but a sickly creeping day. But by the time she heard the house stirring again she had determined what to do.

When she came down to the breakfast-room her father was already in his place with newspapers and letters; and she expected the first words he would utter to be a rebuke to her for having disappeared the night before without taking leave of Mrs. Churchley. Then she saw he wished to be intensely kind, to make every allowance, to conciliate and console her. He knew she had heard from Godfrey, and he got up and kissed her. He told her as quickly as possible, to have it over, stammering a little, with an "I've a piece of news for you that will probably shock you," yet looking even exaggeratedly grave and rather pompous, to inspire the respect he didn't deserve.

When he kissed her she melted, she burst into tears. He held her against him, kissing her again and again, saying tenderly "Yes,

yes, I know, I know." But he didn't know else he couldn't have done it. Beatrice and Muriel came in, frightened when they saw her crying, and still more scared when she turned to them with words and an air that were terrible in their comfortable little lives: "Papa's going to be married; he's going to marry Mrs. Churchley!"

After staring a moment and seeing their father look as strange, on his side, as Adela, though in a different way, the children also began to cry, so that when the servants arrived with tea and boiled eggs these functionaries were greatly embarrassed with their burden, not knowing whether to come in or hang back. They all scraped together a decorum, and as soon as the things had been put on table the Colonel banished the men with a glance. Then he made a little affectionate speech to Beatrice and Muriel, in which he described Mrs. Churchley as the kindest, the most delightful of women, only wanting to make them happy, only wanting to make HIM happy, and convinced that he would be if they were and that they would be if he was.

"What do such words mean?" Adela asked herself. She declared privately that they meant nothing, but she was silent, and everyone was silent, on account of the advent of Miss Flynn the governess, before whom Colonel Chart preferred not to discuss the situation. Adela recognised on the spot that if things were to go as he wished his children would practically never again be alone with him. He would spend all his time with Mrs. Churchley till they were married, and then Mrs. Churchley would spend all her time with him.

Adela was ashamed of him, and that was horrible—all the more that everyone else would be, all his other friends, everyone who had known her mother. But the public dishonour to that high memory shouldn't be enacted; he shouldn't do as he wished.

After breakfast her father remarked to her that it would give him pleasure if in a day or two she would take her sisters to see their friend, and she replied that he should be obeyed. He held her hand a moment, looking at her with an argument in his eyes which presently hardened into sternness. He wanted to know that she forgave him, but also wanted to assure her that he expected her to mind what she did, to go straight. She turned away her eyes; she was indeed ashamed of him.

She waited three days and then conveyed her sisters to the *repaire*, as she would have been ready to term it, of the lioness. That queen of beasts was surrounded with callers, as Adela knew she would be; it was her "day" and the occasion the girl preferred. Before this she had spent all her time with her companions, talking to them about their mother, playing on their memory of her, making them cry and making them laugh, reminding them of blest hours of their early childhood, telling them anecdotes of her own. None the less she confided to them that she believed there was no harm at all in Mrs. Churchley, and that when the time should come she would probably take them out immensely.

She saw with smothered irritation that they enjoyed their visit at Prince's Gate; they had never been at anything so "grown-up," nor seen so many smart bonnets and brilliant complexions. Moreover they were considered with interest, quite as if, being minor elements, yet perceptible ones, of Mrs. Churchley's new life, they had been described in advance and were the heroines of the occasion. There were so many ladies present that this personage didn't talk to them much; she only called them her "chicks" and asked them to hand about tea-cups and bread and butter. All of which was highly agreeable and indeed intensely exciting to Beatrice and Muriel, who had little round red spots in THEIR cheeks when they came away. Adela quivered with the sense that her mother's children were now Mrs. Churchley's "chicks" and a part of the furniture of Mrs. Churchley's dreadful consciousness.

It was one thing to have made up her mind, however; it was another thing to make her attempt. It was when she learned from Godfrey that the day was fixed, the 20th of July, only six weeks removed, that she felt the importance of prompt action. She learned everything from Godfrey now, having decided it would be hypocrisy to question her father. Even her silence was hypocritical, but she couldn't weep and wail. Her father showed extreme tact; taking no notice of her detachment, treating it as a moment of *bouderie* he was bound to allow her and that would pout itself away. She debated much as to whether she should take Godfrey into her confidence; she would have done so without hesitation if he hadn't disappointed her. He was so little what she might have expected, and so perversely preoccupied that she could explain it only by the high pressure at which he was living, his anxiety about his "exam."

He was in a fidget, in a fever, putting on a spurt to come in first; sceptical moreover about his success and cynical about everything else. He appeared to agree to the general axiom that they didn't want a strange woman thrust into their life, but he found Mrs. Churchley "very jolly as a person to know." He had been to see her by himself—he had been to see her three times. He in fact gave it out that he would make the most of her now; he should probably be so little in Seymour Street after these days. What Adela at last determined to give him was her assurance that the marriage would never take place. When he asked what she meant and who was to prevent it she replied that the interesting couple would abandon the idea of themselves, or that Mrs. Churchley at least would after a week or two back out of it.

"That will be really horrid then," Godfrey pronounced. "The only respectable thing, at the point they've come to, is to put it through. Charming for poor Dad to have the air of being 'chucked'!"

This made her hesitate two days more, but she found answers more valid than any objections. The many-voiced answer to everything—it was like the autumn wind round the house—was the affront that fell back on her mother. Her mother was dead but it killed her again. So one morning at eleven o'clock, when she knew her father was writing letters, she went out quietly and, stopping the first hansom she met, drove to Prince's Gate. Mrs. Churchley was at home, and she was shown into the drawing-room with the request that she would wait five minutes. She waited without the sense of breaking down at the last, and the impulse to run away, which were what she had expected to have. In the cab and at the door her heart had beat terribly, but now suddenly, with the game really to play, she found herself lucid and calm.

It was a joy to her to feel later that this was the way Mrs. Churchley found her: not confused, not stammering nor prevaricating, only a little amazed at her own courage, conscious of the immense responsibility of her step and wonderfully older than her years. Her hostess sounded her at first with suspicious eyes, but eventually, to Adela's surprise, burst into tears. At this the girl herself cried, and with the secret happiness of believing they were saved. Mrs. Churchley said she would think over what she had been told, and she promised her young friend, freely enough and very firmly, not to betray the secret of the latter's step to the Colonel. They were saved—they were saved: the words sung themselves in the girl's soul as she came downstairs.

When the door opened for her she saw her brother on the step, and they looked at each other in surprise, each finding it on the part of the other an odd hour for Prince's Gate. Godfrey remarked that Mrs. Churchley would have enough of the family, and Adela answered that she would perhaps have too much. None the less the young man went in while his sister took her way home.

Chapter 3

She saw nothing of him for nearly a week; he had more and more his own times and hours, adjusted to his tremendous responsibilities, and he spent whole days at his crammer's. When she knocked at his door late in the evening he was regularly not in his room. It was known in the house how much he was worried; he was horribly nervous about his ordeal. It was to begin on the 23rd of June, and his father was as worried as himself. The wedding had been arranged in relation to this; they wished poor Godfrey's fate settled first, though they felt the nuptials would be darkened if it shouldn't be settled right.

Ten days after that performance of her private undertaking Adela began to sniff, as it were, a difference in the general air; but as yet she was afraid to exult. It wasn't in truth a difference for the better, so that there might be still a great tension. Her father, since the announcement of his intended marriage, had been visibly pleased with himself, but that pleasure now appeared to have undergone a check. She had the impression known to the passengers on a great steamer when, in the middle of the night, they feel the engines stop.

As this impression may easily sharpen to the sense that something serious has happened, so the girl asked herself what had actually occurred. She had expected something serious; but it was as if she couldn't keep still in her cabin—she wanted to go up and see. On the 20th, just before breakfast, her maid brought her a message from her brother. Mr. Godfrey would be obliged if she would speak to him in his room. She went straight up to him, dreading to find him ill, broken down on the eve of his formidable week.

This was not the case however—he rather seemed already at work, to have been at work since dawn. But he was very white and his eyes had a strange and new expression. Her beautiful young brother looked older; he looked haggard and hard. He met her there as if he had been waiting for her, and he said at once: "Please tell me this, Adela—what was the purpose of your visit the other morning to Mrs. Churchley, the day I met you at her door?"

She stared—she cast about. "The purpose? What's the matter? Why do you ask?"

"They've put it off—they've put it off a month."

"Ah thank God!" said Adela.

"Why the devil do you thank God?" Godfrey asked with a strange impatience.

She gave a strained intense smile. "You know I think it all wrong."

He stood looking at her up and down. "What did you do

there? How did you interfere?"

"Who told you I interfered?" she returned with a deep flush.

"You said something—you did something. I knew you had done it when I saw you come out."

"What I did was my own business."

"Damn your own business!" cried the young man.

She had never in her life been so spoken to, and in advance, had she been given the choice, would have said that she'd rather die than be so handled by Godfrey. But her spirit was high, and for a moment she was as angry as if she had been cut with a whip. She escaped the blow but felt the insult. "And YOUR business then?" she asked. "I wondered what that was when I saw YOU."

He stood a moment longer scowling at her; then with the exclamation "You've made a pretty mess!" he turned away from her and sat down to his books.

They had put it off, as he said; her father was dry and stiff and official about it. "I suppose I had better let you know we've thought it best to postpone our marriage till the end of the summer—Mrs. Churchley has so many arrangements to make": he was not more expansive than that. She neither knew nor greatly cared whether she but vainly imagined or correctly observed him to watch her obliquely for some measure of her receipt of these words. She flattered herself that, thanks to Godfrey's forewarning, cruel as the form of it had been, she was able to repress any crude sign of elation.

She had a perfectly good conscience, for she could now judge what odious elements Mrs. Churchley, whom she had not seen since the morning in Prince's Gate, had already introduced into their dealings. She gathered without difficulty that her father hadn't concurred in the postponement, for he was more restless than before, more absent and distinctly irritable. There was naturally still the question of how much of this condition was to be attributed to his solicitude about Godfrey. That young man took occasion to say a horrible thing to his sister: "If I don't pass it will be your fault." These were dreadful days for the girl, and she asked herself how she could have borne them if the hovering spirit of her mother hadn't been at her side.

Fortunately she always felt it there, sustaining, commending, sanctifying. Suddenly her father announced to her that he wished her to go immediately, with her sisters, down to Brinton, where there was always part of a household and where for a few weeks they would manage well enough. The only explanation he gave of this desire was that he wanted them out of the way. Out of the way of what?" she queried, since there were to be for the time no preparations in Seymour Street. She was willing to take it for out of the way of his nerves.

She never needed urging however to go to Brinton, the dearest old house in the world, where the happiest days of her young life had been spent and the silent nearness of her mother always seemed greatest. She was happy again, with Beatrice and Muriel and Miss Flynn, with the air of summer and the haunted rooms and her mother's garden and the talking oaks and the nightingales. She wrote briefly to her father, giving him, as he had requested, an account of things; and he wrote back that since she was so contented—she didn't recognise having told him that—she had better not return to town at all.

The fag-end of the London season would be unimportant to her, and he was getting on very well. He mentioned that Godfrey had passed his tests, but, as she knew, there would be a tiresome wait before news of results. The poor chap was going abroad for a month with young Sherard—he had earned a little rest and a little fun. He went abroad without a word to Adela, but in his beautiful little hand he took a chaffing leave of Beatrice. The child showed her sister the letter, of which she was very proud and which contained no message for anyone else. This was the worst bitterness of the whole crisis for that somebody—its placing in so strange a light the creature in the world whom, after her mother, she had loved best.

Colonel Chart had said he would "run down" while his children were at Brinton, but they heard no more about it. He only wrote two or three times to Miss Flynn on matters in regard to which Adela was surprised he shouldn't have communicated with herself. Muriel accomplished an upright little letter to Mrs. Churchley—her eldest sister neither fostered nor discouraged the performance—to which Mrs. Churchley replied, after a fortnight, in a meagre and, as Adela thought, illiterate fashion, making no allusion to the approach of any closer tie.

Evidently the situation had changed; the question of the marriage was dropped, at any rate for the time. This idea gave our young woman a singular and almost intoxicating sense of power; she felt as if she were riding a great wave of confidence. She had decided and acted—the greatest could do no more than that. The grand thing was to see one's results, and what else was she doing? These results were in big rich conspicuous lives; the stage was large on which she moved her figures. Such a vision was exciting, and as they had the use of a couple of ponies at Brinton she worked off her excitement by a long gallop.

A day or two after this however came news of which the effect was to rekindle it. Godfrey had come back, the list had been published, he had passed first. These happy tidings proceeded from the young man himself; he announced them by a telegram to Beatrice, who had never in her life before received such a missive and was proportionately inflated. Adela reflected that she herself ought to have felt snubbed, but she was too happy. They were free again, they were themselves, the nightmare of the previous weeks was blown away, the unity and dignity of her father's life restored, and, to round off her sense of success, Godfrey had achieved his first step toward high distinction.

She wrote him the next day as frankly and affectionately as if there had been no estrangement between them, and besides telling him how she rejoiced in his triumph begged him in charity to let them know exactly how the case stood with regard to Mrs. Churchley.

Late in the summer afternoon she walked through the park to the village with her letter, posted it and came back. Suddenly, at one of the turns of the avenue, half-way to the house, she saw a young man hover there as if awaiting her—a young man who proved to be Godfrey on his pedestrian progress over from the station. He had seen her as he took his short cut, and if he had come down to Brinton it wasn't apparently to avoid her. There was nevertheless none of the joy of his triumph in his face as he came a very few steps to meet her; and although, stiffly enough, he let her kiss him and say "I'm so glad—I'm so glad!" she felt this tolerance as not quite the mere calm of the rising diplomatist. He turned toward the house with her and walked on a short distance while she uttered the hope that he had come to stay some days.

"Only till tomorrow morning. They're sending me straight to Madrid. I came down to say goodbye; there's a fellow bringing my bags."

"To Madrid? How awfully nice! And it's awfully nice of you to have come," she said as she passed her hand into his arm.

The movement made him stop, and, stopping, he turned on her in a flash a face of something more than, suspicion—of passionate reprobation. "What I really came for—you might as well know without more delay—is to ask you a question."

"A question?"—she echoed it with a beating heart.

They stood there under the old trees in the lingering light, and, young and fine and fair as they both were, formed a complete superficial harmony with the peaceful English scene. A near view, however, would have shown that Godfrey Chart hadn't taken so much trouble only to skim the surface. He looked deep into his sister's eyes. "What was it you said that morning to Mrs. Churchley?"

She fixed them on the ground a moment, but at last met his own again. "If she has told you, why do you ask?"

"She has told me nothing. I've seen for myself."

"What have you seen?"

"She has broken it off. Everything's over. Father's in the depths."

"In the depths?" the girl quavered.

"Did you think it would make him jolly?" he went on.

She had to choose what to say. "He'll get over it. He'll he glad."

"That remains to be seen. You interfered, you invented something, you got round her. I insist on knowing what you did."

Adela felt that if it was a question of obstinacy there was something within her she could count on; in spite of which, while she stood looking down again a moment, she said to herself "I could be dumb and dogged if I chose, but I scorn to be." She wasn't ashamed of what she had done, but she wanted to be clear. "Are you absolutely certain it's broken off?"

"He is, and she is; so that's as good."

"What reason has she given?"

"None at all—or half a dozen; it's the same thing. She has changed her mind—she mistook her feelings—she can't part with her independence. Moreover he has too many children."

"Did he tell you this?" the girl asked.

"Mrs. Churchley told me. She has gone abroad for a year."

"And she didn't tell you what I said to her?"

Godfrey showed an impatience. "Why should I take this trouble if she had?"

"You might have taken it to make me suffer," said Adela. "That appears to be what you want to do."

"No, I leave that to you—it's the good turn you've done me!" cried the young man with hot tears in his eyes.

She stared, aghast with the perception that there was some dreadful thing she didn't know; but he walked on, dropping the question angrily and turning his back to her as if he couldn't trust himself. She read his disgust in his averted, face, in the way he squared his shoulders and smote the ground with his stick, and she hurried after him and presently overtook him. She kept by him for a moment in silence; then she broke out: "What do you mean? What in the world have I done to you?"

"She would have helped me. She was all ready to help me," Godfrey portentously said.

"Helped you in what?" She wondered what he meant; if he had made debts that he was afraid to confess to his father and-of all horrible things—had been looking to Mrs. Churchley to pay. She turned red with the mere apprehension of this and, on the heels of her guess, exulted again at having perhaps averted such a shame.

"Can't you just see I'm in trouble? Where are your eyes, your senses, your sympathy, that you talk so much about? Haven't you seen these six months that I've a curst worry in my life?"

She seized his arm, made him stop, stood looking up at him like a frightened little girl. "What's the matter, Godfrey?—what IS the matter?"

"You've gone against me so—I could strangle you!" he growled. This image added nothing to her dread; her dread was that he had done some wrong, was stained with some guilt. She uttered it to him with clasped hands, begging him to tell her the worst; but, still more passionately, he cut her short with his own cry: "In God's name, satisfy me! What infernal thing did you do?"

"It wasn't infernal—it was right. I told her mamma had been wretched," said Adela.

"Wretched? You told her such a lie?"

"It was the only way, and she believed me."

"Wretched how?—wretched when?—wretched where?" the young man stammered.

"I told her papa had made her so, and that SHE ought to know it. I told her the question troubled me unspeakably, but that I had made up my mind it was my duty to initiate her." Adela paused, the light of bravado in her face, as if, though struck while the words came with the monstrosity of what she had done, she was incapable of abating a jot of it. "I notified her that he had faults and peculiarities that made mamma's life a long worry—a martyrdom that she hid wonderfully from the world, but that we saw and that I had often pitied. I told her what they were, these faults and peculiarities; I put the dots on the i's. I said it wasn't fair to let another person marry him without a warning. I warned her; I satisfied my conscience. She could do as she liked. My responsibility was over."

Godfrey gazed at her; he listened with parted lips, incredulous and appalled. "You invented such a tissue of falsities and calumnies, and you talk about your conscience? You stand there in your senses and proclaim your crime?"

"I'd have committed any crime that would have rescued us."

"You insult and blacken and ruin your own father?" Godfrey kept on.

"He'll never know it; she took a vow she wouldn't tell him."

"Ah I'll be damned if *I* won't tell him!" he rang out.

Adela felt sick at this, but she flamed up to resent the treachery, as it struck her, of such a menace. "I did right—I did right!" she vehemently declared "I went down on my knees to pray for guidance, and I saved mamma's memory from outrage. But if I hadn't, if I hadn't"—she faltered an instant—"I'm not worse than you, and I'm not so bad, for you've done something that you're ashamed to tell me."

He had taken out his watch; he looked at it with quick intensity, as if not hearing nor heeding her. Then, his calculating eyes raised, he fixed her long enough to exclaim with unsurpassable horror and contempt: "You raving maniac!" He turned away from her; he bounded down the avenue in the direction from which they had come, and, while she watched him, strode away, across the grass, toward the short cut to the station.

Chapter 4

His bags, by the time she got home, had been brought to the house, but Beatrice and Muriel, immediately informed of this, waited for their brother in vain. Their sister said nothing to them of her having seen him, and she accepted after a little, with a calmness that surprised herself, the idea that he had returned to town to denounce her. She believed this would make no difference now—she had done what she had done. She had somehow a stiff faith in Mrs. Churchley. Once that so considerable mass had received its impetus it wouldn't, it couldn't pull up. It represented a heavy-footed person, incapable of further agility. Adela recognised too how well it might have come over her that there were too many children.

Lastly the girl fortified herself with the reflexion, grotesque in the conditions and conducing to prove her sense of humour not high, that her father was after all not a man to be played with. It seemed to her at any rate that if she HAD baffled his unholy purpose she could bear anything—bear imprisonment and bread and water, bear lashes and torture, bear even his life-long reproach. What she could bear least was the wonder of the inconvenience she had inflicted on Godfrey. She had time to turn this over, very vainly, for a succession of days—days more numerous than she had expected, which passed without bringing her from London any summons to come up and take her punishment. She sounded the possible, she compared the degrees of the probable; feeling however that as a cloistered girl she was poorly equipped for speculation.

She tried to imagine the calamitous things young men might do, and could only feel that such things would naturally be connected either with borrowed money or with bad women. She became conscious that after all she knew almost nothing about either of those interests. The worst woman she knew was Mrs. Churchley herself. Meanwhile there was no reverberation from Seymour Street—only a sultry silence.

At Brinton she spent hours in her mother's garden, where she had grown up, where she considered that she was training for old age, since she meant not to depend on whist. She loved the place as, had she been a good Catholic, she would have loved the smell of her parish church; and indeed there was in her passion for flowers something of the respect of a religion. They seemed to her the only things in the world that really respected themselves, unless one made an exception for Nutkins, who had been in command all through her mother's time, with whom she had had a real friendship and who had been affected by their pure example. He was the person left in the world with whom on the whole she could speak most intimately of the dead.

They never had to name her together—they only said "she"; and Nutkins freely conceded that she had taught him everything he knew. When Beatrice and Muriel said "she" they referred to Mrs. Churchley. Adela had reason to believe she should never marry, and that some day she should have about a thousand a year. This made her see in the far future a little garden of her own, under a hill, full of rare and exquisite things, where she would spend most of her old age on her knees with an apron and stout gloves, with a pair of shears and a trowel, steeped in the comfort of being thought mad.

One morning ten days after her scene with Godfrey, on coming back into the house shortly before lunch, she was met by Miss Flynn with the notification that a lady in the drawing-room had been waiting for her for some minutes. "A lady" suggested immediately Mrs. Churchley. It came over Adela that the form in which her penalty was to descend would be a personal explanation with that misdirected woman. The lady had given no name, and Miss Flynn hadn't seen Mrs. Churchley; nevertheless the governess was certain Adela's surmise was wrong.

"Is she big and dreadful?" the girl asked.

Miss Flynn, who was circumspection itself, took her time. "She's dreadful, but she's not big." She added that she wasn't sure she ought to let Adela go in alone; but this young lady took herself throughout for a heroine, and it wasn't in a heroine to shrink from any encounter. Wasn't she every instant in transcendent contact with her mother? The visitor might have no connexion whatever with the drama of her father's frustrated marriage; but everything today for Adela was part of that.

Miss Flynn's description had prepared her for a considerable shock, but she wasn't agitated by her first glimpse of the person who awaited her. A youngish well-dressed woman stood there, and silence was between them while they looked at each other. Before either had spoken however Adela began to see what Miss Flynn had intended. In the light of the drawing-room window the lady was five-and-thirty years of age and had vivid yellow hair. She also had a blue cloth suit with brass buttons, a stick-up collar like a gentleman's, a necktie arranged in a sailor's knot, a golden pin in the shape of a little lawn-tennis racket, and pearl-grey gloves with big black stitchings. Adela's second impression was that she was an actress, and her third that no such person had ever before crossed that threshold.

"I'll tell you what I've come for," said the apparition. "I've come to ask you to intercede." She wasn't an actress; an actress would have had a nicer voice.

"To intercede?" Adela was too bewildered to ask her to sit down.

"With your father, you know. He doesn't know, but he'll have to." Her "have" sounded like "'ave." She explained, with many more such sounds, that she was Mrs. Godfrey, that they had been married seven mortal months. If Godfrey was going abroad she must go with him, and the only way she could go with him would be for his father to do something. He was afraid of his father—that was clear; he was afraid even to tell him. What she had come down for was to see some other member of the family face to face—"fice to fice," Mrs. Godfrey called it—and try if he couldn't be approached by another side. If no one else would act then she would just have to act herself. The Colonel would have to do something—that was the only way out of it.

What really happened Adela never quite understood; what seemed to be happening was that the room went round and round. Through the blur of perception accompanying this effect the sharp stabs of her visitor's revelation came to her like the words heard by a patient "going off" under ether. She afterwards denied passionately even to herself that she had done anything so abject as to faint; but there was a lapse in her consciousness on the score of Miss Flynn's intervention. This intervention had evidently been active, for when they talked the matter over, later in the day, with bated breath and infinite dissimulation for the school-room quarter, the governess had more lurid truths, and still more, to impart than to receive. She was at any rate under the impression that she had athletically contended, in the drawing-room, with the yellow hair—this after removing Adela from the scene and before inducing Mrs. Godfrey to withdraw.

Miss Flynn had never known a more thrilling day, for all the rest of it too was pervaded with agitations and conversations, precautions and alarms. It was given out to Beatrice and Muriel that their sister had been taken suddenly ill, and the governess ministered to her in her room. Indeed Adela had never found herself less at ease, for this time she had received a blow that she couldn't return. There was nothing to do but to take it, to endure the humiliation of her wound.

At first she declined to take it—having, as might appear, the much more attractive resource of regarding her visitant as a mere masquerading person, an impudent impostor. On the face of the matter moreover it wasn't fair to believe till one heard; and to hear in such a case was to hear Godfrey himself. Whatever she had tried to imagine about him she hadn't arrived at anything so belittling as an idiotic secret marriage with a dyed and painted hag. Adela repeated this last word as if it gave her comfort; and indeed where everything was so bad fifteen years of seniority made the case little worse. Miss Flynn was portentous, for Miss Flynn had had it out with the wretch. She had cross-questioned her and had not broken her down.

This was the most uplifted hour of Miss Flynn's life; for whereas she usually had to content herself with being humbly and gloomily in the right she could now be magnanimously and showily so. Her only perplexity was as to what she ought to do—write to Colonel Chart or go up to town to see him. She bloomed with alternatives—she resembled some dull garden-path which under a copious downpour has begun to flaunt with colour. Toward evening Adela was obliged to recognise that her brother's worry, of which he had spoken to her, had appeared bad enough to consist even of a low wife, and to remember that, so far from its being inconceivable a young man in his position should clandestinely take one, she had been present, years before, during her mother's lifetime, when Lady Molesley declared gaily, over a cup of tea, that this was precisely what she expected of her eldest son.

The next morning it was the worst possibilities that seemed clearest; the only thing left with a tatter of dusky comfort being the ambiguity of Godfrey's charge that her own action had "done" for him. That was a matter by itself, and she racked her brains for a connecting link between Mrs. Churchley and Mrs. Godfrey. At last she made up her mind that they were related by blood; very likely, though differing in fortune, they were cousins or even sisters. But even then what did the wretched boy mean?

Arrested by the unnatural fascination of opportunity, Miss Flynn received before lunch a telegram from Colonel Chartan order for dinner and a vehicle; he and Godfrey were to arrive at six o'clock. Adela had plenty of occupation for the interval, since she was pitying her father when she wasn't rejoicing that her mother had gone too soon to know. She flattered herself she made out the providential reason of that cruelty now. She found time however still to wonder for what purpose, given the situation, Godfrey was to he brought down. She wasn't unconscious indeed that she had little general knowledge of what usually was done with young men in that predicament.

One talked about the situation, but the situation was an abyss. She felt this still more when she found, on her father's arrival, that nothing apparently was to happen as she had taken for granted it would. There was an inviolable hush over the whole affair, but no tragedy, no publicity, nothing ugly. The tragedy had been in town—the faces of the two men spoke of it in spite of their other perfunctory aspects; and at present there was only a family dinner, with Beatrice and Muriel and the governesswith almost a company tone too, the result of the desire to avoid publicity.

Adela admired her father; she knew what he was feeling if Mrs. Godfrey had been at him, and yet she saw him positively gallant. He was mildly austere, or rather even—what was it?—august; just as, coldly equivocal, he never looked at his son, so that at moments he struck her as almost sick with sadness. Godfrey was equally inscrutable and therefore wholly different from what he had been as he stood before her in the park. If he was to start on his career (with such a wife!—wouldn't she utterly blight it?) he was already professional enough to know how to wear a mask.

Before they rose from table she felt herself wholly bewildered, so little were such large causes traceable in their effects. She had nerved herself for a great ordeal, but the air was as sweet as an anodyne. It was perfectly plain to her that her father was deadly sore—as pathetic as a person betrayed. He was broken, but he showed no resentment; there was a weight on his heart, but he had lightened it by dressing as immaculately as usual for dinner. She asked herself what immensity of a row there could have been in town to have left his anger so spent.

He went through everything, even to sitting with his son after dinner. When they came out together he invited Beatrice and Muriel to the billiard-room, and as Miss Flynn discreetly withdrew Adela was left alone with Godfrey, who was completely changed and not now in the least of a rage. He was broken too, but not so pathetic as his father. He was only very correct and apologetic he said to his sister: "I'm awfully sorry YOU were annoyed—it was something I never dreamed of."

She couldn't think immediately what he meant; then she grasped the reference to her extraordinary invader. She was uncertain, however, what tone to take; perhaps his father had arranged with him that they were to make the best of it. But she spoke her own despair in the way she murmured "Oh Godfrey, Godfrey, is it true?"

"I've been the most unutterable donkey—you can say what you like to me. You can't say anything worse than I've said to myself."

"My brother, my brother!"—his words made her wail it out. He hushed her with a movement and she asked: "What has father said?"

He looked very high over her head. "He'll give her six hundred a year."

"Ah the angel!"—it was too splendid.

"On condition"—Godfrey scarce blinked—"she never comes near me. She has solemnly promised, and she'll probably leave me alone to get the money. If she doesn't—in diplomacy—I'm lost." He had been turning his eyes vaguely about, this way and that, to avoid meeting hers; but after another instant he gave up the effort and she had the miserable confession of his glance. "I've been living in hell."

"My brother, my brother!" she yearningly repeated.

"I'm not an idiot; yet for her I've behaved like one. Don't ask me—you mustn't know. It was all done in a day, and since then fancy my condition; fancy my work in such a torment; fancy my coming through at all."

"Thank God you passed!" she cried. "You were wonderful!"

"I'd have shot myself if I hadn't been. I had an awful day yesterday with the governor; it was late at night before it was over. I leave England next week. He brought me down here for it to look well—so that the children shan't know."

"HE'S wonderful too!" Adela murmured.

"Wonderful too!" Godfrey echoed.

"Did SHE tell him?" the girl went on.

"She came straight to Seymour Street from here. She saw him alone first; then he called me in. THAT luxury lasted about an hour."

"Poor, poor father!" Adela moaned at this; on which her brother remained silent. Then after he had alluded to it as the scene he had lived in terror of all through his cramming, and she had sighed forth again her pity and admiration for such a mixture of anxieties and such a triumph of talent, she pursued: "Have you told him?"

"Told him what?"

"What you said you would—what *I* did."

Godfrey turned away as if at present he had very little interest in that inferior tribulation. "I was angry with you, but I cooled off. I held my tongue."

She clasped her hands. "You thought of mamma!"

"Oh don't speak of mamma!" he cried as in rueful tenderness.

It was indeed not a happy moment, and she murmured: "No;

if you HAD thought of her—!"

This made Godfrey face her again with a small flare in his eyes. "Oh THEN it didn't prevent. I thought that woman really good. I believed in her."

"Is she VERY bad?"

"I shall never mention her to you again," he returned with dignity.

"You may believe *I* won't speak of her! So father doesn't know?" the girl added.

"Doesn't know what?"

"That I said what I did to Mrs. Churchley."

He had a momentary pause. "I don't think so, but you must find out for yourself."

"I shall find out," said Adela. "But what had Mrs. Churchley to do with it?"

"With MY misery? I told her. I had to tell someone."

"Why didn't you tell me?"

He appeared—though but after an instant—to know exactly why. "Oh you take things so beastly hard—you make such rows." Adela covered her face with her hands and he went on: "What I wanted was comfort—not to be lashed up. I thought I should go mad. I wanted Mrs. Churchley to break it to father, to intercede for me and help him to meet it. She was awfully kind to me, she listened and she understood; she could fancy how it had happened. Without her I shouldn't have pulled through. She liked me, you know," he further explained, and as if it were quite worth mentioning—all the more that it was pleasant to him. "She said she'd do what she could for me. She was full of sympathy and resource. I really leaned on her. But when YOU cut in of course it spoiled everything. That's why I was so furious with you. She couldn't do anything then."

Adela dropped her hands, staring; she felt she had walked in darkness. "So that he had to meet it alone?"

"*Dame!*" said Godfrey, who had got up his French tremendously.

Muriel came to the door to say papa wished the two others

to join them, and the next day Godfrey returned to town. His father remained at Brinton, without an intermission, the rest of the summer and the whole of the autumn, and Adela had a chance to find out, as she had said, whether he knew she had interfered. But in spite of her chance she never found out. He knew Mrs. Churchley had thrown him over and he knew his daughter rejoiced in it, but he appeared not to have divined the relation between the two facts.

It was strange that one of the matters he was clearest about—Adela's secret triumph—should have been just the thing which from this time on justified less and less such a confidence. She was too sorry for him to be consistently glad. She watched his attempts to wind himself up on the subject of shorthorns and drainage, and she favoured to the utmost of her ability his intermittent disposition to make a figure in orchids. She wondered whether they mightn't have a few people at Brinton; but when she mentioned the idea he asked what in the world there would be to attract them.

It was a confoundedly stupid house, he remarked—with all respect to HER cleverness. Beatrice and Muriel were mystified; the prospect of going out immensely had faded so utterly away. They were apparently not to go out at all. Colonel Chart was aimless and bored; he paced up and down and went back to smoking, which was bad for him, and looked drearily out of windows as if on the bare chance that something might arrive. Did he expect Mrs. Churchley to arrive, did he expect her to relent on finding she couldn't live without him? It was Adela's belief that she gave no sign. But the girl thought it really remarkable of her not to have betrayed her ingenious young visitor. Adela's judgement of human nature was perhaps harsh, but she believed that most women, given the various facts, wouldn't have been so forbearing. This lady's conception of the point of honour placed her there in a finer and purer light than had at all originally promised to shine about her.

She meanwhile herself could well judge how heavy her father found the burden of Godfrey's folly and how he was incommoded at having to pay the horrible woman six hundred a year. Doubtless he was having dreadful letters from her; doubtless she threatened them all with hideous exposure. If the matter should be bruited Godfrey's prospects would collapse on the spot. He thought Madrid very charming and curious, but Mrs. Godfrey was in England, so that his father had to face the music. Adela took a dolorous comfort in her mother's being out of that—it would have killed her; but this didn't blind her to the fact that the comfort for her father would perhaps have been greater if he had had someone to talk to about his trouble.

He never dreamed of doing so to her, and she felt she couldn't ask him. In the family life he wanted utter silence about it. Early in the winter he went abroad for ten weeks, leaving her with her sisters in the country, where it was not to be denied that at this time existence had very little savour. She half expected her sister-in-law would again descend on her; but the fear wasn't justified, and the quietude of the awful creature seemed really to vibrate with the ring of gold-pieces. There were sure to be extras. Adela winced at the extras. Colonel Chart went to Paris and to Monte Carlo and then to Madrid to see his boy.

His daughter had the vision of his perhaps meeting Mrs. Churchley somewhere, since, if she had gone for a year, she would still be on the Continent. If he should meet her perhaps the affair would come on again: she caught herself musing over this. But he brought back no such appearance, and, seeing him after an interval, she was struck afresh with his jilted and wasted air. She didn't like it—she resented it. A little more and she would have said that that was no way to treat so faithful a man.

They all went up to town in March, and on one of the first days of April she saw Mrs. Churchley in the Park. She herself remained apparently invisible to that lady—she herself and Beatrice and Muriel, who sat with her in their mother's old bottle-green landau. Mrs. Churchley, perched higher than ever, rode by without a recognition; but this didn't prevent Adela's going to her before the month was over.

As on her great previous occasion she went in the morning,

and she again had the good fortune to be admitted. This time, however, her visit was shorter, and a week after making it—the week was a desolation—she addressed to her brother at Madrid a letter containing these words:

> I could endure it no longer—I confessed and retracted; I explained to her as well as I could the falsity of what I said to her ten months ago and the benighted purity of my motives for saying it. I besought her to regard it as unsaid, to forgive me, not to despise me too much, to take pity on poor PERFECT papa and come back to him. She was more good-natured than you might have expected—indeed she laughed extravagantly. She had never believed me—it was too absurd; she had only, at the time, disliked me. She found me utterly false—she was very frank with me about this—and she told papa she really thought me horrid. She said she could never live with such a girl, and as I would certainly never marry I must be sent away—in short she quite loathed me. Papa defended me, he refused to sacrifice me, and this led practically to their rupture. Papa gave her up, as it were, for ME. Fancy the angel, and fancy what I must try to be to him for the rest of his life! Mrs. Churchley can never come back—she's going to marry Lord Dovedale.

The Middle Years

The April day was soft and bright, and poor Dencombe, happy in the conceit of reasserted strength, stood in the garden of the hotel, comparing, with a deliberation in which however there was still something of languor, the attractions of easy strolls. He liked the feeling of the south so far as you could have it in the north, he liked the sandy cliffs and the clustered pines, he liked even the colourless sea. "Bournemouth as a health-resort" had sounded like a mere advertisement, but he was thankful now for the commonest conveniences. The sociable country postman, passing through the garden, had just given him a small parcel which he took out with him, leaving the hotel to the right and creeping to a bench he had already haunted, a safe recess in the cliff. It looked to the south, to the tinted walls of the Island, and was protected behind by the sloping shoulder of the down.

He was tired enough when he reached it, and for a moment was disappointed; he was better of course, but better, after all, than what? He should never again, as at one or two great moments of the past, be better than himself. The infinite of life was gone, and what remained of the dose a small glass scored like a thermometer by the apothecary. He sat and stared at the sea, which appeared all surface and twinkle, far shallower than the spirit of man. It was the abyss of human illusion that was the real, the tideless deep.

He held his packet, which had come by book-post, unopened on his knee, liking, in the lapse of so many joys—his illness had made him feel his age—to know it was there, but taking for granted there could be no complete renewal of the pleasure, dear to young experience, of seeing one's self "just out." Dencombe, who had a reputation, had come out too often and knew too well in advance how he should look.

His postponement associated itself vaguely, after a little, with a group of three persons, two ladies and a young man, whom, beneath him, straggling and seemingly silent, he could see move slowly together along the sands. The gentleman had his head bent over a book and was occasionally brought to a stop by the charm of this volume, which, as Dencombe could perceive even at a distance, had a cover alluringly red. Then his companions, going a little further, waited for him to come up, poking their parasols into the beach, looking around them at the sea and sky and clearly sensible of the beauty of the day. To these things the young man with the book was still more clearly indifferent; lingering, credulous, absorbed, he was an object of envy to an observer from whose connexion with literature all such artlessness had faded.

One of the ladies was large and mature; the other had the spareness of comparative youth and of a social situation possibly inferior. The large lady carried back Dencombe's imagination to the age of crinoline; she wore a hat of the shape of a mushroom, decorated with a blue veil, and had the air, in her aggressive amplitude, of clinging to a vanished fashion or even a lost cause. Presently her companion produced from under the folds of a mantle a limp portable chair which she stiffened out and of which the large lady took possession. This act, and something in the movement of either party, at once characterised the performers—they performed for Dencombe's recreation—as opulent matron and humble dependent.

Where moreover was the virtue of an approved novelist if one couldn't establish a relation between such figures? the clever theory for instance that the young man was the son of the opulent matron and that the humble dependent, the daughter of a clergyman or an officer, nourished a secret passion for him. Was that not visible from the way she stole behind her protectress to look back at him?—back to where he had let himself come to a full stop when his mother sat down to rest. His book was a novel, it had the catchpenny binding; so that while the romance of life stood neglected at his side he lost himself in that of the circulating library. He moved mechanically to where the sand was softer and ended by plumping down in it to finish his chapter at his ease. The humble dependent, discouraged by his remoteness, wandered with a martyred droop of the head in another direction, and the exorbitant lady, watching the waves, offered a confused resemblance to a flying-machine that had broken down.

When his drama began to fail Dencombe remembered that he had after all another pastime. Though such promptitude on the part of the publisher was rare he was already able to draw from its wrapper his "latest," perhaps his last. The cover of *The Middle Years* was duly meretricious, the smell of the fresh pages the very odour of sanctity; but for the moment he went no further—he had become conscious of a strange alienation. He had forgotten what his book was about. Had the assault of his old ailment, which he had so fallaciously come to Bournemouth to ward off, interposed utter blankness as to what had preceded it? He had finished the revision of proof before quitting London, but his subsequent fortnight in bed had passed the sponge over colour.

He couldn't have chanted to himself a single sentence, couldn't have turned with curiosity or confidence to any particular page. His subject had already gone from him, leaving scarce a superstition behind. He uttered a low moan as he breathed the chill of this dark void, so desperately it seemed to represent the completion of a sinister process. The tears filled his mild eyes; something precious had passed away. This was the pang that had been sharpest during the last few years—the sense of ebbing time, of shrinking opportunity; and now he felt not so much that his last chance was going as that it was gone indeed.

He had done all he should ever do, and yet hadn't done what he wanted. This was the laceration—that practically his career was over: it was as violent as a grip at his throat. He rose from his seat nervously—a creature hunted by a dread; then he fell back in his weakness and nervously opened his book. It was a single volume; he preferred single volumes and aimed at a rare compression. He began to read and, little by little, in this occupation, was pacified and reassured. Everything came back to him, but came back with a wonder, came back above all with a high and magnificent beauty. He read his own prose, he turned his own leaves, and had as he sat there with the spring sunshine on the page an emotion peculiar and intense. His career was over, no doubt, but it was over, when all was said, with THAT.

He had forgotten during his illness the work of the previous year; but what he had chiefly forgotten was that it was extraordinarily good. He dived once more into his story and was drawn down, as by a siren's hand, to where, in the dim underworld of fiction, the great glazed tank of art, strange silent subjects float. He recognised his motive and surrendered to his talent. Never probably had that talent, such as it was, been so fine. His difficulties were still there, but what was also there, to his perception, though probably, alas! to nobody's else, was the art that in most cases had surmounted them.

In his surprised enjoyment of this ability he had a glimpse of a possible reprieve. Surely its force wasn't spent—there was life and service in it yet. It hadn't come to him easily, it had been backward and roundabout. It was the child of time, the nursling of delay; he had struggled and suffered for it, making sacrifices not to be counted, and now that it was really mature was it to cease to yield, to confess itself brutally beaten? There was an infinite charm for Dencombe in feeling as he had never felt before that diligence *vincit omnia*. The result produced in his little book was somehow a result beyond his conscious intention: it was as if he had planted his genius, had trusted his method, and they had grown up and flowered with this sweetness.

If the achievement had been real, however, the process had been painful enough. What he saw so intensely today, what he felt as a nail driven in, was that only now, at the very last, had he come into possession. His development had been abnormally slow, almost grotesquely gradual. He had been hindered and retarded by experience, he had for long periods only groped his way. It had taken too much of his life to produce too little of his art. The art had come, but it had come after everything else. At such a rate a first existence was too short—long enough only to collect material; so that to fructify, to use the material, one should have a second age, an extension. This extension was what poor Dencombe sighed for. As he turned the last leaves of his volume he murmured "Ah for another go, ah for a better chance!"

The three persons drawing his attention to the sands had vanished and then reappeared; they had now wandered up a path, an artificial and easy ascent, which led to the top of the cliff. Dencombe's bench was halfway down, on a sheltered ledge, and the large lady, a massive heterogeneous person with bold black eyes and kind red cheeks, now took a few moments to rest. She wore dirty gauntlets and immense diamond ear-rings; at first she looked vulgar, but she contradicted this announcement in an agreeable off-hand tone. While her companions stood waiting for her she spread her skirts on the end of Dencombe's seat.

The young man had gold spectacles, through which, with his finger still in his red-covered book, he glanced at the volume, bound in the same shade of the same colour, lying on the lap of the original occupant of the bench. After an instant Dencombe felt him struck with a resemblance; he had recognised the gilt stamp on the crimson cloth, was reading *The Middle Years* and now noted that somebody else had kept pace with him. The stranger was startled, possibly even a little ruffled, to find himself not the only person favoured with an early copy.

The eyes of the two proprietors met a moment, and Dencombe borrowed amusement from the expression of those of his competitor, those, it might even be inferred, of his admirer. They confessed to some resentment—they seemed to say: "Hang it, has he got it ALREADY? Of course he's a brute of a reviewer!" Dencombe shuffled his copy out of sight while the opulent matron, rising from her repose, broke out: "I feel already the good of this air!"

"I can't say I do," said the angular lady. "I find myself quite let down."

"I find myself horribly hungry. At what time did you order luncheon?" her protectress pursued.

The young person put the question by. "Doctor Hugh always orders it."

"I ordered nothing today—I'm going to make you diet," said their comrade.

"Then I shall go home and sleep. *Qui dort dine!*"

"Can I trust you to Miss Vernham?" asked Doctor Hugh of his elder companion.

"Don't I trust YOU?" she archly enquired.

"Not too much!" Miss Vernham, with her eyes on the ground, permitted herself to declare. "You must come with us at least to the house," she went on while the personage on whom they appeared to be in attendance began to mount higher. She had got a little out of ear-shot; nevertheless Miss Vernham became, so far as Dencombe was concerned, less distinctly audible to murmur to the young man: "I don't think you realise all you owe the Countess!"

Absently, a moment, Doctor Hugh caused his gold-rimmed spectacles to shine at her. "Is that the way I strike you? I see—I see!"

"She's awfully good to us," continued Miss Vernham, compelled by the lapse of the other's motion to stand there in spite of his discussion of private matters. Of what use would it have been that Dencombe should be sensitive to shades hadn't he detected in that arrest a strange influence from the quiet old convalescent in the great tweed cape? Miss Vernham appeared suddenly to become aware of some such connexion, for she added in a moment: "If you want to sun yourself here you can come back after you've seen us home."

Doctor Hugh, at this, hesitated, and Dencombe, in spite of a desire to pass for unconscious, risked a covert glance at him.

What his eyes met this time, as happened, was, on the part of the young lady, a queer stare, naturally vitreous, which made her remind him of some figure—he couldn't name it—in a play or a novel, some sinister governess or tragic old maid. She seemed to scan him, to challenge him, to say out of general spite: "What have you got to do with us?"

At the same instant the rich humour of the Countess reached them from above: "Come, come, my little lambs; you should follow your old *bergere*!" Miss Vernham turned away for it, pursuing the ascent, and Doctor Hugh, after another mute appeal to Dencombe and a minute's evident demur, deposited his book on the bench as if to keep his place, or even as a gage of earnest return, and bounded without difficulty up the rougher part of the cliff.

Equally innocent and infinite are the pleasures of observation and the resources engendered by the trick of analysing life. It amused poor Dencombe, as he dawdled in his tepid air-bath, to believe himself awaiting a revelation of something at the back of a fine young mind. He looked hard at the book on the end of the bench, but wouldn't have touched it for the world. It served his purpose to have a theory that shouldn't be exposed to refutation. He already felt better of his melancholy; he had, according to his old formula, put his head at the window.

A passing Countess could draw off the fancy when, like the elder of the ladies who had just retreated, she was as obvious as the giantess of a caravan. It was indeed general views that were terrible; short ones, contrary to an opinion sometimes expressed, were the refuge, were the remedy. Doctor Hugh couldn't possibly be anything but a reviewer who had understandings for early copies with publishers or with newspapers. He reappeared in a quarter of an hour with visible relief at finding Dencombe on the spot and the gleam of white teeth in an embarrassed but generous smile.

He was perceptibly disappointed at the eclipse of the other copy of the book; it made a pretext the less for speaking to the quiet gentleman. But he spoke notwithstanding; he held up his own copy and broke out pleadingly: "DO say, if you have occasion to speak of it, that it's the best thing he has done yet!"

Dencombe responded with a laugh: "Done yet" was so amusing to him, made such a grand avenue of the future. Better still, the young man took HIM for a reviewer. He pulled out *The Middle Years* from under his cape, but instinctively concealed any telltale look of fatherhood. This was partly because a person was always a fool for insisting to others on his work. "Is that what you're going to say yourself?" he put to his visitor.

"I'm not quite sure I shall write anything. I don't, as a regular thing—I enjoy in peace. But it's awfully fine."

Dencombe just debated. If the young man had begun to abuse him he would have confessed on the spot to his identity, but there was no harm in drawing out any impulse to praise. He drew it out with such success that in a few moments his new acquaintance, seated by his side, was confessing candidly that the works of the author of the volumes before them were the only ones he could read a second time. He had come the day before from London, where a friend of his, a journalist, had lent him his copy of the last, the copy sent to the office of the journal and already the subject of a "notice" which, as was pretended there—but one had to allow for "swagger"—it had taken a full quarter of an hour to prepare.

He intimated that he was ashamed for his friend, and in the case of a work demanding and repaying study, of such inferior manners; and, with his fresh appreciation and his so irregular wish to express it, he speedily became for poor Dencombe a remarkable, a delightful apparition. Chance had brought the weary man of letters face to face with the greatest admirer in the new generation of whom it was supposable he might boast. The admirer in truth was mystifying, so rare a case was it to find a bristling young doctor—he looked like a German physiologist—enamoured of literary form.

It was an accident, but happier than most accidents, so that Dencombe, exhilarated as well as confounded, spent half an hour in making his visitor talk while he kept himself quiet. He explained his premature possession of *The Middle Years* by an allusion to the friendship of the publisher, who, knowing he was at Bournemouth for his health, had paid him this graceful attention. He allowed he had been ill, for Doctor Hugh would infallibly have guessed it; he even went so far as to wonder if he mightn't look for some hygienic "tip" from a personage combining so bright an enthusiasm with a presumable knowledge of the remedies now in vogue.

It would shake his faith a little perhaps to have to take a doctor seriously who could take HIM so seriously, but he enjoyed this gushing modern youth and felt with an acute pang that there would still be work to do in a world in which such odd combinations were presented. It wasn't true, what he had tried for renunciation's sake to believe, that all the combinations were exhausted. They weren't by any means—they were infinite: the exhaustion was in the miserable artist.

Doctor Hugh, an ardent physiologist, was saturated with the spirit of the age—in other words he had just taken his degree; but he was independent and various, he talked like a man who would have preferred to love literature best. He would fain have made fine phrases, but nature had denied him the trick. Some of the finest in *The Middle Years* had struck him inordinately, and he took the liberty of reading them to Dencombe in support of his plea. He grew vivid, in the balmy air, to his companion, for whose deep refreshment he seemed to have been sent; and was particularly ingenuous in describing how recently he had become acquainted, and how instantly infatuated, with the only man who had put flesh between the ribs of an art that was starving on superstitions.

He hadn't yet written to him—he was deterred by a strain of respect. Dencombe at this moment rejoiced more inwardly than ever that he had never answered the photographers. His visitor's attitude promised him a luxury of intercourse, though he was sure a due freedom for Doctor Hugh would depend not a little on the Countess. He learned without delay what type of Countess was involved, mastering as well the nature of the tie that united the curious trio. The large lady, an Englishwoman by birth and the daughter of a celebrated baritone, whose taste *minus* his talent she had inherited, was the widow of a French nobleman and mistress of all that remained of the handsome fortune, the fruit of her father's earnings, that had constituted her dower. Miss Vernham, an odd creature but an accomplished pianist, was attached to her person at a salary.

The Countess was generous, independent, eccentric; she travelled with her minstrel and her medical man. Ignorant and passionate she had nevertheless moments in which she was almost irresistible. Dencombe saw her sit for her portrait in Doctor Hugh's free sketch, and felt the picture of his young friend's relation to her frame itself in his mind. This young friend, for a representative of the new psychology, was himself easily hypnotised, and if he became abnormally communicative it was only a sign of his real subjection. Dencombe did accordingly what he wanted with him, even without being known as Dencombe.

Taken ill on a journey in Switzerland the Countess had picked him up at an hotel, and the accident of his happening to please her had made her offer him, with her imperious liberality, terms that couldn't fail to dazzle a practitioner without patients and whose resources had been drained dry by his studies. It wasn't the way he would have proposed to spend his time, but it was time that would pass quickly, and meanwhile she was wonderfully kind. She exacted perpetual attention, but it was impossible not to like her.

He gave details about his queer patient, a "type" if there ever was one, who had in connexion with her flushed obesity, and in addition to the morbid strain of a violent and aimless will, a grave organic disorder; but he came back to his loved novelist, whom he was so good as to pronounce more essentially a poet than many of those who went in for verse, with a zeal excited, as all his indiscretion had been excited, by the happy chance of Dencombe's sympathy and the coincidence of their occupation.

Dencombe had confessed to a slight personal acquaintance with the author of *The Middle Years*, but had not felt himself as ready as he could have wished when his companion, who had never yet encountered a being so privileged, began to be eager for particulars. He even divined in Doctor Hugh's eye at that moment a glimmer of suspicion. But the young man was too inflamed to be shrewd and repeatedly caught up the book to exclaim: "Did you notice this?" or "Weren't you immensely struck with that?" "There's a beautiful passage toward the end," he broke out; and again he laid his hand on the volume.

As he turned the pages he came upon something else, while Dencombe saw him suddenly change colour. He had taken up as it lay on the bench Dencombe's copy instead of his own, and his neighbour at once guessed the reason of his start. Doctor Hugh looked grave an instant; then he said: "I see you've been altering the text!"

Dencombe was a passionate corrector, a fingerer of style; the last thing he ever arrived at was a form final for himself. His ideal would have been to publish secretly, and then, on the published text, treat himself to the terrified revise, sacrificing always a first edition and beginning for posterity and even for the collectors, poor dears, with a second. This morning, in *The Middle Years*, his pencil had pricked a dozen lights. He was amused at the effect of the young man's reproach; for an instant it made him change colour. He stammered at any rate ambiguously, then through a blur of ebbing consciousness saw Doctor Hugh's mystified eyes. He only had time to feel he was about to be ill again—that emotion, excitement, fatigue, the heat of the sun, the solicitation of the air, had combined to play him a trick, before, stretching out a hand to his visitor with a plaintive cry, he lost his senses altogether.

Later he knew he had fainted and that Doctor Hugh had got him home in a bath-chair, the conductor of which, prowling within hail for custom, had happened to remember seeing him in the garden of the hotel. He had recovered his perception on the way, and had, in bed that afternoon, a vague recollection of Doctor Hugh's young face, as they went together, bent over him in a comforting laugh and expressive of something more than a suspicion of his identity. That identity was ineffaceable now, and all the more that he was rueful and sore. He had been rash, been stupid, had gone out too soon, stayed out too long. He oughtn't to have exposed himself to strangers, he ought to have taken his servant. He felt as if he had fallen into a hole too deep to descry any little patch of heaven. He was confused about the time that had passed—he pieced the fragments together.

He had seen his doctor, the real one, the one who had treated him from the first and who had again been very kind. His servant was in and out on tiptoe, looking very wise after the fact. He said more than once something about the sharp young gentleman. The rest was vagueness in so far as it wasn't despair. The vagueness, however, justified itself by dreams, dozing anxieties from which he finally emerged to the consciousness of a dark room and a shaded candle.

"You'll be all right again—I know all about you now," said a voice near him that he felt to be young. Then his meeting with Doctor Hugh came back. He was too discouraged to joke about it yet, but made out after a little that the interest was intense for his visitor. "Of course I can't attend you professionally—you've got your own man, with whom I've talked and who's excellent," Doctor Hugh went on. "But you must let me come to see you as a good friend. I've just looked in before going to bed. You're doing beautifully, but it's a good job I was with you on the cliff. I shall come in early tomorrow. I want to do something for you. I want to do everything. You've done a tremendous lot for me." The young man held his hand, hanging over him, and poor Dencombe, weakly aware of this living pressure, simply lay there and accepted his devotion. He couldn't do anything less—he needed help too much.

The idea of the help he needed was very present to him that night, which he spent in a lucid stillness, an intensity of thought that constituted a reaction from his hours of stupor. He was lost, he was lost—he was lost if he couldn't be saved. He wasn't afraid of suffering, of death, wasn't even in love with life; but he had had a deep demonstration of desire. It came over him in the long quiet hours that only with *The Middle Years* had he taken his flight; only on that day, visited by soundless processions, had he recognised his kingdom. He had had a revelation of his range. What he dreaded was the idea that his reputation should stand on the unfinished. It wasn't with his past but with his future that it should properly be concerned.

Illness and age rose before him like spectres with pitiless eyes: how was he to bribe such fates to give him the second chance? He had had the one chance that all men have—he had had the chance of life. He went to sleep again very late, and when he awoke Doctor Hugh was sitting at hand. There was already by this time something beautifully familiar in him.

"Don't think I've turned out your physician," he said; "I'm acting with his consent. He has been here and seen you. Somehow he seems to trust me. I told him how we happened to come together yesterday, and he recognises that I've a peculiar right."

Dencombe felt his own face pressing. "How have you squared the Countess?"

The young man blushed a little, but turned it off. "Oh never mind the Countess!"

"You told me she was very exacting."

Doctor Hugh had a wait. "So she is."

"And Miss Vernham's an *intrigante*."

"How do you know that?"

"I know everything. One HAS to, to write decently!"

"I think she's mad," said limpid Doctor Hugh.

"Well, don't quarrel with the Countess—she's a present help to you."

"I don't quarrel," Doctor Hugh returned. "But I don't get on with silly women." Presently he added: "You seem very much alone."

"That often happens at my age. I've outlived, I've lost by the way."

Doctor Hugh faltered; then surmounting a soft scruple: "Whom have you lost?"

"Every one."

"Ah no," the young man breathed, laying a hand on his arm.

"I once had a wife—I once had a son. My wife died when my child was born, and my boy, at school, was carried off by typhoid."

"I wish I'd been there!" cried Doctor Hugh.

"Well—if you're here!" Dencombe answered with a smile that, in spite of dimness, showed how he valued being sure of his companions's whereabouts.

"You talk strangely of your age. You're not old."

"Hypocrite—so early!"

"I speak physiologically."

"That's the way I've been speaking for the last five years, and it's exactly what I've been saying to myself. It isn't till we ARE old that we begin to tell ourselves we're not."

"Yet I know I myself am young," Doctor Hugh returned.

"Not so well as I!" laughed his patient, whose visitor indeed would have established the truth in question by the honesty with which he changed the point of view, remarking that it must be one of the charms of age—at any rate in the case of high distinction—to feel that one has laboured and achieved. Doctor Hugh employed the common phrase about earning one's rest, and it made poor Dencombe for an instant almost angry. He recovered himself, however, to explain, lucidly enough, that if, ungraciously, he knew nothing of such a balm, it was doubtless because he had wasted inestimable years. He had followed literature from the first, but he had taken a lifetime to get abreast of her. Only today at last had he begun to SEE, so that all he had hitherto shown was a movement without a direction. He had ripened too late and was so clumsily constituted that he had had to teach himself by mistakes.

"I prefer your flowers then to other people's fruit, and your mistakes to other people's successes," said gallant Doctor Hugh. "It's for your mistakes I admire you."

"You're happy—you don't know," Dencombe answered.

Looking at his watch the young man had got up; he named the hour of the afternoon at which he would return. Dencombe warned him against committing himself too deeply, and expressed again all his dread of making him neglect the Countess—perhaps incur her displeasure.

"I want to be like you—I want to learn by mistakes!" Doctor Hugh laughed.

"Take care you don't make too grave a one! But do come back," Dencombe added with the glimmer of a new idea.

"You should have had more vanity!" His friend spoke as if he knew the exact amount required to make a man of letters normal.

"No, no—I only should have had more time. I want another go."

"Another go?"

"I want an extension."

"An extension?" Again Doctor Hugh repeated Dencombe's words, with which he seemed to have been struck.

"Don't you know?—I want to what they call 'live.'"

The young man, for goodbye, had taken his hand, which closed with a certain force. They looked at each other hard. "You WILL live," said Doctor Hugh.

"Don't be superficial. It's too serious!"

"You SHALL live!" Dencombe's visitor declared, turning pale.

"Ah that's better!" And as he retired the invalid, with a troubled laugh, sank gratefully back.

All that day and all the following night he wondered if it mightn't be arranged. His doctor came again, his servant was attentive, but it was to his confident young friend that he felt himself mentally appeal. His collapse on the cliff was plausibly explained and his liberation, on a better basis, promised for the morrow; meanwhile, however, the intensity of his meditations kept him tranquil and made him indifferent. The idea that occupied him was none the less absorbing because it was a morbid fancy. Here was a clever son of the age, ingenious and ardent, who happened to have set him up for connoisseurs to worship.

This servant of his altar had all the new learning in science and all the old reverence in faith; wouldn't he therefore put his knowledge at the disposal of his sympathy, his craft at the disposal of his love? Couldn't he be trusted to invent a remedy for a poor artist to whose art he had paid a tribute? If he couldn't the alternative was hard: Dencombe would have to surrender to silence unvindicated and undivined. The rest of the day and all the next he toyed in secret with this sweet futility. Who would work the miracle for him but the young man who could combine such lucidity with such passion?

He thought of the fairy-tales of science and charmed himself into forgetting that he looked for a magic that was not of this world. Doctor Hugh was an apparition, and that placed him above the law. He came and went while his patient, who now sat up, followed him with supplicating eyes. The interest of knowing the great author had made the young man begin *The Middle Years* afresh and would help him to find a richer sense between its covers.

Dencombe had told him what he "tried for"; with all his intelligence, on a first perusal, Doctor Hugh had failed to guess it. The baffled celebrity wondered then who in the world WOULD guess it: he was amused once more at the diffused massive weight that could be thrown into the missing of an intention. Yet he wouldn't rail at the general mind today—consoling as that ever had been: the revelation of his own slowness had seemed to make all stupidity sacred.

Doctor Hugh, after a little, was visibly worried, confessing, on enquiry, to a source of embarrassment at home. "Stick to the Countess—don't mind me," Dencombe said repeatedly; for his companion was frank enough about the large lady's attitude. She was so jealous that she had fallen ill—she resented such a breach of allegiance. She paid so much for his fidelity that she must have it all: she refused him the right to other sympathies, charged him with scheming to make her die alone, for it was needless to point out how little Miss Vernham was a resource in trouble.

When Doctor Hugh mentioned that the Countess would already have left Bournemouth if he hadn't kept her in bed, poor Dencombe held his arm tighter and said with decision: "Take her straight away." They had gone out together, walking back to the sheltered nook in which, the other day, they had met. The young man, who had given his companion a personal support, declared with emphasis that his conscience was clear—he could ride two horses at once. Didn't he dream for his future of a time when he should have to ride five hundred? Longing equally for virtue, Dencombe replied that in that golden age no patient would pretend to have contracted with him for his whole attention.

On the part of the Countess wasn't such an avidity lawful? Doctor Hugh denied it, said there was no contract, but only a free understanding, and that a sordid servitude was impossible to a generous spirit; he liked moreover to talk about art, and that was the subject on which, this time, as they sat together on the sunny bench, he tried most to engage the author of *The Middle Years*. Dencombe, soaring again a little on the weak wings of convalescence and still haunted by that happy notion of an organised rescue, found another strain of eloquence to plead the cause of a certain splendid "last manner," the very citadel, as it would prove, of his reputation, the stronghold into which his real treasure would be gathered. While his listener gave up the morning and the great still sea ostensibly waited he had a wondrous explanatory hour.

Even for himself he was inspired as he told what his treasure would consist of; the precious metals he would dig from the mine, the jewels rare, strings of pearls, he would hang between the columns of his temple. He was wondrous for himself, so thick his convictions crowded, but still more wondrous for Doctor Hugh, who assured him none the less that the very pages he had just published were already encrusted with gems. This admirer, however, panted for the combinations to come and, before the face of the beautiful day, renewed to Dencombe his guarantee that his profession would hold itself responsible for such a life.

Then he suddenly clapped his hand upon his watch-pocket and asked leave to absent himself for half an hour. Dencombe waited there for his return, but was at last recalled to the actual by the fall of a shadow across the ground. The shadow darkened into that of Miss Vernham, the young lady in attendance on the Countess; whom Dencombe, recognising her, perceived so clearly to have come to speak to him that he rose from his bench to acknowledge the civility. Miss Vernham indeed proved not particularly civil; she looked strangely agitated, and her type was now unmistakeable.

"Excuse me if I do ask," she said, "whether it's too much to hope that you may be induced to leave Doctor Hugh alone." Then before our poor friend, greatly disconcerted, could protest: "You ought to be informed that you stand in his light—that you may do him a terrible injury."

"Do you mean by causing the Countess to dispense with his services?"

"By causing her to disinherit him." Dencombe stared at this, and Miss Vernham pursued, in the gratification of seeing she could produce an impression: "It has depended on himself to come into something very handsome. He has had a grand prospect, but I think you've succeeded in spoiling it."

"Not intentionally, I assure you. Is there no hope the accident may be repaired?" Dencombe asked.

"She was ready to do anything for him. She takes great fancies, she lets herself go—it's her way. She has no relations, she's free to dispose of her money, and she's very ill," said Miss Vernham for a climax.

"I'm very sorry to hear it," Dencombe stammered.

"Wouldn't it be possible for you to leave Bournemouth? That's what I've come to see about."

He sank to his bench. "I'm very ill myself, but I'll try!"

Miss Vernham still stood there with her colourless eyes and the brutality of her good conscience. "Before it's too late, please!" she said; and with this she turned her back, in order, quickly, as if it had been a business to which she could spare but a precious moment, to pass out of his sight.

Oh yes, after this Dencombe was certainly very ill. Miss Vernham had upset him with her rough fierce news; it was the sharpest shock to him to discover what was at stake for a penniless young man of fine parts. He sat trembling on his bench, staring at the waste of waters, feeling sick with the directness of the blow. He was indeed too weak, too unsteady, too alarmed; but he would make the effort to get away, for he couldn't accept the guilt of interference and his honour was really involved. He would hobble home, at any rate, and then think what was to be done.

He made his way back to the hotel and, as he went, had a characteristic vision of Miss Vernham's great motive. The Countess hated women of course—Dencombe was lucid about that; so the hungry pianist had no personal hopes and could only console herself with the bold conception of helping Doctor Hugh in order to marry him after he should get his money or else induce him to recognise her claim for compensation and buy her off. If she had befriended him at a fruitful crisis he would really, as a man of delicacy—and she knew what to think of that point—have to reckon with her.

At the hotel Dencombe's servant insisted on his going back to bed. The invalid had talked about catching a train and had begun with orders to pack; after which his racked nerves had yielded to a sense of sickness. He consented to see his physician, who immediately was sent for, but he wished it to be understood that his door was irrevocably closed to Doctor Hugh. He had his plan, which was so fine that he rejoiced in it after getting back to bed. Doctor Hugh, suddenly finding himself snubbed without mercy, would, in natural disgust and to the joy of Miss Vernham, renew his allegiance to the Countess.

When his physician arrived Dencombe learned that he was feverish and that this was very wrong: he was to cultivate calmness and try, if possible, not to think. For the rest of the day he wooed stupidity; but there was an ache that kept him sentient, the probable sacrifice of his "extension," the limit of his course.

His medical adviser was anything but pleased; his successive relapses were ominous. He charged this personage to put out a strong hand and take Doctor Hugh off his mind—it would contribute so much to his being quiet. The agitating name, in his room, was not mentioned again, but his security was a smothered fear, and it was not confirmed by the receipt, at ten o'clock that evening, of a telegram which his servant opened and read him and to which, with an address in London, the signature of Miss Vernham was attached.

"Beseech you to use all influence to make our friend join us here in the morning. Countess much the worse for dreadful journey, but everything may still be saved."

The two ladies had gathered themselves up and had been capable in the afternoon of a spiteful revolution. They had started for the capital, and if the elder one, as Miss Vernham had announced, was very ill, she had wished to make it clear that she was proportionately reckless. Poor Dencombe, who was not reckless and who only desired that everything should indeed be "saved," sent this missive straight off to the young man's lodging and had on the morrow the pleasure of knowing that he had quitted Bournemouth by an early train.

Two days later he pressed in with a copy of a literary journal in his hand. He had returned because he was anxious and for the pleasure of flourishing the great review of *The Middle Years*. Here at least was something adequate—it rose to the occasion; it was an acclamation, a reparation, a critical attempt to place the author in the niche he had fairly won. Dencombe accepted and submitted; he made neither objection nor enquiry, for old complications had returned and he had had two dismal days. He was convinced not only that he should never again leave his bed, so that his young friend might pardonably remain, but that the demand he should make on the patience of beholders would be of the most moderate.

Doctor Hugh had been to town, and he tried to find in his eyes some confession that the Countess was pacified and his legacy clinched; but all he could see there was the light of his juvenile joy in two or three of the phrases of the newspaper. Dencombe couldn't read them, but when his visitor had insisted on repeating them more than once he was able to shake an unintoxicated head. "Ah no—but they would have been true of what I COULD have done!"

"What people 'could have done' is mainly what they've in fact done," Doctor Hugh contended.

"Mainly, yes; but I've been an idiot!" Dencombe said.

Doctor Hugh did remain; the end was coming fast. Two days later his patient observed to him, by way of the feeblest of jokes, that there would now be no question whatever of a second chance. At this the young man stared; then he exclaimed: "Why it has come to pass—it has come to pass! The second chance has been the public's—the chance to find the point of view, to pick up the pearl!"

"Oh the pearl!" poor Dencombe uneasily sighed. A smile as cold as a winter sunset flickered on his drawn lips as he added: "The pearl is the unwritten—the pearl is the unalloyed, the REST, the lost!"

From that hour he was less and less present, heedless to all appearance of what went on round him. His disease was definitely mortal, of an action as relentless, after the short arrest that had enabled him to fall in with Doctor Hugh, as a leak in a great ship. Sinking steadily, though this visitor, a man of rare resources, now cordially approved by his physician, showed endless art in guarding him from pain, poor Dencombe kept no reckoning of favour or neglect, betrayed no symptom of regret or speculation. Yet toward the last he gave a sign of having noticed how for two days Doctor Hugh hadn't been in his room, a sign that consisted of his suddenly opening his eyes to put a question. Had he spent those days with the Countess?

"The Countess is dead," said Doctor Hugh. "I knew that in a particular contingency she wouldn't resist. I went to her grave."

Dencombe's eyes opened wider. "She left you 'something handsome'?"

The young man gave a laugh almost too light for a chamber

of woe. "Never a penny. She roundly cursed me."

"Cursed you?" Dencombe wailed.

"For giving her up. I gave her up for YOU. I had to choose," his companion explained.

"You chose to let a fortune go?"

"I chose to accept, whatever they might be, the consequences of my infatuation," smiled Doctor Hugh. Then as a larger pleasantry: "The fortune be hanged! It's your own fault if I can't get your things out of my head."

The immediate tribute to his humour was a long bewildered moan; after which, for many hours, many days, Dencombe lay motionless and absent. A response so absolute, such a glimpse of a definite result and such a sense of credit, worked together in his mind and, producing a strange commotion, slowly altered and transfigured his despair. The sense of cold submersion left him—he seemed to float without an effort. The incident was extraordinary as evidence, and it shed an intenser light. At the last he signed to Doctor Hugh to listen and, when he was down on his knees by the pillow, brought him very near. "You've made me think it all a delusion."

"Not your glory, my dear friend," stammered the young man.

"Not my glory—what there is of it! It IS glory—to have been tested, to have had our little quality and cast our little spell. The thing is to have made somebody care. You happen to be crazy of course, but that doesn't affect the law."

"You're a great success!" said Doctor Hugh, putting into his young voice the ring of a marriage-bell.

Dencombe lay taking this in; then he gathered strength to speak once more. "A second chance—THAT'S the delusion. There never was to be but one. We work in the dark—we do what we can—we give what we have. Our doubt is our passion and our passion is our task. The rest is the madness of art."

"If you've doubted, if you've despaired, you've always 'done' it," his visitor subtly argued.

"We've done something or other," Dencombe conceded.

"Something or other is everything. It's the feasible. It's YOU!"

"Comforter!" poor Dencombe ironically sighed.

"But it's true," insisted his friend.

"It's true. It's frustration that doesn't count."

"Frustration's only life," said Doctor Hugh.

"Yes, it's what passes." Poor Dencombe was barely audible, but he had marked with the words the virtual end of his first and only chance.

The Private Life

We talked of London, face to face with a great bristling, primeval glacier. The hour and the scene were one of those impressions which make up a little, in Switzerland, for the modern indignity of travel—the promiscuities and vulgarities, the station and the hotel, the gregarious patience, the struggle for a scrappy attention, the reduction to a numbered state. The high valley was pink with the mountain rose, the cool air as fresh as if the world were young. There was a faint flush of afternoon on undiminished snows, and the fraternizing tinkle of the unseen cattle came to us with a cropped and sun-warmed odour. The balconied inn stood on the very neck of the sweetest pass in the Oberland, and for a week we had had company and weather. This was felt to be great luck, for one would have made up for the other had either been bad.

The weather certainly would have made up for the company; but it was not subjected to this tax, for we had by a happy chance the *fleur des pois*: Lord and Lady Mellifont, Clare Vawdrey, the greatest (in the opinion of many) of our literary glories, and Blanche Adney, the greatest (in the opinion of all) of our theatrical. I mention these first, because they were just the people whom in London, at that time, people tried to 'get'. People endeavoured to 'book' them six weeks ahead, yet on this occasion we had come in for them, we had all come in for each other, without the least wire-pulling.

A turn of the game had pitched us together, the last of August, and we recognized our luck by remaining so, under protection of the barometer. When the golden days were over—that would come soon enough—we should wind down opposite sides of the pass and disappear over the crest of surrounding heights. We were of the same general communion, we participated in the same miscellaneous publicity. We met, in London, with irregular frequency; we were more or less governed by the laws and the language, the traditions and the shibboleths of the same dense social state. I think all of us, even the ladies, 'did' something, though we pretended we didn't when it was mentioned.

Such things are not mentioned indeed in London, but it was our innocent pleasure to be different here. There had to be some way to show the difference, inasmuch as we were under the impression that this was our annual holiday. We felt at any rate that the conditions were more human than in London, or that at least we ourselves were. We were frank about this, we talked about it: it was what we were talking about as we looked at the flushing glacier, just as someone called attention to the prolonged absence of Lord Mellifont and Mrs. Adney. We were seated on the terrace of the inn, where there were benches and little tables, and those of us who were most bent on proving that we had returned to nature were, in the queer Germanic fashion, having coffee before meat.

The remark about the absence of our two companions was not taken up, not even by Lady Mellifont, not even by little Adney, the fond composer; for it had been dropped only in the briefest intermission of Clare Vawdrey's talk. (This celebrity was 'Clarence' only on the title-page.) It was just that revelation of our being after all human that was his theme. He asked the company whether, candidly, every one hadn't been tempted to say to every one else: 'I had no idea you were really so nice.' I had had, for my part, an idea that *he* was, and even a good deal nicer, but that was too complicated to go into then; besides it is exactly my story.

There was a general understanding among us that when Vawdrey talked we should be silent, and not, oddly enough, because he at all expected it. He didn't, for of all abundant talkers he was the most unconscious, the least greedy and professional. It was rather the religion of the host, of the hostess, that prevailed among us: it was their own idea, but they always looked for a listening circle when the great novelist dined with them. On the occasion I allude to there was probably no one present with whom, in London, he had not dined, and we felt the force of this habit. He had dined even with me; and on the evening of that dinner, as on this Alpine afternoon, I had been at no pains to hold my tongue, absorbed as I inveterately was in a study of the question which always rose before me, to such a height, in his fair, square, strong stature.

This question was all the more tormenting that he never suspected himself (I am sure) of imposing it, any more than he had ever observed that every day of his life every one listened to him at dinner. He used to be called 'subjective' in the weekly papers, but in society no distinguished man could have been less so. He never talked about himself; and this was a topic on which, though it would have been tremendously worthy of him, he apparently never even reflected. He had his hours and his habits, his tailor and his hatter, his hygiene and his particular wine, but all these things together never made up an attitude.

Yet they constituted the only attitude he ever adopted, and it was easy for him to refer to our being 'nicer' abroad than at home. *He* was exempt from variations, and not a shade either less or more nice in one place than in another. He differed from other people, but never from himself (save in the extraordinary sense which I will presently explain), and struck me as having neither moods nor sensibilities nor preferences. He might have been always in the same company, so far as he recognized any influence from age or condition or sex: he addressed himself to women exactly as he addressed himself to men, and gossiped with all men alike, talking no better to clever folk than to dull. I used to feel a despair at his way of liking one subject—so far as I could tell—precisely as much as another: there were some I hated so myself.

I never found him anything but loud and cheerful and copious, and I never heard him utter a paradox or express a shade or play with an idea. That fancy about our being 'human' was, in his conversation, quite an exceptional flight. His opinions were sound and second-rate, and of his perceptions it was too mystifying to think. I envied him his magnificent health.

Vawdrey had marched, with his even pace and his perfectly good conscience, into the flat country of anecdote, where stories are visible from afar like windmills and signposts; but I observed after a little that Lady Mellifont's attention wandered. I happened to be sitting next her. I noticed that her eyes rambled a little anxiously over the lower slopes of the mountains. At last, after looking at her watch, she said to me: "Do you know where they went?"

"Do you mean Mrs. Adney and Lord Mellifont?"

"Lord Mellifont and Mrs. Adney." Her ladyship's speech seemed—unconsciously indeed—to correct me, but it didn't occur to me that this was because she was jealous. I imputed to her no such vulgar sentiment: in the first place, because I liked her, and in the second because it would always occur to one quickly that it was right, in any connection, to put Lord Mellifont first. He *was* first—extraordinarily first. I don't say greatest or wisest or most renowned, but essentially at the top of the list and the head of the table. That is a position by itself, and his wife was naturally accustomed to see him in it.

My phrase had sounded as if Mrs. Adney had taken him; but it was not possible for him to be taken—he only took. No one, in the nature of things, could know this better than Lady Mellifont. I had originally been rather afraid of her, thinking her, with her stiff silences and the extreme blackness of almost everything that made up her person, somewhat hard, even a little saturnine. Her paleness seemed slightly grey, and her glossy black hair metallic, like the brooches and bands and combs with which it was inveterately adorned. She was in perpetual mourning, and wore numberless ornaments of jet and onyx, a thousand clicking chains and bugles and beads.

I had heard Mrs. Adney call her the queen of night, and the

term was descriptive if you understood that the night was cloudy. She had a secret, and if you didn't find it out as you knew her better you at least perceived that she was gentle and unaffected and limited, and also rather submissively sad. She was like a woman with a painless malady. I told her that I had merely seen her husband and his companion stroll down the glen together about an hour before, and suggested that Mr. Adney would perhaps know something of their intentions.

Vincent Adney, who, though he was fifty years old, looked like a good little boy on whom it had been impressed that children should not talk before company, acquitted himself with remarkable simplicity and taste of the position of husband of a great exponent of comedy. When all was said about her making it easy for him, one couldn't help admiring the charmed affection with which he took everything for granted. It is difficult for a husband who is not on the stage, or at least in the theatre, to be graceful about a wife who is; but Adney was more than graceful—he was exquisite, he was inspired.

He set his beloved to music; and you remember how genuine his music could be—the only English compositions I ever saw a foreigner take an interest in. His wife was in them, somewhere, always; they were like a free, rich translation of the impression she produced. She seemed, as one listened, to pass laughing, with loosened hair, across the scene. He had been only a little fiddler at her theatre, always in his place during the acts; but she had made him something rare and misunderstood. Their superiority had become a kind of partnership, and their happiness was a part of the happiness of their friends. Adney's one discomfort was that he couldn't write a play for his wife, and the only way he meddled with her affairs was by asking impossible people if *they* couldn't.

Lady Mellifont, after looking across at him a moment, remarked to me that she would rather not put any question to him. She added the next minute: "I had rather people shouldn't see I'm nervous."

"*Are* you nervous?"

"I always become so if my husband is away from me for any time."

"Do you imagine something has happened to him?"

"Yes, always. Of course I'm used to it."

"Do you mean his tumbling over precipices—that sort of thing?"

"I don't know exactly what it is: it's the general sense that he'll never come back."

She said so much and kept back so much that the only way to treat the condition she referred to seemed the jocular. "Surely he'll never forsake you!" I laughed.

She looked at the ground a moment. "Oh, at bottom I'm easy."

"Nothing can ever happen to a man so accomplished, so infallible, so armed at all points," I went on, encouragingly.

"Oh, you don't know how he's armed!" she exclaimed, with such an odd quaver that I could account for it only by her being nervous. This idea was confirmed by her moving just afterwards, changing her seat rather pointlessly, not as if to cut our conversation short, but because she was in a fidget. I couldn't know what was the matter with her, but I was presently relieved to see Mrs. Adney come toward us. She had in her hand a big bunch of wild flowers, but she was not closely attended by Lord Mellifont. I quickly saw, however, that she had no disaster to announce; yet as I knew there was a question Lady Mellifont would like to hear answered, but did not wish to ask, I expressed to her immediately the hope that his lordship had not remained in a crevasse.

"Oh, no; he left me but three minutes ago. He has gone into the house." Blanche Adney rested her eyes on mine an instant—a mode of intercourse to which no man, for himself, could ever object. The interest, on this occasion, was quickened by the particular thing the eyes happened to say. What they usually said was only: 'Oh, yes, I'm charming, I know, but don't make a fuss about it. I only want a new part—I do, I do!' At present they added, dimly, surreptitiously, and of course sweetly—for that was the way they did everything: 'It's all right, but something did happen. Perhaps I'll tell you later.' She turned to Lady Mellifont, and the transition to simple gaiety suggested her mastery of her profession. "I've brought him safe. We had a charming walk."

"I'm so very glad," returned Lady Mellifont, with her faint smile; continuing vaguely, as she got up: "He must have gone to dress for dinner. Isn't it rather near?" She moved away, to the hotel, in her leave-taking, simplifying fashion, and the rest of us, at the mention of dinner, looked at each other's watches, as if to shift the responsibility of such grossness. The head-waiter, essentially, like all head-waiters, a man of the world, allowed us hours and places of our own, so that in the evening, apart under the lamp, we formed a compact, an indulged little circle.

But it was only the Mellifonts who 'dressed' and as to whom it was recognized that they naturally *would* dress: she in exactly the same manner as on any other evening of her ceremonious existence (she was not a woman whose habits could take account of anything so mutable as fitness); and he, on the other hand, with remarkable adjustment and suitability. He was almost as much a man of the world as the head-waiter, and spoke almost as many languages; but he abstained from courting a comparison of dress-coats and white waistcoats, analyzing the occasion in a much finer way—into black velvet and blue velvet and brown velvet, for instance, into delicate harmonies of necktie and subtle informalities of shirt.

He had a costume for every function and a moral for every costume; and his functions and costumes and morals were ever a part of the amusement of life—a part at any rate of its beauty and romance—for an immense circle of spectators. For his particular friends indeed these things were more than an amusement; they were a topic, a social support and of course, in addition, a subject of perpetual suspense. If his wife had not been present before dinner they were what the rest of us probably would have been putting our heads together about.

Clare Vawdrey had a fund of anecdote on the whole question: he had known Lord Mellifont almost from the beginning.

It was a peculiarity of this nobleman that there could be no conversation about him that didn't instantly take the form of anecdote, and a still further distinction that there could apparently be no anecdote that was not on the whole to his honour. If he had come into a room at any moment, people might have said frankly: 'Of course we were telling stories about you!'

As consciences go, in London, the general conscience would have been good. Moreover it would have been impossible to imagine his taking such a tribute otherwise than amiably, for he was always as unperturbed as an actor with the right cue. He had never in his life needed the prompter—his very embarrassments had been rehearsed. For myself, when he was talked about I always had an odd impression that we were speaking of the dead—it was with that peculiar accumulation of relish. His reputation was a kind of gilded obelisk, as if he had been buried beneath it; the body of legend and reminiscence of which he was to be the subject had crystallized in advance.

This ambiguity sprang, I suppose, from the fact that the mere sound of his name and air of his person, the general expectation he created, were, somehow, too exalted to be verified. The experience of his urbanity always came later; the prefigurement, the legend paled before the reality. I remember that on the evening I refer to the reality was particularly operative. The handsomest man of his period could never have looked better, and he sat among us like a bland conductor controlling by an harmonious play of arm an orchestra still a little rough. He directed the conversation by gestures as irresistible as they were vague; one felt as if without him it wouldn't have had anything to call a tone.

This was essentially what he contributed to any occasion—what he contributed above all to English public life. He pervaded it, he coloured it, he embellished it, and without him it would scarcely have had a vocabulary. Certainly it would not have had a style; for a style was what it had in having Lord Mellifont. He *was* a style. I was freshly struck with it as, in the *salle à manger* of the little Swiss inn, we resigned ourselves to inevitable veal. Confronted with his form (I must parenthesize that it was not confronted much), Clare Vawdrey's talk suggested the reporter contrasted with the bard.

It was interesting to watch the shock of characters from which, of an evening, so much would be expected. There was however no concussion—it was all muffled and minimized in Lord Mellifont's tact. It was rudimentary with him to find the solution of such a problem in playing the host, assuming responsibilities which carried with them their sacrifice. He had indeed never been a guest in his life; he was the host, the patron, the moderator at every board. If there was a defect in his manner (and I suggest it under my breath), it was that he had a little more art than any conjunction—even the most complicated-could possibly require. At any rate one made one's reflections in noticing how the accomplished peer handled the situation and how the sturdy man of letters was unconscious that the situation (and least of all he himself as part of it), was handled. Lord Mellifont poured forth treasures of tact, and Clare Vawdrey never dreamed he was doing it.

Vawdrey had no suspicion of any such precaution even when Blanche Adney asked him if he saw yet their third act—an inquiry into which she introduced a subtlety of her own. She had a theory that he was to write her a play and that the heroine, if he would only do his duty, would be the part for which she had immemorially longed. She was forty years old (this could be no secret to those who had admired her from the first), and she could now reach out her hand and touch her uttermost goal. This gave a kind of tragic passion—perfect actress of comedy as she was—to her desire not to miss the great thing.

The years had passed, and still she had missed it; none of the things she had done was the thing she had dreamed of, so that at present there was no more time to lose. This was the canker in the rose, the ache beneath the smile. It made her touching-made her sadness even sweeter than her laughter. She had done the old English and the new French, and had charmed her generation; but she was haunted by the vision of a bigger chance, of something truer to the conditions that lay near her. She was tired of Sheridan and she hated Bowdler; she called for a canvas of a finer grain. The worst of it, to my sense, was that she would never extract her modern comedy from the great mature novelist, who was as incapable of producing it as he was of threading a needle. She coddled him, she talked to him, she made love to him, as she frankly proclaimed; but she dwelt in illusions—she would have to live and die with Bowdler

It is difficult to be cursory over this charming woman, who was beautiful without beauty and complete with a dozen deficiencies. The perspective of the stage made her over, and in society she was like the model off the pedestal. She was the picture walking about, which to the artless social mind was a perpetual surprise—a miracle. People thought she told them the secrets of the pictorial nature, in return for which they gave her relaxation and tea. She told them nothing and she drank the tea; but they had, all the same, the best of the bargain.

Vawdrey was really at work on a play; but if he had begun it because he liked her I think he let it drag for the same reason. He secretly felt the atrocious difficulty—knew that from his hand the finished piece would have received no active life. At the same time nothing could be more agreeable than to have such a question open with Blanche Adney, and from time to time he put something very good into the play. If he deceived Mrs. Adney it was only because in her despair she was determined to be deceived. To her question about their third act he replied that, before dinner, he had written a magnificent passage.

"Before dinner?" I said. "Why, *cher maître,* before dinner you were holding us all spellbound on the terrace."

My words were a joke, because I thought his had been; but for the first time that I could remember I perceived a certain confusion in his face. He looked at me hard, throwing back his head quickly, the least bit like a horse who has been pulled up short. "Oh, it was before that," he replied, naturally enough.

"Before that you were playing billiards with *me*," Lord Mellifont intimated.

"Then it must have been yesterday," said Vawdrey.

But he was in a tight place. "You told me this morning you did nothing yesterday," the actress objected.

"I don't think I really know when I do things." Vawdrey looked vaguely, without helping himself, at a dish that was offered him.

"It's enough if *we* know," smiled Lord Mellifont.

"I don't believe you've written a line," said Blanche Adney.

"I think I could repeat you the scene." Vawdrey helped himself to *haricots verts.*

"Oh, do—oh, do!" two or three of us cried.

"After dinner, in the *salon*; it will be an immense *régal*," Lord Mellifont declared.

"I'm not sure, but I'll try," Vawdrey went on.

"Oh, you lovely man!" exclaimed the actress, who was practising Americanisms, being resigned even to an American comedy.

"But there must be this condition," said Vawdrey: "you must make your husband play."

"Play while you're reading? Never!"

"I've too much vanity," said Adney.

Lord Mellifont distinguished him. "You must give us the overture, before the curtain rises. That's a peculiarly delightful moment."

"I sha'n't read—I shall just speak," said Vawdrey.

"Better still, let me go and get your manuscript," the actress suggested.

Vawdrey replied that the manuscript didn't matter; but an hour later, in the *salon*, we wished he might have had it. We sat expectant, still under the spell of Adney's violin. His wife, in the foreground, on an ottoman, was all impatience and profile, and Lord Mellifont, in the chair—it was always *the* chair, Lord Mellifont's—made our grateful little group feel like a social science congress or a distribution of prizes. Suddenly, instead of beginning, our tame lion began to roar out of tune—he had clean forgotten every word. He was very sorry, but the lines absolutely wouldn't come to him; he was utterly ashamed, but his memory was a blank.

He didn't look in the least ashamed—Vawdrey had never looked ashamed in his life; he was only imperturbably and merrily natural. He protested that he had never expected to make such a fool of himself, but we felt that this wouldn't prevent the incident from taking its place among his jolliest reminiscences. It was only *we* who were humiliated, as if he had played us a premeditated trick. This was an occasion, if ever, for Lord Mellifont's tact, which descended on us all like balm: he told us, in his charming artistic way, his way of bridging over arid intervals (he had a *débit*—there was nothing to approach it in England—like the actors of the *Comédie Française*), of his own collapse on a momentous occasion, the delivery of an address to a mighty multitude, when, finding he had forgotten his memoranda, he fumbled, on the terrible platform, the cynosure of every eye, fumbled vainly in irreproachable pockets for indispensable notes.

But the point of his story was finer than that of Vawdrey's pleasantry; for he sketched with a few light gestures the brilliancy of a performance which had risen superior to embarrassment, had resolved itself, we were left to divine, into an effort recognised at the moment as not absolutely a blot on what the public was so good as to call his reputation.

"Play up—play up!" cried Blanche Adney, tapping her husband and remembering how, on the stage, a *contretemps* is always drowned in music. Adney threw himself upon his fiddle, and I said to Clare Vawdrey that his mistake could easily be corrected by his sending for the manuscript. If he would tell me where it was I would immediately fetch it from his room. To this he replied: "My dear fellow, I'm afraid there *is* no manuscript."

"Then you've not written anything?"

"I'll write it tomorrow."

"Ah, you trifle with us," I said, in much mystification.

Vawdrey hesitated an instant. "If there *is* anything, you'll find it on my table."

At this moment one of the others spoke to him, and Lady

Mellifont remarked audibly, as if to correct gently our want of consideration, that Mr. Adney was playing something very beautiful. I had noticed before that she appeared extremely fond of music; she always listened to it in a hushed transport. Vawdrey's attention was drawn away, but it didn't seem to me that the words he had just dropped constituted a definite permission to go to his room.

Moreover I wanted to speak to Blanche Adney; I had something to ask her. I had to await my chance, however, as we remained silent awhile for her husband, after which the conversation became general. It was our habit to go to bed early, but there was still a little of the evening left. Before it quite waned I found an opportunity to tell the actress that Vawdrey had given me leave to put my hand on his manuscript. She adjured me, by all I held sacred, to bring it immediately, to give it to her; and her insistence was proof against my suggestion that it would now be too late for him to begin to read: besides which the charm was broken—the others wouldn't care. It was not too late for *her* to begin; therefore I was to possess myself, without more delay, of the precious pages. I told her she should be obeyed in a moment, but I wanted her first to satisfy my just curiosity. What had happened before dinner, while she was on the hills with Lord Mellifont?

"How do you know anything happened?"

"I saw it in your face when you came back."

"And they call me an actress!" cried Mrs. Adney.

"What do they call *me*?" I inquired.

"You're a searcher of hearts—that frivolous thing an observer."

"I wish you'd let an observer write you a play!" I broke out.

"People don't care for what you write: you'd break any run of luck."

"Well, I see plays all round me," I declared; "the air is full of them tonight."

"The air? Thank you for nothing! I only wish my table-drawers were."

"Did hemake love to you on the glacier?" I went on.

She stared; then broke into the graduated ecstasy of her laugh. "Lord Mellifont, poor dear? What a funny place! It would indeed be the place for *our* love!"

"Did he fall into a crevasse?" I continued.

Blanche Adney looked at me again as she had done for an instant when she came up, before dinner, with her hands full of flowers. "I don't know into what he fell. I'll tell you tomorrow."

"He did come down, then?"

"Perhaps he went up," she laughed. "It's really strange."

"All the more reason you should tell me to-night."

"I must think it over; I must puzzle it out."

"Oh, if you want conundrums I'll throw in another," I said. "What's the matter with the master?"

"The master of what?"

"Of every form of dissimulation. Vawdrey hasn't written a line."

"Go and get his papers and we'll see."

"I don't like to expose him," I said.

"Why not, if I expose Lord Mellifont?"

"Oh, I'd do anything for that," I conceded. "But why should Vawdrey have made a false statement? It's very curious."

"It's very curious," Blanche Adney repeated, with a musing air and her eyes on Lord Mellifont. Then, rousing herself, she added: "Go and look in his room."

"In Lord Mellifont's?"

She turned to me quickly. "*That* would be a way!"

"A way to what?"

"To find out—to find out!" She spoke gaily and excitedly, but suddenly checked herself. "We're talking nonsense," she said.

"We're mixing things up, but I'm struck with your idea. Get Lady Mellifont to let you."

"Oh, *she* has looked!" Mrs. Adney murmured, with the oddest dramatic expression. Then, after a movement of her beautiful uplifted hand, as if to brush away a fantastic vision, she exclaimed imperiously: "Bring me the scene—bring me the scene!"

"I go for it," I answered; "but don't tell me I can't write a play."

She left me, but my errand was arrested by the approach of a lady who had produced a birthday-book—we had been threatened with it for several evenings—and who did me the honour to solicit my autograph. She had been asking the others, and she couldn't decently leave me out. I could usually remember my name, but it always took me some time to recall my date, and even when I had done so I was never very sure. I hesitated between two days and I remarked to my petitioner that I would sign on both if it would give her any satisfaction. She said that surely I had been born only once; and I replied of course that on the day I made her acquaintance I had been born again.

I mention the feeble joke only to show that, with the obligatory inspection of the other autographs, we gave some minutes to this transaction. The lady departed with her book, and then I became aware that the company had dispersed. I was alone in the little salon that had been appropriated to our use. My first impression was one of disappointment: if Vawdrey had gone to bed I didn't wish to disturb him.

While I hesitated, however, I recognised that Vawdrey had not gone to bed. A window was open, and the sound of voices outside came in to me: Blanche was on the terrace with her dramatist, and they were talking about the stars. I went to the window for a glimpse—the Alpine night was splendid. My friends had stepped out together; the actress had picked up a cloak; she looked as I had seen her look in the wing of the theatre. They were silent awhile, and I heard the roar of a neighbouring torrent. I turned back into the room, and its quiet lamplight gave me an idea.

Our companions had dispersed—it was late for a pastoral country—and we three should have the place to ourselves. Clare Vawdrey had written his scene—it was magnificent; and his reading it to us there, at such an hour, would be an episode intensely memorable. I would bring down his manuscript and meet the two with it as they came in.

I quitted the *salon* for this purpose; I had been in Vawdrey's room and knew it was on the second floor, the last in a long corridor. A minute later my hand was on the knob of his door, which I naturally pushed open without knocking. It was equally natural that in the absence of its occupant the room should be dark; the more so as, the end of the corridor being at that hour unlighted, the obscurity was not immediately diminished by the opening of the door. I was only aware at first that I had made no mistake and that, the window-curtains not being drawn, I was confronted with a couple of vague starlighted apertures.

Their aid, however, was not sufficient to enable me to find what I had come for, and my hand, in my pocket, was already on the little box of matches that I always carried for cigarettes. Suddenly I withdrew it with a start, uttering an ejaculation, an apology. I had entered the wrong room; a glance prolonged for three seconds showed me a figure seated at a table near one of the windows—a figure I had at first taken for a travelling-rug thrown over a chair. I retreated, with a sense of intrusion; but as I did so I became aware, more rapidly than it takes me to express it, in the first place that this was Vawdrey's room and in the second that, most singularly, Vawdrey himself sat before me. Checking myself on the threshold I had a momentary feeling of bewilderment, but before I knew it I had exclaimed: "Hullo! is that you, Vawdrey?"

He neither turned nor answered me, but my question received an immediate and practical reply in the opening of a door on the other side of the passage. A servant, with a candle, had come out of the opposite room, and in this flitting illumination I definitely recognised the man whom, an instant before, I had to the best of my belief left below in conversation with Mrs. Adney. His back was half turned to me, and he bent over the table in the attitude of writing, but I was conscious that I was in no sort of error about his identity.

"I beg your pardon—I thought you were downstairs," I said; and as the personage gave no sign of hearing me I added:

"If you're busy I won't disturb you." I backed out, closing the door—I had been in the place, I suppose, less than a minute. I had a sense of mystification, which however deepened infinitely the next instant. I stood there with my hand still on the knob of the door, overtaken by the oddest impression of my life.

Vawdrey was at his table, writing, and it was a very natural place for him to be; but why was he writing in the dark and why hadn't he answered me? I waited a few seconds for the sound of some movement, to see if he wouldn't rouse himself from his abstraction—a fit conceivable in a great writer—and call out: 'Oh, my dear fellow, is it you?' But I heard only the stillness, I felt only the starlighted dusk of the room, with the unexpected presence it enclosed. I turned away, slowly retracing my steps, and came confusedly downstairs. The lamp was still burning in the salon, but the room was empty. I passed round to the door of the hotel and stepped out. Empty too was the terrace. Blanche Adney and the gentleman with her had apparently come in. I hung about five minutes; then I went to bed.

I slept badly, for I was agitated. On looking back at these queer occurrences (you will see presently that they were queer), I perhaps suppose myself more agitated than I was; for great anomalies are never so great at first as after we have reflected upon them. It takes us some time to exhaust explanations. I was vaguely nervous—I had been sharply startled; but there was nothing I could not clear up by asking Blanche Adney, the first thing in the morning, who had been with her on the terrace.

Oddly enough, however, when the morning dawned—it dawned admirably—I felt less desire to satisfy myself on this point than to escape, to brush away the shadow of my stupefaction. I saw the day would be splendid, and the fancy took me to spend it, as I had spent happy days of youth, in a lonely mountain ramble. I dressed early, partook of conventional coffee, put a big roll into one pocket and a small flask into the other, and, with a stout stick in my hand, went forth into the high places.

My story is not closely concerned with the charming hours I passed there—hours of the kind that make intense memories.

If I roamed away half of them on the shoulders of the hills, I lay on the sloping grass for the other half and, with my cap pulled over my eyes (save a peep for immensities of view), listened, in the bright stillness, to the mountain bee and felt most things sink and dwindle. Clare Vawdrey grew small, Blanche Adney grew dim, Lord Mellifont grew old, and before the day was over I forgot that I had ever been puzzled. When in the late afternoon I made my way down to the inn there was nothing I wanted so much to find out as whether dinner would not soon be ready. Tonight I dressed, in a manner, and by the time I was presentable they were all at table.

In their company again my little problem came back to me, so that I was curious to see if Vawdrey wouldn't look at me the least bit queerly. But he didn't look at me at all; which gave me a chance both to be patient and to wonder why I should hesitate to ask him my question across the table. I did hesitate, and with the consciousness of doing so came back a little of the agitation I had left behind me, or below me, during the day. I wasn't ashamed of my scruple, however: it was only a fine discretion. What I vaguely felt was that a public inquiry wouldn't have been fair. Lord Mellifont was there, of course, to mitigate with his perfect manner all consequences; but I think it was present to me that with these particular elements his lordship would not be at home. The moment we got up, therefore, I approached Mrs. Adney, asking her whether, as the evening was lovely, she wouldn't take a turn with me outside.

"You've walked a hundred miles; had you not better be quiet?" she replied.

"I'd walk a hundred miles more to get you to tell me something."

She looked at me an instant, with a little of the queerness that I had sought, but had not found, in Clare Vawdrey's eyes. "Do you mean what became of Lord Mellifont?"

"Of Lord Mellifont?" With my new speculation I had lost that thread.

"Where's your memory, foolish man? We talked of it last

evening."

"Ah, yes!" I cried, recalling; "we shall have lots to discuss." I drew her out to the terrace, and before we had gone three steps I said to her: "Who was with you here last night?"

"Last night?" she repeated, as wide of the mark as I had been.

"At ten o'clock—just after our company broke up. You came out here with a gentleman; you talked about the stars."

She stared a moment; then she gave her laugh. "Are you jealous of dear Vawdrey?"

"Then it was he?"

"Certainly it was."

"And how long did he stay?"

"You have it badly. He stayed about a quarter of an hour-perhaps rather more. We walked some distance; he talked about his play. There you have it all; that is the only witchcraft I have used."

"And what did Vawdrey do afterwards?"

"I haven't the least idea. I left him and went to bed."

"At what time did you go to bed?"

"At what time did *you*? I happen to remember that I parted from Mr. Vawdrey at ten twenty-five," said Mrs. Adney. "I came back into the salon to pick up a book, and I noticed the clock."

"In other words you and Vawdrey distinctly lingered here from about five minutes past ten till the hour you mention?"

"I don't know how distinct we were, but we were very jolly. *Où voulez-vous en venir?*" Blanche Adney asked.

"Simply to this, dear lady: that at the time your companion was occupied in the manner you describe, he was also engaged in literary composition in his own room."

She stopped short at this, and her eyes had an expression in the darkness. She wanted to know if I challenged her veracity; and I replied that, on the contrary, I backed it up—it made the case so interesting. She returned that this would only be if she should back up mine; which, however, I had no difficulty in persuading her to do, after I had related to her circumstantially the incident of my quest of the manuscript—the manuscript which, at the time, for a reason I could now understand, appeared to have passed so completely out of her own head.

"His talk made me forget it—I forgot I sent you for it. He made up for his fiasco in the *salon*: he declaimed me the scene," said my companion. She had dropped on a bench to listen to me and, as we sat there, had briefly cross-examined me. Then she broke out into fresh laughter "Oh, the eccentricities of genius!"

"They seem greater even than I supposed."

"Oh, the mysteries of greatness!"

"You ought to know all about them, but they take me by surprise."

"Are you absolutely certain it was Mr. Vawdrey?" my companion asked.

"If it wasn't he, who in the world was it? That a strange gentleman, looking exactly like him, should be sitting in his room at that hour of the night and writing at his table *in the dark*," I insisted, "would be practically as wonderful as my own contention."

"Yes, why in the dark?" mused Mrs. Adney.

"Cats can see in the dark," I said.

She smiled at me dimly. "Did it look like a cat?"

"No, dear lady, but I'll tell you what it did look like—it looked like the author of Vawdrey's admirable works. It looked infinitely more like him than our friend does himself," I declared.

"Do you mean it was somebody he gets to do them?"

"Yes, while he dines out and disappoints you."

"Disappoints me?" murmured Mrs. Adney artlessly.

"Disappoints *me*—disappoints everyone who looks in him for the genius that created the pages they adore. Where is it in his talk?"

"Ah, last night he was splendid," said the actress.

"He's always splendid, as your morning bath is splendid, or a sirloin of beef, or the railway service to Brighton. But he's never rare."

"I see what you mean."

"That's what makes you such a comfort to talk to. I've often wondered—now I know. There are two of them."

"What a delightful idea!"

"One goes out, the other stays at home. One is the genius, the other's the *bourgeois*, and it's only the *bourgeois* whom we personally know. He talks, he circulates, he's awfully popular, he flirts with you—"

"Whereas it's the genius *you* are privileged to see!" Mrs. Adney broke in. "I'm much obliged to you for the distinction."

I laid my hand on her arm. "See him yourself. Try it, test it, go to his room."

"Go to his room? It wouldn't be proper!" she exclaimed, in the tone of her best comedy.

"Anything is proper in such an inquiry. If you see him, it settles it."

"How charming—to settle it!" She thought a moment, then she sprang up. "Do you mean *now*?"

"Whenever you like."

"But suppose I should find the wrong one?" said Blanche Adney, with an exquisite effect.

"The wrong one? Which one do you call the right?"

"The wrong one for a lady to go and see. Suppose I shouldn't find—the genius?"

"Oh, I'll look after the other," I replied. Then, as I had happened to glance about me, I added: "Take care—here comes Lord Mellifont."

"I wish you'd look after *him*," my interlocutress murmured.

"What's the matter with him?"

"That's just what I was going to tell you."

"Tell me now; he's not coming."

Blanche Adney looked a moment. Lord Mellifont, who appeared to have emerged from the hotel to smoke a meditative cigar, had paused, at a distance from us, and stood admiring the wonders of the prospect, discernible even in the dusk. We strolled slowly in another direction, and she presently said: "My idea is almost as droll as yours."

"I don't call mine droll: it's beautiful."

"There's nothing so beautiful as the droll," Mrs. Adney declared.

"You take a professional view. But I'm all ears." My curiosity was indeed alive again.

"Well then, my dear friend, if Clare Vawdrey is double (and I'm bound to say I think that the more of him the better), his lordship there has the opposite complaint: he isn't even whole."

We stopped once more, simultaneously. "I don't understand."

"No more do I. But I have a fancy that if there are two of Mr. Vawdrey, there isn't so much as one, all told, of Lord Mellifont."

I considered a moment, then I laughed out. "I think I see what you mean!"

"That's what makes *you* a comfort. Did you ever see him alone?"

I tried to remember. "Oh, yes; he has been to see me."

"Ah, then he wasn't alone."

"And I've been to see him, in his study."

"Did he know you were there?"

"Naturally—I was announced."

Blanche Adney glanced at me like a lovely conspirator. "You mustn't be announced!" With this she walked on.

I rejoined her, breathless. "Do you mean one must come upon him when he doesn't know it?"

"You must take him unawares. You must go to his room-that's what you must do."

If I was elated by the way our mystery opened out, I was also, pardonably, a little confused. "When I know he's not there?"

"When you know he *is*."

"And what shall I see?"

"You won't see anything!" Mrs. Adney cried as we turned round.

We had reached the end of the terrace, and our movement brought us face to face with Lord Mellifont, who, resuming his walk, had now, without indiscretion, overtaken us. The sight of him at that moment was illuminating, and it kindled a great backward train, connecting itself with one's general impression of the personage. As he stood there smiling at us and waving a practised hand into the transparent night (he introduced the view as if it had been a candidate and 'supported' the very Alps), as he rose before us in the delicate fragrance of his cigar and all his other delicacies and fragrances, with more perfections, somehow, heaped upon his handsome head than one had ever seen accumulated before, he struck me as so essentially, so conspicuously and uniformly the public character that I read in a flash the answer to Blanche Adney's riddle.

He was all public and had no corresponding private life, just as Clare Vawdrey was all private and had no corresponding public one. I had heard only half my companion's story, yet as we joined Lord Mellifont (he had followed us—he liked Mrs. Adney; but it was always to be conceived of him that he accepted society rather than sought it), as we participated for half an hour in the distributed wealth of his conversation, I felt with unabashed duplicity that we had, as it were, found him out. I was even more deeply diverted by that whisk of the curtain to which the actress had just treated me than I had been by my own discovery; and if I was not ashamed of my share of her secret any more than of having divided my own with her (though my own was, of the two mysteries, the more glorious for the personage involved), this was because there was no cruelty in my advantage, but on the contrary an extreme tenderness and a positive compassion.

Oh, he was safe with me, and I felt moreover rich and enlightened, as if I had suddenly put the universe into my pocket. I had learned what an affair of the spot and the moment a great appearance may be. It would doubtless be too much to say that I had always suspected the possibility, in the background of his lordship's being, of some such beautiful instance; but it is at least a fact that, patronising as it sounds, I had been conscious of a certain reserve of indulgence for him. I had secretly pitied him for the perfection of his performance, had wondered what blank face such a mask had to cover, what was left to him for the immitigable hours in which a man sits down with himself, or, more serious still, with that intenser self, his lawful wife. How was he at home and what did he do when he was alone?

There was something in Lady Mellifont that gave a point to these researches—something that suggested that even to her he was still the public character and that she was haunted by similar questionings. She had never cleared them up: that was her eternal trouble. We therefore knew more than she did, Blanche Adney and I; but we wouldn't tell her for the world, nor would she probably thank us for doing so. She preferred the relative grandeur of uncertainty. She was not at home with him, so she couldn't say; and with her he was not alone, so he couldn't show her.

He represented to his wife and he was a hero to his servants, and what one wanted to arrive at was what really became of him when no eye could see. He rested, presumably; but what form of rest could repair such a plenitude of presence? Lady Mellifont was too proud to pry, and as she had never looked through a keyhole she remained dignified and unassuaged.

It may have been a fancy of mine that Blanche Adney drew out our companion, or it may be that the practical irony of our relation to him at such a moment made me see him more vividly: at any rate he never had struck me as so dissimilar from what he would have been if we had not offered him a reflection of his image. We were only a concourse of two, but he had never been more public. His perfect manner had never been more perfect, his remarkable tact had never been more remarkable.

I had a tacit sense that it would all be in the morning papers, with a leader, and also a secretly exhilarating one that I knew something that wouldn't be, that never could be, though any enterprising journal would give one a fortune for it. I must add, however, that in spite of my enjoyment—it was almost sensual, like that of a consummate dish—I was eager to be alone again with Mrs. Adney, who owed me an anecdote. It proved impossible, that evening, for some of the others came out to see what we found so absorbing; and then Lord Mellifont bespoke a little music from the fiddler, who produced his violin and played to us divinely, on our platform of echoes, face to face with the ghosts of the mountains.

Before the concert was over I missed our actress and, glancing into the window of the *salon*, saw that she was established with Vawdrey, who was reading to her from a manuscript. The great scene had apparently been achieved and was doubtless the more interesting to Blanche from the new lights she had gathered about its author. I judged it discreet not to disturb them, and I went to bed without seeing her again. I looked out for her betimes the next morning and, as the promise of the day was fair, proposed to her that we should take to the hills, reminding her of the high obligation she had incurred. She recognised the obligation and gratified me with her company; but before we had strolled ten yards up the pass she broke out with intensity: "My dear friend, you've no idea how it works in me! I can think of nothing else."

"Than your theory about Lord Mellifont?"

"Oh, bother Lord Mellifont! I allude to yours about Mr. Vawdrey, who is much the more interesting person of the two. I'm fascinated by that vision of his—what-do-you-call-it?"

"His alternative identity?"

"His other self: that's easier to say."

"You accept it, then, you adopt it?"

"Adopt it? I rejoice in it! It became tremendously vivid to me last evening."

"While he read to you there?"

"Yes, as I listened to him, watched him. It simplified everything, explained everything."

"That's indeed the blessing of it. Is the scene very fine?"

"Magnificent, and he reads beautifully."

"Almost as well as the other one writes!" I laughed.

This made my companion stop a moment, laying her hand on my arm. "You utter my very impression. I felt that he was reading me the work of another man."

"What a service to the other man!"

"Such a totally different person," said Mrs. Adney. We talked of this difference as we went on, and of what a wealth it constituted, what a resource for life, such a duplication of character.

"It ought to make him live twice as long as other people," I observed.

"Ought to make which of them?"

"Well, both; for after all they're members of a firm, and one of them couldn't carry on the business without the other. Moreover mere survival would be dreadful for either."

Blanche Adney was silent a little; then she exclaimed: "I don't know—I wish he *would* survive!"

"May I, on my side, inquire which?"

"If you can't guess I won't tell you."

"I know the heart of woman. You always prefer the other."

She halted again, looking round her. "Off here, away from my husband, I *can* tell you. I'm in love with him!"

"Unhappy woman, he has no passions," I answered.

"That's exactly why I adore him. Doesn't a woman with my history know that the passions of others are insupportable? An actress, poor thing, can't care for any love that's not all on *her* side; she can't afford to be repaid. My marriage proves that: marriage is ruinous. Do you know what was in my mind last night, all the while Mr Vawdrey was reading me those beautiful speeches? An insane desire to see the author." And dramatically, as if to hide her shame, Blanche Adney passed on.

"We'll manage that," I returned. "I want another glimpse of him myself. But meanwhile please remember that I've been waiting more than forty-eight hours for the evidence that supports your sketch, intensely suggestive and plausible, of Lord Mellifont's private life."

"Oh, Lord Mellifont doesn't interest me."

"He did yesterday," I said.

"Yes, but that was before I fell in love. You blotted him out with your story."

"You'll make me sorry I told it. Come," I pleaded, "if you don't let me know how your idea came into your head I shall imagine you simply made it up."

"Let me recollect then, while we wander in this grassy valley."

We stood at the entrance of a charming crooked gorge, a portion of whose level floor formed the bed of a stream that was smooth with swiftness. We turned into it, and the soft walk beside the clear torrent drew us on and on; till suddenly, as we continued and I waited for my companion to remember, a bend of the valley showed us Lady Mellifont coming toward us. She was alone, under the canopy of her parasol, drawing her sable train over the turf; and in this form, on the devious ways, she was a sufficiently rare apparition. She usually took a footman, who marched behind her on the highroads and whose livery was strange to the mountaineers. She blushed on seeing us, as if she ought somehow to justify herself; she laughed vaguely and said she had come out for a little early stroll. We stood together a moment, exchanging platitudes, and then she remarked that she had thought she might find her husband.

"Is he in this quarter?" I inquired.

"I supposed he would be. He came out an hour ago to sketch."

"Have you been looking for him?" Mrs. Adney asked.

"A little; not very much," said Lady Mellifont.

Each of the women rested her eyes with some intensity, as it seemed to me, on the eyes of the other.

"We'll look for him *for* you, if you like," said Mrs. Adney.

"Oh, it doesn't matter. I thought I'd join him."

"He won't make his sketch if you don't," my companion hinted.

"Perhaps he will if *you* do," said Lady Mellifont.

"Oh, I dare say he'll turn up," I interposed.

"He certainly will if he knows we're here!" Blanche Adney retorted.

"Will you wait while we search?" I asked of Lady Mellifont.

She repeated that it was of no consequence; upon which Mrs. Adney went on: "We'll go into the matter for our own pleasure."

"I wish you a pleasant expedition," said her ladyship, and was turning away when I sought to know if we should inform her husband that she had followed him. She hesitated a moment; then she jerked out oddly: "I think you had better not." With this she took leave of us, floating a little stiffly down the gorge.

My companion and I watched her retreat, then we exchanged a stare, while a light ghost of a laugh rippled from the actress's lips. "She might be walking in the shrubberies at Mellifont!"

"She suspects it, you know," I replied.

"And she doesn't want him to know it. There won't be any sketch."

"Unless we overtake him," I subjoined. "In that case we shall find him producing one, in the most graceful attitude, and the queer thing is that it will be brilliant."

"Let us leave him alone—he'll have to come home without it."

"He'd rather never come home. Oh, he'll find a public!"

"Perhaps he'll do it for the cows," Blanche Adney suggested; and as I was on the point of rebuking her profanity she went on: "That's simply what I happened to discover."

"What are you speaking of?"

"The incident of day before yesterday."

"Ah, let's have it at last!"

"That's all it was—that I was like Lady Mellifont: I couldn't find him."

"Did you lose him?"

"He lost *me*—that appears to be the way of it. He thought I was gone."

"But you did find him, since you came home with him."

"It was he who found *me*. That again is what must happen. He's there from the moment he knows somebody else is."

"I understand his intermissions," I said after a short reflection, "but I don't quite seize the law that governs them."

"Oh, it's a fine shade, but I caught it at that moment. I had started to come home. I was tired, and I had insisted on his not coming back with me. We had found some rare flowers—those I brought home—and it was he who had discovered almost all of them. It amused him very much, and I knew he wanted to get more; but I was weary and I quitted him. He let me go—where else would have been his tact?—and I was too stupid then to have guessed that from the moment I was not there no flower would be gathered. I started homeward, but at the end of three minutes I found I had brought away his penknife—he had lent it to me to trim a branch—and I knew he would need it. I turned back a few steps, to call him, but before I spoke I looked about for him. You can't understand what happened then without having the place before you."

"You must take me there," I said.

"We may see the wonder here. The place was simply one that offered no chance for concealment—a great gradual hillside, without obstructions or trees. There were some rocks below me, behind which I myself had disappeared, but from which on coming back I immediately emerged again."

"Then he must have seen you."

"He was too utterly gone, for some reason best known to himself. It was probably some moment of fatigue—he's getting on, you know, so that, with the sense of returning solitude, the reaction had been proportionately great, the extinction proportionately complete. At any rate the stage was as bare as your hand."

"Could he have been somewhere else?"

"He couldn't have been, in the time, anywhere but where I had left him. Yet the place was utterly empty—as empty as this stretch of valley before us. He had vanished—he had ceased to be. But as soon as my voice rang out (I uttered his name), he rose before me like the rising sun."

"And where did the sun rise?"

"Just where it ought to—just where he would have been and where I should have seen him had he been like other people."

I had listened with the deepest interest, but it was my duty to think of objections. "How long a time elapsed between the moment you perceived his absence and the moment you called?"

"Oh, only an instant. I don't pretend it was long."

"Long enough for you to be sure?" I said.

"Sure he wasn't there?"

"Yes, and that you were not mistaken, not the victim of some hocus-pocus of your eyesight."

"I may have been mistaken, but I don't believe it. At any rate, that's just why I want you to look in his room."

I thought a moment. "How *can* I, when even his wife doesn't dare to?"

"She *wants* to; propose it to her. It wouldn't take much to make her. She does suspect."

I thought another moment. "Did he seem to know?"

"That I had missed him? So it struck me, but he thought he had been quick enough."

"Did you speak of his disappearance?"

"Heaven forbid! It seemed to me too strange."

"Quite right. And how did he look?"

Trying to think it out again and reconstitute her miracle, Blanche Adney gazed abstractedly up the valley. Suddenly she exclaimed: "Just as he looks now!" and I saw Lord Mellifont stand before us with his sketch-block. I perceived, as we met him, that he looked neither suspicious nor blank: he looked simply, as he did always, everywhere, the principal feature of the scene. Naturally he had no sketch to show us, but nothing could better have rounded off our actual conception of him than the way he fell into position as we approached. He had been selecting his point of view; he took possession of it with a flourish of the pencil.

He leaned against a rock; his beautiful little box of water-colours reposed on a natural table beside him, a ledge of the bank which showed how inveterately nature ministered to his convenience. He painted while he talked and he talked while he painted; and if the painting was as miscellaneous as the talk, the talk would equally have graced an album. We waited while the exhibition went on, and it seemed indeed as if the conscious profiles of the peaks were interested in his success. They grew as black as silhouettes in paper, sharp against a livid sky from which, however, there would be nothing to fear till Lord Mellifont's sketch should be finished.

Blanche Adney communed with me dumbly, and I could read the language of her eyes: 'Oh, if *we* could only do it as well as that! He fills the stage in a way that beats us.' We could no more have left him than we could have quitted the theatre till the play was over; but in due time we turned round with him and strolled back to the inn, before the door of which his lordship, glancing again at his picture, tore the fresh leaf from the block and presented it with a few happy words to Mrs. Adney. Then he went into the house; and a moment later, looking up from where we stood, we saw him, above, at the window of his sitting-room (he had the best apartments), watching the signs of the weather.

"He'll have to rest after this," Blanche said, dropping her eyes on her water-colour.

"Indeed he will!" I raised mine to the window: Lord Mellifont had vanished. "He's already reabsorbed."

"Reabsorbed?" I could see the actress was now thinking of something else.

"Into the immensity of things. He has lapsed again; there's an *entr'acte*"

"It ought to be long." Mrs. Adney looked up and down the terrace, and at that moment the head-waiter appeared in the doorway. Suddenly she turned to this functionary with the question: "Have you seen Mr. Vawdrey lately?"

The man immediately approached. "He left the house five minutes ago—for a walk, I think. He went down the pass; he had a book."

I was watching the ominous clouds. "He had better have had an umbrella."

The waiter smiled. "I recommended him to take one."

"Thank you," said Mrs. Adney; and the Oberkellner withdrew. Then she went on, abruptly: "Will you do me a favour?"

"Yes, if you'll do *me* one. Let me see if your picture is signed."

She glanced at the sketch before giving it to me. "For a wonder it isn't."

"It ought to be, for full value. May I keep it awhile?"

"Yes, if you'll do what I ask. Take an umbrella and go after Mr. Vawdrey."

"To bring him to Mrs. Adney?"

"To keep him out—as long as you can."

"I'll keep him as long as the rain holds off."

"Oh, never mind the rain!" my companion exclaimed.

"Would you have us drenched?"

"Without remorse." Then with a strange light in her eyes she added: "I'm going to try."

"To try?"

"To see the real one. Oh, if I can get at him!" she broke out with passion.

"Try, try!" I replied. "I'll keep our friend all day."

"If I can get at the one who does it"—and she paused, with shining eyes—"if I can have it out with him I shall get my part!"

"I'll keep Vawdrey forever!" I called after her as she passed quickly into the house.

Her audacity was communicative, and I stood there in a glow of excitement. I looked at Lord Mellifont's water-colour and I looked at the gathering storm; I turned my eyes again to his lordship's windows and then I bent them on my watch. Vawdrey had so little the start of me that I should have time to overtake him—time even if I should take five minutes to go up to Lord Mellifont's sitting-room (where we had all been hospitably received), and say to him, as a messenger, that Mrs. Adney begged he would bestow upon his sketch the high consecration of his signature.

As I again considered this work of art I perceived there was something it certainly did lack: what else then but so noble an autograph? It was my duty to supply the deficiency without delay, and in accordance with this conviction I instantly re-entered the hotel. I went up to Lord Mellifont's apartments; I reached the door of his salon. Here, however, I was met by a difficulty of which my extravagance had not taken account. If I were to knock I should spoil everything; yet was I prepared to dispense with this ceremony? I asked myself the question, and it embarrassed me; I turned my little picture round and round, but it didn't give me the answer I wanted.

I wanted it to say: 'Open the door gently, gently, without a sound, yet very quickly: then you will see what you will see.' I had gone so far as to lay my hand upon the knob when I became aware (having my wits so about me), that exactly in the manner I was thinking of—gently, gently, without a sound—another door had moved, on the opposite side of the hall. At the same instant I found myself smiling rather constrainedly upon Lady Mellifont, who, on seeing me, had checked herself on the threshold of her room.

For a moment, as she stood there, we exchanged two or three ideas that were the more singular for being unspoken. We had caught each other hovering, and we understood each other; but as I stepped over to her (so that we were separated from the sitting-room by the width of the hall), her lips formed the almost soundless entreaty: "Don't!" I could see in her conscious eyes everything that the word expressed—the confession of her own curiosity and the dread of the consequences of mine. "*Don't!*" she repeated, as I stood before her.

From the moment my experiment could strike her as an act of violence I was ready to renounce it; yet I thought I detected in her frightened face a still deeper betrayal—a possibility of disappointment if I should give way. It was as if she had said: 'I'll let you do it if you'll take the responsibility. Yes, with someone else I'd surprise him. But it would never do for him to think it was I.'

"We soon found Lord Mellifont," I observed, in allusion to our encounter with her an hour before, "and he was so good as to give this lovely sketch to Mrs. Adney, who has asked me to come up and beg him to put in the omitted signature."

Lady Mellifont took the drawing from me, and I could guess the struggle that went on in her while she looked at it. She was silent for some time; then I felt that all her delicacies and dignities, all her old timidities and pieties were fighting against her opportunity. She turned away from me and, with the drawing, went back to her room. She was absent for a couple of minutes, and when she reappeared I could see that she had vanquished her temptation; that even, with a kind of resurgent horror, she had shrunk from it. She had deposited the sketch in the room. "If you will kindly leave the picture with me, I will see that Mrs. Adney's request is attended to," she said, with great courtesy and sweetness, but in a manner that put an end to our colloquy.

I assented, with a somewhat artificial enthusiasm perhaps, and then, to ease off our separation, remarked that we were going to have a change of weather.

"In that case we shall go—we shall go immediately," said Lady Mellifont. I was amused at the eagerness with which she made this declaration: it appeared to represent a coveted flight into safety, an escape with her threatened secret. I was the more surprised therefore when, as I was turning away, she put out her hand to take mine. She had the pretext of bidding me farewell, but as I shook hands with her on this supposition I felt that what the movement really conveyed was: 'I thank you for the help you would have given me, but it's better as it is. If I should know, who would help me then?' As I went to my room to get my umbrella I said to myself : 'She's sure, but she won't put it to the proof.'

A quarter of an hour later I had overtaken Clare Vawdrey in the pass, and shortly after this we found ourselves looking for refuge. The storm had not only completely gathered, but it had broken at the last with extraordinary rapidity. We scrambled up a hillside to an empty cabin, a rough structure that was hardly more than a shed for the protection of cattle. It was a tolerable shelter however, and it had fissures through which we could watch the splendid spectacle of the tempest. This entertainment lasted an hour—an hour that has remained with me as full of odd disparities. While the lightning played with the thunder and the rain gushed in on our umbrellas, I said to myself that Clare Vawdrey was disappointing.

I don't know exactly what I should have predicated of a great author exposed to the fury of the elements, I can't say what particular Manfred attitude I should have expected my companion to assume, but it seemed to me somehow that I shouldn't have looked to him to regale me in such a situation with stories (which I had already heard), about the celebrated Lady Ringrose. Her ladyship formed the subject of Vawdrey's conversation during this prodigious scene, though before it was quite over he had launched out on Mr. Chafer, the scarcely less notorious reviewer. It broke my heart to hear a man like Vawdrey talk of reviewers.

The lightning projected a hard clearness upon the truth, familiar to me for years, to which the last day or two had added transcendent support—the irritating certitude that for personal relations this admirable genius thought his second-best good enough. It *was*, no doubt, as society was made, but there was a contempt in the distinction which could not fail to be galling to an admirer. The world was vulgar and stupid, and the real man would have been a fool to come out for it when he could gossip and dine by deputy. None the less my heart sank as I felt my companion practice this economy. I don't know exactly what I wanted; I suppose I wanted him to make an exception for *me*. I almost believed he would, if he had known how I worshipped his talent. But I had never been able to translate this to him, and his application of his principle was relentless. At any rate I was more than ever sure that at such an hour his chair at home was not empty: *there* was the Manfred attitude, *there* were the responsive flashes. I could only envy Mrs. Adney her presumable enjoyment of them.

The weather drew off at last, and the rain abated sufficiently to allow us to emerge from our asylum and make our way back to the inn, where we found on our arrival that our prolonged absence had produced some agitation. It was judged apparently that the fury of the elements might have placed us in a predicament. Several of our friends were at the door, and they seemed a little disconcerted when it was perceived that we were only drenched. Clare Vawdrey, for some reason, was wetter than I, and he took his course to his room.

Blanche Adney was among the persons collected to look out for us, but as Vawdrey came toward her she shrank from him, without a greeting; with a movement that I observed as almost one of estrangement she turned her back on him and went quickly into the salon. Wet as I was I went in after her; on which she immediately flung round and faced me. The first thing I saw was that she had never been so beautiful. There was a light of inspiration in her face, and she broke out to me in the quickest whisper, which was at the same time the loudest cry, I have ever heard: "I've got my *part*!"

"You went to his room—I was right?"

"Right?" Blanche Adney repeated. "Ah, my dear fellow!" she murmured.

"He was there—you saw him?"

"He saw me. It was the hour of my life!"

"It must have been the hour of his, if you were half as lovely as you are at this moment."

"He's splendid," she pursued, as if she didn't hear me. "He *is* the one who does it!" I listened, immensely impressed, and she added: "We understood each other."

"By flashes of lightning?"

"Oh, I didn't see the lightning then!"

"How long were you there?" I asked with admiration.

"Long enough to tell him I adore him."

"Ah, that's what I've never been able to tell him!" I exclaimed ruefully.

"I shall have my part—I shall have my part!" she continued, with triumphant indifference; and she flung round the room with the joy of a girl, only checking herself to say: "Go and change your clothes."

"You shall have Lord Mellifont's signature," I said.

"Oh, bother Lord Mellifont's signature! He's far nicer than Mr Vawdrey," she went on irrelevantly.

"Lord Mellifont?" I pretended to inquire.

"Confound Lord Mellifont!" And Blanche Adney, in her elation, brushed by me, whisking again through the open door. Just outside of it she came upon her husband; whereupon, with a charming cry of "We're talking of you, my love!" she threw herself upon him and kissed him.

I went to my room and changed my clothes, but I remained there till the evening. The violence of the storm had passed over us, but the rain had settled down to a drizzle. On descending to dinner I found that the change in the weather had already broken up our party. The Mellifonts had departed in a carriage and four, they had been followed by others, and several vehicles had been bespoken for the morning. Blanche Adney's was one of them, and on the pretext that she had preparations to make she quitted us directly after dinner.

Clare Vawdrey asked me what was the matter with her—she suddenly appeared to dislike him. I forget what answer I gave, but I did my best to comfort him by driving away with him the next day. Mrs. Adney had vanished when we came down; but they made up their quarrel in London, for he finished his play, which she produced. I must add that she is still, nevertheless, in want of the great part. I have a beautiful one in my head, but she doesn't come to see me to stir me up about it. Lady Mellifont always drops me a kind word when we meet, but that doesn't console me.

The Right Thing

Chapter 1

When the porter's wife (she used to answer the house-bell), announced "A gentleman—with a lady, sir," I had, as I often had in those days, for the wish was father to the thought, an immediate vision of sitters. Sitters my visitors in this case proved to be; but not in the sense I should have preferred. However, there was nothing at first to indicate that they might not have come for a portrait. The gentleman, a man of fifty, very high and very straight, with a moustache slightly grizzled and a dark grey walking-coat admirably fitted, both of which I noted professionally—I don't mean as a barber or yet as a tailor—would have struck me as a celebrity if celebrities often were striking. It was a truth of which I had for some time been conscious that a figure with a good deal of frontage was, as one might say, almost never a public institution. A glance at the lady helped to remind me of this paradoxical law: she also looked too distinguished to be a "personality." Moreover one would scarcely come across two variations together.

Neither of the pair spoke immediately—they only prolonged the preliminary gaze which suggested that each wished to give the other a chance. They were visibly shy; they stood there letting me take them in—which, as I afterwards perceived, was the most practical thing they could have done. In this way their embarrassment served their cause. I had seen people painfully reluctant to mention that they desired anything so gross as to be represented on canvas; but the scruples of my new friends appeared almost insurmountable. Yet the gentleman might have said "I should like a portrait of my wife," and the lady might have said "I should like a portrait of my husband." Perhaps they were not husband and wife—this naturally would make the matter more delicate. Perhaps they wished to be done together—in which case they ought to have brought a third person to break the news.

"We come from Mr. Rivet," the lady said at last, with a dim smile which had the effect of a moist sponge passed over a "sunk" piece of painting, as well as of a vague allusion to vanished beauty. She was as tall and straight, in her degree, as her companion, and with ten years less to carry. She looked as sad as a woman could look whose face was not charged with expression; that is her tinted oval mask showed friction as an exposed surface shows it. The hand of time had played over her freely, but only to simplify. She was slim and stiff, and so well-dressed, in dark blue cloth, with lappets and pockets and buttons, that it was clear she employed the same tailor as her husband. The couple had an indefinable air of prosperous thrift—they evidently got a good deal of luxury for their money. If I was to be one of their luxuries it would behove me to consider my terms.

"Ah, Claude Rivet recommended me?" I inquired; and I added that it was very kind of him, though I could reflect that, as he only painted landscape, this was not a sacrifice.

The lady looked very hard at the gentleman, and the gentleman looked round the room. Then staring at the floor a moment and stroking his moustache, he rested his pleasant eyes on me with the remark:

"He said you were the right one."

"I try to be, when people want to sit."

"Yes, we should like to," said the lady anxiously.

"Do you mean together?"

My visitors exchanged a glance. "If you could do anything with ME, I suppose it would be double," the gentleman stammered.

"Oh yes, there's naturally a higher charge for two figures than for one."

"We should like to make it pay," the husband confessed.

"That's very good of you," I returned, appreciating so unwonted a sympathy—for I supposed he meant pay the artist.

A sense of strangeness seemed to dawn on the lady. "We mean for the illustrations—Mr Rivet said you might put one in."

"Put one in—an illustration?" I was equally confused.

"Sketch her off, you know," said the gentleman, colouring.

It was only then that I understood the service Claude Rivet had rendered me; he had told them that I worked in black and white, for magazines, for story-books, for sketches of contemporary life, and consequently had frequent employment for models. These things were true, but it was not less true (I may confess it now—whether because the aspiration was to lead to everything or to nothing I leave the reader to guess), that I couldn't get the honours, to say nothing of the emoluments, of a great painter of portraits out of my head.

My "illustrations" were my pot-boilers; I looked to a different branch of art (far and away the most interesting it had always seemed to me), to perpetuate my fame. There was no shame in looking to it also to make my fortune; but that fortune was by so much further from being made from the moment my visitors wished to be "done" for nothing. I was disappointed; for in the pictorial sense I had immediately SEEN them. I had seized their type—I had already settled what I would do with it. Something that wouldn't absolutely have pleased them, I afterwards reflected.

"Ah, you're—you're—a—?" I began, as soon as I had mastered my surprise. I couldn't bring out the dingy word "models"; it seemed to fit the case so little.

"We haven't had much practice," said the lady.

"We've got to DO something, and we've thought that an artist in your line might perhaps make something of us," her husband threw off. He further mentioned that they didn't know many artists and that they had gone first, on the off-chance (he painted views of course, but sometimes put in figures—perhaps

I remembered), to Mr. Rivet, whom they had met a few years before at a place in Norfolk where he was sketching.

"We used to sketch a little ourselves," the lady hinted.

"It's very awkward, but we absolutely MUST do something," her husband went on.

"Of course, we're not so VERY young," she admitted, with a wan smile.

With the remark that I might as well know something more about them, the husband had handed me a card extracted from a neat new pocket-book (their appurtenances were all of the freshest) and inscribed with the words "Major Monarch." Impressive as these words were they didn't carry my knowledge much further; but my visitor presently added: "I've left the army, and we've had the misfortune to lose our money. In fact our means are dreadfully small."

"It's an awful bore," said Mrs. Monarch.

They evidently wished to be discreet—to take care not to swagger because they were gentlefolks. I perceived they would have been willing to recognise this as something of a drawback, at the same time that I guessed at an underlying sense—their consolation in adversity—that they HAD their points. They certainly had; but these advantages struck me as preponderantly social; such for instance as would help to make a drawing-room look well. However, a drawing-room was always, or ought to be, a picture.

In consequence of his wife's allusion to their age Major Monarch observed: "Naturally, it's more for the figure that we thought of going in. We can still hold ourselves up." On the instant I saw that the figure was indeed their strong point. His "naturally" didn't sound vain, but it lighted up the question. "SHE has got the best," he continued, nodding at his wife, with a pleasant after-dinner absence of circumlocution. I could only reply, as if we were in fact sitting over our wine, that this didn't prevent his own from being very good; which led him in turn to rejoin: "We thought that if you ever have to do people like us, we might be something like it. SHE, particularly—for a lady in a book, you know."

I was so amused by them that, to get more of it, I did my best to take their point of view; and though it was an embarrassment to find myself appraising physically, as if they were animals on hire or useful blacks, a pair whom I should have expected to meet only in one of the relations in which criticism is tacit, I looked at Mrs. Monarch judicially enough to be able to exclaim, after a moment, with conviction: "Oh yes, a lady in a book!" She was singularly like a bad illustration.

"We'll stand up, if you like," said the Major; and he raised himself before me with a really grand air.

I could take his measure at a glance—he was six feet two and a perfect gentleman. It would have paid any club in process of formation and in want of a stamp to engage him at a salary to stand in the principal window. What struck me immediately was that in coming to me they had rather missed their vocation; they could surely have been turned to better account for advertising purposes. I couldn't of course see the thing in detail, but I could see them make someone's fortune—I don't mean their own. There was something in them for a waistcoat-maker, an hotel-keeper or a soap-vendor. I could imagine "We always use it" pinned on their bosoms with the greatest effect; I had a vision of the promptitude with which they would launch a *table d'hôte*.

Mrs. Monarch sat still, not from pride but from shyness, and presently her husband said to her: "Get up my dear and show how smart you are." She obeyed, but she had no need to get up to show it. She walked to the end of the studio, and then she came back blushing, with her fluttered eyes on her husband. I was reminded of an incident I had accidentally had a glimpse of in Paris—being with a friend there, a dramatist about to produce a play—when an actress came to him to ask to be intrusted with a part. She went through her paces before him, walked up and down as Mrs. Monarch was doing.

Mrs. Monarch did it quite as well, but I abstained from applauding. It was very odd to see such people apply for such poor pay. She looked as if she had ten thousand a year. Her husband had used the word that described her: she was, in the London current jargon, essentially and typically "smart." Her figure was, in the same order of ideas, conspicuously and irreproachably "good." For a woman of her age her waist was surprisingly small; her elbow moreover had the orthodox crook. She held her head at the conventional angle; but why did she come to ME? She ought to have tried on jackets at a big shop. I feared my visitors were not only destitute, but "artistic"— which would be a great complication. When she sat down again I thanked her, observing that what a draughtsman most valued in his model was the faculty of keeping quiet.

"Oh, SHE can keep quiet," said Major Monarch. Then he added, jocosely: "I've always kept her quiet."

"I'm not a nasty fidget, am I?" Mrs. Monarch appealed to her husband.

He addressed his answer to me. "Perhaps it isn't out of place to mention—because we ought to be quite business-like, oughtn't we?—that when I married her she was known as the Beautiful Statue."

"Oh dear!" said Mrs. Monarch, ruefully.

"Of course I should want a certain amount of expression," I rejoined.

"Of COURSE!" they both exclaimed.

"And then I suppose you know that you'll get awfully tired."

"Oh, we NEVER get tired!" they eagerly cried.

"Have you had any kind of practice?"

They hesitated—they looked at each other. "We've been photographed, IMMENSELY," said Mrs. Monarch.

"She means the fellows have asked us," added the Major.

"I see—because you're so good-looking."

"I don't know what they thought, but they were always after us."

"We always got our photographs for nothing," smiled Mrs. Monarch.

"We might have brought some, my dear," her husband remarked.

"I'm not sure we have any left. We've given quantities away," she explained to me.

"With our autographs and that sort of thing," said the Major.

"Are they to be got in the shops?" I inquired, as a harmless pleasantry.

"Oh, yes; hers—they used to be."

"Not now," said Mrs. Monarch, with her eyes on the floor.

Chapter 2

I could fancy the "sort of thing" they put on the presentation-copies of their photographs, and I was sure they wrote a beautiful hand. It was odd how quickly I was sure of everything that concerned them. If they were now so poor as to have to earn shillings and pence, they never had had much of a margin. Their good looks had been their capital, and they had good-humouredly made the most of the career that this resource marked out for them. It was in their faces, the blankness, the deep intellectual repose of the twenty years of country-house visiting which had given them pleasant intonations. I could see the sunny drawing-rooms, sprinkled with periodicals she didn't read, in which Mrs. Monarch had continuously sat; I could see the wet shrubberies in which she had walked, equipped to admiration for either exercise.

I could see the rich covers the Major had helped to shoot and the wonderful garments in which, late at night, he repaired to the smoking-room to talk about them. I could imagine their leggings and waterproofs, their knowing tweeds and rugs, their rolls of sticks and cases of tackle and neat umbrellas; and I could evoke the exact appearance of their servants and the compact variety of their luggage on the platforms of country stations.

They gave small tips, but they were liked; they didn't do anything themselves, but they were welcome. They looked so well everywhere; they gratified the general relish for stature, complexion and "form." They knew it without fatuity or vulgarity, and they respected themselves in consequence. They were not superficial; they were thorough and kept themselves up—it had been their line. People with such a taste for activity had to have some line. I could feel how, even in a dull house, they could have been counted upon for cheerfulness.

At present something had happened—it didn't matter what, their little income had grown less, it had grown least—and they had to do something for pocket-money. Their friends liked them, but didn't like to support them. There was something about them that represented credit—their clothes, their manners, their type; but if credit is a large empty pocket in which an occasional chink reverberates, the chink at least must be audible. What they wanted of me was to help to make it so. Fortunately they had no children—I soon divined that. They would also perhaps wish our relations to be kept secret: this was why it was "for the figure"—the reproduction of the face would betray them.

I liked them—they were so simple; and I had no objection to them if they would suit. But, somehow, with all their perfections I didn't easily believe in them. After all they were amateurs, and the ruling passion of my life was the detestation of the amateur. Combined with this was another perversity—an innate preference for the represented subject over the real one: the defect of the real one was so apt to be a lack of representation. I liked things that appeared; then one was sure. Whether they WERE or not was a subordinate and almost always a profitless question. There were other considerations, the first of which was that I already had two or three people in use, notably a young person with big feet, in alpaca, from Kilburn, who for a couple of years had come to me regularly for my illustrations and with whom I was still—perhaps ignobly—satisfied.

I frankly explained to my visitors how the case stood; but they had taken more precautions than I supposed. They had reasoned out their opportunity, for Claude Rivet had told them of the projected edition *de luxe* of one of the writers of our day—the rarest of the novelists—who, long neglected by the multitudinous vulgar and dearly prized by the attentive (need I mention Philip Vincent?) had had the happy fortune of seeing, late in life, the dawn and then the full light of a higher criticism—an estimate in which, on the part of the public, there was something really of expiation.

The edition in question, planned by a publisher of taste, was practically an act of high reparation; the wood-cuts with which it was to be enriched were the homage of English art to one of the most independent representatives of English letters. Major and Mrs. Monarch confessed to me that they had hoped I might be able to work THEM into my share of the enterprise. They knew I was to do the first of the books, *Rutland Ramsay,* but I had to make clear to them that my participation in the rest of the affair—this first book was to be a test—was to depend on the satisfaction I should give.

If this should be limited my employers would drop me without a scruple. It was therefore a crisis for me, and naturally I was making special preparations, looking about for new people, if they should be necessary, and securing the best types. I admitted however that I should like to settle down to two or three good models who would do for everything.

"Should we have often to—a—put on special clothes?" Mrs. Monarch timidly demanded.

"Dear, yes—that's half the business."

"And should we be expected to supply our own costumes?"

"Oh, no; I've got a lot of things. A painter's models put on—or put off—anything he likes."

"And do you mean—a—the same?"

"The same?"

Mrs. Monarch looked at her husband again.

"Oh, she was just wondering," he explained, "if the costumes are in GENERAL use." I had to confess that they were, and I mentioned further that some of them (I had a lot of genuine, greasy last-century things), had served their time, a hundred years ago, on living, world-stained men and women. "We'll put on anything that fits," said the Major.

"Oh, I arrange that—they fit in the pictures."

"I'm afraid I should do better for the modern books. I would come as you like," said Mrs. Monarch.

"She has got a lot of clothes at home: they might do for contemporary life," her husband continued.

"Oh, I can fancy scenes in which you'd be quite natural." And indeed I could see the slipshod rearrangements of stale properties—the stories I tried to produce pictures for without the exasperation of reading them—whose sandy tracts the good lady might help to people. But I had to return to the fact that for this sort of work—the daily mechanical grind—I was already equipped; the people I was working with were fully adequate.

"We only thought we might be more like SOME characters," said Mrs. Monarch mildly, getting up.

Her husband also rose; he stood looking at me with a dim wistfulness that was touching in so fine a man. "Wouldn't it be rather a pull sometimes to have—a—to have—?" He hung fire; he wanted me to help him by phrasing what he meant. But I couldn't—I didn't know. So he brought it out, awkwardly: "The REAL thing; a gentleman, you know, or a lady." I was quite ready to give a general assent—I admitted that there was a great deal in that.

This encouraged Major Monarch to say, following up his appeal with an unacted gulp: "It's awfully hard—we've tried everything." The gulp was communicative; it proved too much for his wife. Before I knew it Mrs. Monarch had dropped again upon a divan and burst into tears. Her husband sat down beside her, holding one of her hands; whereupon she quickly dried her eyes with the other, while I felt embarrassed as she looked up at me. "There isn't a confounded job I haven't applied for-waited for—prayed for. You can fancy we'd be pretty bad first. Secretaryships and that sort of thing? You might as well ask for a peerage. I'd be ANYTHING—I'm strong; a messenger or a coalheaver. I'd put on a gold-laced cap and open carriage-doors in front of the haberdasher's; I'd hang about a station, to carry portmanteaus; I'd be a postman. But they won't LOOK at you;

there are thousands, as good as yourself, already on the ground. GENTLEMEN, poor beggars, who have drunk their wine, who have kept their hunters!"

I was as reassuring as I knew how to be, and my visitors were presently on their feet again while, for the experiment, we agreed on an hour. We were discussing it when the door opened and Miss Churm came in with a wet umbrella. Miss Churm had to take the omnibus to Maida Vale and then walk half-a-mile. She looked a trifle blowsy and slightly splashed. I scarcely ever saw her come in without thinking afresh how odd it was that, being so little in herself, she should yet be so much in others. She was a meagre little Miss Churm, but she was an ample heroine of romance. She was only a freckled cockney, but she could represent everything, from a fine lady to a shepherdess; she had the faculty, as she might have had a fine voice or long hair.

She couldn't spell, and she loved beer, but she had two or three "points," and practice, and a knack, and mother-wit, and a kind of whimsical sensibility, and a love of the theatre, and seven sisters, and not an ounce of respect, especially for the H. The first thing my visitors saw was that her umbrella was wet, and in their spotless perfection they visibly winced at it. The rain had come on since their arrival.

"I'm all in a soak; there WAS a mess of people in the 'bus. I wish you lived near a stytion," said Miss Churm. I requested her to get ready as quickly as possible, and she passed into the room in which she always changed her dress. But before going out she asked me what she was to get into this time.

"It's the Russian princess, don't you know?" I answered; "the one with the 'golden eyes,' in black velvet, for the long thing in the *Cheapside*."

"Golden eyes? I SAY!" cried Miss Churm, while my companions watched her with intensity as she withdrew. She always arranged herself, when she was late, before I could turn round; and I kept my visitors a little, on purpose, so that they might get an idea, from seeing her, what would be expected of themselves. I mentioned that she was quite my notion of an excellent model—she was really very clever.

"Do you think she looks like a Russian princess?" Major Monarch asked, with lurking alarm.

"When I make her, yes."

"Oh, if you have to MAKE her—!" he reasoned, acutely.

"That's the most you can ask. There are so many that are not makeable."

"Well now, HERE'S a lady"—and with a persuasive smile he passed his arm into his wife's—"who's already made!"

"Oh, I'm not a Russian princess," Mrs. Monarch protested, a little coldly. I could see that she had known some and didn't like them. There, immediately, was a complication of a kind that I never had to fear with Miss Churm.

This young lady came back in black velvet—the gown was rather rusty and very low on her lean shoulders—and with a Japanese fan in her red hands. I reminded her that in the scene I was doing she had to look over someone's head. "I forget whose it is; but it doesn't matter. Just look over a head."

"I'd rather look over a stove," said Miss Churm; and she took her station near the fire. She fell into position, settled herself into a tall attitude, gave a certain backward inclination to her head and a certain forward droop to her fan, and looked, at least to my prejudiced sense, distinguished and charming, foreign and dangerous. We left her looking so, while I went downstairs with Major and Mrs. Monarch.

"I think I could come about as near it as that," said Mrs. Monarch.

"Oh, you think she's shabby, but you must allow for the alchemy of art."

However, they went off with an evident increase of comfort, founded on their demonstrable advantage in being the real thing. I could fancy them shuddering over Miss Churm. She was very droll about them when I went back, for I told her what they wanted.

"Well, if SHE can sit I'll tyke to bookkeeping," said my model.

"She's very lady-like," I replied, as an innocent form of aggravation.

"So much the worse for YOU. That means she can't turn round."

"She'll do for the fashionable novels."

"Oh yes, she'll DO for them!" my model humorously declared. "Ain't they had enough without her?" I had often sociably denounced them to Miss Churm.

Chapter 3

It was for the elucidation of a mystery in one of these works that I first tried Mrs. Monarch. Her husband came with her, to be useful if necessary—it was sufficiently clear that as a general thing he would prefer to come with her. At first I wondered if this were for "propriety's" sake—if he were going to be jealous and meddling. The idea was too tiresome, and if it had been confirmed it would speedily have brought our acquaintance to a close. But I soon saw there was nothing in it and that if he accompanied Mrs. Monarch it was (in addition to the chance of being wanted), simply because he had nothing else to do.

When she was away from him his occupation was gone—she never HAD been away from him. I judged, rightly, that in their awkward situation their close union was their main comfort and that this union had no weak spot. It was a real marriage, an encouragement to the hesitating, a nut for pessimists to crack. Their address was humble (I remember afterwards thinking it had been the only thing about them that was really professional), and I could fancy the lamentable lodgings in which the Major would have been left alone. He could bear them with his wife-he couldn't bear them without her.

He had too much tact to try and make himself agreeable when he couldn't be useful; so he simply sat and waited, when I was too absorbed in my work to talk. But I liked to make him talk—it made my work, when it didn't interrupt it, less sordid, less special. To listen to him was to combine the excitement of going out with the economy of staying at home. There was only one hindrance: that I seemed not to know any of the people he and his wife had known. I think he wondered extremely, during the term of our intercourse, whom the deuce I DID know. He hadn't a stray sixpence of an idea to fumble for; so we didn't spin it very fine—we confined ourselves to questions of leather and even of liquor (saddlers and breeches-makers and how to get good claret cheap), and matters like "good trains" and the habits of small game. His lore on these last subjects was astonishing, he managed to interweave the station-master with the ornithologist. When he couldn't talk about greater things he could talk cheerfully about smaller, and since I couldn't accompany him into reminiscences of the fashionable world he could lower the conversation without a visible effort to my level.

So earnest a desire to please was touching in a man who could so easily have knocked one down. He looked after the fire and had an opinion on the draught of the stove, without my asking him, and I could see that he thought many of my arrangements not half clever enough. I remember telling him that if I were only rich I would offer him a salary to come and teach me how to live. Sometimes he gave a random sigh, of which the essence was: "Give me even such a bare old barrack as THIS, and I'd do something with it!"

When I wanted to use him he came alone; which was an illustration of the superior courage of women. His wife could bear her solitary second floor, and she was in general more discreet; showing by various small reserves that she was alive to the propriety of keeping our relations markedly professional—not letting them slide into sociability. She wished it to remain clear that she and the Major were employed, not cultivated, and if she approved of me as a superior, who could be kept in his place, she never thought me quite good enough for an equal.

She sat with great intensity, giving the whole of her mind to it, and was capable of remaining for an hour almost as motionless as if she were before a photographer's lens. I could see she had been photographed often, but somehow the very habit that made her good for that purpose unfitted her for mine. At first I was extremely pleased with her lady-like air, and it was a satisfaction, on coming to follow her lines, to see how good they were and how far they could lead the pencil. But after a few times I began to find her too insurmountably stiff; do what I would with it my drawing looked like a photograph or a copy of a photograph. Her figure had no variety of expression—she herself had no sense of variety. You may say that this was my business, was only a question of placing her.

I placed her in every conceivable position, but she managed to obliterate their differences. She was always a lady certainly, and into the bargain was always the same lady. She was the real thing, but always the same thing. There were moments when I was oppressed by the serenity of her confidence that she WAS the real thing. All her dealings with me and all her husband's were an implication that this was lucky for ME.

Meanwhile I found myself trying to invent types that approached her own, instead of making her own transform itself—in the clever way that was not impossible, for instance, to poor Miss Churm. Arrange as I would and take the precautions I would, she always, in my pictures, came out too tall—landing me in the dilemma of having represented a fascinating woman as seven feet high, which, out of respect perhaps to my own very much scantier inches, was far from my idea of such a personage.

The case was worse with the Major—nothing I could do would keep HIM down, so that he became useful only for the representation of brawny giants. I adored variety and range, I cherished human accidents, the illustrative note; I wanted to characterise closely, and the thing in the world I most hated was the danger of being ridden by a type. I had quarrelled with some of my friends about it—I had parted company with them for maintaining that one HAD to be, and that if the type was beautiful (witness Raphael and Leonardo), the servitude was only a gain. I was neither Leonardo nor Raphael; I might only be a presumptuous young modern searcher, but I held that everything was to be sacrificed sooner than character. When they averred that the haunting type in question could easily BE character, I retorted, perhaps superficially: "Whose?" It couldn't be everybody's—it might end in being nobody's.

After I had drawn Mrs. Monarch a dozen times I perceived more clearly than before that the value of such a model as Miss Churm resided precisely in the fact that she had no positive stamp, combined of course with the other fact that what she did have was a curious and inexplicable talent for imitation. Her usual appearance was like a curtain which she could draw up at request for a capital performance. This performance was simply suggestive; but it was a word to the wise—it was vivid and pretty. Sometimes, even, I thought it, though she was plain herself, too insipidly pretty; I made it a reproach to her that the figures drawn from her were monotonously (*betement*, as we used to say) graceful. Nothing made her more angry: it was so much her pride to feel that she could sit for characters that had nothing in common with each other. She would accuse me at such moments of taking away her "reputytion."

It suffered a certain shrinkage, this queer quantity, from the repeated visits of my new friends. Miss Churm was greatly in demand, never in want of employment, so I had no scruple in putting her off occasionally, to try them more at my ease. It was certainly amusing at first to do the real thing—it was amusing to do Major Monarch's trousers. They WERE the real thing, even if he did come out colossal. It was amusing to do his wife's back hair (it was so mathematically neat,) and the particular "smart" tension of her tight stays. She lent herself especially to positions in which the face was somewhat averted or blurred; she abounded in lady-like back views and *profils perdus*.

When she stood erect she took naturally one of the attitudes in which court-painters represent queens and princesses; so that I found myself wondering whether, to draw out this accomplishment, I couldn't get the editor of the *Cheapside* to publish a really royal romance, *A Tale of Buckingham Palace*. Sometimes, however, the real thing and the make-believe came into contact; by which I mean that Miss Churm, keeping an appointment or coming to make one on days when I had much work in hand, encountered her invidious rivals.

The encounter was not on their part, for they noticed her no more than if she had been the housemaid; not from intentional loftiness, but simply because, as yet, professionally, they didn't know how to fraternise, as I could guess that they would have liked—or at least that the Major would. They couldn't talk about the omnibus—they always walked; and they didn't know what else to try—she wasn't interested in good trains or cheap claret. Besides, they must have felt—in the air—that she was amused at them, secretly derisive of their ever knowing how. She was not a person to conceal her scepticism if she had had a chance to show it. On the other hand Mrs. Monarch didn't think her tidy; for why else did she take pains to say to me (it was going out of the way, for Mrs. Monarch), that she didn't like dirty women?

One day when my young lady happened to be present with my other sitters (she even dropped in, when it was convenient, for a chat), I asked her to be so good as to lend a hand in getting tea—a service with which she was familiar and which was one of a class that, living as I did in a small way, with slender domestic resources, I often appealed to my models to render. They liked to lay hands on my property, to break the sitting, and sometimes the china—I made them feel Bohemian.

The next time I saw Miss Churm after this incident she surprised me greatly by making a scene about it—she accused me of having wished to humiliate her. She had not resented the outrage at the time, but had seemed obliging and amused, enjoying the comedy of asking Mrs. Monarch, who sat vague and silent, whether she would have cream and sugar, and putting an exaggerated simper into the question. She had tried intonations—as if she too wished to pass for the real thing; till I was afraid my other visitors would take offence.

Oh, THEY were determined not to do this; and their touching patience was the measure of their great need. They would sit by the hour, uncomplaining, till I was ready to use them; they would come back on the chance of being wanted and would walk away cheerfully if they were not. I used to go to the door with them to see in what magnificent order they retreated. I tried to find other employment for them—I introduced them to several artists.

But they didn't "take," for reasons I could appreciate, and I became conscious, rather anxiously, that after such disappointments they fell back upon me with a heavier weight. They did me the honour to think that it was I who was most THEIR form. They were not picturesque enough for the painters, and in those days there were not so many serious workers in black and white. Besides, they had an eye to the great job I had mentioned to them—they had secretly set their hearts on supplying the right essence for my pictorial vindication of our fine novelist. They knew that for this undertaking I should want no costume-effects, none of the frippery of past ages—that it was a case in which everything would be contemporary and satirical and, presumably, genteel. If I could work them into it their future would be assured, for the labour would of course be long and the occupation steady.

One day Mrs. Monarch came without her husband—she explained his absence by his having had to go to the City. While she sat there in her usual anxious stiffness there came, at the door, a knock which I immediately recognised as the subdued appeal of a model out of work. It was followed by the entrance of a young man whom I easily perceived to be a foreigner and who proved in fact an Italian acquainted with no English word but my name, which he uttered in a way that made it seem to include all others. I had not then visited his country, nor was I proficient in his tongue; but as he was not so meanly constituted—what Italian is?—as to depend only on that member for expression he conveyed to me, in familiar but graceful mimicry, that he was in search of exactly the employment in which the lady before me was engaged.

I was not struck with him at first, and while I continued to draw I emitted rough sounds of discouragement and dismissal. He stood his ground, however, not importunately, but with a dumb, dog-like fidelity in his eyes which amounted to innocent impudence—the manner of a devoted servant (he might have been in the house for years), unjustly suspected. Suddenly I saw that this very attitude and expression made a picture, whereupon I told him to sit down and wait till I should be free. There was another picture in the way he obeyed me, and I observed as I worked that there were others still in the way he looked wonderingly, with his head thrown back, about the high studio. He might have been crossing himself in St. Peter's. Before I finished I said to myself: "The fellow's a bankrupt orange-monger, but he's a treasure."

When Mrs. Monarch withdrew he passed across the room like a flash to open the door for her, standing there with the rapt, pure gaze of the young Dante spellbound by the young Beatrice. As I never insisted, in such situations, on the blankness of the British domestic, I reflected that he had the making of a servant (and I needed one, but couldn't pay him to be only that), as well as of a model; in short I made up my mind to adopt my bright adventurer if he would agree to officiate in the double capacity. He jumped at my offer, and in the event my rashness (for I had known nothing about him), was not brought home to me. He proved a sympathetic though a desultory ministrant, and had in a wonderful degree the sentiment *de la pose*.

It was uncultivated, instinctive; a part of the happy instinct which had guided him to my door and helped him to spell out my name on the card nailed to it. He had had no other introduction to me than a guess, from the shape of my high north window, seen outside, that my place was a studio and that as a studio it would contain an artist. He had wandered to England in search of fortune, like other itinerants, and had embarked, with a partner and a small green handcart, on the sale of penny ices. The ices had melted away and the partner had dissolved in their train.

My young man wore tight yellow trousers with reddish stripes and his name was Oronte. He was sallow but fair, and when I put him into some old clothes of my own he looked like an Englishman. He was as good as Miss Churm, who could look, when required, like an Italian.

CHAPTER 4

I thought Mrs. Monarch's face slightly convulsed when, on her coming back with her husband, she found Oronte installed. It was strange to have to recognise in a scrap of a *lazzarone* a competitor to her magnificent Major. It was she who scented danger first, for the Major was anecdotically unconscious. But Oronte gave us tea, with a hundred eager confusions (he had never seen such a queer process), and I think she thought better of me for having at last an "establishment." They saw a couple of drawings that I had made of the establishment, and Mrs. Monarch hinted that it never would have struck her that he had sat for them.

"Now the drawings you make from US, they look exactly like us," she reminded me, smiling in triumph; and I recognised that this was indeed just their defect. When I drew the Monarchs I couldn't, somehow, get away from them—get into the character I wanted to represent; and I had not the least desire my model should be discoverable in my picture. Miss Churm never was, and Mrs. Monarch thought I hid her, very properly, because she was vulgar; whereas if she was lost it was only as the dead who go to heaven are lost—in the gain of an angel the more.

By this time I had got a certain start with *Rutland Ramsay*, the first novel in the great projected series; that is I had produced a dozen drawings, several with the help of the Major and his wife, and I had sent them in for approval. My understanding with the publishers, as I have already hinted, had been that I was to be left to do my work, in this particular case, as I liked, with the whole book committed to me; but my connection with the rest of the series was only contingent. There were moments when, frankly, it WAS a comfort to have the real thing under one's hand; for there were characters in *Rutland Ramsay* that were very much like it. There were people presumably as straight as the Major and women of as good a fashion as Mrs. Monarch. There was a great deal of country-house life—treated, it is true, in a fine, fanciful, ironical, generalised way—and there was a considerable implication of knickerbockers and kilts.

There were certain things I had to settle at the outset; such things for instance as the exact appearance of the hero, the particular bloom of the heroine. The author of course gave me a lead, but there was a margin for interpretation. I took the Monarchs into my confidence, I told them frankly what I was about, I mentioned my embarrassments and alternatives. "Oh, take HIM!" Mrs. Monarch murmured sweetly, looking at her husband; and "What could you want better than my wife?" the Major inquired, with the comfortable candour that now prevailed between us.

I was not obliged to answer these remarks—I was only obliged to place my sitters. I was not easy in mind, and I postponed, a little timidly perhaps, the solution of the question. The book was a large canvas, the other figures were numerous, and I worked off at first some of the episodes in which the hero and the heroine were not concerned. When once I had set THEM up I should have to stick to them—I couldn't make my young man seven feet high in one place and five feet nine in another. I inclined on the whole to the latter measurement, though the Major more than once reminded me that HE looked about as young as anyone. It was indeed quite possible to arrange him, for the figure, so that it would have been difficult to detect his age.

After the spontaneous Oronte had been with me a month, and after I had given him to understand several different times that his native exuberance would presently constitute an insurmountable barrier to our further intercourse, I waked to a sense of his heroic capacity. He was only five feet seven, but the remaining inches were latent. I tried him almost secretly at first, for I was really rather afraid of the judgment my other models would pass on such a choice. If they regarded Miss Churm as little better than a snare, what would they think of the representation by a person so little the real thing as an Italian street-vendor of a protagonist formed by a public school?

If I went a little in fear of them it was not because they bullied me, because they had got an oppressive foothold, but because in their really pathetic decorum and mysteriously permanent newness they counted on me so intensely. I was therefore very glad when Jack Hawley came home: he was always of such good counsel. He painted badly himself, but there was no one like him for putting his finger on the place. He had been absent from England for a year; he had been somewhere—I don't remember where—to get a fresh eye. I was in a good deal of dread of any such organ, but we were old friends; he had been away for months and a sense of emptiness was creeping into my life. I hadn't dodged a missile for a year.

He came back with a fresh eye, but with the same old black velvet blouse, and the first evening he spent in my studio we smoked cigarettes till the small hours. He had done no work himself, he had only got the eye; so the field was clear for the production of my little things. He wanted to see what I had done for the *Cheapside*, but he was disappointed in the exhibition. That at least seemed the meaning of two or three comprehensive groans which, as he lounged on my big divan, on a folded leg, looking at my latest drawings, issued from his lips with the smoke of the cigarette.

"What's the matter with you?" I asked.

"What's the matter with YOU?"

"Nothing save that I'm mystified."

"You are indeed. You're quite off the hinge. What's the meaning of this new fad?" And he tossed me, with visible irreverence, a drawing in which I happened to have depicted both my majestic models. I asked if he didn't think it good, and he replied that it struck him as execrable, given the sort of thing I had always represented myself to him as wishing to arrive at; but I let that pass, I was so anxious to see exactly what he meant. The two figures in the picture looked colossal, but I supposed this was NOT what he meant, inasmuch as, for aught he knew to the contrary, I might have been trying for that.

I maintained that I was working exactly in the same way as

when he last had done me the honour to commend me. "Well, there's a big hole somewhere," he answered; "wait a bit and I'll discover it." I depended upon him to do so: where else was the fresh eye? But he produced at last nothing more luminous than "I don't know—I don't like your types." This was lame, for a critic who had never consented to discuss with me anything but the question of execution, the direction of strokes and the mystery of values.

"In the drawings you've been looking at I think my types are very handsome."

"Oh, they won't do!"

"I've had a couple of new models."

"I see you have. THEY won't do."

"Are you very sure of that?"

"Absolutely—they're stupid."

"You mean *I* am—for I ought to get round that."

"You CAN'T—with such people. Who are they?"

I told him, as far as was necessary, and he declared, heartlessly: "*Ce sont des gens qu'il faut mettre a la porte.*"

"You've never seen them; they're awfully good," I compassionately objected.

"Not seen them? Why, all this recent work of yours drops to pieces with them. It's all I want to see of them."

"No one else has said anything against it—the *Cheapside* people are pleased."

"Everyone else is an ass, and the *Cheapside* people the biggest asses of all. Come, don't pretend, at this time of day, to have pretty illusions about the public, especially about publishers and editors. It's not for SUCH animals you work—it's for those who know, *coloro che sanno*; so keep straight for ME if you can't keep straight for yourself. There's a certain sort of thing you tried for from the first—and a very good thing it is. But this twaddle isn't IN it." When I talked with Hawley later about *Rutland Ramsay* and its possible successors he declared that I must get back into my boat again or I would go to the bottom. His voice in short was the voice of warning.

I noted the warning, but I didn't turn my friends out of doors. They bored me a good deal; but the very fact that they bored me admonished me not to sacrifice them—if there was anything to be done with them—simply to irritation. As I look back at this phase they seem to me to have pervaded my life not a little. I have a vision of them as most of the time in my studio, seated, against the wall, on an old velvet bench to be out of the way, and looking like a pair of patient courtiers in a royal ante-chamber. I am convinced that during the coldest weeks of the winter they held their ground because it saved them fire. Their newness was losing its gloss, and it was impossible not to feel that they were objects of charity.

Whenever Miss Churm arrived they went away, and after I was fairly launched in *Rutland Ramsay* Miss Churm arrived pretty often. They managed to express to me tacitly that they supposed I wanted her for the low life of the book, and I let them suppose it, since they had attempted to study the work-it was lying about the studio—without discovering that it dealt only with the highest circles. They had dipped into the most brilliant of our novelists without deciphering many passages. I still took an hour from them, now and again, in spite of Jack Hawley's warning: it would be time enough to dismiss them, if dismissal should be necessary, when the rigour of the season was over.

Hawley had made their acquaintance—he had met them at my fireside—and thought them a ridiculous pair. Learning that he was a painter they tried to approach him, to show him too that they were the real thing; but he looked at them, across the big room, as if they were miles away: they were a compendium of everything that he most objected to in the social system of his country. Such people as that, all convention and patent-leather, with ejaculations that stopped conversation, had no business in a studio. A studio was a place to learn to see, and how could you see through a pair of feather beds?

The main inconvenience I suffered at their hands was that, at first, I was shy of letting them discover how my artful little servant had begun to sit to me for *Rutland Ramsay*. They knew that I had been odd enough (they were prepared by this time to allow oddity to artists,) to pick a foreign vagabond out of the streets, when I might have had a person with whiskers and credentials; but it was some time before they learned how high I rated his accomplishments. They found him in an attitude more than once, but they never doubted I was doing him as an organ-grinder. There were several things they never guessed, and one of them was that for a striking scene in the novel, in which a footman briefly figured, it occurred to me to make use of Major Monarch as the menial. I kept putting this off, I didn't like to ask him to don the livery—besides the difficulty of finding a livery to fit him.

At last, one day late in the winter, when I was at work on the despised Oronte (he caught one's idea in an instant), and was in the glow of feeling that I was going very straight, they came in, the Major and his wife, with their society laugh about nothing (there was less and less to laugh at), like country-callers—they always reminded me of that—who have walked across the park after church and are presently persuaded to stay to luncheon. Luncheon was over, but they could stay to tea—I knew they wanted it. The fit was on me, however, and I couldn't let my ardour cool and my work wait, with the fading daylight, while my model prepared it. So I asked Mrs. Monarch if she would mind laying it out—a request which, for an instant, brought all the blood to her face.

Her eyes were on her husband's for a second, and some mute telegraphy passed between them. Their folly was over the next instant; his cheerful shrewdness put an end to it. So far from pitying their wounded pride, I must add, I was moved to give it as complete a lesson as I could. They bustled about together and got out the cups and saucers and made the kettle boil. I know they felt as if they were waiting on my servant, and when the tea was prepared I said: "He'll have a cup, please—he's tired." Mrs. Monarch brought him one where he stood, and he took it from her as if he had been a gentleman at a party, squeezing a crush-hat with an elbow.

Then it came over me that she had made a great effort for me—made it with a kind of nobleness—and that I owed her a compensation. Each time I saw her after this I wondered what the compensation could be. I couldn't go on doing the wrong thing to oblige them. Oh, it WAS the wrong thing, the stamp of the work for which they sat—Hawley was not the only person to say it now. I sent in a large number of the drawings I had made for *Rutland Ramsay*, and I received a warning that was more to the point than Hawley's. The artistic adviser of the house for which I was working was of opinion that many of my illustrations were not what had been looked for.

Most of these illustrations were the subjects in which the Monarchs had figured. Without going into the question of what HAD been looked for, I saw at this rate I shouldn't get the other books to do. I hurled myself in despair upon Miss Churm, I put her through all her paces. I not only adopted Oronte publicly as my hero, but one morning when the Major looked in to see if I didn't require him to finish a figure for the *Cheapside*, for which he had begun to sit the week before, I told him that I had changed my mind—I would do the drawing from my man. At this my visitor turned pale and stood looking at me. "Is HE your idea of an English gentleman?" he asked.

I was disappointed, I was nervous, I wanted to get on with my work; so I replied with irritation: "Oh, my dear Major—I can't be ruined for YOU!"

He stood another moment; then, without a word, he quitted the studio. I drew a long breath when he was gone, for I said to myself that I shouldn't see him again. I had not told him definitely that I was in danger of having my work rejected, but I was vexed at his not having felt the catastrophe in the air, read with me the moral of our fruitless collaboration, the lesson that, in the deceptive atmosphere of art, even the highest respectability may fail of being plastic.

I didn't owe my friends money, but I did see them again. They reappeared together, three days later, and under the circumstances there was something tragic in the fact. It was a proof to me that they could find nothing else in life to do. They had threshed the matter out in a dismal conference—they had digested the bad news that they were not in for the series. If they were not useful to me even for the *Cheapside* their function seemed difficult to determine, and I could only judge at first that they had come, forgivingly, decorously, to take a last leave. This made me rejoice in secret that I had little leisure for a scene; for I had placed both my other models in position together and I was pegging away at a drawing from which I hoped to derive glory.

It had been suggested by the passage in which Rutland Ramsay, drawing up a chair to Artemisia's piano-stool, says extraordinary things to her while she ostensibly fingers out a difficult piece of music. I had done Miss Churm at the piano before—it was an attitude in which she knew how to take on an absolutely poetic grace. I wished the two figures to "compose" together, intensely, and my little Italian had entered perfectly into my conception. The pair were vividly before me, the piano had been pulled out; it was a charming picture of blended youth and murmured love, which I had only to catch and keep. My visitors stood and looked at it, and I was friendly to them over my shoulder.

They made no response, but I was used to silent company and went on with my work, only a little disconcerted (even though exhilarated by the sense that THIS was at least the ideal thing), at not having got rid of them after all. Presently I heard Mrs. Monarch's sweet voice beside, or rather above me: "I wish her hair was a little better done." I looked up and she was staring with a strange fixedness at Miss Churm, whose back was turned to her. "Do you mind my just touching it?" she went on—a question which made me spring up for an instant, as with the instinctive fear that she might do the young lady a harm. But she quieted me with a glance I shall never forget—I confess I should like to have been able to paint THAT—and went for a moment to my model.

She spoke to her softly, laying a hand upon her shoulder and bending over her; and as the girl, understanding, gratefully assented, she disposed her rough curls, with a few quick passes, in such a way as to make Miss Churm's head twice as charming. It was one of the most heroic personal services I have ever seen rendered. Then Mrs. Monarch turned away with a low sigh and, looking about her as if for something to do, stooped to the floor with a noble humility and picked up a dirty rag that had dropped out of my paint-box.

The Major meanwhile had also been looking for something to do and, wandering to the other end of the studio, saw before him my breakfast things, neglected, unremoved. "I say, can't I be useful HERE?" he called out to me with an irrepressible quaver. I assented with a laugh that I fear was awkward and for the next ten minutes, while I worked, I heard the light clatter of china and the tinkle of spoons and glass. Mrs. Monarch assisted her husband—they washed up my crockery, they put it away. They wandered off into my little scullery, and I afterwards found that they had cleaned my knives and that my slender stock of plate had an unprecedented surface.

When it came over me, the latent eloquence of what they were doing, I confess that my drawing was blurred for a moment—the picture swam. They had accepted their failure, but they couldn't accept their fate. They had bowed their heads in bewilderment to the perverse and cruel law in virtue of which the real thing could be so much less precious than the unreal; but they didn't want to starve. If my servants were my models, my models might be my servants. They would reverse the parts—the others would sit for the ladies and gentlemen, and THEY would do the work. They would still be in the studio—it was an intense dumb appeal to me not to turn them out. "Take us on," they wanted to say—"we'll do ANYTHING."

When all this hung before me the afflatus vanished—my pencil dropped from my hand. My sitting was spoiled and I got rid of my sitters, who were also evidently rather mystified and awestruck. Then, alone with the Major and his wife, I had a most uncomfortable moment, He put their prayer into a single sentence: "I say, you know—just let US do for you, can't you?" I couldn't—it was dreadful to see them emptying my slops; but I pretended I could, to oblige them, for about a week. Then I gave them a sum of money to go away; and I never saw them again. I obtained the remaining books, but my friend Hawley repeats that Major and Mrs. Monarch did me a permanent harm, got me into a second-rate trick. If it be true I am content to have paid the price—for the memory.

The Romance of Certain Old Clothes

1

Towards the middle of the eighteenth century there lived in the Province of Massachusetts a widowed gentlewoman, the mother of three children, by name Mrs. Veronica Wingrave. She had lost her husband early in life, and had devoted herself to the care of her progeny. These young persons grew up in a manner to reward her tenderness and to gratify her highest hopes. The first-born was a son, whom she had called Bernard, in remembrance of his father. The others were daughters—born at an interval of three years apart. Good looks were traditional in the family, and this youthful trio were not likely to allow the tradition to perish.

The boy was of that fair and ruddy complexion and that athletic structure which in those days (as in these) were the sign of good English descent—a frank, affectionate young fellow, a deferential son, a patronising brother, a steadfast friend. Clever, however, he was not; the wit of the family had been apportioned chiefly to his sisters. The late Mr. William Wingrave had been a great reader of Shakespeare, at a time when this pursuit implied more freedom of thought than at the present day, and in a community where it required much courage to patronise the drama even in the closet; and he had wished to call attention to his admiration of the great poet by calling his daughters out of his favourite plays. Upon the elder he had bestowed the romantic name of Rosalind, and the younger he had called Perdita, in memory of a little girl born between them, who had lived but a few weeks.

When Bernard Wingrave came to his sixteenth year his mother put a brave face upon it and prepared to execute her husband's last injunction. This had been a formal command that, at the proper age, his son should be sent out to England, to complete his education at the university of Oxford, where he himself had acquired his taste for elegant literature. It was Mrs. Wingrave's belief that the lad's equal was not to be found in the two hemispheres, but she had the old traditions of literal obedience. She swallowed her sobs, and made up her boy's trunk and his simple provincial outfit, and sent him on his way across the seas. Bernard presented himself at his father's college, and spent five years in England, without great honour, indeed, but with a vast deal of pleasure and no discredit.

On leaving the university he made the journey to France. In his twenty-fourth year he took ship for home, prepared to find poor little New England (New England was very small in those days) a very dull, unfashionable residence. But there had been changes at home, as well as in Mr. Bernard's opinions. He found his mother's house quite habitable, and his sisters grown into two very charming young ladies, with all the accomplishments and graces of the young women of Britain, and a certain native-grown originality and wildness, which, if it was not an accomplishment, was certainly a grace the more. Bernard privately assured his mother that his sisters were fully a match for the most genteel young women in the old country; whereupon poor Mrs. Wingrave, you may be sure, bade them hold up their heads.

Such was Bernard's opinion, and such, in a tenfold higher degree, was the opinion of Mr. Arthur Lloyd. This gentleman was a college-mate of Mr. Bernard, a young man of reputable family, of a good person and a handsome inheritance; which latter appurtenance he proposed to invest in trade in the flourishing colony. He and Bernard were sworn friends; they had crossed the ocean together, and the young American had lost no time in presenting him at his mother's house, where he had made quite as good an impression as that which he had received and of which I have just given a hint.

The two sisters were at this time in all the freshness of their youthful bloom; each wearing, of course, this natural brilliancy in the manner that became her best. They were equally dissimilar in appearance and character. Rosalind, the elder—now in her twenty-second year—was tall and white, with calm gray eyes and auburn tresses; a very faint likeness to the Rosalind of Shakespeare's comedy, whom I imagine a brunette (if you will), but a slender, airy creature, full of the softest, quickest impulses. Miss Wingrave, with her slightly lymphatic fairness, her fine arms, her majestic height, her slow utterance, was not cut out for adventures. She would never have put on a man's jacket and hose; and, indeed, being a very plump beauty, she may have had reasons apart from her natural dignity.

Perdita, too, might very well have exchanged the sweet melancholy of her name against something more in consonance with her aspect and disposition. She had the cheek of a gipsy and the eye of an eager child, as well as the smallest waist and lightest foot in all the country of the Puritans. When you spoke to her she never made you wait, as her handsome sister was wont to do (while she looked at you with a cold fine eye), but gave you your choice of a dozen answers before you had uttered half your thought.

The young girls were very glad to see their brother once more; but they found themselves quite able to spare part of their attention for their brother's friend. Among the young men their friends and neighbours, the *belle jeunesse* of the Colony, there were many excellent fellows, several devoted swains, and some two or three who enjoyed the reputation of universal charmers and conquerors. But the homebred arts and somewhat boisterous gallantry of these honest colonists were completely eclipsed by the good looks, the fine clothes, the punctilious courtesy, the perfect elegance, the immense information, of Mr. Arthur Lloyd.

He was in reality no paragon; he was a capable, honourable, civil youth, rich in pounds sterling, in his health and complacency and his little capital of uninvested affections. But he was a gentleman; he had a handsome person; he had studied and travelled; he spoke French, he played on the flute, and he read verses aloud with very great taste. There were a dozen reasons why Miss Wingrave and her sister should have thought their other male acquaintance made but a poor figure before such a perfect man of the world. Mr. Lloyd's anecdotes told our little New England maidens a great deal more of the ways and means of people of fashion in European capitals than he had any idea of doing.

It was delightful to sit by and hear him and Bernard talk about the fine people and fine things they had seen. They would all gather round the fire after tea, in the little wainscoted parlour, and the two young men would remind each other, across the rug, of this, that and the other adventure. Rosalind and Perdita would often have given their ears to know exactly what adventure it was, and where it happened, and who was there, and what the ladies had on; but in those days a well-bred young woman was not expected to break into the conversation of her elders, or to ask too many questions; and the poor girls used therefore to sit fluttering behind the more languid—or more discreet-curiosity of their mother.

2

That they were both very fine girls Arthur Lloyd was not slow to discover; but it took him some time to make up his mind whether he liked the big sister or the little sister best. He had a strong presentiment—an emotion of a nature entirely too cheerful to be called a foreboding—that he was destined to stand up before the parson with one of them; yet he was unable to arrive at a preference, and for such a consummation a preference was certainly necessary, for Lloyd had too much young blood in his veins to make a choice by lot and be cheated of the satisfaction of falling in love. He resolved to take things as they came—to let his heart speak.

Meanwhile he was on a very pleasant footing. Mrs. Wingrave showed a dignified indifference to his 'intentions', equally remote from a carelessness of her daughter's honour and from that sharp alacrity to make him come to the point, which, in his quality of a young man of property, he had too often encountered in the worldly matrons of his native islands. As for Bernard, all that he asked was that his friend should treat his sisters as his own; and as for the poor girls themselves, however each may have secretly longed that their visitor should do or say something 'marked', they kept a very modest and contented demeanour.

Towards each other, however, they were somewhat more on the offensive. They were good friends enough, and accommodating bedfellows (they shared the same four-poster), betwixt whom it would take more than a day for the seeds of jealousy to sprout and bear fruit; but they felt that the seeds had been sown on the day that Mr. Lloyd came into the house. Each made up her mind that, if she should be slighted, she would bear her grief in silence, and that no one should be any the wiser; for if they had a great deal of ambition, they had also a large share of pride. But each prayed in secret, nevertheless, that upon *her* the selection, the distinction, might fall.

They had need of a vast deal of patience, of self-control, of dissimulation. In those days a young girl of decent breeding could make no advances whatever, and barely respond, indeed, to those that were made. She was expected to sit still in her chair, with her eyes on the carpet, watching the spot where the mystic handkerchief should fall. Poor Arthur Lloyd was obliged to carry on his wooing in the little wainscoted parlour, before the eyes of Mrs. Wingrave, her son, and his prospective sister-in-law. But youth and love are so cunning that a hundred signs and tokens might travel to and fro, and not one of these three pairs of eyes detect them in their passage.

The two maidens were almost always together, and had plenty of chances to betray themselves. That each knew she was being watched, however, made not a grain of difference in the little offices they mutually rendered, or in the various household tasks they performed in common. Neither flinched nor fluttered beneath the silent battery of her sister's eyes. The only apparent change in their habits was that they had less to say to each other. It was impossible to talk about Mr. Lloyd, and it was ridiculous to talk about anything else. By tacit agreement they began to wear all their choice finery, and to devise such little implements of conquest, in the way of ribbons and top-knots and kerchiefs, as were sanctioned by indubitable modesty.

They executed in the same inarticulate fashion a contract of fair play in this exciting game. "Is it better so?" Rosalind would ask, tying a bunch of ribbons on her bosom, and turning about from her glass to her sister. Perdita would look up gravely from her work and examine the decoration. "I think you had better give it another loop," she would say, with great solemnity, looking hard at her sister with eyes that added, 'upon my honour!' So they were forever stitching and trimming their petticoats, and pressing out their muslins, and contriving washes and ointments and cosmetics, like the ladies in the household of the vicar of Wakefield. Some three or four months went by; it grew to be midwinter, and as yet Rosalind knew that if Perdita had nothing more to boast of than she, there was not much to be feared from her rivalry. But Perdita by this time—the charming Perdita—felt that her secret had grown to be tenfold more precious than her sister's.

One afternoon Miss Wingrave sat alone—that was a rare accident—before her toilet-glass, combing out her long hair. It was getting too dark to see; she lit the two candles in their sockets, on the frame of her mirror, and then went to the window to draw her curtains. It was a gray December evening; the landscape was bare and bleak, and the sky heavy with snow-clouds. At the end of the large garden into which her window looked was a wall with a little postern door, opening into a lane. The door stood ajar, as she could vaguely see in the gathering darkness, and moved slowly to and fro, as if someone were swaying it from the lane without.

It was doubtless a servant-maid who had been having a tryst with her sweetheart. But as she was about to drop her curtain Rosalind saw her sister step into the garden and hurry along the path which led to the house. She dropped the curtain, all save a little crevice for her eyes. As Perdita came up the path she seemed to be examining something in her hand, holding it close to her eyes. When she reached the house she stopped a moment, looked intently at the object, and pressed it to her lips.

Poor Rosalind slowly came back to her chair and sat down before her glass, where, if she had looked at it less abstractedly, she would have seen her handsome features sadly disfigured by jealousy. A moment afterwards the door opened behind her and her sister came into the room, out of breath, and her cheeks aglow with the chilly air.

Perdita started. "Ah," said she, "I thought you were with our mother." The ladies were to go to a tea-party, and on such occasions it was the habit of one of the young girls to help their mother to dress. Instead of coming in, Perdita lingered at the door.

"Come in, come in," said Rosalind. "We have more than an hour yet. I should like you very much to give a few strokes to my hair." She knew that her sister wished to retreat, and that she could see in the glass all her movements in the room. "Nay, just help me with my hair," she said, "and I will go to mamma."

Perdita came reluctantly, and took the brush. She saw her sister's eyes, in the glass, fastened hard upon her hands. She had not made three passes when Rosalind clapped her own right hand upon her sister's left, and started out of her chair. "Whose ring is that?" she cried, passionately, drawing her towards the light.

On the young girl's third finger glistened a little gold ring, adorned with a very small sapphire. Perdita felt that she need no longer keep her secret, yet that she must put a bold face on her avowal. "It's mine," she said proudly.

"Who gave it to you?" cried the other.

Perdita hesitated a moment. "Mr. Lloyd."

"Mr. Lloyd is generous, all of a sudden."

"Ah no," cried Perdita, with spirit, "not all of a sudden! He offered it to me a month ago."

"And you needed a month's begging to take it?" said Rosalind, looking at the little trinket, which indeed was not especially elegant, although it was the best that the jeweller of the Province could furnish. "I wouldn't have taken it in less than two."

"It isn't the ring," Perdita answered, "it's what it means!"

"It means that you are not a modest girl!" cried Rosalind. "Pray, does your mother know of your intrigue? does Bernard?"

"My mother has approved my 'intrigue', as you call it. Mr. Lloyd has asked for my hand, and mamma has given it. Would you have had him apply to you, dearest sister?"

Rosalind gave her companion a long look, full of passionate envy and sorrow. Then she dropped her lashes on her pale cheeks and turned away. Perdita felt that it had not been a pretty scene; but it was her sister's fault. However, the elder girl rapidly called back her pride, and turned herself about again. "You have my very best wishes," she said, with a low curtsey. "I wish you every happiness, and a very long life."

Perdita gave a bitter laugh. "Don't speak in that tone!" she cried. "I would rather you should curse me outright. Come, Rosy," she added, "he couldn't marry both of us."

"I wish you very great joy," Rosalind repeated, mechanically, sitting down to her glass again, "and a very long life, and plenty of children."

There was something in the sound of these words not at all to Perdita's taste. "Will you give me a year to live at least?" she said. "In a year I can have one little boy—or one little girl at least. If you will give me your brush again I will do your hair."

"Thank you," said Rosalind. "You had better go to mamma. It isn't becoming that a young lady with a promised husband should wait on a girl with none."

"Nay," said Perdita, good-humouredly, "I have Arthur to wait upon me. You need my service more than I need yours."

But her sister motioned her away, and she left the room. When she had gone poor Rosalind fell on her knees before her dressing-table, buried her head in her arms, and poured out a flood of tears and sobs. She felt very much the better for this effusion of sorrow. When her sister came back she insisted upon helping her to dress—on her wearing her prettiest things. She forced upon her acceptance a bit of lace of her own, and declared that now that she was to be married she should do her best to appear worthy of her lover's choice. She discharged these offices in stern silence; but, such as they were, they had to do duty as an apology and an atonement; she never made any other.

Now that Lloyd was received by the family as an accepted suitor nothing remained but to fix the wedding-day. It was appointed for the following April, and in the interval preparations were diligently made for the marriage. Lloyd, on his side, was busy with his commercial arrangements, and with establishing a correspondence with the great mercantile house to which he had attached himself in England. He was therefore not so frequent a visitor at Mrs. Wingrave's as during the months of his diffidence and irresolution, and poor Rosalind had less to suffer than she had feared from the sight of the mutual endearments of the young lovers.

Touching his future sister-in-law Lloyd had a perfectly clear conscience. There had not been a particle of love-making between them, and he had not the slightest suspicion that he had dealt her a terrible blow. He was quite at his ease; life promised so well, both domestically and financially. The great revolt of the Colonies was not yet in the air, and that his connubial felicity should take a tragic turn it was absurd, it was blasphemous, to apprehend. Meanwhile, at Mrs. Wingrave's, there was a greater rustling of silks, a more rapid clicking of scissors and flying of needles, than ever. The good lady had determined that her daughter should carry from home the genteelest outfit that her money could buy or that the country could furnish.

All the sage women in the Province were convened, and their united taste was brought to bear on Perdita's wardrobe. Rosalind's situation, at this moment, was assuredly not to be envied.

The poor girl had an inordinate love of dress, and the very best taste in the world, as her sister perfectly well knew. Rosalind was tall, she was stately and sweeping, she was made to carry stiff brocade and masses of heavy lace, such as belong to the toilet of a rich man's wife. But Rosalind sat aloof, with her beautiful arms folded and her head averted, while her mother and sister and the venerable women aforesaid worried and wondered over their materials, oppressed by the multitude of their resources.

One day there came in a beautiful piece of white silk, brocaded with heavenly blue and silver, sent by the bridegroom himself—it not being thought amiss in those days that the husband-elect should contribute to the bride's *trousseau*. Perdita could think of no form or fashion which would do sufficient honour to the splendour of the material.

"Blue's your colour, sister, more than mine," she said, with appealing eyes. "It's a pity it's not for you. You would know what to do with it."

Rosalind got up from her place and looked at the great shining fabric, as it lay spread over the back of a chair. Then she took it up in her hands and felt it—lovingly, as Perdita could see—and turned about toward the mirror with it. She let it roll down to her feet, and flung the other end over her shoulder, gathering it in about her waist with her white arm, which was bare to the elbow. She threw back her head, and looked at her image, and a hanging tress of her auburn hair fell upon the gorgeous surface of the silk.

It made a dazzling picture. The women standing about uttered a little "Look, look!" of admiration. "Yes, indeed," said Rosalind, quietly, "blue is my colour." But Perdita could see that her fancy had been stirred, and that she would now fall to work and solve all their silken riddles. And indeed she behaved very well, as Perdita, knowing her insatiable love of millinery, was quite ready to declare. Innumerable yards of lustrous silk and satin, of muslin, velvet and lace, passed through her cunning hands, without a jealous word coming from her lips. Thanks to her industry, when the wedding-day came Perdita was prepared to espouse more of the vanities of life than any fluttering young bride who had yet received the sacramental blessing of a New England divine.

It had been arranged that the young couple should go out and spend the first days of their wedded life at the country-house of an English gentleman—a man of rank and a very kind friend to Arthur Lloyd. He was a bachelor; he declared he should be delighted to give up the place to the influence of Hymen. After the ceremony at church—it had been performed by an English clergyman—young Mrs. Lloyd hastened back to her mother's house to change her nuptial robes for a riding-dress. Rosalind helped her to effect the change, in the little homely room in which they had spent their undivided younger years. Perdita then hurried off to bid farewell to her mother, leaving Rosalind to follow.

The parting was short; the horses were at the door, and Arthur was impatient to start. But Rosalind had not followed, and Perdita hastened back to her room, opening the door abruptly. Rosalind, as usual, was before the glass, but in a position which caused the other to stand still, amazed. She had dressed herself in Perdita's cast-off wedding veil and wreath, and on her neck she had hung the full string of pearls which the young girl had received from her husband as a wedding-gift. These things had been hastily laid aside, to await their possessor's disposal on her return from the country. Bedizened in this unnatural garb Rosalind stood before the mirror, plunging a long look into its depths and reading heaven knows what audacious visions. Perdita was horrified. It was a hideous image of their old rivalry come to life again. She made a step toward her sister, as if to pull off the veil and the flowers. But catching her eyes in the glass, she stopped.

"Farewell, sweetheart," she said. "You might at least have waited till I had got out of the house!" And she hurried away from the room.

Mr. Lloyd had purchased in Boston a house which to the taste of those days appeared as elegant as it was commodious;

and here he very soon established himself with his young wife. He was thus separated by a distance of twenty miles from the residence of his mother-in-law. Twenty miles, in that primitive era of roads and conveyances, were as serious a matter as a hundred at the present day, and Mrs. Wingrave saw but little of her daughter during the first twelvemonth of her marriage. She suffered in no small degree from Perdita's absence; and her affliction was not diminished by the fact that Rosalind had fallen into terribly low spirits and was not to be roused or cheered but by change of air and company.

The real cause of the young lady's dejection the reader will not be slow to suspect. Mrs. Wingrave and her gossips, however, deemed her complaint a mere bodily ill, and doubted not that she would obtain relief from the remedy just mentioned. Her mother accordingly proposed, on her behalf, a visit to certain relatives on the paternal side, established in New York, who had long complained that they were able to see so little of their New England cousins. Rosalind was despatched to these good people, under a suitable escort, and remained with them for several months. In the interval her brother Bernard, who had begun the practice of the law, made up his mind to take a wife.

Rosalind came home to the wedding, apparently cured of her heartache, with bright roses and lilies in her face and a proud smile on her lips. Arthur Lloyd came over from Boston to see his brother-in-law married, but without his wife, who was expecting very soon to present him with an heir. It was nearly a year since Rosalind had seen him. She was glad—she hardly knew why—that Perdita had stayed at home. Arthur looked happy, but he was more grave and important than before his marriage. She thought he looked 'interesting'—for although the word, in its modern sense, was not then invented, we may be sure that the idea was.

The truth is, he was simply anxious about his wife and her coming ordeal. Nevertheless, he by no means failed to observe Rosalind's beauty and splendour, and to note how she effaced the poor little bride. The allowance that Perdita had enjoyed for her dress had now been transferred to her sister, who turned it to wonderful account. On the morning after the wedding he had a lady's saddle put on the horse of the servant who had come with him from town, and went out with the young girl for a ride. It was a keen, clear morning in January; the ground was bare and hard, and the horses in good condition—to say nothing of Rosalind, who was charming in her hat and plume, and her dark blue riding coat, trimmed with fur. They rode all the morning, they lost their way, and were obliged to stop for dinner at a farmhouse.

The early winter dusk had fallen when they got home. Mrs. Wingrave met them with a long face. A messenger had arrived at noon from Mrs. Lloyd; she was beginning to be ill, she desired her husband's immediate return. The young man, at the thought that he had lost several hours, and that by hard riding he might already have been with his wife, uttered a passionate oath. He barely consented to stop for a mouthful of supper, but mounted the messenger's horse and started off at a gallop.

He reached home at midnight. His wife had been delivered of a little girl. "Ah, why weren't you with me?" she said, as he came to her bedside.

"I was out of the house when the man came. I was with Rosalind," said Lloyd, innocently.

Mrs. Lloyd made a little moan, and turned away. But she continued to do very well, and for a week her improvement was uninterrupted. Finally, however, through some indiscretion in the way of diet or exposure, it was checked, and the poor lady grew rapidly worse. Lloyd was in despair. It very soon became evident that she was breathing her last. Mrs. Lloyd came to a sense of her approaching end, and declared that she was reconciled with death.

On the third evening after the change took place she told her husband that she felt she should not get through the night. She dismissed her servants, and also requested her mother to withdraw—Mrs. Wingrave having arrived on the preceding day. She had had her infant placed on the bed beside her, and she lay on her side, with the child against her breast, holding her husband's hands. The night-lamp was hidden behind the heavy curtains of the bed, but the room was illumined with a red glow from the immense fire of logs on the hearth.

"It seems strange not to be warmed into life by such a fire as that," the young woman said, feebly trying to smile. "If I had but a little of it in my veins! But I have given all *my* fire to this little spark of mortality." And she dropped her eyes on her child. Then raising them she looked at her husband with a long, penetrating gaze. The last feeling which lingered in her heart was one of suspicion. She had not recovered from the shock which Arthur had given her by telling her that in the hour of her agony he had been with Rosalind. She trusted her husband very nearly as well as she loved him; but now that she was called away forever she felt a cold horror of her sister. She felt in her soul that Rosalind had never ceased to be jealous of her good fortune; and a year of happy security had not effaced the young girl's image, dressed in her wedding-garments, and smiling with simulated triumph.

Now that Arthur was to be alone, what might not Rosalind attempt? She was beautiful, she was engaging; what arts might she not use, what impression might she not make upon the young man's saddened heart? Mrs. Lloyd looked at her husband in silence. It seemed hard, after all, to doubt of his constancy. His fine eyes were filled with tears; his face was convulsed with weeping; the clasp of his hands was warm and passionate. How noble he looked, how tender, how faithful and devoted! 'Nay,' thought Perdita, 'he's not for such a one as Rosalind. He'll never forget me. Nor does Rosalind truly care for him; she cares only for vanities and finery and jewels.' And she lowered her eyes on her white hands, which her husband's liberality had covered with rings, and on the lace ruffles which trimmed the edge of her night-dress. 'She covets my rings and my laces more than she covets my husband.'

At this moment the thought of her sister's rapacity seemed to cast a dark shadow between her and the helpless figure of her little girl. "Arthur," she said, "you must take off my rings.

I shall not be buried in them. One of these days my daughter shall wear them—my rings and my laces and silks. I had them all brought out and shown me today. It's a great wardrobe—there's not such another in the Province; I can say it without vanity, now that I have done with it. It will be a great inheritance for my daughter when she grows into a young woman. There are things there that a man never buys twice, and if they are lost you will never again see the like. So you will watch them well. Some dozen things I have left to Rosalind; I have named them to my mother. I have given her that blue and silver; it was meant for her; I wore it only once, I looked ill in it.

"But the rest are to be sacredly kept for this little innocent. It's such a providence that she should be my colour; she can wear my gowns; she has her mother's eyes. You know the same fashions come back every twenty years. She can wear my gowns as they are. They will lie there quietly waiting till she grows into them—wrapped in camphor and rose-leaves, and keeping their colours in the sweet-scented darkness. She shall have black hair, she shall wear my carnation satin. Do you promise me, Arthur?"

"Promise you what, dearest?"

"Promise me to keep your poor little wife's old gowns."

"Are you afraid I shall sell them?"

"No, but that they may get scattered. My mother will have them properly wrapped up, and you shall lay them away under a double-lock. Do you know the great chest in the attic, with the iron bands? There is no end to what it will hold. You can put them all there. My mother and the housekeeper will do it, and give you the key. And you will keep the key in your secretary, and never give it to anyone but your child. Do you promise me?"

"Ah, yes, I promise you," said Lloyd, puzzled at the intensity with which his wife appeared to cling to this idea.

"Will you swear?" repeated Perdita.

"Yes, I swear."

"Well—I trust you—I trust you," said the poor lady, looking

into his eyes with eyes in which, if he had suspected her vague apprehensions, he might have read an appeal quite as much as an assurance.

Lloyd bore his bereavement rationally and manfully. A month after his wife's death, in the course of business, circumstances arose which offered him an opportunity of going to England. He took advantage of it, to change the current of his thoughts. He was absent nearly a year, during which his little girl was tenderly nursed and guarded by her grandmother. On his return he had his house again thrown open, and announced his intention of keeping the same state as during his wife's lifetime.

It very soon came to be predicted that he would marry again, and there were at least a dozen young women of whom one may say that it was by no fault of theirs that, for six months after his return, the prediction did not come true. During this interval he still left his little daughter in Mrs. Wingrave's hands, the latter assuring him that a change of residence at so tender an age would be full of danger for her health. Finally, however, he declared that his heart longed for his daughter's presence and that she must be brought up to town. He sent his coach and his housekeeper to fetch her home.

Mrs. Wingrave was in terror lest something should befall her on the road; and, in accordance with this feeling, Rosalind offered to accompany her. She could return the next day. So she went up to town with her little niece, and Mr. Lloyd met her on the threshold of his house, overcome with her kindness and with paternal joy. Instead of returning the next day Rosalind stayed out the week; and when at last she reappeared, she had only come for her clothes. Arthur would not hear of her coming home, nor would the baby. That little person cried and choked if Rosalind left her; and at the sight of her grief Arthur lost his wits, and swore that she was going to die. In fine, nothing would suit them but that the aunt should remain until the little niece had grown used to strange faces.

It took two months to bring this consummation about; for it was not until this period had elapsed that Rosalind took leave of her brother-in-law. Mrs. Wingrave had shaken her head over her daughter's absence; she had declared that it was not becoming, that it was the talk of the whole country. She had reconciled herself to it only because, during the girl's visit, the household enjoyed an unwonted term of peace. Bernard Wingrave had brought his wife home to live, between whom and her sister-in-law there was as little love as you please. Rosalind was perhaps no angel; but in the daily practice of life she was a sufficiently good-natured girl, and if she quarrelled with Mrs. Bernard, it was not without provocation.

Quarrel, however, she did, to the great annoyance not only of her antagonist, but of the two spectators of these constant altercations. Her stay in the household of her brother-in-law, therefore, would have been delightful, if only because it removed her from contact with the object of her antipathy at home. It was doubly—it was ten times—delightful, in that it kept her near the object of her early passion. Mrs. Lloyd's sharp suspicions had fallen very far short of the truth. Rosalind's sentiment had been a passion at first, and a passion it remained—a passion of whose radiant heat, tempered to the delicate state of his feelings, Mr. Lloyd very soon felt the influence. Lloyd, as I have hinted, was not a modern Petrarch; it was not in his nature to practise an ideal constancy.

He had not been many days in the house with his sister-in-law before he began to assure himself that she was, in the language of that day, a devilish fine woman. Whether Rosalind really practised those insidious arts that her sister had been tempted to impute to her it is needless to inquire. It is enough to say that she found means to appear to the very best advantage. She used to seat herself every morning before the big fireplace in the dining-room, at work upon a piece of tapestry, with her little niece disporting herself on the carpet at her feet, or on the train of her dress, and playing with her woollen balls.

Lloyd would have been a very stupid fellow if he had remained insensible to the rich suggestions of this charming picture. He was exceedingly fond of his little girl, and was never weary of taking her in his arms and tossing her up and down, and making her crow with delight. Very often, however, he would venture upon greater liberties than the young lady was yet prepared to allow, and then she would suddenly vociferate her displeasure. Rosalind, at this, would drop her tapestry, and put out her handsome hands with the serious smile of the young girl whose virgin fancy has revealed to her all a mother's healing arts. Lloyd would give up the child, their eyes would meet, their hands would touch, and Rosalind would extinguish the little girl's sobs upon the snowy folds of the kerchief that crossed her bosom. Her dignity was perfect, and nothing could be more discreet than the manner in which she accepted her brother-in-law's hospitality. It may almost be said, perhaps, that there was something harsh in her reserve.

Lloyd had a provoking feeling that she was in the house and yet was unapproachable. Half-an-hour after supper, at the very outset of the long winter evenings, she would light her candle, make the young man a most respectful curtsey, and march off to bed. If these were arts, Rosalind was a great artist. But their effect was so gentle, so gradual, they were calculated to work upon the young widower's fancy with a *crescendo* so finely shaded, that, as the reader has seen, several weeks elapsed before Rosalind began to feel sure that her returns would cover her outlay. When this became morally certain she packed up her trunk and returned to her mother's house.

For three days she waited; on the fourth Mr. Lloyd made his appearance—a respectful but pressing suitor. Rosalind heard him to the end, with great humility, and accepted him with infinite modesty. It is hard to imagine that Mrs. Lloyd would have forgiven her husband; but if anything might have disarmed her resentment it would have been the ceremonious continence of this interview. Rosalind imposed upon her lover but a short probation. They were married, as was becoming, with great privacy—almost with secrecy—in the hope perhaps, as was waggishly remarked at the time, that the late Mrs. Lloyd wouldn't hear of it.

The marriage was to all appearance a happy one, and each party obtained what each had desired—Lloyd 'a devilish fine woman', and Rosalind—but Rosalind's desires, as the reader will have observed, had remained a good deal of a mystery. There were, indeed, two blots upon their felicity, but time would perhaps efface them. During the first three years of her marriage Mrs. Lloyd failed to become a mother, and her husband on his side suffered heavy losses of money. This latter circumstance compelled a material retrenchment in his expenditure, and Rosalind was perforce less of a fine lady than her sister had been. She contrived, however, to carry it like a woman of considerable fashion.

She had long since ascertained that her sister's copious wardrobe had been sequestrated for the benefit of her daughter, and that it lay languishing in thankless gloom in the dusty attic. It was a revolting thought that these exquisite fabrics should await the good pleasure of a little girl who sat in a high chair and ate bread-and-milk with a wooden spoon. Rosalind had the good taste, however, to say nothing about the matter until several months had expired. Then, at last, she timidly broached it to her husband. Was it not a pity that so much finery should be lost?—for lost it would be, what with colours fading, and moths eating it up, and the change of fashions.

But Lloyd gave her so abrupt and peremptory a refusal, that she saw, for the present, her attempt was vain. Six months went by, however, and brought with them new needs and new visions. Rosalind's thoughts hovered lovingly about her sister's relics. She went up and looked at the chest in which they lay imprisoned. There was a sullen defiance in its three great padlocks and its iron bands which only quickened her cupidity. There was something exasperating in its incorruptible immobility. It was like a grim and grizzled old household servant, who locks his jaws over a family secret.

And then there was a look of capacity in its vast extent, and a sound as of dense fullness, when Rosalind knocked its side with the toe of her little shoe, which caused her to flush with baffled longing. "It's absurd," she cried; "it's improper, it's wicked"; and she forthwith resolved upon another attack upon her husband. On the following day, after dinner, when he had had his wine, she boldly began it. But he cut her short with great sternness.

"Once for all, Rosalind," said he, "it's out of the question. I shall be gravely displeased if you return to the matter."

"Very good," said Rosalind. "I am glad to learn the esteem in which I am held. Gracious heaven," she cried, "I am a very happy woman! It's an agreeable thing to feel one's self sacrificed to a caprice!" And her eyes filled with tears of anger and disappointment.

Lloyd had a good-natured man's horror of a woman's sobs, and he attempted—I may say he condescended—to explain. "It's not a caprice, dear, it's a promise," he said—"an oath."

"An oath? It's a pretty matter for oaths! and to whom, pray?"

"To Perdita," said the young man, raising his eyes for an instant, but immediately dropping them.

"Perdita—ah, Perdita!" and Rosalind's tears broke forth. Her bosom heaved with stormy sobs—sobs which were the long-deferred sequel of the violent fit of weeping in which she had indulged herself on the night when she discovered her sister's betrothal. She had hoped, in her better moments, that she had done with her jealousy; but her temper, on that occasion, had taken an ineffaceable fold. "And pray, what right had Perdita to dispose of my future?" she cried. "What right had she to bind you to meanness and cruelty? Ah, I occupy a dignified place, and I make a very fine figure! I am welcome to what Perdita has left! And what has she left? I never knew till now how little! Nothing, nothing, nothing."

This was very poor logic, but it was very good as a 'scene'. Lloyd put his arm around his wife's waist and tried to kiss her, but she shook him off with magnificent scorn. Poor fellow! he had coveted a 'devilish fine woman', and he had got one. Her scorn was intolerable. He walked away with his ears tingling-irresolute, distracted. Before him was his secretary, and in it the sacred key which with his own hand he had turned in the triple lock. He marched up and opened it, and took the key from a secret drawer, wrapped in a little packet which he had sealed with his own honest bit of blazonry. *Je garde*, said the motto—*I keep*. But he was ashamed to put it back. He flung it upon the table beside his wife.

"Put it back!" she cried. "I want it not. I hate it!"

"I wash my hands of it," cried her husband. "God forgive me!"

Mrs. Lloyd gave an indignant shrug of her shoulders, and swept out of the room, while the young man retreated by another door. Ten minutes later Mrs. Lloyd returned, and found the room occupied by her little step-daughter and the nursery-maid. The key was not on the table. She glanced at the child. Her little niece was perched on a chair, with the packet in her hands. She had broken the seal with her own small fingers. Mrs. Lloyd hastily took possession of the key.

At the habitual supper-hour Arthur Lloyd came back from his counting-room. It was the month of June, and supper was served by daylight. The meal was placed on the table, but Mrs. Lloyd failed to make her appearance. The servant whom his master sent to call her came back with the assurance that her room was empty, and that the women informed him that she had not been seen since dinner. They had, in truth, observed her to have been in tears, and, supposing her to be shut up in her chamber, had not disturbed her. Her husband called her name in various parts of the house, but without response.

At last it occurred to him that he might find her by taking the way to the attic. The thought gave him a strange feeling of discomfort, and he bade his servants remain behind, wishing no witness in his quest. He reached the foot of the staircase leading to the topmost flat, and stood with his hand on the banisters, pronouncing his wife's name. His voice trembled. He called again louder and more firmly. The only sound which disturbed the absolute silence was a faint echo of his own tones, repeating his question under the great eaves. He nevertheless felt irresistibly moved to ascend the staircase. It opened upon a wide hall, lined with wooden closets, and terminating in a window which looked westward, and admitted the last rays of the sun. Before the window stood the great chest.

Before the chest, on her knees, the young man saw with amazement and horror the figure of his wife. In an instant he crossed the interval between them, bereft of utterance. The lid of the chest stood open, exposing, amid their perfumed napkins, its treasure of stuffs and jewels. Rosalind had fallen backward from a kneeling posture, with one hand supporting her on the floor and the other pressed to her heart. On her limbs was the stiffness of death, and on her face, in the fading light of the sun, the terror of something more than death. Her lips were parted in entreaty, in dismay, in agony; and on her blanched brow and cheeks there glowed the marks of ten hideous wounds from two vengeful ghostly hands.

Brooksmith

We are scattered now, the friends of the late Mr Oliver Offord but whenever we chance to meet I think we are conscious of a certain esoteric respect for each other. 'Yes, you too have been in Arcadia,' we seem not too grumpily to allow. When I pass the house in Mansfield Street I remember that Arcadia was there. I don't know who has it now, and I don't want to know; it's enough to be so sure that if I should ring the bell there would be no such luck for me as that Brooksmith should open the door. Mr. Offord, the most agreeable, the most lovable of bachelors, was a retired diplomatist, living on his pension, confined by his infirmities to his fireside and delighted to be found there any afternoon in the year by such visitors as Brooksmith allowed to come up.

Brooksmith was his butler and his most intimate friend, to whom we all stood, or I should say sat, in the same relation in which the subject of the sovereign finds himself to the prime minister. By having been for years, in foreign lands, the most delightful Englishman any one had ever known, Mr. Offord had, in my opinion, rendered signal service to his country. But I suppose he had been too much liked—liked even by those who didn't like *it*—so that as people of that sort never get titles or dotations for the horrid things they have not done, his principal reward was simply that we went to see him.

Oh, we went perpetually, and it was not our fault if he was not overwhelmed with this particular honour. Any visitor who came once came again—to come merely once was a slight which nobody, I am sure, had ever put upon him. His circle, therefore, was essentially composed of *habitués*, who were *habitués* for each other as well as for him, as those of a happy *salon* should be. I remember vividly every element of the place, down to the intensely Londonish look of the grey opposite houses, in the gap of the white curtains of the high windows, and the exact spot where, on a particular afternoon, I put down my tea-cup for Brooksmith, lingering an instant, to gather it up as if he were plucking a flower. Mr. Offord's drawing-room was indeed Brooksmith's garden, his pruned and tended human *parterre*, and if we all flourished there and grew well in our places it was largely owing to his supervision.

Many persons have heard much, though most have doubtless seen little, of the famous institution of the *salon*, and many are born to the depression of knowing that this finest flower of social life refuses to bloom where the English tongue is spoken. The explanation is usually that our women have not the skill to cultivate it—the art to direct, between suggestive shores, the course of the stream of talk. My affectionate, my pious memory of Mr. Offord contradicts this induction only, I fear, more insidiously to confirm it. The very sallow and slightly smoked drawing-room in which he spent so large a portion of the last years of his life certainly deserved the distinguished name; but on the other hand it could not be said at all to owe its stamp to the soft pressure of the indispensable sex.

The dear man had indeed been capable of one of those sacrifices to which women are deemed peculiarly apt; he had recognised (under the influence, in some degree, it is true, of physical infirmity), that if you wished people to find you at home you must manage not to be out. He had in short accepted the fact which many dabblers in the social art are slow to learn, that you must really, as they say, take a line and that the only way to be at home is to stay at home. Finally his own fireside had become a summary of his habits. Why should he ever have left it?—since this would have been leaving what was notoriously pleasantest in London, the compact charmed cluster (thinning away indeed into casual couples), round the fine old last century chimney-piece which, with the exception of the remarkable collection of miniatures, was the best thing the place contained. Mr. Offord was not rich; he had nothing but his pension and the use for life of the somewhat superannuated house.

When I am reminded by some uncomfortable contrast of to-day how perfectly we were all handled there I ask myself once more what had been the secret of such perfection. One had taken it for granted at the time, for anything that is supremely good produces more acceptance than surprise. I felt we were all happy, but I didn't consider how our happiness was managed. And yet there were questions to be asked, questions that strike me as singularly obvious now that there is nobody to answer them. Mr. Offord had solved the insoluble; he had, without feminine help (save in the sense that ladies were dying to come to him and he saved the lives of several), established a *salon*; but I might have guessed that there was a method in his madness—a law in his success. He had not hit it off by a mere fluke. There was an art in it all, and how was the art so hidden? Who, indeed, if it came to that, was the occult artist? Launching this inquiry the other day, I had already got hold of the tail of my reply. I was helped by the very wonder of some of the conditions that came back to me—those that used to seem as natural as sunshine in a fine climate.

How was it, for instance, that we never were a crowd, never either too many or too few, always the right people *with* the right people (there must really have been no wrong people at all), always coming and going, never sticking fast nor overstaying, yet never popping in or out with an indecorous familiarity? How was it that we all sat where we wanted and moved when we wanted and met whom we wanted and escaped whom we wanted; joining, according to the accident of inclination, the general circle or falling in with a single talker on a convenient sofa? Why were all the sofas so convenient, the accidents so happy, the talkers so ready, the listeners so willing, the subjects presented to you in a rotation as quickly fore-ordained as the courses at dinner? A dearth of topics would have been as unheard of as a lapse in the service. These speculations couldn't fail to lead me to the fundamental truth that Brooksmith had been somehow at the bottom of the mystery. If he had not established the *salon* at least he had carried it on. Brooksmith, in short, was the artist!

We felt this, covertly, at the time, without formulating it, and were conscious, as an ordered and prosperous community, of his evenhanded justice, untainted with flunkeyism. He had none of that vulgarity—his touch was infinitely fine. The delicacy of it was clear to me on the first occasion my eyes rested, as they were so often to rest again, on the domestic revealed, in the turbid light of the street, by the opening of the house-door. I saw on the spot that though he had plenty of school he carried it without arrogance—he had remained articulate and human. *L'Ecole Anglaise*, Mr. Offord used to call him, laughing, when, later, it happened more than once that we had some conversation about him. But I remember accusing Mr. Offord of not doing him quite ideal justice.

That he was not one of the giants of the school, however, my old friend, who really understood him perfectly and was devoted to him, as I shall show, quite admitted; which doubtless poor Brooksmith had himself felt, to his cost, when his value in the market was originally determined. The utility of his class in general is estimated by the foot and the inch, and poor Brooksmith had only about five feet two to put into circulation. He acknowledged the inadequacy of this provision, and I am sure was penetrated with the everlasting fitness of the relation between service and stature. If *he* had been Mr. Offord he certainly would have found Brooksmith wanting, and indeed the laxity of his employer on this score was one of many things which he had had to condone and to which he had at last indulgently adapted himself.

I remember the old man's saying to me: "Oh, my servants, if they can live with me a fortnight they can live with me forever. But it's the first fortnight that tries 'em." It was in the first fortnight, for instance, that Brooksmith had had to learn that he was exposed to being addressed as 'my dear fellow' and 'my poor child'. Strange and deep must such a probation have been to him, and he doubtless emerged from it tempered and purified. This was written to a certain extent in his appearance; in his spare, brisk little person, in his cloistered white face and extraordinarily polished hair, which told of responsibility, looked as if it were kept up to the same high standard as the plate; in his small, clear, anxious eyes, even in the permitted, though not exactly encouraged tuft on his chin.

"He thinks me rather mad, but I've broken him in, and now he likes the place, he likes the company," said the old man.

I embraced this fully after I had become aware that Brooksmith's main characteristic was a deep and shy refinement, though I remember I was rather puzzled when, on another occasion, Mr. Offord remarked: "What he likes is the talk—mingling in the conversation." I was conscious that I had never seen Brooksmith permit himself this freedom, but I guessed in a moment that what Mr. Offord alluded to was a participation more intense than any speech could have represented—that of being perpetually present on a hundred legitimate pretexts, errands, necessities, and breathing the very atmosphere of criticism, the famous criticism of life.

"Quite an education, sir, isn't it, sir?" he said to me one day at the foot of the stairs, when he was letting me out; and I have always remembered the words and the tone as the first sign of the quickening drama of poor Brooksmith's fate. It was indeed an education, but to what was this sensitive young man of thirty-five, of the servile class, being educated?

Practically and inevitably, for the time, to companionship, to the perpetual, the even exaggerated reference and appeal of a person brought to dependence by his time of life and his infirmities and always addicted moreover (this was the exaggeration) to the art of giving you pleasure by letting you do things for him. There were certain things Mr. Offord was capable of pretending he liked you to do, even when he didn't, if he thought *you* liked them. If it happened that you didn't either (this was rare, but it might be), of course there were cross-purposes; but Brooksmith was there to prevent their going very far.

This was precisely the way he acted as moderator: he averted misunderstandings or cleared them up. He had been capable, strange as it may appear, of acquiring for this purpose an insight into the French tongue, which was often used at Mr. Offord's; for besides being habitual to most of the foreigners, and they were many, who haunted the place or arrived with letters (letters often requiring a little worried consideration, of which Brooksmith always had cognisance), it had really become the primary language of the master of the house. I don't know if all the *malentendus* were in French, but almost all the explanations were, and this didn't a bit prevent Brooksmith from following them.

I know Mr. Offord used to read passages to him from *Montaigne* and *Saint Simon*, for he read perpetually when he was alone—when they were alone, I should say—and Brooksmith was always about. Perhaps you'll say no wonder Mr. Offord's butler regarded him as 'rather mad'. However, if I'm not sure what he thought about Montaigne I'm convinced he admired Saint-Simon. A certain feeling for letters must have rubbed off on him from the mere handling of his master's books, which he was always carrying to and fro and putting back in their places.

I often noticed that if an anecdote or a quotation, much more a lively discussion, was going forward, he would, if busy with the fire or the curtains, the lamp or the tea, find a pretext for remaining in the room till the point should be reached. If his purpose was to catch it you were not discreet to call him off, and I shall never forget the look, a hard, stony stare (I caught it in its passage), which, one day when there were a good many people in the room, he fastened upon the footman who was helping him in the service and who, in an undertone, had asked him some irrelevant question.

It was the only manifestation of harshness that I ever observed on Brooksmith's part, and at first I wondered what was the matter. Then I became conscious that Mr. Offord was relating a very curious anecdote, never before perhaps made so public, and imparted to the narrator by an eye-witness of the fact, bearing upon Lord Byron's life in Italy. Nothing would induce me to reproduce it here; but Brooksmith had been in danger of losing it. If I ever should venture to reproduce it I shall feel how much I lose in not having my fellow-auditor to refer to.

The first day Mr. Offord's door was closed was therefore a dark date in contemporary history. It was raining hard and my umbrella was wet, but Brooksmith took it from me exactly as if this were a preliminary for going upstairs. I observed however that instead of putting it away he held it poised and trickling over the rug, and then I became aware that he was looking at me with deep, acknowledging eyes—his air of universal responsibility. I immediately understood; there was scarcely need of the question and the answer that passed between us. When I did understand that the old man had given up, for the first time, though only for the occasion, I exclaimed dolefully: "What a difference it will make—and to how many people!"

"I shall be one of them, sir!" said Brooksmith; and that was the beginning of the end.

Mr. Offord came down again, but the spell was broken, and the great sign of it was that the conversation was, for the first time, not directed. It wandered and stumbled, a little frightened, like a lost child—it had let go the nurse's hand. "The worst of it is that now we shall talk about my health—*c'est la fin du tout*," Mr. Offord said, when he reappeared; and then I recognised what a sign of change that would be—for he had never tolerated anything so provincial. The talk became ours, in a word—not his; and as ours, even when *he* talked, it could only be inferior. In this form it was a distress to Brooksmith, whose attention now wandered from it altogether: he had so much closer a vision of his master's intimate conditions than our superficialities represented.

There were better hours, and he was more in and out of the room, but I could see that he was conscious that the great institution was falling to pieces. He seemed to wish to take counsel with me about it, to feel responsible for its going on in some form or other. When for the second period—the first had lasted several days—he had to tell me that our old friend didn't receive, I half expected to hear him say after a moment: "Do you think I ought to, sir, in his place?"—as he might have asked me, with the return of autumn, if I thought he had better light the drawing-room fire.

He had a resigned philosophic sense of what his guests—our guests, as I came to regard them in our colloquies—would expect. His feeling was that he wouldn't absolutely have approved of himself as a substitute for the host; but he was so saturated with the religion of habit that he would have made, for our friends, the necessary sacrifice to the divinity. He would take them on a little further, till they could look about them. I think I saw him also mentally confronted with the opportunity to deal—for once in his life—with some of his own dumb preferences, his limitations of sympathy, *weeding* a little, in prospect, and returning to a purer tradition. It was not unknown to me that he considered that toward the end of Mr. Offord's career a certain laxity of selection had crept in.

At last it came to be the case that we all found the closed door more often than the open one; but even when it was closed Brooksmith managed a crack for me to squeeze through; so that practically I never turned away without having paid a visit. The difference simply came to be that the visit was to Brooksmith. It took place in the hall, at the familiar foot of the stairs, and we didn't sit down—at least Brooksmith didn't; moreover it was devoted wholly to one topic and always had the air of being already over—beginning, as it were, at the end. But it was always interesting—it always gave me something to think about. It is true that the subject of my meditation was ever the same—ever 'It's all very well, but what *will* become of Brooksmith?' Even my private answer to this question left me still unsatisfied.

No doubt Mr. Offord would provide for him, but *what* would he provide? that was the great point. He couldn't provide society; and society had become a necessity of Brooksmith's nature.

I must add that he never showed a symptom of what I may call sordid solicitude—anxiety on his own account. He was rather livid and intensely grave, as befitted a man before whose eyes the 'shade of that which once was great' was passing away. He had the solemnity of a person winding up, under depressing circumstances, a long established and celebrated business; he was a kind of social executor or liquidator. But his manner seemed to testify exclusively to the uncertainty of our future. I couldn't in those days have afforded it—I lived in two rooms in Jermyn Street and didn't 'keep a man'; but even if my income had permitted I shouldn't have ventured to say to Brooksmith (emulating Mr. Offord), 'My dear fellow, I'll take you on.' The whole tone of our intercourse was so much more an implication that it was *I* who should now want a lift. Indeed there was a tacit assurance in Brooksmith's whole attitude that he would have me on his mind.

One of the most assiduous members of our circle had been Lady Kenyon, and I remember his telling me one day that her ladyship had, in spite of her own infirmities, lately much aggravated, been in person to inquire. In answer to this I remarked that she would feel it more than any one. Brooksmith was silent a moment; at the end of which he said, in a certain tone (there is no reproducing some of his tones), "I'll go and see her." I went to see her myself, and I learned that he had waited upon her; but when I said to her, in the form of a joke but with a core of earnest, that when all was over some of us ought to combine, to club together to set Brooksmith up on his own account, she replied a trifle disappointingly: "Do you mean in a public-house?"

I looked at her in a way that I think Brooksmith himself would have approved, and then I answered: "Yes, the Offord Arms." What I had meant, of course, was that, for the love of art itself, we ought to look to it that such a peculiar faculty and so much acquired experience should not be wasted. I really think that if we had caused a few black-edged cards to be struck off and circulated—'Mr Brooksmith will continue to receive on the old premises from four to seven; business carried on as usual during the alterations'—the majority of us would have rallied.

Several times he took me upstairs—always by his own proposal—and our dear old friend, in bed, in curious flowered and brocaded *casaque* which made him, especially as his head was tied up in a handkerchief to match, look, to my imagination, like the dying Voltaire, held for ten minutes a sadly shrunken little *salon*. I felt indeed each time, as if I were attending the last *coucher* of some social sovereign. He was royally whimsical about his sufferings and not at all concerned—quite as if the Constitution provided for the case—about his successor. He glided over *our* sufferings charmingly, and none of his jokes—it was a gallant abstention, some of them would have been so easy—were at our expense.

Now and again, I confess, there was one at Brooksmith's, but so pathetically sociable as to make the excellent man look at me in a way that seemed to say: 'Do exchange a glance with me, or I sha'n't be able to stand it.' What he was not able to stand was not what Mr. Offord said about him, but what he wasn't able to say in return. His notion of conversation, for himself, was giving you the convenience of speaking to him; and when he went to 'see' Lady Kenyon, for instance, it was to carry her the tribute of his receptive silence. Where would the speech of his betters have been if proper service had been a manifestation of sound? In that case the fundamental difference would have had to be shown by their dumbness, and many of them, poor things, were dumb enough without that provision. Brooksmith took an unfailing interest in the preservation of the fundamental difference; it was the thing he had most on his conscience.on his conscience.

What had become of it, however, when Mr. Offord passed away like any inferior person—was relegated to eternal stillness like a butler upstairs? His aspect for several days after the expected event may be imagined, and the multiplication by funereal observance of the things he didn't say. When everything was over—it was late the same day—I knocked at the door of the house of mourning as I so often had done before. I could never call on Mr. Offord again, but I had come, literally, to call on Brooksmith. I wanted to ask him if there was anything I could do for him, tainted with vagueness as this inquiry could only be. My wild dream of taking him into my own service had died away: my service was not worth his being taken into. My offer to him could only be to help him to find another place, and yet there was an indelicacy, as it were, in taking for granted that his thoughts would immediately be fixed on another. I had a hope that he would be able to give his life a different form—though certainly not the form, the frequent result of such bereavements, of his setting up a little shop.

That would have been dreadful; for I should have wished to further any enterprise that he might embark in, yet how could I have brought myself to go and pay him shillings and take back coppers over a counter? My visit then was simply an intended compliment. He took it as such, gratefully and with all the tact in the world. He knew I really couldn't help him and that I knew he knew I couldn't, but we discussed the situation—with a good deal of elegant generality—at the foot of the stairs, in the hall already dismantled, where I had so often discussed other situations with him. The executors were in possession, as was still more apparent when he made me pass for a few minutes into the dining-room, where various objects were muffled up for removal.

Two definite facts, however, he had to communicate; one being that he was to leave the house for ever that night (servants, for some mysterious reason, seem always to depart by night), and the other—he mentioned it only at the last, with hesitation-that he had already been informed his late master had left him a legacy of eighty pounds. "I'm very glad." I said, and Brooksmith rejoined: "It was so like him to think of me." This was all that passed between us on the subject, and I know nothing of his judgement of Mr. Offord's memento. Eighty pounds are always eighty pounds, and no one has ever left *me* an equal sum; but, all the same, for Brooksmith, I was disappointed. I don't know what

I had expected—in short I was disappointed.

Eighty pounds might stock a little shop—a *very* little shop; but, I repeat, I couldn't bear to think of that. I asked my friend if he had been able to save a little, and he replied: "No, sir; I have had to do things." I didn't inquire what things he had had to do; they were his own affair, and I took his word for them as assentingly as if he had had the greatness of an ancient house to keep up; especially as there was something in his manner that seemed to convey a prospect of further sacrifice.

"I shall have to turn round a bit, sir—I shall have to look about me," he said; and then he added, indulgently, magnanimously: "If you should happen to hear of anything for me—"

I couldn't let him finish; this was, in its essence, too much in the really grand manner. It would be a help to my getting him off my mind to be able to pretend I *could* find the right place, and that help he wished to give me, for it was doubtless painful to him to see me in so false a position. I interposed with a few words to the effect that I was well aware that wherever he should go, whatever he should do, he would miss our old friend terribly—miss him even more than I should, having been with him so much more. This led him to make the speech that I have always remembered as the very text of the whole episode.

"Oh, sir, it's sad for *you*, very sad, indeed, and for a great many gentlemen and ladies; that it is, sir. But for me, sir, it is, if I may say so, still graver even than that: it's just the loss of something that was everything. For me, sir," he went on, with rising tears, "he was just *all*, if you know what I mean, sir. You have others, sir, I daresay—not that I would have you understand me to speak of them as in any way tantamount. But you have the pleasures of society, sir; if it's only in talking about him, sir, as I daresay you do freely—for all his blessed memory has to fear from it—with gentlemen and ladies who have had the same honour. That's not for me, sir, and I have to keep my associations to myself. Mr. Offord was *my* society, and now I have no more. You go back to conversation, sir, after all, and I go back to my place," Brooksmith stammered, without exaggerated irony or dramatic bitterness, but with a flat, unstudied veracity and his hand on the knob of the street-door. He turned it to let me out and then he added: "I just go downstairs, sir, again, and I stay there."

"My poor child," I replied, in my emotion, quite as Mr. Offord used to speak, "my dear fellow, leave it to me; we'll look after you, we'll all do something for you."

"Ah, if you could give me some one *like* him! But there ain't two in the world," said Brooksmith as we parted.

He had given me his address—the place where he would be to be heard of. For a long time I had no occasion to make use of the information; for he proved indeed, on trial, a very difficult case. In a word the people who knew him and had known Mr. Offord, didn't want to take him, and yet I couldn't bear to try to thrust him among people who didn't know him. I spoke to many of our old friends about him, and I found them all governed by the odd mixture of feelings of which I myself was conscious, and disposed, further, to entertain a suspicion that he was 'spoiled', with which I then would have nothing to do. In plain terms a certain embarrassment, a sensible awkwardness, when they thought of it, attached to the idea of using him as a menial: they had met him so often in society.

Many of them would have asked him, and did ask him, or rather did ask me to ask him, to come and see them; but a mere visiting-list was not what I wanted for him. He was too short for people who were very particular; nevertheless I heard of an opening in a diplomatic household which led me to write him a note, though I was looking much less for something grand than for something human. Five days later I heard from him. The secretary's wife had decided, after keeping him waiting till then, that she couldn't take a servant out of a house in which there had not been a lady. The note had a P.S.: 'It's a good job there wasn't, sir, such a lady as some.'

A week later he came to see me and told me he was 'suited'-committed to some highly respectable people (they were something very large in the City), who lived on the Bayswater side of the Park. "I daresay it will be rather poor, sir," he admitted; "but

I've seen the fireworks, haven't I, sir?—it can't be fireworks *every* night. After Mansfield Street there ain't much choice." There was a certain amount, however, it seemed; for the following year, going one day to call on a country cousin, a lady of a certain age who was spending a fortnight in town with some friends of her own, a family unknown to me and resident in Chester Square, the door of the house was opened, to my surprise and gratification, by Brooksmith in person. When I came out I had some conversation with him, from which I gathered that he had found the large City people too dull for endurance, and I guessed, though he didn't say it, that he had found them vulgar as well. I don't know what judgement he would have passed on his actual patrons if my relative had not been their friend; but under the circumstances he abstained from comment.

None was necessary, however, for before the lady in question brought her visit to a close they honoured me with an invitation to dinner, which I accepted. There was a largeish party on the occasion, but I confess I thought of Brooksmith rather more than of the seated company. They required no depth of attention—they were all referable to usual, irredeemable, inevitable types. It was the world of cheerful commonplace and conscious gentility and prosperous density, a full-fed, material, insular world, a world of hideous florid plate and ponderous order and thin conversation. There was not a word said about Byron. Nothing would have induced me to look at Brooksmith in the course of the repast, and I felt sure that not even my overturning the wine would have induced him to meet my eye. We were in intellectual sympathy—we felt, as regards each other, a kind of social responsibility. In short we had been in Arcadia together, and we had both come to *this*!

No wonder we were ashamed to be confronted. When he helped on my overcoat, as I was going away, we parted, for the first time since the earliest days in Mansfield Street, in silence. I thought he looked lean and wasted, and I guessed that his new place was not more 'human' than his previous one. There was plenty of beef and beer, but there was no reciprocity. The question for him to have asked before accepting the position would have been not 'How many footmen are kept?' but 'How much imagination?'

The next time I went to the house—I confess it was not very soon—I encountered his successor, a personage who evidently enjoyed the good fortune of never having quitted his natural level. Could any be higher? he seemed to ask—over the heads of three footmen and even of some visitors. He made me feel as if Brooksmith were dead; but I didn't dare to inquire—I couldn't have borne his 'I haven't the least idea, sir.' I despatched a note to the address Brooksmith had given me after Mr. Offord's death, but I received no answer. Six months later, however, I was favoured with a visit from an elderly, dreary, dingy person, who introduced herself to me as Mr. Brooksmith's aunt and from whom I learned that he was out of place and out of health and had allowed her to come and say to me that if I could spare half-an-hour to look in at him he would take it as a rare honour.

I went the next day—his messenger had given me a new address—and found my friend lodged in a short sordid street in Marylebone, one of those corners of London that wear the last expression of sickly meanness. The room into which I was shown was above the small establishment of a dyer and cleaner who had inflated kid gloves and discoloured shawls in his shop-front. There was a great deal of grimy infant life up and down the place, and there was a hot, moist smell within, as of the 'boiling' of dirty linen. Brooksmith sat with a blanket over his legs at a clean little window, where, from behind stiff bluish-white curtains, he could look across at a huckster's and a tinsmith's and a small greasy public-house.

He had passed through an illness and was convalescent, and his mother, as well as his aunt, was in attendance on him. I liked the mother, who was bland and intensely humble, but I didn't much fancy the aunt, whom I connected, perhaps unjustly, with the opposite public-house (she seemed somehow to be greasy with the same grease), and whose furtive eye followed every movement of my hand, as if to see if it were not going into my pocket. It didn't take this direction—I couldn't, unsolicited, put myself at that sort of ease with Brooksmith. Several times the door of the room opened, and mysterious old women peeped in and shuffled back again. I don't know who they were; poor Brooksmith seemed encompassed with vague, prying, beery females.

He was vague himself, and evidently weak, and much embarrassed, and not an allusion was made between us to Mansfield Street. The vision of the *salon* of which he had been an ornament hovered before me, however, by contrast, sufficiently. He assured me that he was really getting better, and his mother remarked that he would come round if he could only get his spirits up. The aunt echoed this opinion, and I became more sure that in her own case she knew where to go for such a purpose. I'm afraid I was rather weak with my old friend, for I neglected the opportunity, so exceptionally good, to rebuke the levity which had led him to throw up honourable positions—fine, stiff, steady berths, with morning prayers, as I knew, attached to one of them—in Bayswater and Belgravia.

Very likely his reasons had been profane and sentimental; he didn't want morning prayers, he wanted to be somebody's dear fellow; but I couldn't be the person to rebuke him. He shuffled these episodes out of sight—I saw that he had no wish to discuss them. I perceived further, strangely enough, that it would probably be a questionable pleasure for him to see me again: he doubted now even of my power to condone his aberrations. He didn't wish to have to explain; and his behaviour, in future, was likely to need explanation.

When I bade him farewell he looked at me a moment with eyes that said everything: 'How can I talk about those exquisite years in this place, before these people, with the old women poking their heads in? It was very good of you to come to see me—it wasn't my idea; *she* brought you. We've said everything; it's over; you'll lose all patience with me, and I'd rather you shouldn't see the rest.' I sent him some money, in a letter, the next day, but I saw the rest only in the light of a barren sequel.

A whole year after my visit to him I became aware once, in dining out, that Brooksmith was one of the several servants who hovered behind our chairs. He had not opened the door of the house to me, and I had not recognised him in the cluster of retainers in the hall. This time I tried to catch his eye, but he never gave me a chance, and when he handed me a dish I could only be careful to thank him audibly. Indeed I partook of two *entrées* of which I had my doubts, subsequently converted into certainties, in order not to snub him. He looked well enough in health, but much older, and wore, in an exceptionally marked degree, the glazed and expressionless mask of the British domestic *de race.*

I saw with dismay that if I had not known him I should have taken him, on the showing of his countenance, for an extravagant illustration of irresponsive servile gloom. I said to myself that he had become a reactionary, gone over to the Philistines, thrown himself into religion, the religion of his 'place', like a foreign lady *sur le retour.* I divined moreover that he was only engaged for the evening—he had become a mere waiter, had joined the band of the white-waistcoated who 'go out'. There was something pathetic in this fact, and it was a terrible vulgarisation of Brooksmith. It was the mercenary prose of butlerhood; he had given up the struggle for the poetry. If reciprocity was what he had missed, where was the reciprocity now? Only in the bottoms of the wine-glasses and five shillings (or whatever they get), clapped into his hand by the permanent man.

However, I supposed he had taken up a precarious branch of his profession because after all it sent him less downstairs. His relations with London society were more superficial, but they were of course more various. As I went away, on this occasion, I looked out for him eagerly among the four or five attendants whose perpendicular persons, fluting the walls of London passages, are supposed to lubricate the process of departure; but he was not on duty. I asked one of the others if he were not in the house, and received the prompt answer: "Just left, sir. Anything I can do for you, sir?" I wanted to say 'Please give him my kind regards;' but I abstained; I didn't want to compromise him, and I never came across him again..

Often and often, in dining out, I looked for him, sometimes accepting invitations on purpose to multiply the chances of my meeting him. But always in vain; so that as I met many other members of the casual class over and over again, I at last adopted the theory that he always procured a list of expected guests beforehand and kept away from the banquets which he thus learned I was to grace. At last I gave up hope, and one day, at the end of three years, I received another visit from his aunt. She was drearier and dingier, almost squalid, and she was in great tribulation and want. Her sister, Mrs Brooksmith, had been dead a year, and three months later her nephew had disappeared. He had always looked after her a bit—since her troubles; I never knew what her troubles had been—and now she hadn't so much as a petticoat to pawn.

She had also a niece, to whom she had been everything, before her troubles, but the niece had treated her most shameful. These were details; the great and romantic fact was Brooksmith's final evasion of his fate. He had gone out to wait one evening, as usual, in a white waistcoat she had done up for him with her own hands, being due at a large party up Kensington way. But he had never come home again, and had never arrived at the large party, or at any party that anyone could make out. No trace of him had come to light—no gleam of the white waistcoat had pierced the obscurity of his doom.

This news was a sharp shock to me, for I had my ideas about his real destination. His aged relative had promptly, as she said, guessed the worst. Somehow and somewhere he had got out of the way altogether, and now I trust that, with characteristic deliberation, he is changing the plates of the immortal gods. As my depressing visitant also said, he never *had* got his spirits up. I was fortunately able to dismiss her with her own somewhat improved. But the dim ghost of poor Brooksmith is one of those that I see. He had indeed been spoiled.

Maud-Evelyn

On some allusion to a lady who, though unknown to myself, was known to two or three of the company, it was asked by one of these if we had heard the odd circumstance of what she had just 'come in for'—the piece of luck suddenly overtaking, in the grey afternoon of her career, so obscure and lonely a personage. We were at first, in our ignorance, mainly reduced to crude envy; but old Lady Emma, who for a while had said nothing, scarcely even appearing to listen and letting the chatter, which was indeed plainly beside the mark, subside of itself, came back from a mental absence to observe that if what had happened to Lavinia was wonderful, certainly, what had for years gone before it, led up to it, had likewise not been without some singular features. From this we perceived that Lady Emma had a story—a story moreover out of the ken even of those of her listeners acquainted with the quiet person who was the subject of it.

Almost the oddest thing—as came out afterwards—was that such a situation should, for the world, have remained so in the background of this person's life. By 'afterwards' I mean simply before we separated; for what came out came on the spot, under encouragement and pressure, our common, eager solicitation. Lady Emma, who always reminded me of a fine old instrument that has first to be tuned, agreed, after a few of our scrapings and fingerings, that, having said so much, she couldn't, without wantonly tormenting us, forbear to say all. She had known Lavinia, whom she mentioned throughout only by that name, from far away, and she had also known—. But what she had known I must give as nearly as possible as she herself gave it. She talked to us from her corner of the sofa, and the flicker of the firelight in her face was like the glow of memory, the play of fancy, from within.

1

"Then why on earth don't you take him?" I asked. I think that was the way that, one day when she was about twenty—before some of you perhaps were born—the affair, for me, must have begun. I put the question because I knew she had had a chance, though I didn't know how great a mistake her failure to embrace it was to prove. I took an interest because I liked them both—you see how I like young people still—and because, as they had originally met at my house, I had in a manner to answer to each for the other. I'm afraid I'm thrown baldly back on the fact that if the girl was the daughter of my earliest, almost my only governess, to whom I had remained much attached and who, after leaving me, had married—for a governess—'well', Marmaduke (it isn't *his* real name!) was the son of one of the clever men who had—I was charming then, I assure you I was—wanted, years before, and this one as a widower, to marry me.

I hadn't cared, somehow, for widowers, but even after I had taken somebody else I was conscious of a pleasant link with the boy whose stepmother it had been open to me to become and to whom it was perhaps a little a matter of vanity with me to show that I should have been for him one of the kindest. This was what the woman his father eventually did marry was not, and that threw him upon me the more.

Lavinia was one of nine, and her brothers and sisters, who have never done anything for her, help, actually, in different countries and on something, I believe, of that same scale, to people the globe. There were mixed in her then, in a puzzling way, two qualities that mostly exclude each other—an extreme timidity and, as the smallest fault that could qualify a harmless creature for a world of wickedness, a self-complacency hard in tiny, unexpected spots, for which I used sometimes to take her up, but which, I subsequently saw, would have done something for the flatness of her life had they not evaporated with everything else. She was at any rate one of those persons as to whom you don't know whether they might have been attractive if they had been happy, or might have been happy if they had been attractive.

If I was a trifle vexed at her not jumping at Marmaduke, it was probably rather less because I expected wonders of him than because I thought she took her own prospect too much for granted. She had made a mistake and, before long, admitted it; yet I remember that when she expressed to me a conviction that he would ask her again, I also thought this highly probable, for in the meantime I had spoken to him. "She does care for you," I declared; and I can see at this moment, long ago though it be, his handsome empty young face look, on the words, as if, in spite of itself for a little, it really thought. I didn't press the matter, for he had, after all, no great things to offer; yet my conscience was easier, later on, for having not said less. He had three hundred and fifty a year from his mother, and one of his uncles had promised him something—I don't mean an allowance, but a place, if I recollect, in a business. He assured me that he loved as a man loves—a man of twenty-two!—but once. He said it, at all events, as a man says it but once.

"Well, then," I replied, "your course is clear."

"To speak to her again, you mean?"

"Yes—try it."

He seemed to try it a moment in imagination; after which, a little to my surprise, he asked: "Would it be very awful if she should speak to *me*?"

I stared. "Do you mean pursue you—overtake you? Ah, if you're running away—"

"I'm not running away!"—he was positive as to that. "But when a fellow has gone so far—"

"He can't go any further? Perhaps," I replied dryly. "But in that case he shouldn't talk of 'caring'."

"Oh, but I do, I do."

I shook my head. "Not if you're too proud!" On which I

turned away, looking round at him again, however, after he had surprised me by a silence that seemed to accept my judgement. Then I saw he had not accepted it; I perceived it indeed to be essentially absurd. He expressed more, on this, than I had yet seen him do—had the queerest, frankest, and, for a young man of his conditions, saddest smile.

"I'm *not* proud. It isn't *in* me. If you're not, you're not, you know. I don't think I'm proud enough."

It came over me that this was, after all, probable; yet somehow I didn't at the moment like him the less for it, though I spoke with some sharpness. "Then what's the matter with you?"

He took a turn or two about the room, as if what he had just said had made him a little happier. "Well, how can a man say more?" Then, just as I was on the point of assuring him that I didn't know what he had said, he went on: "I swore to her that I would never marry. Oughtn't that to be enough?"

"To make her come after you?"

"No—I suppose scarcely that; but to make her feel sure of me—to make her wait."

"Wait for what?"

"Well, till I come back."

"Back from where?"

"From Switzerland—haven't I told you? I go there next month with my aunt and my cousin."

He was quite right about not being proud—this was an alternative distinctly humble.

2

And yet see what it brought forth—the beginning of which was something that, early in the autumn, I learned from poor Lavinia. He had written to her, they were still such friends; and thus it was that she knew his aunt and his cousin to have come back without him. He had stayed on—stayed much longer and travelled much further: he had been to the Italian lakes and to Venice; he was now in Paris. At this I vaguely wondered, knowing that he was always short of funds and that he must, by his uncle's beneficence, have started on the journey on a basis of expenses paid. "Then whom has he picked up?" I asked; but feeling sorry, as soon as I had spoken, to have made Lavinia blush. It was almost as if he had picked up some improper lady, though in this case he wouldn't have told her, and it wouldn't have saved him money.

"Oh, he makes acquaintance so quickly, knows people in two minutes," the girl said. "And every one always wants to be nice to him."

This was perfectly true, and I saw what she saw in it. "Ah, my dear, he will have an immense circle ready for you!"

"Well," she replied, "if they do run after us I'm not likely to suppose it will ever be for me. It will be for *him*, and they may do to me what they like. My pleasure will be—but you'll see." I already saw—saw at least what she supposed she herself saw: her drawing-room crowded with female fashion and her attitude angelic. "Do you know what he said to me again before he went?" she continued.

I wondered; he *had* then spoken to her. "That he will never, never marry—"

"Anyone but *me*!" She ingenuously took me up. "Then you knew?"

It might be. "I guessed."

"And don't you believe it?"

Again I hesitated. "Yes." Yet all this didn't tell me why she had changed colour. "Is it a secret—whom he's with?"

"Oh no, they seem so nice. I was only struck with the way you know him—your seeing immediately that it must be a new friendship that has kept him over. It's the devotion of the Dedricks," Lavinia said. "He's travelling with them."

Once more I wondered. "Do you mean they're taking him about?"

"Yes—they've invited him."

No, indeed, I reflected—he wasn't proud. But what I said was: "Who in the world are the Dedricks?"

"Kind, good people whom, last month, he accidentally met. He was walking some Swiss pass—a long, rather stupid one, I believe, without his aunt and his cousin, who had gone round some other way and were to meet him somewhere. It came on to rain in torrents, and while he was huddling under a shelter he was overtaken by some people in a carriage, who kindly made him get in. They drove him, I gather, for several hours; it began an intimacy, and they've continued to be charming to him."

I thought a moment. "Are they ladies?"

Her own imagination meanwhile had also strayed a little. "I think about forty."

"Forty ladies?"

She quickly came back. "Oh no; I mean Mrs Dedrick is."

"About forty? Then Miss Dedrick—"

"There isn't any Miss Dedrick."

"No daughter?"

"Not with them, at any rate. No one but the husband."

I thought again. "And how old is *he*?"

Lavinia followed my example. "Well, about forty, too."

"About forty-two?" We laughed, but "That's all right!" I said; and so, for the time, it seemed.

He continued absent, none the less, and I saw Lavinia repeatedly, and we always talked of him, though this represented a greater concern with his affairs than I had really supposed myself committed to. I had never sought the acquaintance of his father's people, nor seen either his aunt or his cousin, so that the account given by these relatives of the circumstances of their separation reached me at last only through the girl, to whom, also—for she knew them as little—it had circuitously come. They considered, it appeared, the poor ladies he had started with, that he had treated them ill and thrown them over, sacrificing them selfishly to company picked up on the road—a reproach deeply resented by Lavinia, though about the company too I could see she was not much more at her ease.

"How can he help it if he's so taking?" she asked; and to be properly indignant in one quarter she had to pretend to be delighted in the other. Marmaduke *was* 'taking'; yet it also came out between us at last that the Dedricks must certainly be extraordinary. We had scant added evidence, for his letters stopped, and that naturally was one of our signs. I had meanwhile leisure to reflect—it was a sort of study of the human scene I always liked—on what to be taking consisted of. The upshot of my meditations, which experience has only confirmed, was that it consisted simply of itself. It was a quality implying no others. Marmaduke *had* no others. What indeed was his need of any?

3

He at last, however, turned up; but then it happened that if, on his coming to see me, his immediate picture of his charming new friends quickened even more than I had expected my sense of the variety of the human species, my curiosity about them failed to make me respond when he suggested I should go to see them. It's a difficult thing to explain, and I don't pretend to put it successfully, but doesn't it often happen that one may think well enough of a person without being inflamed with the desire to meet—on the ground of any such sentiment—other persons who think still better? Somehow—little harm as there was in Marmaduke—it was but half a recommendation of the Dedricks that they were crazy about him. I didn't say this—I was careful to say little; which didn't prevent his presently asking if he mightn't then bring them to *me*. "If not, why not?" he laughed. He laughed about everything.

"Why not? Because it strikes me that your surrender doesn't require any backing. Since you've done it you must take care of yourself."

"Oh, but they're as safe," he returned, "as the Bank of England. They're wonderful—for respectability and goodness."

"Those are precisely qualities to which my poor intercourse can contribute nothing." He hadn't, I observed, gone so far as to tell me they would be 'fun', and he *had*, on the other hand, promptly mentioned that they lived in Westbourne Terrace. They were not forty—they were forty-five; but Mr Dedrick had already, on considerable gains, retired from some primitive profession. They were the simplest, kindest, yet most original and unusual people, and nothing could exceed, frankly, the fancy they had taken to him. Marmaduke spoke of it with a placidity of resignation that was almost irritating. I suppose I should have despised him if, after benefits accepted, he had said they bored him; yet their not boring him vexed me even more than it puzzled. "Whom do they know?"

"No one but me. There are people in London like that."

"Who know no one but you?"

"No—I mean no one at all. There are extraordinary people in London, and awfully nice. You haven't an idea. You people don't know every one. They lead their lives—they go their way. One finds—what do you call it?—refinement, books, cleverness, don't you know, and music, and pictures, and religion, and an excellent table—all sorts of pleasant things. You only come across them by chance; but it's all perpetually going on."

I assented to this: the world was very wonderful, and one must certainly see what one could. In my own quarter too I found wonders enough. "But are you," I asked, "as fond of them—"

"As they are of *me*?" He took me up promptly, and his eyes were quite unclouded. "I'm quite sure I shall become so."

"Then are you taking Lavinia—?"

"Not to see them—no." I saw, myself, the next minute, of course, that I had made a mistake. "On what footing *can* I?"

I bethought myself. "I keep forgetting you're not engaged."

"Well," he said after a moment, "I shall never marry another."

It somehow, repeated again, gave on my nerves. "Ah, but what good will that do her, or me either, if you don't marry *her*?"

He made no answer to this—only turned away to look at something in the room; after which, when he next faced me, he had a heightened colour. "She ought to have taken me that day," he said gravely and gently; fixing me also as if he wished to say more.

I remember that his very mildness irritated me; some show of resentment would have been a promise that the case might still be righted. But I dropped it, the silly case, without letting him say more, and, coming back to Mr and Mrs Dedrick asked him how in the world, without either occupation or society, they passed so much of their time. My question appeared for a moment to leave him at a loss, but he presently found light; which, at the same time, I saw on my side, really suited him better than further talk about Lavinia. "Oh, they live for Maud-Evelyn."

"And who's Maud-Evelyn?"

"Why, their daughter."

"Their daughter?" I had supposed them childless.

He partly explained. "Unfortunately they've lost her."

"Lost her?" I required more.

He hesitated again. "I mean that a great many people would take it that way. But *they* don't—they won't."

I speculated. "Do you mean other people would have given her up?"

"Yes—perhaps even tried to forget her. But the Dedricks can't."

I wondered what she had done: had it been anything very bad? However, it was none of my business, and I only said: "They communicate with her?"

"Oh, all the while."

"Then why isn't she with them?"

Marmaduke thought. "She *is*—now."

"'Now'? Since when?"

"Well, this last year."

"Then why do you say they've lost her?"

"Ah," he said, smiling sadly, "*I* should call it that. I, at any rate," he went on, "don't see her."

Still more I wondered. "They keep her apart?"

He thought again. "No, it's not that. As I say, they live for her."

"But they don't want *you* to—is that it?"

At this he looked at me for the first time, as I thought, a little strangely. "How *can* I?"

He put it to me as if it were bad of him, somehow, that he shouldn't; but I made, to the best of my ability, a quick end of that. "You can't. Why in the world *should* you? Live for *my* girl.

Live for Lavinia."

4

I had unfortunately run the risk of boring him again with that idea, and, though he had not repudiated it at the time, I felt in my having returned to it the reason why he never reappeared for weeks. I saw 'my girl', as I had called her, in the interval, but we avoided with much intensity the subject of Marmaduke. It was just this that gave me my perspective for finding her constantly full of him. It determined me, in all the circumstances, not to rectify her mistake about the childlessness of the Dedricks. But whatever I left unsaid, her naming the young man was only a question of time, for at the end of a month she told me he had been twice to her mother's and that she had seen him on each of these occasions.

"Well then?"

"Well then, he's very happy."

"And still taken up—"

"As much as ever, yes, with those people. He didn't tell me so, but I could see it."

I could too, and her own view of it. "What, in that case, did he tell you?"

"Nothing—but I think there's something he wants to. Only not what *you* think," she added.

I wondered then if it were what I had had from him the last time. "Well, what prevents him?" I asked.

"From bringing it out? I don't know."

It was in the tone of this that she struck, to my ear, the first note of an acceptance so deep and a patience so strange that they gave me, at the end, even more food for wonderment than the rest of the business. "If he can't speak, why does he come?"

She almost smiled. "Well. I think I *shall* know."

I looked at her; I remember that I kissed her. "You're admirable; but it's very ugly."

"Ah," she replied, "he only wants to be kind!"

"To *them*? Then he should let others alone. But what I call ugly is his being content to be so 'beholden'—"

"To Mr and Mrs Dedrick?" She considered as if there might be many sides to it. "But mayn't he do them some good?"

The idea failed to appeal to me. "What good can Marmaduke do? There's one thing," I went on, "in case he should want you to know them. Will you promise me to refuse?"

She only looked helpless and blank. "Making their acquaintance?"

"Seeing them, going near them—ever, ever."

Again she brooded. "Do you mean *you* won't?"

"Never, never."

"Well, then, I don't think I want to."

"Ah, but that's not a promise." I kept her up to it. "I want your word."

She demurred a little. "But why?"

"So that at least he shan't make use of you," I said with energy.

My energy overbore her, though I saw how she would really have given herself. "I promise, but it's only because it's something I know he will never ask."

I differed from her at the time, believing the proposal in question to have been exactly the subject she had supposed him to be wishing to broach; but on our very next meeting I heard from her of quite another matter, upon which, as soon as she came in, I saw her to be much excited.

"You know then about the daughter without having told me? He called again yesterday," she explained as she met my stare at her unconnected plunge, "and now I know that he *has* wanted to speak to me. He at last brought it out."

I continued to stare. "Brought what?"

"Why, everything." She looked surprised at my face. "Didn't he tell you about Maud-Evelyn?"

I perfectly recollected, but I momentarily wondered. "He spoke of there being a daughter, but only to say that there's something the matter with her. What is it?"

The girl echoed my words. "What 'is' it?—you dear, strange thing! The matter with her is simply that she's dead."

"Dead?" I was naturally mystified. "When then did she die?"

"Why, years and years ago—fifteen, I believe. As a little girl. Didn't you understand it so?"

"How *should* I?—when he spoke of her as 'with' them and said that they lived for her!"

"Well," my young friend explained, "that's just what he meant—they live for her memory. She *is* with them in the sense that they think of nothing else."

I found matter for surprise in this correction, but also, at first, matter for relief. At the same time it left, as I turned it over, a fresh ambiguity. "If they think of nothing else, how can they think so much of Marmaduke?"

The difficulty struck her, though she gave me even then a dim impression of being already, as it were, rather on Marmaduke's side, or, at any rate—almost as against herself—in sympathy with the Dedricks. But her answer was prompt: "Why, that's just their reason—that they can talk to him so much about her."

"I see." Yet still I wondered. "But what's *his* interest—?"

"In being drawn into it?" Again Lavinia met her difficulty. "Well, that she was so interesting! It appears she was lovely."

I doubtless fairly gaped. "A little girl in a pinafore?"

"She was out of pinafores; she was, I believe, when she died, about fourteen. Unless it was sixteen! She was at all events wonderful for beauty."

"That's the rule. But what good does it do him if he has never seen her?"

She thought a moment, but this time she had no answer. "Well, you must ask him!"

I determined without delay to do so; but I had before me meanwhile other contradictions. "Hadn't I better ask him on the same occasion what he means by their 'communicating'?"

Oh, this was simple. "They go in for 'mediums', don't you know, and raps, and sittings. They began a year or two ago."

"Ah, the idiots!" I remember, at this, narrow-mindedly exclaiming. "Do they want to drag *him* in—?"

"Not in the least; they don't desire it, and he has nothing to do with it."

"Then where does his fun come in?"

Lavinia turned away; again she seemed at a loss. At last she brought out: "Make him show you her little photograph."

But I remained unenlightened. "Is her little photograph his fun?"

Once more she coloured for him. "Well, it represents a young loveliness!"

"That he goes about showing?"

She hesitated. "I think he has only shown it to *me*."

"Ah, you're just the last one!" I permitted myself to observe.

"Why so, if I'm also struck?"

There was something about her that began to escape me, and I must have looked at her hard. "It's very good of you to be struck!"

"I don't only mean by the beauty of the face," she went on; "I mean by the whole thing—by that also of the attitude of the parents, their extraordinary fidelity and the way that, as he says, they have made of her memory a real religion. That was what, above all, he came to tell me about."

I turned away from her now, and she soon afterwards left me; but I couldn't help its dropping from me before we parted that I had never supposed him to be *that* sort of fool.

5

If I were really the perfect cynic you probably think me I should frankly say that the main interest of the rest of this matter lay for me in fixing the sort of fool I *did* suppose him. But I'm afraid, after all, that my anecdote amounts mainly to a presentation of my own folly. I shouldn't be so in possession of the whole spectacle had I not ended by accepting it, and I shouldn't have accepted it had it not, for my imagination, been saved somehow from grotesqueness. Let me say at once, however, that grotesqueness, and even indeed something worse, did at first appear to me strongly to season it.

After that talk with Lavinia I immediately addressed to our friend a request that he would come to see me; when I took the liberty of challenging him outright on everything she had told me. There was one point in particular that I desired to clear up and that seemed to me much more important even than the colour of Maud-Evelyn's hair or the length of her pinafores: the question, I of course mean, of my young man's good faith. Was he altogether silly or was he only altogether mercenary? I felt my choice restricted for the moment to these alternatives.

After he had said to me "It's as ridiculous as you please, but they've simply adopted me" I had it out with him, on the spot, on the issue of common honesty, the question of what he was conscious, so that his self-respect should be saved, of being able to give such benefactors in return for such bounty. I'm obliged to say that to a person so inclined at the start to quarrel with him his amiability could yet prove persuasive. His contention was that the equivalent he represented was something for his friends alone to measure. He didn't for a moment pretend to sound deeper than the fancy they had taken to him. He had not, from the first, made up to them in any way: it was all their own doing, their own insistence, their own eccentricity, no doubt, and even, if I liked, their own insanity.

Wasn't it enough that he was ready to declare to me, looking me straight in the eye, that he was 'really and truly' fond of them and that they didn't bore him a mite? I had evidently—didn't I see?—an ideal for him that he wasn't at all, if I didn't mind, the fellow to live up to. It was he himself who put it so, and it drew from me the pronouncement that there *was* something irresistible in the refinement of his impudence.

"I don't go near Mrs. Jex," he said—Mrs. Jex was their favourite medium: "I do find *her* ugly and vulgar and tiresome, and I hate that part of the business. Besides," he added in words that I afterwards remembered, "I don't require it: I do beautifully without it. But my friends themselves," he pursued, "though they're of a type you've never come within miles of, are not ugly, are not vulgar, are not in any degree whatever any sort of a 'dose'. They're, on the contrary, in their own unconventional way, the very best company. They're endlessly amusing. They're delightfully queer and quaint and kind—they're like people in some old story or of some old time. It's at any rate our own affair—mine and theirs—and I beg you to believe that I should make short work of a remonstrance on the subject from anyone but you."

I remember saying to him three months later: "You've never yet told me what they really want of you"; but I'm afraid this was a form of criticism that occurred to me precisely because I had already begun to guess. By that time indeed I had had great initiations, and poor Lavinia had had them as well—hers in fact throughout went further than mine—and we had shared them together, and I had settled down to a tolerably exact sense of what I was to see. It was what Lavinia added to it that really made the picture.

The portrait of the little dead girl had evoked something attractive, though one had not lived so long in the world without hearing of plenty of little dead girls; and the day came when I felt as if I had actually sat with Marmaduke in each of the rooms converted by her parents—with the aid not only of the few small, cherished relics, but that of the fondest figments and fictions, ingenious imaginary mementoes and tokens, the unexposed make-believes of the sorrow that broods and the passion that clings—into a temple of grief and worship.

The child, incontestably beautiful, had evidently been passionately loved, and in the absence from their lives—I suppose originally a mere accident—of such other elements, either new pleasures or new pains, as abound for most people, their feeling had drawn to itself their whole consciousness: it had become mildly maniacal. The idea was fixed, and it kept others out. The world, for the most part, allows no leisure for such a ritual, but the world had consistently neglected this plain, shy couple, who were sensitive to the wrong things and whose sincerity and fidelity, as well as their tameness and twaddle, were of a rigid, antique pattern.

I must not represent that either of these objects of interest, or my care for their concerns, took up all my leisure; for I had many claims to meet and many complications to handle, a hundred preoccupations and much deeper anxieties. My young woman, on her side, had other contacts and contingencies-other troubles too, poor girl; and there were stretches of time in which I neither saw Marmaduke nor heard a word of the Dedricks.

Once, only once, abroad, in Germany at a railway-station, I met him in their company. They were colourless, commonplace, elderly Britons, of the kind you identify by the livery of their footman or the labels of their luggage, and the mere sight of them justified me to my conscience in having avoided, from the first, the stiff problem of conversation with them. Marmaduke saw me on the spot and came over to me. There was no doubt whatever of *his* vivid bloom. He had grown fat—or almost, but not with grossness—and might perfectly have passed for the handsome, happy, full-blown son of doting parents who couldn't let him out of view and to whom he was a model of respect and solicitude. They followed him with placid, pleased eyes when he joined me, but asking nothing at all for themselves and quite fitting into his own manner of saying nothing about them.

It had its charm, I confess, the way he could be natural and easy, and yet intensely conscious too, on such a basis. What he was conscious of was that there were things I by this time knew; just as, while we stood there and good-humouredly sounded each other's faces—for, having accepted everything at last, I was only a little curious—I knew that he measured my insight. When he returned again to his doting parents I had to admit that, doting as they were, I felt him not to have been spoiled. It was incongruous in such a career, but he was rather more of a man.

There came back to me with a shade of regret after I had got on this occasion into my train, which was not theirs, a memory of some words that, a couple of years before, I had uttered to poor Lavinia. She had said to me, speaking in reference to what was then our frequent topic and on some fresh evidence that I have forgotten: "He feels now, you know, about Maud-Evelyn quite as the old people themselves do."

"Well," I had replied, "it's only a pity he's paid for it!"

"Paid?" She had looked very blank.

"By all the luxuries and conveniences," I had explained, "that he comes in for through living with them. For that's what he practically does."

At present I saw how wrong I had been. He was paid, but paid differently, and the mastered wonder of that was really what had been between us in the waiting-room of the station. Step by step, after this, I followed.

6

I can see Lavinia for instance in her ugly new mourning immediately after her mother's death. There had been long anxieties connected with this event, and she was already faded, already almost old. But Marmaduke, on her bereavement, had been to her, and she came straightway to me.

"Do you know what he thinks now?" she soon began. "He thinks he knew her."

"Knew the child?" It came to me as if I had half expected it.

"He speaks of her now as if she hadn't been a child." My visitor gave me the strangest fixed smile. "It appears that she wasn't so young—it appears she had grown up."

I stared. "How can it 'appear'? They *know*, at least! There were the facts."

"Yes," said Lavinia, "but they seem to have come to take a different view of them. He talked to me a long time, and all about *her*. He told me things."

"What kind of things? Not trumpery stuff, I hope, about 'communicating'—about his seeing or hearing her?"

"Oh no, he doesn't go in for that; he leaves it to the old couple, who, I believe, cling to their mediums, keep up their sittings and their rappings and find in it all a comfort, an amusement, that he doesn't grudge them and that he regards as harmless. I mean anecdotes—memories of his own. I mean things she said to him and that they did together—places they went to. His mind is full of them."

I turned it over. "Do you think he's decidedly mad?"

She shook her head with her bleached patience. "Oh no, it's too beautiful!"

"Then are *you* taking it up? I mean the preposterous theory—"

"It *is* a theory," she broke in, "but it isn't necessarily preposterous. Any theory has to suppose something," she sagely pursued, "and it depends at any rate on what it's a theory *of*. It's wonderful to see this one work."

"Wonderful always to see the growth of a legend!" I laughed. "This is a rare chance to watch one in formation. They're all three in good faith building it up. Isn't that what you made out from him?"

Her tired face fairly lighted. "Yes—you understand it; and you put it better than I. It's the gradual effect of brooding over the past; the past, that way, grows and grows. They make it and make it. They've persuaded each other—the parents—of so many things that they've at last also persuaded *him*. It has been contagious."

"It's you who put it well," I returned. "It's the oddest thing I ever heard of, but it is, in its way, a reality. Only we mustn't speak of it to others."

She quite accepted that precaution. "No—to nobody. *He* doesn't. He keeps it only for me."

"Conferring on you thus," I again laughed, "such a precious privilege!"

She was silent a moment, looking away from me. "Well, he has kept his vow."

"You mean of not marrying? Are you very sure?" I asked. "Didn't he perhaps—?" But I faltered at the boldness of my joke.

The next moment I saw I needn't. "He *was* in love with her," Lavinia brought out.

I broke now into a peal which, however provoked, struck even my own ear at the moment as rude almost to profanity. "He literally tells you outright that he's making believe?"

She met me effectively enough. "I don't think he *knows* he is.

He's just completely in the current."

"The current of the old people's twaddle?"

Again my companion hesitated; but she knew what she thought. "Well, whatever we call it, I like it. It isn't so common, as the world goes, for any one—let alone for two or three—to feel and to care for the dead as much as that. It's self-deception, no doubt, but it comes from something that—well," she faltered again, "is beautiful when one does hear of it. They make her out older, so as to imagine they had her longer; and they make out that certain things really happened to her, so that she shall have had more life. They've invented a whole experience for her, and Marmaduke has become a part of it. There's one thing, above all, they want her to have had." My young friend's face, as she analysed the mystery, fairly grew bright with her vision. It came to me with a faint dawn of awe that the attitude of the Dedricks *was* contagious. "And she did have it!" Lavinia declared.

I positively admired her, and if I could yet perfectly be rational without being ridiculous, it was really, more than anything else, to draw from her the whole image. "She had the bliss of knowing Marmaduke? Let us agree to it, then, since she's not here to contradict us. But what I don't get over is the scant material for *him*!" It may easily be conceived how little, for the moment, I could get over it. It was the last time my impatience was to be too much for me, but I remember how it broke out. "A man who might have had *you*!"

For an instant I feared I had upset her—thought I saw in her face the tremor of a wild wail. But poor Lavinia was magnificent. "It wasn't that he might have had 'me'—that's nothing: it was, at the most, that I might have had *him*. Well, isn't that just what has happened? He's mine from the moment no one else has him. I give up the past, but don't you see what it does for the rest of life? I'm surer than ever that he won't marry."

"Of course, he won't—to quarrel, with those people!"

For a minute she answered nothing; then, "Well, for whatever reason!" she simply said. Now, however, I had gouged out of her a couple of still tears, and I pushed away the whole obscure comedy.

7

I might push it away, but I couldn't really get rid of it; nor, on the whole, doubtless, did I want to, for to have in one's life, year after year, a particular question or two that one couldn't comfortably and imposingly make up one's mind about was just the sort of thing to keep one from turning stupid. There had been little need of my enjoining reserve upon Lavinia: she obeyed, in respect to impenetrable silence save with myself, an instinct, an interest of her own. We never therefore gave poor Marmaduke, as you call it, 'away'; we were much too tender, let alone that she was also too proud; and, for himself, evidently, there was not, to the end, in London, another person in his confidence.

No echo of the queer part he played ever came back to us; and I can't tell you how this fact, just by itself, brought home to me little by little a sense of the charm he was under. I met him 'out' at long intervals—met him usually at dinner. He had grown like a person with a position and a history. Rosy and rich-looking, fat, moreover, distinctly fat at last, there was almost in him something of the bland—yet not too bland—young head of an hereditary business.

If the Dedricks had been bankers he might have constituted the future of the house. There was none the less a long middle stretch during which, though we were all so much in London, he dropped out of my talks with Lavinia. We were conscious, she and I, of his absence from them; but we clearly felt in each quarter that there are things after all unspeakable, and the fact, in any case, had nothing to do with her seeing or not seeing our friend. I was sure, as it happened, that she did see him. But there were moments that for myself still stand out.

One of these was a certain Sunday afternoon when it was so dismally wet that, taking for granted I should have no visitors, I had drawn up to the fire with a book—a successful novel of the day—that I promised myself comfortably to finish. Suddenly, in my absorption, I heard a firm rat-tat-tat; on which I remember giving a groan of inhospitality. But my visitor proved in due course Marmaduke, and Marmaduke proved—in a manner even less, at the point we had reached, to have been counted on—still more attaching than my novel. I think it was only an accident that he became so; it would have been the turn of a hair either way.

He hadn't come to speak—he had only come to talk, to show once more that we could continue good old friends without his speaking. But somehow there were the circumstances: the insidious fireside, the things in the room, with their reminders of his younger time; perhaps even too the open face of my book, looking at him from where I had laid it down for him and giving him a chance to feel that he could supersede Wilkie Collins. There was at all events a promise of intimacy, of opportunity for him in the cold lash of the windows by the storm. We should be alone; it was cosy; it was safe.

The action of these impressions was the more marked that what was touched by them, I afterwards saw, was not at all a desire for an effect—was just simply a spirit of happiness that needed to overflow. It had finally become too much for him. His past, rolling up year after year, had grown too interesting. But he was, all the same, directly stupefying. I forget what turn of our preliminary gossip brought it out, but it came, in explanation of something or other, as it had not yet come: "When a man has had for a few months what *I* had, you know!" The moral appeared to be that nothing in the way of human experience of the exquisite could again particularly matter. He saw, however, that I failed immediately to fit his reflection to a definite case, and he went on with the frankest smile: "You look as bewildered as if you suspected me of alluding to some sort of thing that isn't usually spoken of; but I assure you I mean nothing more reprehensible than our blessed engagement itself."

"Your blessed engagement?" I couldn't help the tone in which I took him up; but the way he disposed of that was something of which I feel to this hour the influence. It was only a look, but it put an end to my tone for ever. It made me, on my side, after an instant, look at the fire—look hard and even turn a little red.

During this moment I saw my alternatives and I chose; so that when I met his eyes again I was fairly ready. "You still feel," I asked with sympathy, "how much it did for you?"

I had no sooner spoken than I saw that that would be from that moment the right way. It instantly made all the difference. The main question would be whether I could keep it up. I remember that only a few minutes later, for instance, this question gave a flare. His reply had been abundant and imperturbable—had included some glance at the way death brings into relief even the faintest things that have preceded it; on which I felt myself suddenly as restless as if I had grown afraid of him.

I got up to ring for tea; he went on talking—talking about Maud-Evelyn and what she had been for him; and when the servant had come up I prolonged, nervously, on purpose, the order I had wished to give. It made time, and I could speak to the footman sufficiently without thinking: what I thought of really was the risk of turning right round with a little outbreak. The temptation was strong; the same influences that had worked for my companion just worked, in their way, during that minute or two, for me. *Should* I, taking him unaware, flash at him a plain 'I say, just settle it for me once for all. *Are* you the boldest and basest of fortune-hunters, or have you only, more innocently and perhaps more pleasantly, suffered your brain slightly to soften?'

But I missed the chance—which I didn't in fact afterwards regret. My servant went out, and I faced again to my visitor, who continued to converse. I met his eyes once more, and their effect was repeated. If anything had happened to his brain this effect was perhaps the domination of the madman's stare. Well, he was the easiest and gentlest of madmen. By the time the footman came back with tea I was in for it; I was in for everything. By 'everything' I mean my whole subsequent treatment of the case. It *was*—the case was—really beautiful.

So, like all the rest, the hour comes back to me: the sound of the wind and the rain; the look of the empty, ugly, cabless square and of the stormy spring light; the way that, uninterrupted and absorbed, we had tea together by my fire. So it was that he found me receptive and that I found myself able to look merely grave and kind when he said, for example: "Her father and mother, you know, really, that first day—the day they picked me up on the *Splügen*—recognised me as the proper one."

"The proper one?"

"To make their son-in-law. They wanted her so," he went on, "to have had, don't you know, just everything."

"Well, if she did have it"—I tried to be cheerful—"isn't the whole thing then all right?"

"Oh, it's all right *now*," he replied—"now that we've got it all there before us. You see, they couldn't like me so much"—he wished me thoroughly to understand—"without wanting me to have been the man."

"I see—that was natural."

"Well," said Marmaduke, "it prevented the possibility of any-one else."

"Ah, that would never have done!" I laughed.

His own pleasure at it was impenetrable, splendid. "You see, they couldn't do much, the old people—and they can do still less now—with the future; so they had to do what they could with the past."

"And they seem to have done," I concurred, "remarkably much."

"Everything, simply. Everything," he repeated. Then he had an idea, though without insistence or importunity—I noticed it just flicker in his face. "If you *were* to come to Westbourne Terrace—"

"Oh, don't speak of that!" I broke in. "It wouldn't be decent now. I should have come, if at all, ten years ago."

But he saw, with his good humour, further than this. "I see what you mean. But there's much more in the place now than then."

"I dare say. People get new things. All the same—!" I was at bottom but resisting my curiosity.

Marmaduke didn't press me, but he wanted me to know. "There are our rooms—the whole set; and I don't believe you ever saw anything more charming, for *her* taste was extraordinary. I'm afraid too that I myself have had much to say to them." Then as he made out that I was again a little at sea, "I'm talking," he went on, "of the suite prepared for her marriage." He 'talked' like a crown prince. "They were ready, to the last touch—there was nothing more to be done. And they're just as they were—not an object moved, not an arrangement altered, not a person but ourselves coming in: they're only exquisitely kept. All our presents are there—I should have liked you to see them."

It had become a torment by this time—I saw that I had made a mistake. But I carried it off. "Oh, I couldn't have borne it!"

"They're not sad," he smiled—"they're too lovely to be sad. They're happy. And the things—!" He seemed, in the excitement of our talk, to have them before him.

"They're so very wonderful?"

"Oh, selected with a patience that makes them almost priceless. It's really a museum. There was nothing they thought too good for her."

I had lost the museum, but I reflected that it could contain no object so rare as my visitor. "Well, you've helped them—you could do *that*."

He quite eagerly assented. "I could do that, thank God—I could do that! I felt it from the first, and it's what I *have* done." Then as if the connection were direct: "All *my* things are there."

I thought a moment. "Your presents?"

"Those I made her. She loved each one, and I remember about each the particular thing she said. Though I do say it," he continued, "none of the others, as a matter of fact, come near mine. I look at them every day, and I assure you I'm not ashamed." Evidently, in short, he had spared nothing, and he talked on and on. He really quite swaggered.

8

In relation to times and intervals I can only recall that if this visit of his to me had been in the early spring it was one day in the late autumn—a day, which couldn't have been in the same year, with the difference of hazy, drowsy sunshine and brown and yellow leaves—that, taking a short cut across Kensington Gardens, I came, among the untrodden ways, upon a couple occupying chairs under a tree, who immediately rose at the sight of me. I had been behind them at recognition, the fact that Marmaduke was in deep mourning having perhaps, so far as I had observed it, misled me. In my desire both not to look flustered at meeting them and to spare their own confusion I bade them again be seated and asked leave, as a third chair was at hand, to share a little their rest.

Thus it befell that after a minute Lavinia and I had sat down, while our friend, who had looked at his watch, stood before us among the fallen foliage and remarked that he was sorry to have to leave us. Lavinia said nothing, but I expressed regret; I couldn't, however, as it struck me, without a false or a vulgar note speak as if I had interrupted a tender passage or separated a pair of lovers. But I could look him up and down, take in his deep mourning. He had not made, for going off, any other pretext than that his time was up and that he was due at home. 'Home', with him now, had but one meaning: I knew him to be completely quartered in Westbourne Terrace. "I hope nothing has happened," I said—"that you've lost no one whom *I* know."

Marmaduke looked at my companion, and she looked at Marmaduke. "He has lost his wife," she then observed.

Oh, this time, I fear, I had a small quaver of brutality; but it was at him I directed it. "Your wife? I didn't know you had *had* a wife!"

"Well," he replied, positively gay in his black suit, his black gloves, his high hatband, "the more we live in the past, the more things we find in it. That's a literal fact. You would see the truth of it if your life had taken such a turn."

"*I* live in the past," Lavinia put in gently and as if to help us both.

"But with the result, my dear," I returned, "of not making, I hope, such extraordinary discoveries!" It seemed absurd to be afraid to be light.

"May none of her discoveries be more fatal than mine!" Marmaduke wasn't uproarious, but his treatment of the matter had the good taste of simplicity. "They've wanted it so for her," he continued to me wonderfully, "that we've at last seen our way to it—I mean to what Lavinia has mentioned." He hesitated but three seconds—he brought it brightly out. "Maud-Evelyn had *all* her young happiness."

I stared, but Lavinia was, in her peculiar manner, as brilliant. "The marriage *did* take place," she quietly, stupendously explained to me.

Well, I was determined not to be left. "So you're a widower," I gravely asked, "and these are the signs?"

"Yes; I shall wear them always now."

"But isn't it late to have begun?"

My question had been stupid, I felt the next instant; but it didn't matter—he was quite equal to the occasion. "Oh, I had to wait, you know, till all the facts about my marriage had given me the right." And he looked at his watch again. "Excuse me—I *am* due. Goodbye, goodbye." He shook hands with each of us, and as we sat there together watching him walk away I was struck with his admirable manner of looking the character. I felt indeed as our eyes followed him that we were at one on this, and I said nothing till he was out of sight. Then by the same impulse we turned to each other.

"I thought he was never to marry!" I exclaimed to my friend.

Her fine wasted face met me gravely. "He isn't—ever. He'll be still more faithful."

"Faithful this time to whom?"

"Why, to Maud-Evelyn." I said nothing—I only checked an ejaculation; but I put out a hand and took one of hers, and for a minute we kept silence. "Of course it's only an idea," she began again at last, "but it seems to me a beautiful one." Then she continued resignedly and remarkably: "And now *they* can die."

"Mr and Mrs Dedrick?" I pricked up my ears. "Are they dying?"

"Not quite, but the old lady, it appears, is failing, steadily weakening; less, as I understand it, from any definite ailment than because she just feels her work done and her little sum of passion, as Marmaduke calls it, spent. Fancy, with her convictions, all her reasons for wanting to die! And if she goes, he says, Mr Dedrick won't long linger. It will be quite '*John Anderson my jo*'"

"Keeping her company down the hill, to lie beside her at the foot?"

"Yes, having settled all things."

I turned these things over as we walked away, and how they had settled them—for Maud-Evelyn's dignity and Marmaduke's high advantage; and before we parted that afternoon—we had taken a cab in the Bayswater Road and she had come home with me—I remember saying to her: "Well then, when they die won't he be free?"

She seemed scarce to understand. "Free?"

"To do what he likes."

She wondered. "But he does what he likes now."

"Well then, what *you* like!"

"Oh, you know what *I* like—!"

Ah, I closed her mouth! "You like to tell horrid fibs—yes, I know it!"

What she had then put before me, however, came in time to pass: I heard in the course of the next year of Mrs. Dedrick's extinction, and some months later, without, during the interval, having seen a sign of Marmaduke, wholly taken up with his bereaved patron, learned that her husband had touchingly followed her. I was out of England at the time; we had had to put into practice great economies and let our little place; so that, spending three winters successively in Italy, I devoted the periods between, at home, altogether to visits among people, mainly relatives, to whom these friends of mine were not known. Lavinia of course wrote to me—wrote, among many things, that Marmaduke was ill and had not seemed at all himself since the loss of his 'family', and this in spite of the circumstance, which she had already promptly communicated, that they had left him, by will, 'almost everything'. I knew before I came back to remain that she now saw him often and, to the extent of the change that had overtaken his strength and his spirits, greatly ministered to him. As soon as we at last met I asked for news of him; to which she replied: "He's gradually going." Then on my surprise: "He has had his life."

"You mean that, as he said of Mrs. Dedrick, his sum of passion is spent?"

At this she turned away. "You've never understood."

I *had*, I conceived; and when I went subsequently to see him I was moreover sure. But I only said to Lavinia on this first occasion that I would immediately go; which was precisely what brought out the climax, as I feel it to be, of my story. "He's not now, you know," she turned round to admonish me, "in Westbourne Terrace. He has taken a little old house in Kensington."

"Then he hasn't kept the things?"

"He has kept everything." She looked at me still more as if I had never understood.

"You mean he has moved them?"

She was patient with me. "He has moved nothing. Everything is as it was, and kept with the same perfection."

I wondered. "But if he doesn't live there?"

"It's just what he does."

"Then how can he be in Kensington?"

She hesitated, but she had still more than her old grasp of it. "He's in Kensington—without living."

"You mean that at the other place—?"

"Yes, he spends most of his time. He's driven over there every day—he remains there for hours. He keeps it for that."

"I see—it's still the museum."

"It's still the temple!" Lavinia replied with positive austerity.

"Then why did he move?"

"Because, you see, there"—she faltered again—"I could come to him. And he wants me," she said with admirable simplicity.

Little by little I took it in. "After the death of the parents, even, you never went?"

"Never."

"So you haven't seen anything?"

"Anything of hers? Nothing."

I understood, oh perfectly; but I won't deny that I was disappointed: I had hoped for an account of his wonders and I immediately felt that it wouldn't be for me to take a step that she had declined. When, a short time later, I saw them together in Kensington Square—there were certain hours of the day that she regularly spent with him—I observed that everything about him was new, handsome and simple. They were, in their strange, final union—if union it could be called—very natural and very touching; but he was visibly stricken—he had his ailment in his eyes. She moved about him like a sister of charity—at all events like a sister. He was neither robust nor rosy now, nor was his attention visibly very present, and I privately and fancifully asked myself where it wandered and waited. But poor Marmaduke was a gentleman to the end—he wasted away with an excellent manner. He died twelve days ago; the will was opened; and last week, having meanwhile heard from her of its contents, I saw Lavinia. He leaves her everything that he himself had inherited. But she spoke of it all in a way that caused me to say in surprise: "You haven't yet been to the house?"

"Not yet. I've only seen the solicitors, who tell me there will be no complications."

There was something in her tone that made me ask more. "Then you're not curious to see what's there?"

She looked at me with a troubled—almost a pleading—sense, which I understood; and presently she said: "Will you go with me?"

"Some day, with pleasure—but not the first time. You must go alone then. The 'relics' that you'll find there," I added—for I had read her look—"you must think of now not as hers—"

"But as his?"

"Isn't that what his death—with his so close relation them-has made them for you?"

Her face lighted—I saw it was a view she could thank me for putting into words. "I see—I see. They *are* his. I'll go."

She went, and three days ago she came to me. They're really marvels, it appears, treasures extraordinary, and she has them all. Next week I go with her—I shall see them at last. Tell *you* about them, you say? My dear man, everything.

The Tone of Time

1

I was too pleased with what it struck me that, as an old, old friend, I had done for her, not to go to her that very afternoon with the news. I knew she worked late, as in general I also did; but I sacrificed for her sake a good hour of the February daylight. She was in her studio, as I had believed she would be, where her card ('Mary J. Tredick'—not Mary Jane, but Mary Juliana) was manfully on the door; a little tired, a little old and a good deal spotted, but with her ugly spectacles taken off, as soon as I appeared, to greet me. She kept on, while she scraped her palette and wiped her brushes, the big stained apron that covered her from head to foot and that I have often enough before seen her retain in conditions giving the measure of her renunciation of her desire to dazzle.

Every fresh reminder of this brought home to me that she had given up everything but her work, and that there had been in her history some reason. But I was as far from the reason as ever. She had given up too much; this was just why one wanted to lend her a hand. I told her, at any rate, that I had a lovely job for her.

"To copy something I do like?"

Her complaint, I knew, was that people only gave orders, if they gave them at all, for things she did not like. But this wasn't a case of copying—not at all, at least, in the common sense. "It's for a portrait—quite in the air."

"Ah, you do portraits yourself!"

"Yes, and you know how. My trick won't serve for this. What's wanted is a pretty picture."

"Then of whom?"

"Of nobody. That is of anybody. Anybody you like."

She naturally wondered. "Do you mean I'm myself to choose my sitter?"

"Well, the oddity is that there is to *be* no sitter."

"Whom then is the picture to represent?"

"Why, a handsome, distinguished, agreeable man, of not more than forty, clean-shaven, thoroughly well-dressed, and a perfect gentleman."

She continued to stare. "And I'm to find him myself?"

I laughed at the term she used. "Yes, as you 'find' the canvas, the colours and the frame." After which I immediately explained. "I've just had the 'rummest' visit, the effect of which was to make me think of you. A lady, unknown to me and unintroduced, turned up at my place at three o'clock. She had come straight, she let me know, without preliminaries, on account of one's high reputation—the usual thing—and of her having admired one's work. Of course I instantly saw—I mean I saw it as soon as she named her affair—that she hadn't understood my work at all. What am I good for in the world but just the impression of the given, the presented case? I can do but the face I see."

"And do you think I can do the face I don't?"

"No, but you see so many more. You see them in fancy and memory, and they come out, for you, from all the museums you've haunted and all the great things you've studied. I *know* you'll be able to see the one my visitor wants and to give it-what's the *crux* of the business—the tone of time."

She turned the question over. "What does she want it for?"

"Just *for* that—for the tone of time. And, except that it's to hang over her chimney, she didn't tell me. I've only my idea that it's to represent, to symbolise, as it were, her husband, who's not alive and who perhaps never was. This is exactly what will give you a free hand."

"With nothing to go by—no photographs or other portraits?"

"Nothing."

"She only proposes to describe him?"

"Not even; she wants the picture itself to do that. Her only condition is that he be a *très-bel homme*."

She had begun at last, a little thoughtfully, to remove her apron. "Is she French?"

"I don't know. I give it up. She calls herself Mrs. Bridgenorth."

Mary wondered. "*Connais pas*! I never heard of her."

"You wouldn't."

"You mean it's not her real name?"

I hesitated. "I mean that she's a very downright fact, full of the implication that she'll pay a downright price. It's clear to me that you can ask what you like; and it's therefore a chance that I can't consent to your missing." My friend gave no sign either way, and I told my story. "She's a woman of fifty, perhaps of more, who has been pretty, and who still presents herself, with her grey hair a good deal powdered, as I judge, to carry it off, extraordinarily well. She was a little frightened and a little free; the latter because of the former. But she did uncommonly well, I thought, considering the oddity of her wish.

This oddity she quite admits; she began indeed by insisting on it so in advance that I found myself expecting I didn't know what. She broke at moments into French, which was perfect, but no better than her English, which isn't vulgar; not more at least than that of everybody else. The things people *do* say, and the way they say them, to artists! She wanted immensely, I could see, not to fail of her errand, not to be treated as absurd; and she was extremely grateful to me for meeting her so far as I did. She was beautifully dressed and she came in a *brougham*."

My listener took it in; then, very quietly, "Is she respectable?" she inquired.

"Ah, there you are!" I laughed; "and how you always pick the point right out, even when one has endeavoured to diffuse a specious glamour! She's extraordinary," I pursued after an instant; "and just what she wants of the picture, I think, is to make her a little less so."

"Who is she, then? What is she?" my companion simply went on.

It threw me straightway back on one of my hobbies. "Ah, my dear, what is so interesting as life? What is, above all, so stupendous as London? There's everything in it, everything in the world, and nothing too amazing not some day to pop out at you. What is a woman, faded, preserved, pretty, powdered, vague, odd, dropping on one without credentials, but with a carriage and very good lace? What is such a person but a person who *may* have had adventures, and have made them, in one way or another, pay? They're, however, none of one's business; it's scarcely on the cards that one should ask her. I should like, with Mrs. Bridgenorth, to see a fellow ask! She goes in for propriety, the real thing. If I suspect her of being the creation of her own talents, she has clearly, on the other hand, seen a lot of life. Will you meet her?" I next demanded.

My hostess waited. "No."

"Then you won't try?"

"Need I meet her to try?" And the question made me guess that, so far as she had understood, she began to feel herself a little taken. "It seems strange," she none the less mused, "to attempt to please her on such a basis. To attempt," she presently added, "to please her at all. It's your idea that she's not married?" she, with this, a trifle inconsequently asked.

"Well," I replied, "I've only had an hour to think of it, but I somehow already see the scene. Not immediately, not the day after, or even perhaps the year after the thing she desires is set up there, but in due process of time and on convenient opportunity, the transfiguration will occur. 'Who is that awfully handsome man?' 'That? Oh, that's an old sketch of my dear dead husband.' Because I told her—insidiously sounding her—that she would want it to look old, and that the tone of time is exactly what you're full of."

"I believe I am," Mary sighed at last.

"Then put on your hat." I had proposed to her on my arrival to come out to tea with me, and it was when left alone in the studio while she went to her room that I began to feel sure of the success of my errand. The vision that had an hour before determined me grew deeper and brighter for her while I moved about and looked at her things. There were more of them there on her hands than one liked to see; but at least they sharpened my confidence, which was pleasant for me in view of that of my visitor, who had accepted without reserve my plea for Miss Tredick. Four or five of her copies of famous portraits—ornaments of great public and private collections—were on the walls, and to see them again together was to feel at ease about my guarantee.

The mellow manner of them was what I had had in my mind in saying, to excuse myself to Mrs. Bridgenorth, "Oh, my things, you know, look as if they had been painted tomorrow!" It made no difference that Mary's Vandykes and Gainsboroughs were reproductions and replicas, for I had known her more than once to amuse herself with doing the thing quite, as she called it, off her own bat. She had copied so bravely so many brave things that she had at the end of her brush an extraordinary bag of tricks. She had always replied to me that such things were mere clever humbug, but mere clever humbug was what our client happened to want. The thing was to let her have it—one could trust her for the rest.

And at the same time that I mused in this way I observed to myself that there was already something more than, as the phrase is, met the eye in such response as I felt my friend had made. I had touched, without intention, more than one spring; I had set in motion more than one impulse. I found myself indeed quite certain of this after she had come back in her hat and her jacket. She was different—her idea had flowered; and she smiled at me from under her tense veil, while she drew over her firm, narrow hands a pair of fresh gloves, with a light distinctly new. "Please tell your friend that I'm greatly obliged to both of you and that

I take the order."

"Good. And to give him all his good looks?"

"It's just to do *that* that I accept. I shall make him supremely beautiful—and supremely base."

"Base?" I just demurred.

"The finest gentleman you'll ever have seen, and the worst friend."

I wondered, as I was startled; but after an instant I laughed for joy. "Ah well, so long as he's not mine! I see we *shall* have him," I said as we went, for truly I had touched a spring. In fact I had touched *the* spring.

It rang, more or less, I was presently to find, all over the place. I went, as I had promised, to report to Mrs. Bridgenorth on my mission, and though she declared herself much gratified at the success of it I could see she a little resented the apparent absence of any desire on Miss Tredick's part for a preliminary conference. "I only thought she might have liked just to see me, and have imagined I might like to see *her*."

But I was full of comfort. "You'll see her when it's finished. You'll see her in time to thank her."

"And to pay her, I suppose," my hostess laughed, with an asperity that was, after all, not excessive. "Will she take very long?"

I thought. "She's so full of it that my impression would be that she'll do it off at a heat."

"She *is* full of it then?" she asked; and on hearing to what tune, though I told her but half, she broke out with admiration. "You artists are the most extraordinary people!" It was almost with a bad conscience that I confessed we indeed were, and while she said that what she meant was that we seemed to understand everything, and I rejoined that this was also what *I* meant, she took me into another room to see the place for the picture—a proceeding of which the effect was singularly to confirm the truth in question. The place for the picture—in her own room, as she called it, a *boudoir* at the back, overlooking the general garden of the approved modern row and, as she said, only just wanting that touch—proved exactly the place (the space of a large panel in the white woodwork over the mantel) that I had spoken of to my friend.

She put it quite candidly, "Don't you see what it will do?" and looked at me, wonderfully, as for a sign that I could sympathetically take from her what she didn't literally say. She said it, poor woman, so very nearly that I had no difficulty whatever. The portrait, tastefully enshrined there, of the finest gentleman one should ever have seen, would do even more for herself than it would do for the room.

I may as well mention at once that my observation of Mrs. Bridgenorth was not in the least of a nature to unseat me from the hobby I have already named. In the light of the impression she made on me life seemed quite as prodigious and London quite as amazing as I had ever contended, and nothing could have been more in the key of that experience than the manner in which everything was vivid between us and nothing expressed. We remained on the surface with the tenacity of shipwrecked persons clinging to a plank.

Our plank was our concentrated gaze at Mrs. Bridgenorth's mere present. We allowed her past to exist for us only in the form of the prettiness that she had gallantly rescued from it and to which a few scraps of its identity still adhered. She was amiable, gentle, consistently proper. She gave me more than anything else the sense, simply, of waiting. She was like a house so freshly and successfully 'done up' that you were surprised it wasn't occupied. She was waiting for something to happen—for somebody to come. She was waiting, above all, for Mary Tredick's work. She clearly counted that it would help her.

I had foreseen the fact—the picture was produced at a heat; rapidly, directly, at all events, for the sort of thing it proved to be. I left my friend alone at first, left the ferment to work, troubling her with no questions and asking her for no news; two or three weeks passed, and I never went near her. Then at last, one afternoon as the light was failing, I looked in. She immediately knew what I wanted. "Oh yes, I'm doing him."

"Well," I said, "I've respected your intensity, but I *have* felt curious."

I may not perhaps say that she was never so sad as when she laughed, but it's certain that she always laughed when she was sad. When, however, poor dear, for that matter, was she, secretly, not? Her little gasps of mirth were the mark of her worst moments. But why should she have one of these just now? "Oh, I know your curiosity!" she replied to me; and the small chill of her amusement scarcely met it. "He's coming out, but I can't show him to you yet. I must muddle it through in my own way. It has insisted on being, after all, a 'likeness'," she added. "But nobody will ever know."

"Nobody?"

"Nobody *she* sees."

"Ah, she doesn't, poor thing," I returned, "seem to see anybody!"

"So much the better. I'll risk it." On which I felt I should have to wait, though I had suddenly grown impatient. But I still hung about, and while I did so she explained. "If what I've done is really a portrait, the conditions itself prescribed it. If I was to do the most beautiful man in the world I could do but one."

We looked at each other; then I laughed. "It can scarcely be *me*! But you're getting," I asked, "the great thing?"

"The infamy? Oh yes, please God."

It took away my breath a little, and I even for the moment scarce felt at liberty to press. But one could always be cheerful. "What I meant is the tone of time."

"Getting it, my dear man? Didn't I get it long ago? Don't I *show* it—the tone of time?" she suddenly, strangely sighed at me, with something in her face I had never yet seen. "I can't give it to him more than—for all these years—he was to have given it to *me*."

I scarce knew what smothered passion, what remembered wrong, what mixture of joy and pain my words had accidentally quickened. Such an effect of them could only become, for me, an instant pity, which, however, I brought out but indirectly. "It's the tone," I smiled, "in which you're speaking now."

This served, unfortunately, as something of a check. "I didn't mean to speak now." Then with her eyes on the picture, "I've said everything there. Come back," she added, "in three days. He'll be all right."

He was indeed when at last I saw him. She had produced an extraordinary thing—a thing wonderful, ideal, for the part it was to play. My only reserve, from the first, was that it was too fine for its part, that something much less 'sincere' would equally have served Mrs. Bridgenorth's purpose, an that relegation to that lady's 'own room'—whatever charm it was to work there—might only mean for it cruel obscurity. The picture is before me now, so that I could describe it if description availed. It represents a man of about five-and-thirty, seen only as to the head and shoulders, but dressed, the observer gathers, in a fashion now almost antique and which was far from contemporaneous with the date of the work. His high, slightly narrow face, which would be perhaps too aquiline but for the beauty of the forehead and the sweetness of the mouth, has a charm that even, after all these years, still stirs my imagination.

His type has altogether a distinction that you feel to have been firmly caught and yet not vulgarly emphasised. The eyes are just too near together, but they are, in a wondrous way, both careless and intense, while lip, cheek, and chin, smooth and clear, are admirably drawn. Youth is still, you see, in all his presence, the joy and pride of life, the perfection of a high spirit and the expectation of a great fortune, which he takes for granted with unconscious insolence. Nothing has ever happened to humiliate or disappoint him, and if my fancy doesn't run away with me the whole presentation of him is a guarantee that he will die without having suffered. He is so handsome, in short, that you can scarcely say what he means, and so happy that you can scarcely guess what he feels.

It is of course, I hasten to add, an appreciably feminine rendering, light, delicate, vague, imperfectly synthetic—insistent and evasive, above all, in the wrong places; but the composition, none the less, is beautiful and the suggestion infinite. The grandest air of the thing struck me in fact, when first I saw it, as coming from the high artistic impertinence with which it offered itself as painted about 1850. It would have been a rare flower of refinement for that dark day. The 'tone'—that of such a past as it pretended to—was there almost to excess, a brown bloom into which the image seemed mysteriously to retreat.

The subject of it looks at me now across more years and more knowledge, but what I felt at the moment was that he managed to be at once a triumphant trick and a plausible evocation. He hushed me, I remember, with so many kinds of awe that I shouldn't have dreamt of asking who he was. All I said, after my first incoherences of wonder at my friend's practised skill, was: "And you've arrived at this truth without documents?"

"It depends on what you call documents."

"Without notes, sketches, studies?"

"I destroyed them years ago."

"Then you once had them?"

She just hung fire. "I once had everything."

It told me both more and less than I had asked; enough at all events to make my next question, as I uttered it, sound even to myself a little foolish. "So that it's all memory?"

From where she stood she looked once more at her work; after which she jerked away and, taking several steps, came back to me with something new—whatever it was I had already seen-in her air and answer. "It's all *hate*!" she threw at me, and then went out of the room. It was not till she had gone that I quite understood why. Extremely affected by the impression visibly made on me, she had burst into tears but had wished me not to see them.

She left me alone for some time with her wonderful subject, and I again, in her absence, made things out. He was dead—he had been dead for years; the sole humiliation, as I have called it, that he was to know had come to him in that form. The canvas held and cherished him, in any case, as it only holds the dead. She had suffered from him, it came to me, the worst that a woman can suffer, and the wound he had dealt her, though hidden, had never effectually healed. It had bled again while she worked. Yet when she at last reappeared there was but one thing to say. "The beauty, heaven knows, I see. But I don't see what you call the infamy."

She gave him a last look—again she turned away. "Oh, he was like that."

"Well, whatever he was like," I remember replying, "I wonder you can bear to part with him. Isn't it better to let her see the picture first here?"

As to this she doubted. "I don't think I want her to come."

I wondered. "You continue to object so to meet her?"

"What good will it do? It's quite impossible I should alter him for her."

"Oh, she won't want *that*!" I laughed. "She'll adore him as he is."

"Are you quite sure of your idea?"

"That he's to figure as Mr. Bridgenorth? Well, if I hadn't been from the first, my dear lady, I should be now. Fancy, with the chance, her *not* jumping at him! Yes, he'll figure as Mr. Bridgenorth."

"Mr. Bridgenorth!" she echoed, making the sound, with her small, cold laugh, grotesquely poor for him. He might really have been a prince, and I wondered if he hadn't been. She had, at all events, a new notion. "Do you mind my having it taken to your place and letting her come to see it there?" Which—as I immediately embraced her proposal, deferring to her reasons, whatever they were—was what was speedily arranged.

2

The next day therefore I had the picture in charge, and on the following Mrs. Bridgenorth, whom I had notified, arrived. I had placed it, framed and on an easel, well in evidence, and I have never forgotten the look and the cry that, as she became aware of it, leaped into her face and from her lips. It was an extraordinary moment, all the more that it found me quite unprepared—so extraordinary that I scarce knew at first what had happened. By the time I really perceived, moreover, more things had happened than one, so that when I pulled myself together it was to face the situation as a whole. She had recognised on the instant the subject; that came first and was irrepressibly vivid in her. Her recognition had, for the length of a flash, lighted for her the possibility that the stroke had been directed.

That came second, and she flushed with it as with a blow in the face. What came third—and it was what was really most wondrous—was the quick instinct of getting both her strange recognition and her blind suspicion well in hand. She couldn't control, however, poor woman, the strong colour in her face and the quick tears in her eyes. She could only glare at the canvas, gasping, grimacing, and try to gain time. Whether in surprise or in resentment she intensely reflected, feeling more than anything else how little she might prudently show; and I was conscious even at the moment that nothing of its kind could have been finer than her effort to swallow her shock in ten seconds.

How many seconds she took I didn't measure; enough, assuredly, for me also to profit. I gained more time than she, and the greatest oddity doubtless was my own private manoeuvre—the quickest calculation that, acting from a mere confused instinct, I had ever made. If she had known the great gentleman represented there and yet had determined on the spot to carry herself as ignorant, all my loyalty to Mary Tredick came to the surface in a prompt counter-move. What gave me opportunity was the red in her cheek. "Why, you've known him!"

I saw her ask herself for an instant if she mightn't successfully make her startled state pass as the mere glow of pleasure-her natural greeting to her acquisition. She was pathetically, yet at the same time almost comically, divided. Her line was so to cover her tracks that every avowal of a past connection was a danger; but it also concerned her safety to learn, in the light of our astounding coincidence, how far she already stood exposed. She meanwhile begged the question. She smiled through her tears. "He's too magnificent!"

But I gave her, as I say, all too little time. "Who is he? Who *was* he?"

It must have been my look still more than my words that determined her. She wavered but an instant longer, panted, laughed, cried again, and then, dropping into the nearest seat, gave herself up so completely that I was almost ashamed. "Do you think I'd tell you his *name*?" The burden of the backward years—all the effaced and ignored—lived again, almost like an accent unlearned but freshly breaking out at a touch, in the very sound of the words. These perceptions she, however, the next thing showed me, were a game at which two could play. She had to look at me but an instant. "Why, you really *don't* know it!"

I judged best to be frank. "I don't know it."

"Then how does *she*?"

"How do you?" I laughed. "I'm a different matter."

She sat a minute turning things round, staring at the picture. "The likeness, the likeness!" It was almost too much.

"It's so true?"

"Beyond everything."

I considered. "But a resemblance to a known individual-that wasn't what you wanted."

She sprang up at this in eager protest. "Ah, no one else would see it."

I showed again, I fear, my amusement. "No one but you and she?"

"It's her doing *him*!" She was held by her wonder. "Doesn't she, on your honour, know?"

"That his is the very head you would have liked if you had dared? Not a bit. How *should* she? She knows nothing—on my honour."

Mrs. Bridgenorth continued to marvel. "She just painted him for the kind of face—?"

"That corresponds with my description of what you wished? Precisely."

"But *how*—after so long? From memory? As a friend?"

"As a reminiscence—yes. Visual memory, you see, in our uncanny race, is wonderful. As the ideal thing, simply, for your purpose. You *are* then suited?" I after an instant added.

She had again been gazing, and at this turned her eyes on me; but I saw she couldn't speak, couldn't do more at least than sound, unutterably, 'Suited!' so that I was positively not surprised when suddenly—just as Mary had done, the power to produce this effect seeming a property of the model—she burst into tears. I feel no harsher in relating it, however I may appear, than I did at the moment, but it is a fact that while she just wept I literally had a fresh inspiration on behalf of Miss Tredick's interests. I knew exactly, moreover, before my companion had recovered herself, what she would next ask me; and I consciously brought this appeal on in order to have it over.

I explained that I had not the least idea of the identity of our artist's sitter, to which she had given me no clue. I had nothing but my impression that she had known him—known him well; and, from whatever material she had worked, the fact of his having also been known to Mrs. Bridgenorth was a coincidence pure and simple. It partook of the nature of prodigy, but such prodigies did occur. My visitor listened with avidity and credulity. She was so far reassured. Then I saw her question come. "Well, if she doesn't dream he was ever anything to me—or what he will be now—I'm going to ask you, as a very particular favour, never to tell her. She will want to know of course exactly how I've been struck. You'll naturally say that I'm delighted, but may I exact from you that you say nothing else?"

There was supplication in her face, but I had to think. "There are conditions I must put to you first, and one of them is also a question, only more frank than yours. Was this mysterious personage—frustrated by death—to have married you?"

She met it bravely. "Certainly, if he had lived."

I was only amused at an artlessness in her 'certainly'. "Very good. But why do you wish the coincidence—"

"Kept from her?" She knew exactly why. "Because if she suspects it she won't let me have the picture. Therefore," she added with decision, "you must let me pay for it on the spot."

"What do you mean by on the spot?"

"I'll send you a cheque as soon as I get home."

"Oh," I laughed, "let us understand. Why do you consider she won't let you have the picture?"

She made me wait a little for this, but when it came it was perfectly lucid. "Because she'll then see how much more I must want it."

"How much less—wouldn't it be rather, since the bargain was, as the more convenient thing, not for a likeness?"

"Oh," said Mrs. Bridgenorth with impatience, "the likeness will take care of itself. She'll put this and that together." Then she brought out her real apprehension. "She'll be jealous."

"Oh!" I laughed. But I was startled.

"She'll hate me!"

I wondered. "But I don't think she liked him."

"Don't think?" She stared at me, with her echo, over all that might be in it, then seemed to find little enough. "I *say*!"

It was almost comically the old Mrs. Bridgenorth. "But I gather from her that he was bad."

"Then what was *she*?"

I barely hesitated. "What were *you*?"

"That's my own business." And she turned again to the picture. "He was good enough for her to do *that* of him."

I took it in once more. "Artistically speaking, for the way it's done, it's one of the most curious things I've ever seen."

"It's a grand treat!" said poor Mrs. Bridgenorth more simply.

It was, it *is* really; which is exactly what made the case so interesting. "Yet I feel somehow that, as I say, it wasn't done with love."

It was wonderful how she understood. "It was done with rage."

"Then what have you to fear?"

She knew again perfectly. "What happened when he made *me* jealous. So much," she declared, "that if you'll give me your word for silence—"

"Well?"

"Why, I'll double the money."

"Oh," I replied, taking a turn about in the excitement of our concurrence, "that's exactly what—to do a still better stroke for her—it had just come to *me* to propose!"

"It's understood then, on your oath as a gentleman?" She was so eager that practically this settled it, though I moved to and fro a little while she watched me in suspense. It vibrated all round us that she had gone out to the thing in a stifled flare, that a whole close relation had in the few minutes revived. We know it of the truly amiable person that he will strain a point for another that he wouldn't strain for himself. The stroke to put in for Mary was positively prescribed. The work represented really much more than had been covenanted, and if the purchaser chose so to value it this was her own affair. I decided. "If it's understood also on *your* word."

We were so at one that we shook hands on it. "And when may I send?"

"Well, I shall see her this evening. Say early tomorrow."

"Early tomorrow." And I went with her to her brougham, into which, I remember, as she took leave, she expressed regret that she mightn't then and there have introduced the canvas for removal. I consoled her with remarking that she couldn't have got it in—which was not quite true.

I saw Mary Tredick before dinner, and though I was not quite ideally sure of my present ground with her I instantly brought out my news. "She's so delighted that I felt I must in conscience do something still better for you. She's not to have it on the original terms. I've put up the price."

Mary wondered. "But to what?"

"Well, to four hundred. If you say so I'll try even for five."

"Oh, she'll never give that."

"I beg your pardon."

"After the agreement?" She looked grave. "I don't like such leaps and bounds."

"But, my dear child, they're yours. You contracted for a decorative trifle and you've produced a breathing masterpiece."

She thought. "Is that what she calls it?" Then, as having to think too, I hesitated, "What does she know?" she pursued.

"She knows she wants it."

"So much as that?"

At this I had to brace myself a little. "So much that she'll send me the cheque this afternoon, and that you'll have mine by the first post in the morning."

"Before she has even received the picture?"

"Oh, she'll send for it to-morrow." And as I was dining out and had still to dress, my time was up. Mary came with me to the door, where I repeated my assurance. "You shall receive my cheque by the first post." To which I added: "If it's little enough for a lady so much in need to pay for *any* husband, it isn't worth mentioning as the price of such a one as you've given her!"

I was in a hurry, but she held me. "Then you've felt your idea confirmed?"

"My idea?"

"That that's what I *have* given her?"

I suddenly fancied I had perhaps gone too far; but I had kept my cab and was already in it. "Well, put it," I called with excess of humour over the front, "that you've, at any rate, given *him* a wife!"

When on my return from dinner that night I let myself in, my first care, in my dusky studio, was to make light for another look at Mary's subject. I felt the impulse to bid him good-night, but, to my astonishment, he was no longer there. His place was a void—he had already disappeared. I saw, however, after my first surprise, what had happened—saw it moreover, frankly, with some relief. As my servants were in bed I could ask no questions, but it was clear that Mrs. Bridgenorth, whose note, containing its cheque, lay on my table, had been after all unable to wait.

The note, I found, mentioned nothing but the enclosure; but it had come by hand, and it was her silence that told the tale. Her messenger had been instructed to 'act'; he had come with a vehicle, he had transferred to it canvas and frame. The prize was now therefore landed and the incident closed. I didn't altogether, the next morning, know why, but I had slept the better for the sense of these things, and as soon as my attendant came in I asked for details. It was on this that his answer surprised me. "No, sir, there was no man; she came herself. She had only a four-wheeler, but I helped her, and we got it in. It was a squeeze, sir, but she *would* take it."

I wondered. "She had a four-wheeler? and not her servant?"

"No, no, sir. She came, as you may say, single-handed."

"And not even in her brougham, which would have been larger?"

My man, with his habit, weighed it. "But *have* she a brougham, sir?"

"Why, the one she was here in yesterday."

Then light broke. "Oh, *that* lady! It wasn't her, sir. It was Miss Tredick."

Light broke, but darkness a little followed it—a darkness that, after breakfast, guided my steps back to my friend. There, in its own first place, I met her creation; but I saw it would be a different thing meeting *her*. She immediately put down on a table, as if she had expected me, the cheque I had sent her overnight. "Yes, I've brought it away. And I can't take the money."

I found myself in despair. "You want to keep him?"

"I don't understand what has happened."

"You just back out?"

"I don't understand," she repeated, "what has happened." But what I had already perceived was, on the contrary, that she very nearly, that she in fact quite remarkably, did understand. It was as if in my zeal I had given away my case, and I felt that my test was coming. She had been thinking all night with intensity, and Mrs. Bridgenorth's generosity, coupled with Mrs. Bridgenorth's promptitude, had kept her awake. Thence, for a woman nervous and critical, imaginations, visions, questions. "Why, in writing me last night, did you take for granted it was *she* who had swooped down? Why," asked Mary Tredick, "should she swoop?"

Well, if I could drive a bargain for Mary I felt I could *a fortiori* lie for her. "Because it's her way. She does swoop. She's impatient and uncontrolled. And it's affectation for you to pretend," I said with diplomacy, "that you see no reason for her falling in love—"

"Falling in love?" She took me straight up.

"With that gentleman. Certainly. What woman wouldn't? What woman didn't? I really don't see, you know, your right to back out."

"I won't back out," she presently returned, "if you'll answer me a question. Does she know the man represented?" Then as I hung fire: "It has come to me that she must. It would account for so much. For the strange way I feel," she went on, "and for the extraordinary sum you've been able to extract from her."

It was a pity, and I flushed with it, besides wincing at the word she used. But Mrs. Bridgenorth and I, between us, had clearly made the figure too high. "You think that, if she *had* guessed, I would naturally work it to 'extract' more?"

She turned away from me on this and, looking blank in her trouble, moved vaguely about. Then she stopped. "I see him set up there. I hear her say it. What you said she would make him pass for."

I believe I foolishly tried—though only for an instant—to look as if I didn't remember what I had said. "Her husband?"

"He wasn't."

The next minute I had risked it. "Was he yours?"

I don't know what I had expected, but I found myself surprised at her mere pacific head-shake. "No."

"Then why mayn't he have been—?"

"Another woman's? Because he died, to my absolute knowledge, unmarried." She spoke as quietly. "He had known many women, and there was one in particular with whom he became—and too long remained—ruinously intimate. She tried to make him marry her, and he was very near it. Death, however, saved him. But she was the reason—"

"Yes?" I feared again from her a wave of pain, and I went on while she kept it back. "Did you know her?"

"She was one I wouldn't." Then she brought it out. "She was

the reason he failed me." Her successful detachment somehow said all, reduced me to a flat, kind "Oh!" that marked my sense of her telling me, against my expectation, more than I knew what to do with. But it was just while I wondered how to turn her confidence that she repeated, in a changed voice, her challenge of a moment before. "Does she know the man represented?"

"I haven't the least idea." And having so acquitted myself I added, with what strikes me now as futility: "She certainly—yesterday—didn't name him."

"Only recognised him?"

"If she did she brilliantly concealed it."

"So that you got nothing from her?"

It was a question that offered me a certain advantage. "I thought you accused me of getting too much."

She gave me a long look, and I now saw everything in her face. "It's very nice—what you're doing for me, and you do it handsomely. It's beautiful—beautiful, and I thank you with all my heart. But I know."

"And what do you know?"

She went about now preparing her usual work. "What he must have been to her."

"You mean she was the person?"

"Well," she said, putting on her old spectacles, "she was one of them."

"And you accept so easily the astounding coincidence—?"

"Of my finding myself, after years, in so extraordinary a relation with her? What do you call easily? I've passed a night of torment."

"But what put it into your head—?"

"That I had so blindly and strangely given him back to her? *You* put it—yesterday."

"And how?"

"I can't tell you. You didn't in the least mean to—on the contrary. But you dropped the seed. The plant, after you had gone," she said with a business-like pull at her easel, "the plant began to grow. I *saw* them there—in your studio—face to face."

"You were jealous?" I laughed.

She gave me through her glasses another look, and they seemed, from this moment, in their queerness, to have placed her quite on the other side of the gulf of time. She was firm there; she was settled; I couldn't get at her now. "I see she told you I *would* be." I doubtless kept down too little my start at it, and she immediately pursued. "You say I accept the coincidence, which is of course prodigious. But such things happen. Why shouldn't I accept it if you do?"

"*Do* I?" I smiled.

She began her work in silence, but she presently exclaimed: "I'm glad I didn't meet her!"

"I don't yet see why you wouldn't."

"Neither do I. It was an instinct."

"Your instincts"—I tried to be ironic—"are miraculous."

"They *have* to be, to meet such accidents. I must ask you kindly to tell her, when you return her gift, that now I have done the picture I find I must after all keep it for myself."

"Giving no reason?"

She painted away. "She'll know the reason."

Well, by this time I knew it too; I knew so many things that I fear my resistance was weak. If our wonderful client hadn't been his wife in fact, she was not to be helped to become his wife in fiction. I knew almost more than I can say, more at any rate than I could then betray. He had been bound in common mercy to stand by my friend, and he had basely forsaken her. This indeed brought up the obscure, into which I shyly gazed. "Why, even granting your theory, should you grudge her the portrait? It was painted in bitterness."

"Yes. Without that—!"

"It wouldn't have come? Precisely. Is it in bitterness, then, you'll keep it?"

She looked up from her canvas. "In what would *you* keep it?"

It made me jump. "Do you mean I *may*?" Then I had my idea. "I'd give you her price for it!"

Her smile through her glasses was beautiful. "And afterwards make it over to her? You shall have it when I die." With which she came away from her easel, and I saw that I was staying her work and should properly go. So I put out my hand to her. "It took—whatever you will!—to paint it," she said, "but I shall keep it in joy." I could answer nothing now—had to cease to pretend; the thing was in her hands. For a moment we stood there, and I had again the sense, melancholy and final, of her being, as it were, remotely glazed and fixed into what she had done. "He's taken from me, and for all those years he's kept. Then she herself, by a prodigy—!" She lost herself again in the wonder of it.

"Unwittingly gives him back?"

She fairly, for an instant over the marvel, closed her eyes. "Gives him back."

Then it was I saw how he would be kept! But it was the end of my vision. I could only write, ruefully enough, to Mrs. Bridgenorth, whom I never met again, but of whose death—preceding by a couple of years Mary Tredick's—I happened to hear. This is an old man's tale. I have inherited the picture, in the deep beauty of which, however, darkness still lurks. No one, strange to say, has ever recognised the model, but everyone asks his name. I don't even know it.

Master Eustace

Having handed me my cup of tea, she proceeded to make her own; an operation she performed with a delicate old-maidish precision I delighted to observe.

The story is not my own—she then began—but that of persons with whom for a time I was intimately connected. I have led a quiet life. This is my only romance—and it's the romance of others. When I was a young woman of twenty-two my poor mother died, after a long, weary illness, and I found myself obliged to seek a new home. Making a home requires time and money. I had neither to spare, so I advertised for a "situation," rating my accomplishments modestly, and asking rather for kind treatment than high wages. Mrs. Gamyer immediately answered my advertisement. She offered me a fair salary and a peaceful asylum.

I was to teach her little boy the rudiments of my slender stock of sciences and to make myself generally useful. Something in her tone and manner assured me that in accepting this latter condition I was pledging myself to no very onerous servitude, and I never found reason to repent of my bargain. I had always valued my freedom before all things, and it seemed to me that in trading it away even partially I was surrendering a priceless treasure; but Mrs. Gamyer made service easy. I liked her from the first, and I doubt that she ever fairly measured my fidelity and affection. She knew that she could trust me, and she always spoke of me as "a good creature"; but she never estimated the trouble I saved her, or the little burdens I lifted from her pretty, feeble shoulders. Both in her position and her person there was something singularly appealing.

She was in those days—indeed she always remained—a very pretty little woman. But she had grace even more than beauty. She was young, and looked even younger than her years; slight, light of tread and of gesture, though not at all rapid (for in all her movements there was a kind of pathetic morbid languor), and fairer, whiter, purer in complexion than any woman I have seen. She reminded me of a sketch from which the "shading" has been omitted. She had her shadows indeed, as well as her lights; but they were all turned inward. She might have seemed compounded of the airy substance of lights and shadows. Nature in making her had left out that wholesome leaden ballast of will, of logic, of worldly zeal, with which we are all more or less weighted.

Experience, however, had given her a burden to carry; she was evidently sorrow-laden. She shifted the cruel weight from shoulder to shoulder, she ached and sighed under it, and in the depths of her sweet natural smile you saw it pressing the tears from her soul. Mrs. Gamyer's trouble, I confess, was in my eyes an added charm. I was desperately fond of a bit of romance, and as I was plainly never to have one of my own, I made the most of my neighbour's. This secret sadness of hers would have covered more sins than I ever had to forgive her. At first, naturally, I connected her unavowed sorrow with the death of her husband; but as time went on, I found reason to believe that there had been little love between the pair.

She had married against her will. Mr. Gamyer was fifteen years her senior, and, as she frankly intimated, coarsely and cruelly dissipated. Their married life had lasted but three years, and had come to an end to her great and obvious relief. Had he done her while it lasted some irreparable wrong? I fancied so; she was like a garden rose with half its petals plucked. He had left her with diminished means, though her property (mostly her own) was still ample for her needs. These, with those of her son, were extremely simple. To certain little luxuries she was obstinately attached; but her manner of life was so monotonous and frugal that she must have spent but a fraction of her income.

It was her single son—the heir of her hopes, the apple of her eye—that she intrusted to my care. He was five years old, and she had taught him his letters—a great feat, she seemed to think; she was as proud of it as if she had invented the alphabet for the occasion. She had called him Eustace, for she meant that he should have the best of everything—the prettiest clothes, the prettiest playthings, and the prettiest name. He was himself as pretty as his name, though but little like his mother. He was slight like her, but far more nervous and decided, and he had neither her features nor her colouring. Least of all had he her expression.

Mrs. Gamyer's attitude was one of tender, pensive sufferance modified by hopes—a certain half-mystical hope which seemed akin to religion, but which was not all religion, for the heaven she dreamed of was lodged here below. The boy from his early childhood wore an air of defiance and authority. He was not one to wait for things, good or evil, but to snatch boldly at the one sort and snap his fingers at the other. He had a pale, dark skin, not altogether healthy in tone; a mass of fine brown hair, which seemed given him just to emphasize by its dancing sweep the petulant little nods and shakes of his head; and a deep, wilful, malicious eye. His eyes told me from the first that I should have no easy work with him; and in spite of a vast expense of tact and tenderness, no easy work it turned out to be.

His wits were so quick, however, and his imagination so lively, that I gradually managed to fill out his mother's meagre little programme of study. This had been drawn up with a sparing hand; her only fear was of his being overworked. The poor lady had but a dim conception of what a man of the world is expected to know. She thought, I believe, that with his handsome face, his handsome property, and his doting mother, he would need to know little more than how to sign that pretty name of Eustace to replies to invitations to dinners. I wonder now that with her constant interference I contrived to set the child intellectually on his legs. Later, when he had a tutor, I received a compliment for my perseverance.

The truth is, I became fond of him; his very imperfections fascinated me. He would soon enough have to take his chance of the world's tolerance, and society would cease to consist for him of a couple of coaxing women. I told Mrs. Gamyer that there was never an easier child to spoil, and that those caressing hands of hers would sow a crop of formidable problems for future years. But Mrs. Gamyer was utterly incapable of taking a rational view of matters, or of sacrificing today to to-morrow; and her folly was the more incurable as it was founded on a strange, moonshiny little principle—a crude, passionate theory that love, love, pure love is the sum and substance of maternal duty; and that the love which reasons and exacts and denies is cruel and wicked and hideous.

"I know you think I'm a silly goose," she said, "and not fit to have a child at all. But you're wrong—I promise you you're wrong. I'm very reasonable, I'm very patient; I have a great deal to bear—more than you know—and I bear it very well. But one can't be always on the stretch—always hard and wise and good. In some things one must break down and be one's poor, natural, lonely self. Eustace can't turn out wrong; it's impossible; it would be too cruel. You mustn't say it nor hint it. I shall do with him as my heart bids me; he's all I have; he consoles me."

My notions perhaps were a little old-fashioned; but surely it will never altogether go out of fashion to teach a child that he is not to have the moon by crying for it. Now Eustace had a particular fancy for the moon—for everything bright and inaccessible and absurd. His will was as sharp as a steel spring, and it was vain to attempt to bend it or break it. He had an indefeasible conviction that he was number one among men; and if he had been born in the purple, as they say, of some far-off Eastern court, or the last consummate fruit of a shadowy line of despots, he couldn't have been more closely curtained in this superb illusion. I pierced it here and there as roughly as I dared; but his mother's light fingers speedily repaired my punctures.

The poor child had no sense of justice. He had the graceful virtues, but not the legal ones. He could condescend, he could forgive, he could permit this, that, and the other, with due leave asked; but he couldn't endure the hint of conflicting right. Poor puny little mortal, sitting there wrapped in his golden mist, listening to the petty trickle of his conscious favour and damming it—a swelling fountain of privileges! He could love, love passionately; but he was so jealous and exacting that his love cost you very much more than it was worth. I found it no sinecure to possess the confidence I had striven so cunningly to obtain. He fancied it a very great honour that he should care to harness me up as his horse, to throw me his ball by the hour, to have me joggle with him (sitting close to the middle) on the see-saw till my poor bones ached.

Nevertheless, in this frank, childish arrogance there was an almost irresistible charm, and I was absurdly flattered by enjoying his favour. Poor me! at twenty-three I was his first "conquest"—the first in a long list, as I believe it came to be. If he demanded great license, he used it with a peculiar grace of his own, and he admitted the corresponding obligation of being clever and brilliant. As a child even, he seemed to be in a sort of occult sympathy with the picturesque. His talents were excellent, and teaching him, whatever it may have been, was at least not dull work. It was indeed less to things really needful than to the luxuries of learning that he took most kindly. He had an excellent ear for music, and though he never fairly practised, he turned off an air as neatly as you could have wished.

In this he resembled his mother, who was a natural musician. She, however, was always at the piano, and whenever I think of her in those early years, I see her sitting before it musingly, half sadly, with her pretty head on one side, her fair braids thrust behind her ears—ears from which a couple of small but admirable diamonds were never absent—and her white hands wandering over the notes, seeking vaguely for an air which they seemed hardly to dare to remember. Eustace had an insatiable appetite for stories, though he was one of the coolest and most merciless of critics. I can fancy him now at my knee with his big, superbly-expectant eyes fastened on my lips, demanding more wonders and more, till my poor little short-winded invention had to cry mercy for its impotence.

Do my best, I could never startle him; my giants were never big enough and my fairies never small enough, and my enchanters, my prisoners, my castles never on the really grand scale of his own imaginative needs. I felt pitifully prosaic. At last he would always open his wilful little mouth and gape in my face with a dreadfully dry want of conviction. I felt flattered when by chance I had pleased him, for, by a precocious instinct, he knew tinsel from gold. "Look here," he would say, "you're dreadfully ugly; what makes you so ugly? Your nose is so big at the end." (You needn't protest; I was ugly. Like most very plain women, I have improved with time.)

Of course I used to rebuke him for his rudeness, though I secretly thanked it, for it taught me a number of things. Once he said something, I forget what, which made me burst into tears. It was the first time, and the last; for I found that, instead of stirring his pity, tears only moved his contempt, and apparently a kind of cynical, physical disgust. The best way was to turn the tables on him by pretending to be cool and indifferent and superior. In that case he himself would condescend to tears—bitter, wrathful tears. Then you had perhaps gained nothing, but you had lost nothing. In every other case you had.

Of course these close relations lasted but a couple of years. I had made him very much wiser than myself; he was growing tall and boyish and terribly inquisitive. My poor little stories ceased to have any illusion for him; and he would spend hours lying on his face on the carpet, kicking up his neat little legs and poring over the *Arabian Nights*, the *Fairy Queen*, the dozen prime enchanters of childhood. My advice would have been to pack him off to school; but I might as well have asked his mother to send him to the penitentiary. He was to be educated en prince; he was to have a teacher to himself.

I thought sympathetically of the worthy pedagogue who was

to enjoy Eustace without concurrence. But such a one was easily found—in fact, he was found three times over. Three private tutors came and went successively. They fell in love, categorically, with Mrs. Gamyer. Their love indeed she might have put up with; but unhappily, unlike Viola, they told their love—by letter—with an offer of their respective hands. Their letters were different, but to Mrs. Garnyer their hands were all alike, and alike distasteful.

"The horrid creatures!" was her invariable commentary. "I wouldn't speak to them for the world. My dear, you must do it." And I, who had never declined an offer on my own account, went to work in this wholesale fashion for my friend! You will say that young as she was, pretty, independent, lovely, Mrs. Gamyer would have looked none the worse for a spice of coquetry. Nay, in her own eyes, she would have been hideous.

Her greatest charm for me was a brave little passion of scorn for this sort of levity, and indeed a general contempt for cheap sentimental effects. It was as if, from having drunk at the crystal head-spring, she had lost her taste for standing water. She was absolutely indifferent to attention; in fact, she seemed to shrink from it. She hadn't a trace of personal vanity; she was even without visible desire to please.

Unfortunately, as you see, she pleased in spite of herself. As regards love, she had an imposing array of principles; on this one point her floating imagination found anchorage. "It's either a passion," she said, "or it's nothing. You can know it by being willing to give up everything for it—name and fame, past and future, this world and the next. Do you keep back a feather's weight of tenderness and trust? Then you're not in love. You must risk everyrthing, for you get everything—if you're happy. I can't understand a woman trifling with love. They talk about the unpardonable sin; that's it, it seems to me. Do you know the word in the language I most detest? Flirtation, Poh! it makes me ill."

When Mrs. Gamyer uttered this hint of an esoteric doctrine, her clear blue eyes would become clouded with the gathered mists of memory. In this matter she understood herself and meant what she said. Defiant as she was of admiration, she saw little of the world. She met her few friends but two or three times a year, and was without a single intimate. As time went on, she came to care more for me than for anyone. When Eustace had outgrown my teaching, she insisted on my remaining in any capacity I chose—as housekeeper, companion, seam- stress, guest; I might make my own terms. I became a little of each of these, and with the increasing freedom of our intercourse grew to regard her as a younger and weaker sister. I gave her, for what it was worth, my frankest judgment on all things. Her own confidence always stopped short of a certain point.

A little curtain of reticence seemed always to hang between us. Sometimes I fancied it growing thinner and thinner, becoming almost transparent and revealing the figures behind it. Sometimes it seemed to move and flutter in the murmur of our talk, so that in a moment it might drop or melt away into air. But it was a magical web; it played a hundred tormenting tricks, and year after year it hung in its place. Of course this inviolate mystery stirred my curiosity, but I can't say more for the disinterested tenderness I felt for Mrs. Gamyer than that it never unduly irritated it. I lingered near the door of her Blue-Beard's chamber, but I never peeped through the keyhole. She was a poor lady with a secret; I took her into my heart, secret and all. She proclaimed that her isolation was her own choice, and pretended to be vastly content that society let her so well alone.

She made her widowhood serve as a motive for her lonesome days, and declared that her boy's education amply filled them. She was a widow, however, who never of her own accord mentioned her husband's name, and she wore her weeds very lightly. She was very fond of white, and for six months of the year was rarely seen in a dark dress. Occasionally, on certain fixed days, she would flame forth in some old-fashioned piece of finery from a store which she religiously preserved, and would flash about the house in rose-colour or blue. One day, her boy's birthday, she kept with fantastic solemnity. It fell in the middle of September.

On this occasion she would put on a faded ball-dress, overload herself with jewels and trinkets, and dress her hair with flowers. Eustace, too, she would trick out in a suit of crimson velvet, and in this singular guise the pair would walk with prodigious gravity about the gar- den and up and down the avenue. Every now and then she would stoop and give him a convulsive hug. The child himself seemed to feel the magnitude of this festival, and played his part with precocious discretion. He would appear at dark with the curl still in his hair, his velvet trousers unstained, his ruffles uncrumpled.

In the evening the coachman let off rockets in the garden; we feasted on icecream, and a bottle of champagne was sent to the kitchen. No wonder Master Eustace took on the graces of an heir-apparent! Once, I remember, the mother and son were overtaken in the festal promenade by some people who had come to live in the neighbourhood, and who drove up rather officiously to leave their cards. They stared in amazement from the carriage window, and were told Mrs. Gamyer was not at home. A few days later we heard that Mrs. Gamyer was out of her mind; she had been found masquerading in her grounds with her little boy, in the most indecent costume.

From time to time she received an invitation, and occasionally she accepted one. When she went out she deepened her mourning, but she always came home in a fret. "It is the last house I will go to," she declared, as I helped her to undress. "People's neglect I can bear, and thank them for it; but Heaven deliver me from their kindness! I won't be patronized—I won't, I won't! Shall I, my boy? We'll wait till you grow up, shan't we, my darling? Then his poor little mother shan't be patronized, shall she, my brave little man?" The child was constantly dangling at his mother's skirts, and was seldom beyond the reach of some such passionate invocation.

A preceptor had at last been found of a less inflammable composition than the others—a worthy, elderly German of fair attainments, with a stout, sentimental wife—she gave music lessons in town—who monopolized his ardours. He was a mild, patient man—a nose of wax, as the saying is. A pretty nose it grew to be in Eustace's supple fingers! I'll answer for it that in all those years he never carried a point. I believe that, like me, he had begun with tears; but finding this an altogether losing game, he was content now to take off his spectacles, drop his head on one side, look imploringly at his pupil with his weak blue eyes, and then exhale his renunciation in a plaintive *Lieber Gott*!

Under this discipline the boy bloomed like a flower. But it was to my sense a kind of hothouse growth. His tastes were sedentary, and he lived largely within doors. He kept a horse and took long lonely rides; but most of the time he spent lounging over a book, trifling at the piano, or fretting over a water- colour sketch, which he was sure to throw aside in disgust. One amusement he pursued with unwearying constancy; it was a sign of especial good humour, and I never knew it to fail him. He would sit for hours lounging in a chair, with his head thrown back and his legs extended, staring at vacancy, or what seemed to us so, but a vacancy filled with the silent revel of his fancy and the images it evoked. What was the substance of these beatific visions? The broad, happy life before him, the great world whose far-off murmurs caressed his ear—the joys of consummate manhood—pleasure, success, prosperity—kind of triumphant and transfigured egotism.

His reveries swarmed with ideal shapes and transcendent delights; his handsome young face, his idle, insolent smile were the cold reflections of their brightness. His mother, after watching him for a while in these moods, would steal up behind him and kiss him softly on the forehead, as if to marry his sweet illusions to sweet reality. For my part, I wanted to divorce them. It was a sad pity, I thought, that desire and occasion in the lad's life played so deftly into each other's hands. I longed to spoil the game, to shuffle the cards afresh and give him a taste of bad luck. I felt as if between them—she by her measureless concessions, he by his consuming arrogance—they were sowing a crop of dragon's teeth. This sultry summer of youth couldn't last forever, and I knew that the poor lady would be the first to suffer by a change of weather.

He would turn someday in his passionate vanity and rend the gentle creature who had fed it with the delusive wine of her love. And yet he had a better angel as well as a worse. It was a marvel to see how this sturdy seraph tussled with the fiends, and, in spite of bruises and ruffled pinions, returned again and again to the onset. There were days when his generous, boyish gayety—the natural sunshine of youth and intelligence—warmed our women's hearts to their depths and kindled our most trusting smiles. Me, as he grew older, he treated as a licensed old-time friend. I was the prince's jester. I used to tell him his truths, as the French say. He believed them just enough to feel an agreeable irritation in listening; for the rest, doubtless, they seemed as vague and remote as a croaking good-wife's gossip.

There were moments, I think, when the eternal blue sky of his mother's temper wearied his capricious brain. At such times he would come and sprawl on the sofa near my little work-table, clipping my threads, mixing my spools, mislaying my various utensils, and criticizing my work without reserve—chattering, gossiping, complaining, boasting. With all his faults Eustace had one sovereign merit—that merit without which even the virtues he lacked lose half their charms: he was superbly frank. He was only too transparent. The light of truth played through his rank pretensions, and against it they stood relieved in his hard tenacity, like young trees against a sunset. He uttered his passions, and uttered them only too loudly; you received ample notice of his vengeance. It came as a matter of course; he never took it out in talk; but you were warned.

If these intense meditations of which I have spoken followed exclusively the vista of his personal fortunes, his conversation was hardly more disinterested. It was altogether about himself—his ambitions, his ailments, his dreams, his needs, his intentions. He talked a great deal of his property, and, though he had a great aversion to figures, he knew the amount of his expectations before he was out of jackets. He had a shrewd relish for luxury—

and indeed, as he respected pretty things and used them with a degree of tenderness which he by no means lavished upon animated objects, saving, sparing, and preserving them, this seemed to me one of his most human traits, though, I admit, an expensive virtue—and he promised to spend his fortune in books and pictures, in art and travel.

His mother was imperiously appealed to to do the honours of his castles in the air. She would look at him always with her doting smile, and with a little glow of melancholy in her eyes—a faint tribute to some shadowy chance that even her Eustace might reckon without his host. She would shake her head tenderly, or lean it on his shoulder and murmur, "Who knows, who knows? It's perhaps as foolish, my son, to try and forecast happiness as to attempt to take the measure of misery. We know them each when they come. Whatever comes to us, at all events, we shall meet it together."

Resting in this delicious contact, with her arm round his neck and her cheek on his hair, she would close her eyes in a kind of tremor of ecstasy. As I have never had a son myself, I can speak of maternity but by hear- say; but I feel as if I knew some of its secrets, as if I had gained from Mrs. Gamyer a revelation of maternal passion. The perfect humility of her devotion, indeed, seemed to me to point to some motive deeper than vulgar motherhood. It looked like a kind of penance, a kind of pledge. Had she done him some early wrong? Did she meditate some wrong to come? Did she wish to purchase pardon for the past or impunity for the future?

One might have fancied from the lad's calm relish of her incense—as if it were the fumes of some perfumed *chibouque* palpitating lazily through his own lips—that he had a comfortable sense of some- thing to forgive. In fact, he had something to forgive us all—our dullness, our vulgarity, our not guessing his unuttered desires—the want of a super-celestial harmony between our wills and his. I fancied, however, that there were even moments when he turned dizzy on the cope of this awful gulf of his mother's self-sacrifice. Fixing his eyes, then, an instant to steady himself, he took comfort in the thought that she had ceased to suffer—her personal ambitions lay dead at the bottom. He could vaguely see them—distant, dim, motionless. It was to be hoped that no adventurous ghost of these shuflfled passions would climb upward to the light.

A frequent source of complaint with Eustace, when he had no more immediate displeasure, was that he had not known his father. He had formed a mental image of the late Mr. Gamyer which I am afraid hardly tallied at all points with the original. He knew that his father had been a man of pleasure, and he had painted his portrait in ideal hues. What a charming father—a man of pleasure! the boy thought, fancying that gentlemen of this stamp take their pleasure in the nursery. What pleasure they might have shared; what rides, what talks, what games, what adventures—what far other hours than those he passed in the deserted billiard-room (this had been one of Mr. Gamyer's pleasures) clicking the idle balls in the stillness. He learned to talk very early of shaping his life on his father's. What he had done his son would do.

A dozen odds and ends which had belonged to Mr. Gamyer he carried to his room, where he arranged them on his mantelshelf like relics on a high altar. When he had turned seventeen he began to smoke an old silver-mounted pipe which had his father's initials embossed on the bowl.

"It would be a great blessing," he said as he puffed this pipe—it made him dismally sick, for he hated tobacco—"to have some man in the house. It's so fearfully womanish here. No one but you two and Hauff, and what's he but an old woman? Mother, why have you always lived in this way? What's the matter with you? You've got no savoir vivre. What are you blushing about? That comes of moping here all your days—that you blush for nothing. I don't want my mother to blush for anything or anyone, not even for me. But I give you notice, I can stand it no longer. Now I'm seventeen, it's time I should see the world. I'm going to travel. My father travelled; he went all over Europe. There's a little French book upstairs, the poems of Pamy—it's awfully French, too— with 'Henry Gamyer, Paris, 1802,' on the fly-leaf.

"I must go to Paris. I shan't go to college. I've never been to school. I want to be complete—privately educated altogether. Very few people are, here; it's quite a distinction. Besides, I know all I want to know. Hauff brought me out some college catalogues. They're absurd; he laughs at them. We did all that three years ago. I know more about books than most young fellows; what I want is knowledge of the world. My father had it, and you haven't, mother. But he had plenty of taste, too. Hauff says that little edition of Pamy is very rare. I shall bring home lots of such things. You'll see!"

Mrs. Gamyer listened to such effusions of filial emulation in sad, distracted silence. I couldn't but pity her. She knew that her husband was no proper model for her child; yet she couldn't in decency turn his heart again his father's memory. She took refuge in that attitude of tremulous contemplation which committed her neither to condemnation of her husband nor to approval with her son.

She had recourse at this period, as I have known her to do before, to a friend attached to a mercantile house in India—an old friend, she had told me; "in fact," she had added, "my only friend, a man to whom I am under immense obligations." Once in six months there came to her from this distant benefactor a large square letter, heavily sealed and covered with foreign post-marks. I used to fancy it a kind of bulletin of advice for the coming half year. Advice about what? Her cares were so few, her habits so simple, that they offered scanty matter for discussion. But now, of course, came a packet of counsel as to Eustace's absence.

I knew that she dreaded it; but since her oracle had spoken, she wore a brave face. She was certainly a devout postulant. She concealed from Eustace the extent of her dependence on this far-away adviser, for the boy would have resented such interference, even though it favoured his own schemes. She had always read her friend's letters in secret; this was the only practice of her life she failed to share with her son. Me she now for the first time admitted into her confidence. "Mr. Cope strongly recommends my letting him go," she said. "He says it will make a man of him. He needs to rub against other men. I suppose at least," she cried with her usual sweet fatuity, "it will do other men no harm! Perhaps I don't love him as I ought, and that I must lose him awhile to learn to prize him. If I only get him back again! It would be monstrous that I shouldn't! But why are we cursed with these frantic woes and fears? It's a weary life!" She would have said more if she had known that it was not his departure but his return that was to be cruel.

The excellent Mr. Hauff was deemed too mild and infirm to cope with the hazards of travel; but a companion was secured in the person of his nephew, an amiable young German who claimed to possess erudition and discretion in equal manner. For a week before he left us Eustace was so serene and joyous of humour as to double his mother's sense of loss. "I give her into your care," he said to me. "If anything happens to her, I shall hold you responsible. She is very woebegone just now, but she'll cheer up yet But, mother, you're not to be too cheerful, mind. You're not to forget me an instant If you do, I'll never forgive you. I insist on being missed. There's little enough merit in loving me when I'm here; I wish to be loved in my absence."

For many weeks after he left, he might have been satisfied. His mother wandered about like a churchyard ghost keeping watch near a buried treasure. When his letters began to come, she read them over a dozen times, and sat for hours with her eyes closed holding them in her hand. They were wretchedly meagre and hurried; but their very brevity gratified her. He was prosperous and happy, and could snatch but odd moments from his pleasure-taking.

One morning, after he had been away some three months, there came two letters, one from Eustace, the other from India, the latter very much in advance of its time. Mrs. Gamyer opened the Indian letter first. I was pouring out tea; I observed her from behind the urn. As her eyes ran over the pages she turned deadly pale; then raising her glance she met mine. Immediately her paleness turned to crimson. She rose to her feet and hurried out of the room, leaving Eustace's letter untouched on the table. This little fact was eloquent, and my curiosity was aroused. Later in the day it was partially satisfied. She came to me with a singular conscious look—the look of a sort of oppression of happiness—and announced that Mr. Cope was coming home. He had obtained release from his engagements in India, and would arrive in a fortnight.

She uttered herewith no words of rejoicing, but I fancied her joy was of the unutterable sort. As the days elapsed, however, her emotion betrayed itself in a restless, aimless flutter of movement, so intense as to seem to me almost painful. She roamed about the house singing to herself, gazing out of the windows, shifting the chairs and tables, smoothing the curtains, trying vaguely to brighten the faded look of things. Before every mirror she paused and inspected herself, with that frank audacity of pretty women which I have always envied, tucking up a curl of her blond hair or smoothing a crease in those muslins which she always kept so fresh. Of Eustace for the moment she rarely spoke; the boy's prediction had not been so very much amiss.

Who was this wonderful Mr. Cope, this mighty magician? I very soon learned. He arrived on the day he had fixed, and took up his lodging in the house. From the moment I looked at him, I felt that here was a man I should like. My poor unflattered soul, I suppose, was won by the kindness of his greeting. He had often heard of me, he said; he knew how good a friend I had been to Mrs. Gamyer; he begged to bespeak a proportionate friendship for himself. I felt as if I were amply thanked for my years of household zeal. But in spite of this pleasant assurance, I had a sense of being for the moment altogether *de trop*.

He was united to his friend by a closer bond than I had suspected. I left them alone with their mutual secrets and effusions, and confined myself to my own room; though indeed I had noticed between them a sort of sentimental intelligence, so deep and perfect that many words were exchanged without audible speech. Mrs. Gamyer underwent a singular change; I seemed to know her now for the first time. It was as if she had flung aside a veil which muffled her tones and blurred her features. There was a new decision in her tread, a deeper meaning in her smile. So, at thirty-eight her girlhood had come back to her! She was as full of blushes and random prattle and foolish falterings for very pleasure as a young bride.

Upon Mr. Cope the years had set a more ineffaceable seal. He was a man of forty-five, but you would have given him ten years more. He had that look which I have always liked of people who have lived in hot climates, a bronzed complexion, and a pool deliberate gait, as if he had learned to think twice before moving. He was tall and lean, yet extremely massive in shape, like a stout man emaciated by circumstances. His hair was thin and perfectly white, and he wore a grizzled moustache. He dressed in loose, light-coloured garments of those fine Eastern stuffs.

I had a singular impression of having seen him before, but I could never say when or where. He was extremely deaf—so deaf that I had to force my voice; though I observed that Mrs. Garnyer easily made him hear by speaking slowly and looking at him. He had peculiarly that patient appealing air which you find in very deaf persons less frequently than in the blind, but which has with them an even deeper eloquence, enforced as it is by the normal pathos of the eye.

It has an especially mild dignity where, as in Mr. Cope, it overlies a truly masculine mind. He had been obliged to make good company of himself, and the glimpses that one got of this blessed fellowship in stillness were of a kind to make one long to share it. But with others, too, he was a charming talker, though he was obliged to keep the talk in his own hands. He took your response for granted with a kind of conciliating bonhomie, guessed with a glance at your opinion, and phrased it usually more wittily than you would have done.

For ten years I had been pitying Mrs. Gamyer; it was odd to find myself envying her. Patient waiting is no loss; at last her day had come. I had always rather wondered at her patience; it was spiced with a logic all its own. But she had lived by precept and example, by chapter and verse; for his sake it was easy to be wise. I say for "his" sake, because as a matter of course I now connected her visitor with that undefined secret which had been one of my earliest impressions of Mrs. Gamyer. Mr. Cope's presence renewed my memory of it I fitted the key to the lock, but on coming to open the casket I was disappointed to find that the best of the mystery had evaporated.

Mr. Cope, I imagined, had been her first and only love. Her parents had frowned on him and forced her into a marriage with poor dissolute Mr. Gamyer—a course the more untender as he had already spent half his own property and was likely to make sad havoc with his wife's. He had a high social value, which the girl's own family, who were plain enough people to have had certain primitive scruples in larger measure, deemed a compensation for his vices. The discarded lover, thinking she had not resisted as firmly as she might, embarked for India, and there, half in spite, half in despair, married as sadly remiss as herself. She had trifled with his happiness; he lived to repent.

His wife lived as well to perpetuate his misery; it was my belief that she had only recently died, and that this event was the occasion of his return. When he arrived he wore a weed on his hat; the next day it had disappeared. Reunion had come to them in the afternoon of life, when the tricks and graces of passion are no longer becoming; but when these have spent themselves something of passion still is left, and this they were free to enjoy. They had begun to enjoy it with the chastened zeal of which I caught the aroma. Such was my reading of the riddle. Right or not, at least it made sense.

I had promised Eustace to write to him, and one afternoon as I sat alone, well pleased to have a theme, I despatched him a long letter full of the praises of Mr. Cope, and by implication of the echo of his mother's happiness. I wished to anticipate his possible suspicions and reconcile him with the altered situation. But after I had posted my letter, it seemed to me that I had spoken too frankly. I doubted whether, even amid the wholesome novelty of travel, he had unlearned the old trick of jealousy. Jealousy surely would have been quite misplaced, for Mr. Cope's affection for his hostess embraced her boy in its ample scope. He regretted the lad's absence; he manifested the kindliest interest in everything that spoke of him; he turned over his books, he looked at his sketches, he examined and compared the half dozen portraits which the fond mother had caused to be executed at various stages of his growth.

One hot day, when poor old Mr. Hauff travelled out from town for news of his pupil, he made a point of being introduced and of shaking his. hand. The old man stayed to dinner, and on Mr. Cope's proposition we drank the boy's health in brimming glasses. The old German of course wept profusely; it was Eustace's mission to make people cry. I fancied too I saw a tear on Mr. Cope's lid. The cup of his contentment was full; at a touch it overflowed. On the whole, however, he took this bliss of reunion more quietly than his friend. He was a melancholy man. He had the air of one for whom the moral of this fable of life has greater charms than the plot, and who has made up his mind to ask no favours of destiny.

When he met me, he used to smile gently, frankly, saying little; but I had a vast relish for his smile. It seemed to say much—to murmur, "Receive my compliments. You and I are a couple of tested souls; we understand each other. We are not agog with the privileges of existence, like charity children on a picnic. We have had, each of us, to live for years without the thing we once fancied gave life its only value. We have tasted of bondage, and patience, taken up as a means, has grown grateful as an end. It has cured us of eagerness." So easily it gossiped, the smile of our guest. No wonder I liked it.

One evening, a month after his advent, Mrs. Gamyer came to me with a strange embarrassed smile. "I have something to tell you," she said; "something that will surprise you. Do you consider me a very old woman? I am old enough to be wiser, you'll say. But I've never been so wise as today. I'm engaged to Mr. Cope. There! make the best of it. I have no apologies to make to anyone," she went on with a kind of defiant manner. "It's between ourselves. If we suit each other, it's no one's business. I know what I'm about. He means to remain in this country; we should be constantly together and extremely intimate. As he says, I'm young enough to be—what do they call it? —compromised. Of course, therefore, I'm young enough to marry. It will make no difference with you; you'll stay with me all the same. Who cares, after all, what I do? No one but Eustace, and he will thank me for giving him such a father. Ah, I shall do well by my boy !" she cried, clasping her hands with ecstasy. "I shall do better than he knows. My property, it appears, is dreadfully entangled.

"Mr. Gamyer did as he pleased with it; I was given to him with my hands tied. Mr. Cope has been looking into it, and he tells me that it will be a long labour to restore order. I have been living all these years at the mercy of unprincipled strangers. But now I have given up everything to Mr. Cope. He'll drive the moneychangers from the temple! It's a small reward to marry him. Eustace has no head for money matters; he only knows how to spend. For years now he needn't think of them. Mr. Cope is our providence. Don't be afraid; Eustace won't blaspheme! and at last he'll have a companion—the best, the wisest, the kindest.

"You know how he used to long for one—how tired he was of me and you. It will be a new life. Oh, I'm a happy mother—at last—at last! Don't look at me so hard; I'm a blushing bride, remember. Smile, laugh, kiss me. There! You're a good creature. I shall make my boy a present—the handsomest that ever was made! Poor Mr. Cope! I'm happier than he. I have had my boy all these years, and he has had none. He has the heart of a father. He has longed for a son. Do you know," she added with a strange deepening of her smile, "that I think he marries me as much for my son's sake as for my own? He marries me at all events, boy and all."

This speech was uttered with a forced and hurried animation which betrayed the effort to cheat herself into pure enthusiasm. The matter was not quite so simple as she tried to believe.

Nevertheless, I was deeply pleased, and I kissed her in genuine sympathy. The more I thought of it the better I liked the marriage. It relieved me personally of a burdensome sense of ineffectual care, and it filled out solidly a kind of defenceless breach which had always existed on the worldly face of Mrs. Gamyer's position. Moreover, it promised to be full of wholesome profit for Eustace.

It was a pity that Eustace had but a slender relish for wholesome profit. I ventured to hope, however, that his high esteem for his father's memory had been, at bottom, the expression of a need for counsel and support, and of a capacity to grant respect if there should be something of inspiration in it. Yet I took the liberty of suggesting to Mrs. Gamyer that she perhaps counted too implicitly on her son's concurrence; that he was always in opposition; that a margin should be left for his possible jealousy. Of course I was called a suspicious wretch for my pains.

"For what do you take him?" she cried. "He'll thank me on his knees. I shall place them face to face. Eustace has instinct! A word to the wise, says the proverb. I know what I'm about."

She knew it, I think, hardly as well as she declared. I had deemed it my duty to make a modest little speech of congratulation to the bridegroom elect. He blushed—somewhat to my surprise—but he answered me with a grave, grateful bow. He was preoccupied; Mrs. Gamyer was of a dozen different minds about her wedding-day. I had taken for granted that they would wait for Eustace's return; but I was somewhat startled on learning that Mr. Cope disapproved of further delay. They had waited twenty years! Mrs. Garnyer told me that she had not announced the news to Eustace. She wished it to be a "surprise."

She seemed, however, not altogether to believe in her surprise. Poor lady! she had made herself a restless couch. One evening, coming into the library, I found Mr. Cope pleading his cause. For the first time I saw him excited. This hint of autumnal ardour was very becoming. He turned appealingly to me. "You have great authority with this lady," he said. "Plead my case. Are we people to care for Mrs. Grundy? Has she been so very civil to us? We don't marry to please her. I don't see why she should arrange the wedding. Mrs. Gamyer has no *trousseau* to buy, no cards to send. Indeed, I think any more airs and graces are rather ridiculous. They don't belong to our years. There's little Master Grundy, I know," he went on, smiling—"a most honourable youth! But I'll take charge of him. I should like vastly, of course, to have him at the wedding; but one of these days I shall make up for the breach of ceremony by punctually attending his own."

It was only an hour before this, as it happened, that I had received Eustace's answer to my letter. It was brief and hasty, but he had found time to insert some such words as this:

> I don't at all thank you for your news of Mr. Cope. I knew that my mother only wanted a chance to forget me and console herself, as they say in France. Demonstrative mothers always do. I'm like Hamlet—I don't approve of mothers consoling themselves. Mr. Cope may be an excellent fellow—I've no doubt he is; but I do hope he will have made his visit by the time I get back. The house isn't large enough for both of us. You'll find me a bigger man than when I left home. I give you warning. I've got a roaring black moustache, and I'm proportionately fiercer.

I said nothing about this letter. A week later they were married. The time will always be memorable to me, apart from this matter of my story, from the intense and overwhelming heat which then prevailed. It had lasted several days when the wedding took place; it bade fair to continue unbroken. The ceremony was performed by the little old Episcopal clergyman whose ministrations Mrs. Gamyer had regularly attended, and who had always given her a vague parochial countenance. His sister, a mature spinster who wore her hair cut short, and called herself "strong-minded," and, thus qualified, had made overtures to Mrs. Gamyer—this lady and myself were the only witnesses.

The marriage had nothing of a festive air; it seemed a grave sacrifice to the unknown god. Mrs. Gamyer was very much oppressed by the heat; in the vestibule, on leaving the church, she fainted. They had arranged to go for a week to the seaside, to a place they had known of old. When she had revived we placed her in the carriage, and they immediately started. I, of course, remained in charge of the empty house, vastly envying them their seaside breezes.

On the morning after the wedding, sitting alone in the darkened library, I heard a rapid tread in the hall. My first thought of course was of burglars—my second of Eustace. In a moment he came striding into the room. His step, his glance, his whole outline foretold trouble. He was amazingly changed, and all for the better. He seemed taller, older, manlier. He was bronzed by travel and dressed with great splendour. The moustache he had mentioned, though but a slender thing as yet, gave him, to my eye, a formidable foreign look. He gave me no greeting.

"Where's my mother?" he cried.

My heart rose to my throat; his tone seemed to put us horribly in the wrong. "She's away—for a day," I said. "But you"—and I took his hand—pray, where have you dropped from?"

From New York, from shipboard, from Southampton. Is this the way my mother receives me?"

"Why, she never dreamed you were coming."

★'She got no letter? I wrote from New York."

★★Your letter never came. She left town yesterday, for a week."

He looked at me hard. "How comes it you're; not with her?"

"I am not needed. She has—she has—" But I faltered.

"Say it—say it!" he cried; and he stamped his foot. "She has a companion."

"Mr. Cope went with her," I said, in a still, small voice. I was ashamed of my tremor, I was outraged by his imperious manner, but the thought of worse to come unnerved me.

"Mr. Cope—ah!" he answered, with an indefinable accent. He looked about the room with a kind of hungry desire to detect some invidious difference as a trace of Mr. Cope's passage. Then flinging himself into a chair, "What infernal heat!" he went on. "What a hideous climate you've got here! Do bring me a glass of water."

I brought him his glass, and stood before him as he quickly drank it. "Don't think you're not welcome," I ventured to say, "if I ask what has brought you home so suddenly."

He gave me another hard look over the top of his glass. "A suspicion. It's none too soon. Tell me what is going on between my mother and Mr. Cope."

"Eustace," I said, "before I answer you, let me remind you of the respect which under all circumstances you owe your mother."

He sprang from his chair. "Respect! I'm right, then. They mean to marry! Speak!" And as I hesitated, "You needn't speak," he cried. "I see it in your face. Thank God I'm here!"

His violence aroused me. "If you have a will to enforce in the matter," I said, "you are indeed none too soon. You're too late. Your mother is married." I spoke passionately, but in a moment I repented of my words.

"Married!" the poor boy shouted. "Married, you say!" He turned deadly pale and stood staring at me with his mouth wide open. Then, trembling in all his limbs, he dropped into a chair. For some moments he was silent, gazing at me with fierce stupefaction, overwhelmed by the treachery of fate. "Married!" he went on. "When, where, how? Without me—without notice—without shame! And you stood and watched it, as you stand and tell me now! I called you friend!" he cried, with the bitterest reproach. "But if my mother betrays me, what can I expect of *you*? Married!" he repeated "Is the devil in it? I'll unmarry her! When—when—when?" And he seized me by the arm.

"Yesterday, Eustace. I entreat you to be calm."

"Calm? Is it a case for calmness? *She* was calm enough—that she couldn't wait for her son!" He flung aside the hand I had laid upon his to soothe him, and began a furious march about the room. "What has come to her? Is she mad? Has she lost her head, her heart, her memory—all that made her mine?

You're joking—come, it's a horrible dream?" And he stopped before me, glaring through fiery tears. "Did she hope to keep it a secret? Did she hope to hide away her husband in a cupboard? Her husband! And I—I—I—what has she done with me? Where am I in this devil's game? Standing here crying like a schoolboy for a cut finger—for the bitterest of disappointments! She has blighted my life—she has blasted my rights. She has insulted me—dishonoured me. Am I a man to treat in that fashion? Am I a man to be made light of? Brought up as a flower and trampled as a weed! Bound in cotton and steeped in vitriol! You needn't speak"—I had tried, for pity, to remonstrate.

"You can say nothing but bald folly. There's nothing to be said but this—that I'm *insulted*. Do you understand ?" He uttered the word with a concentrated agony of vanity. "I guessed it from the first. I knew it was coming. Mr. Cope—Mr. Cope—always Mr. Cope. It poisoned my journey—it poisoned my pleasure—it poisoned Italy. You don't know what that means. But what matter, so long as it has poisoned my home? I held my tongue—I swallowed my rage; I was patient, I was gentle, I forbore. And for this! I could have damned him with a word! At the seaside, hey? Enjoying the breezes—splashing in the surf—picking up shells. It's idyllic, it's ideal—great heavens, it's fabulous, it's monstrous! It's well she's not here. I don't answer for myself. Yes, madam, stare, stare, wring your hands! You see an angry man, an outraged man, but a man, mind you! He means to act as one."

This sweeping torrent of unreason I had vainly endeavoured to arrest. He pushed me aside, strode out of the room, and went bounding upstairs to his own chamber, where I heard him close the door with a terrible bang and turn the key. My hope was that his passion would expend itself in this first explosion; I was glad to bear the brunt of it. But I deemed it my duty to communicate with his mother. I wrote her a hurried line: "Eustace is back—very ill. Come home." This I intrusted to the coachman, with injunctions to carry it in person to the place of her sojourn. I believed that if she started immediately on the receipt of it, she might reach home late at night. Those were days of private conveyances.

Meanwhile I did my best to pacify the poor young man. There was something terrible and portentous in his rage; he seemed absolutely rabid. This was the sweet compliance, the fond assent, on which his mother had counted; this was the "surprise"! I went repeatedly to his chamber door with soft speeches and urgent prayers and offers of luncheon, of wine, of vague womanly comfort. But there came no answer but shouts and imprecations, and finally a sullen silence. Late in the day I heard him from the window order the gardener to saddle his horse; and in a short time he came stamping downstairs, booted and spurred, pale, dishevelled, with bloodshot eyes. "Where are you going," I said, "in this awful heat?"

"To ride—ride—ride myself cool!" he cried. "There's nothing so hot as my rage!" And in a moment he was in the saddle and bounding out of the gate. I went up to his room. It's wild disorder bore vivid evidence of the tumult of his temper. A dozen things were strewn broken on the floor; old letters were lying crumpled and torn; I was sickened by the sight of a pearl necklace, snatched from his gaping valise, and evidently purchased as a present to his mother, ground into fragments on the carpet as if by his boot-heels.

His father's relics were standing in a row untouched on the mantelshelf, save for a couple of pistols mounted with his initials in silver, which were tossed upon the table. I made a brave effort to thrust them into a drawer and turn the key, but to my eternal regret I was afraid to touch them. Evening descended and wore away; but neither Eustace nor his mother returned. I sat gloomily enough on the verandah, listening for wheels or hoofs. Toward midnight a carriage rattled over the gravel; my friend descended with her husband at the door. She fluttered into my arms with a kind of shrinking yet impetuous dread, "Where is he—how is he?" she cried.

I was spared the pain of answering, for at the same moment I heard Eustace's horse clatter into the stable-yard. He had rapidly dismounted and passed into the house by one of the side windows, which opened from the *piazza* into the drawing- room. There the lamps were lighted. I led in my companions. Eustace had crossed the threshold of the window; the lamplight fell upon him, relieving him against the darkness. His mother with a shriek flung herself toward him, but in an instant with a deeper cry she stopped short, pressing her hand to her heart. He had raised his hand, and, with a gesture which had all the spiritual force of a blow, he had cast her off. "Ah, my son, my son!" she cried with a piteous moan, and looking round at us in wild bewilderment.

"I'm not your son !" said the boy in a voice half stifled with passion. "I give you up! You're not my mother! Don't touch me! You've cheated me—you've betrayed me—you've insulted me!" In this mad peal of imprecations, it was still the note of vanity which rang clearest.

I looked at Mr. Cope. He was deadly pale. He had seen the lad's gesture; he was unable to hear his words. He sat down in the nearest chair and eyed him wonderingly. I hurried to his poor wife's relief. She seemed smitten with a sudden tremor, a deadly chill. She clasped her hands, but she could barely find her voice. "Eustace—my boy—my darling—my own—do you know what you say? Listen, listen, Eustace. It's all for you—that you should love me more. I've done my best. I seem to have been hasty, but hasty to do for you—to do for you " Her strength deserted her; she burst into tears. "He curses me—he denies me!" she cried. "He has killed me!"

"Cry, cry!" Eustace retorted; "cry as I've been crying! But don't be falser than you have been. That you couldn't even wait! And you prate of my happiness! Is my happiness in a broken home—in a disputed heart—in a bullying stepfather! You've chosen him big and strong! Cry your eyes out—you're no mother of mine."

"He's killing me—he's killing me," groaned his mother. "O Heaven! if I dared to speak, I should kill him!" She turned to her husband. "Go to him—go to him !" she cried. "He's ill, he's mad—he doesn't know what he says. Take his hand in yours—

look at him, soothe him, heal him. It's the hot weather," she rambled on. "Let him feel your touch! Eustace, Eustace, be healed!"

Poor Mr. Cope had risen to his feet, passing his handkerchief over his forehead, on which the perspiration stood in great drops. He went slowly toward the young man, bending his eyes on him half in entreaty, half in command. Before him he stopped and frankly held out his hand. Eustace eyed him defiantly from head to foot—him and his proffered friendship, enforced as it was by a gaze of the most benignant authority. Then pushing his hand savagely down, "Hypocrite!" he roared close to his face—"can you hear that?" and marched bravely out of the room. Mr. Cope shook his head with a world of tragic meaning, and for an instant exchanged with his wife a long look brimming with anguish. She fell upon his neck shaken with resounding sobs. But soon recovering herself, "Go to him," she urged, "follow him; say everything, spare nothing. No matter for me; I've got my blow."

I helped her up to her room. Her strength had completely left her; she but half undressed and let me lay her on her bed. She was in a state of the intensest excitement. Every nerve in her body was thrilling and ringing. She kept murmuring to herself, with a kind of heart-breaking incoherency. "Nothing can hurt me now; I needn't be spared. Nothing can disgrace me—or grace me. I've got my blow. It's my fault—all, all, all! I heaped up folly on folly and weakness on weakness. My heart's broken; it will never serve again. You have been right, my dear—I perverted him, I taught him to strike. Oh, what a blow! He's hard—he's hard. He's cruel. He has no heart. He's blind with vanity and egotism. But it matters little now; I shan't live to suffer. I've suffered enough. I'm dying, my friend, I'm dying."

In this broken strain the poor lady poured out the bitterness of her grief. I used every art to soothe and console her, but I felt that the tenderest spot in her gentle heart had received an irreparable bruise. "I don't want to live," she murmured. "I'm disillusioned. It could never be patched up; we should never be the same. He has shown the bottom of his soul. It's bad."

In spite of my efforts to restore her to calmness, she became—not more excited, for her strength seemed to be ebbing and her voice was low—but more painfully and incoherently garrulous. Nevertheless, from her distressing murmur I gathered the glimmer of a meaning. She seemed to wish to make a kind of supreme confession. I sat on the cope of her bed, with her hand in mine. From time to time, above her loud whispers, I heard the sound of the two gentlemen's voices. Adjoining her chamber was a large dressing-room; beyond this was Eustace's apartment. The three rooms opened upon a long uncovered balcony.

Mr. Cope had followed the young man to his own chamber, and was addressing him in a low, steady voice. Eustace apparently was silent; but there was something sullen and portentous to my ear in this unnatural absence of response.

"What have you thought of me, my friend, all these years?" his mother asked. "Have I seemed to you like other women? I haven't been like others. I have tried to be so—and you see—you see! Let me tell you. It don't matter whether you despise me—I shan't know it. These are my last words; let them be frank."

They were not, however, so frank as she intended.

She seemed to lose herself in a dim wilderness of memories; her faculty wandered, faltered, stumbled. Not from her words—they were ambiguous—but from her silence and from the rebound of my own impassioned sympathy, as it were, I guessed the truth. It blossomed into being vivid and distinct; it exhaled a long illuminating glow upon the past—a lurid light upon the present. Strange it seemed now that my suspicions had been so late to bear fruit; but our imagination is always too timid. Now all things were clear! Heaven knows that in this unpitying light I felt no contempt for the poor woman who lay before me, panting from her violated soul.

Poor victims of destiny! If I could only bring them to terms! For the moment, however, the unhappy mother and wife demanded all my attention. I left her and passed along the balcony, intending to summon her husband. The light in Eustace's room showed me the young man and his companion. They sat facing each other in momentary silence. Mr. Cope's two hands were on his knees, his eyes were fixed on the carpet, his teeth were set—as if, baffled, irate, desperate, he were pre- paring to play his last card. Eustace was looking at him hard, with a terribly untender gaze. It made me sick. I was on the point of rushing in and adjuring Eustace by the truth. But suddenly Mr. Cope raised his eyes and exchanged with the boy a look with which he seemed to read his very soul. He waved his hand in the air as if to dismiss fond patience.

"If you were to see yourself as I see you," he said, "you would be vastly amazed; you would know your absurd appearance. Young as you are, you are rotten with arrogance and pride. What would you say if I were to tell you that, least of men, you have reason to be proud? Your stable boy there has more. There's a leak in your vanity; there's a blot on your escutcheon! You force me to strong measures. Let me tell you, in the teeth of your monstrous egotism, what you are. You're a ——"

I knew what was coming, but I hadn't the heart to hear it. The word, ringing out, overtook my ear as I hurried back to Mrs. Cope. It was followed by a loud, incoherent cry, the sound, prolonged for some moments, of a scuffle, and then the report of a pistol. This was lost in the noise of crashing glass. Mrs. Cope rose erect in bed and shrieked aloud, "He has killed him—and me." I caught her in my arms; she breathed her last. I laid her gently on the bed and made my trembling way, by the balcony, to Eustace's room. The first glance reassured me. Neither of the men was visibly injured; the pistol lay smoking on the floor. Eustace had sunk into a chair with his head buried in his hands. I saw his face crimson through his fingers.

"It's not murder," Mr. Cope said to me as I crossed the threshold, "but it has just missed being suicide. It has been fatal only to the looking-glass." The mirror was shivered.

"It is murder," I answered, seizing Eustace by the arm and forcing him to rise. "You have killed your mother. This is your father!"

My friend paused and looked at me with a triumphant air, as

if she was very proud of her effect. Of course I had foreseen it half an hour ago. "What a dismal tale," I said. "But it's interesting. Of course Mrs. Cope recovered."

She was silent an instant. "You're like me," she answered. "Your imagination is timid."

"I confess," I rejoined, "I am rather at a loss how to dispose of our friend Eustace. I don't see how the two could very well shake hands—nor yet how they couldn't."

"They did once—and but once. They were for years, each in his way, lonely men. They were never reconciled. The trench had been dug too deep. Even the poor lady buried there didn't avail to fill it up. Yet the son was forgiven—the father never!"

www.ingramcontent.com/pod-product-compliance
Lightning Source LLC
Chambersburg PA
CBHW030348030726
47497CB00002B/229
* 9 7 8 0 8 5 7 0 6 0 3 9 6 *